The Rise of the Raven

Of the Ravens of Berengar

Robin John Morgan

www.heirstothekingdom.com

First published in the UK in 2021 by Violet Circle Publishing.

Manchester, England, UK.

Print ISBN: 978-1-910299-30-2
Digital ISBN: 978-1-910299-31-9

British Library Cataloguing in Publication Data.
A catalogue record for this book is available from the British Library.

All papers used in the production of this book are sourced only from wood grown in sustainable forests.

www.violetcirclepublishing.co.uk

*The Act of Betrayal,
only comes for those in which we placed our trust.
For everyone,
who has felt the pain caused by it, and suffered.*

Author's Note

The Rise of the Raven, was inspired mainly out of necessity, as I began to write the final instalment of my fantasy adventure series Heirs to the Kingdom. Having spent over ten years writing the series, I had accumulated a lot of background material, which gave full explanations to certain previous events within the story. I then referenced these backstories in a more edited format within the books. When I arrived at the final eighth book, I realised that I only had a very slim selection of bullet points to outline the past of the villainous family faced by our hero.

It was clear that I needed a more detailed account in order to reference the history of this dark line in the book, and so in order to ensure I maintained the same standard of explanation in my final instalment, I began to write the history in full detail of this dark family line. What occurred was the simultaneous writing of two books, the final Heirs to the Kingdom book, which would become entitled "The Circle of Darkness, and what is contained within this book, The Rise of the Raven.

The more I thought about this particular piece of my puzzle, which was a requirement to enable me to complete the last book, a process that also brought to my attention the fact that it was indeed one of the most important aspects relating to the start of Heirs to the Kingdom, it was clear that going backwards to the start, was the only real way to complete the tale. So, in order to finish my series of stories, I also had to look to the start of it, which is why I made the decision to publish this particular part of the back story to the series. In many ways this is a separate story of deception betrayal and deviousness, which can be read as a standalone story by someone who has not read Heirs to the Kingdom, but it is also a pivotal part of Heirs to the Kingdom's birth, and it is my hope it will indeed provide greater enjoyment and depth, as well as a fuller picture as to how everything came about.

Robin John Morgan.

Eve sat on a rock with her feet in the cool water at the edge of a stream, deep within the Woodland Realm. She turned, and smiled a caring loving smile at him, and then paused. "What is it my Love?"

He stared momentarily as his thoughts cleared. "Your hair, you have changed the colour." Her bright violet eyes flickered with glee.

"Do you like it? I have been watching the trees and how their shapes change colour with the new season you created to match my aura, so I made my hair copy them."

Her hair was caught for a moment in the reflection of the sun in the water, and the deep copper red burned almost like fire edged with gold, casting glints of firelight across her pale skin. "It makes me feel happy, especially since Tide left, her mooning around seemed to affect me so deeply, I wanted the restful feelings of your trees."

She slipped her feet from the water and lifted herself off the rock, and stood before him with a questioning look in her eyes. "If you do not like it, I can change it back." He shook his head slowly as he looked upon her pale form, surrounded by the long falls of her fiery hair.

"No, my dear you look more beautiful than anything I have seen."

She gave a bright smile and scampered across the grass to him, where she slipped into his arms, and he embraced her, as his thoughts gently strolled through his acute mind. He held her warm slight figure in his arms for a few moments, before she slid back and looked up at his lined face.

"What troubles you, my Love?"

He shook his head, freeing him from his momentary thoughts, and looked down into her bright violet eyes that sparkled with life. "What is mooning?" She gave a giggle.

"It is a new word I have made just for Tide." Her face looked serious for a second. "She is so filled with some kind of feeling I do not understand, it is almost like there is something inside her that has crept in and stolen her joy, and I have no word for it, so I made a new one which seems to fit her... I call it mooning; I think it shall mean like the day and night, sometimes bright and sometimes dark, like the ball of light in the sky she lives within. It is alright to do this isn't it? If you do not like it, I will stop."

The young green man of the trees smiled. "It is fine, and I think you are right, it does seem to sound like she has been of late, we shall add it to the words we use, and teach your brother the word and explain it to him."

Eve gave a big smile and lifted up on her toes, and kissed him on the lips, and then with a giggle, she turned and skipped out of his embrace and ran back to the water's edge.

(Heirs to the Kingdom, The Circle of Darkness.)

Introduction.

My life has been spent in the service of the House
of Scribes. It has been my privilege to serve my people
translating the parchments from the start of our time, as
I help record the history of my people. I have always seen
this task as an honourable one, and I have served with
dedication and duty, and yet it is with the completion of
the task to transcribe the first and second books of Branna,
written by my mentor Ariel of the line of Enaria, that I
find myself searching my soul and my very being, for the
understanding to shape my wisdom.

In the world of men, they say that history is always
written by the victor, and so therefore it is accurate and the
truth. Many books portray the victor as just, and have the
love of their god on their side, which is why they emerged
victorious. By contrast, the loser also always believes that
their cause is also just, and their god is on their side, are
they less likely to be right or are they wrong, which is why
they lost?

The same could be said for Rhiannon and Branna, both
of them believed each other to have committed acts of great
evil. Ariel even agreed that Branna was right and not to
blame, and there was a great deal of evidence to suggest that
Rhiannon caused much of the hatred and resentment she
faced from her people, by her own actions. Even her own
son Rayne, made a deal with Queen Bridget in secret against
his mother, so who is right and who is wrong?

The simple fact is that it matters not, what matters is that
the tale told is accurate, and also detailed enough to allow

those who hear it to judge for themselves, hence here in these pages, the tale is told as an accurate account of what happened, and is true to the tales that have been passed down from father to son for many long generations, as well as recorded by Ariel herself.

You must decide, you must close your ears to those that would confound them, and make the choice having witnessed the facts, because this is not a tale that is black and white, there is indeed many grey areas that will test you to the core, so my advice as the teller of this tale, is judge for yourself, and once the tale is told, only then will you see the full truth of life, death, and all that exists in between.

(Tila, Scribe to the House of Scribes, Florae 2078)

Chapter One.

New Truce, New Realms.

*T*he charts and books of modern man tell one story. It is called the history of the ages, and it speaks of the world through Iron, bronze, and dark ages. It is a tale embroiled with the dogma forced on the men of those times, by those who bore the symbol of a crucifix. In truth the ages set by modern man fall short of the mark, for long before those times are the tales of truth brought into the world by those who carried the history of their tribes within them. These are the tales passed down from father to son, and they speak of strange times, when wizards and fairies walked openly amongst the people.

*O*ne such tale was of five spirits of power, and the creations and gifts of life they brought into the world. These are tales of a spirit devastated by the loss of a love who left her, and how in her solitary time alone in the emptiness above the earth, she was seduced by the darkness, as her heart ached for her lost love so much, that she gave up her earthly body known then as her garment, and fled out in to the universe to seek the one she loved the most.

When the garment was discovered, it was taken to earth and fashioned into two new garments to create new lines of beings to walk besides the men of the earth, and they were known simply as Fae. The word meant fairy in the old tongues long since forgotten, and they brought peace and harmony, and taught skills of weaving, growing, and metal fashioning to men to aid them and help them prosper. In those times long before the cross became the symbol of all things, the world was settled and at peace.

The two lines of the Fae were ruled by separate entities, Rhiannon ruled the Fae Ofmoon from high up above the earth, sat in the seat of the departed spirit, and down below on in the Forest of Time, and later on the Isle of Erin in the world of men, Bridge or Bridget Violet as her people named her, ruled the Fae of Earth, with her husband, Malcolm

Lord of Fae, a fair folk at ease with the world around them, who worked the land and planted the earth to give it more beauty.

Rhiannon ruled her people with an iron grip, for she held within her great power, and she sent her Fae to earth to tunnel and mine below the surface, and her halls grew beautiful with gold and emeralds and countless precious stones. Her warriors were the most skilled in combat, and yet they required little use, for the Fae of Earth kept the balance, as they journeyed throughout the tribes of men bringing order, culture, and harmony. It came as a huge surprise, to find that Rhiannon and Bridget had disagreed and argued to a point that both the lines of Fae separated, and no longer worked together to promote harmony. Rhiannon closed her realm hidden within the moon, and Bridget seeing the troubles caused amongst the kings of Erin by Rhiannon's interference, moved her people across the water and established them on a small isle off the northern coast, and they named it Violet Isle in tribute to their queen.

For many years, the conflict between the two lines of Fae caused an impact on the world of men, until in frustration the high White Lord Albanlin visited the realm of Rhiannon and demanded entry. When she refused him, his rage erupted out of him, and he blew off the gates to her realm, and confronted the cowering queen. In her fear of the powerful head of the ruling council, she agreed to all his terms that she should come down to the earth, and he demanded that Bridget and Rhiannon attend a meeting with him, and the two remaining ruling spirits, and also the old wizard Merlin, to meet to settle the problem, and bring back harmony to the world.

*O*n the highest peak of the first realm created, where the land was flat, Albanlin built a large plinth from the rock, and on it placed a table of white stone, which sat under a huge dome of crystal, and all the summoned members sat and drank wine and ate fruit, as he gave his opening speech. For all the time as he spoke, he watched from under his black hood, and he warned them all of the danger, and that their stubbornness would bring yet more chaos to the world created by Hearne and Eve. When he had spoken his piece, he then sat back and stared at the assembled group.

"This must be settled at this hour, I cannot and will not tolerate this bickering and ignoring of your races." He turned to Bridget Violet. "It was your words that insulted the Queen of the Fae Ofmoon, and even though you yourself lead the Fae of this Earth, I will not tolerate this silence between your races any longer."

Rhiannon gave a smirk, but Albanlin turned on her. Although he had no earthly form, from under the dark black cloak and hood, his displeasure could be felt.

"You are no better Queen of the Moon, you preach wisdom, and yet I see little of late. Have I not warned all of you about what lives in the darkness beyond these realms? All of you must find a peace and work together once again, for if what lurks in the darkness ever finds its way to these realms, all of you will see pain and misery on a scale never known to any of you." Rhiannon lowered her head and prodded the grapes on her wooden plate, the voice of Eve lifted with her love into the air and around the table.

"I do not think two women of great power should act such, both of you are my friends and dear to me, and yet I have a pain in my soul watching you as I have, will you not remember the bonds you swore to each other and honour the code of Fellowship and Earth?" Merlin gave a resounding nod.

"The Lady of Life speaks the truth; it is time to end this feud and join again. Bridge you are a friend and I know you want only harmony, and offered your advice to our Queen of the Moon in good faith. Rhiannon long have we walked the stars and talked of the future, and I know of your determination to bring your people the best a life can offer, but you too must look into yourself and the choices you make. I feel here at this table we can all see that there have been errors and misunderstandings, can we not forge a new pact and walk from this place as we once did, as friends?" Bridget smiled.

"My Lord as always you speak with honour and truth, and for my part I will admit I have been far too stubborn, and I am sorry for my part and would happily look to make peace with all the lines of Fae once again." Albanlin looked to Rhiannon.

"What say you my Queen of the Moon, can you walk with glad hearts once again from this table?" Rhiannon gave a solemn nod.

"We can My Lord, I too am sorry for my part in this, yet I feel that the stance I have taken in the ruling of my people is still the right one. For my part, I will gladly accept the words of my friend and sister of the Earth, and would seek to forge a new future with her." Hearne gave a deep rumbling cough and cleared his throat.

"So may it be… But I must at this point add that I have discussed this with all of you, and I for my part, feel it is hard to form a union with a queen who is well outside the realms we have created. All of the realms connect in one fashion or another to each other, all except the realm of the moon, and so it is my thought that this first realm built at the start of all things should contain a door to your realm my Queen of the Moon. In so doing, I will hand this land to the peoples of Fae Ofmoon to rule over, for this place is directly connected to the realm of men, and therefore all other realms." Rhiannon looked round in great surprise.

"My Lord that is a mighty gift to hand to my people, I have no words that can adequately express my gratitude." Eve smiled.

"Bring peace and harmony to this land, for it contains many things that your people have great skill in the working of. Bring your people down and work this land into a place of great wonder to the sky and the earth, for here you can trade with all of the realms. This is my heart's desire my friend as it will bring you closer to Bridge, and once again you can flourish as the sisters you are."

And so it was done. The peace was settled and a new Age of Knowledge began, Rhiannon made her peace and travelled back to her realm, to plan the building of a realm for the people of her race in the First Realm. Bridget travelled back to her Isle having made her peace with Rhiannon and spoke with her husband and children, and it was decreed that the Fae of the Earth should travel far and wide and aid the world of men, to bring them to the new realm of the Queen of the Moon in peace to trade and learn. Albanlin was satisfied and returned to his seat of watch, and Rhiannon prepared with her husband to plan the new world for her people.

Within the year, Bridget was rewarded with a new realm of her own, which she named Florae. It was connected to the Violet Isle, and was a place of great wonder and lush green life. As her husband Malcolm began work on the realm, she invested her time in selecting one person she could trust more than any for the position of ambassador to the realm of Avalon, the name Rhiannon had chosen for her new seat. One moon cycle later in the heart of the new realm of Florae, Bridget stood beside her dearest friend and watched as the final steps were added to the newly built House of Scribes, Ariel could only marvel at the size and scale of the wooden building that stood on great stilts before her.

"It is beautiful." Bridget smiled.

"Finally, you and all your researchers will have a place large enough to actually house the mountain of scrolls you have collaborated on. This is an important place for our people Ariel, as here will house not only the history of our people but of the others also, for I feel the time has come for us to start to document all things." Ariel gave a gasp.

"That is a hefty project, I mean we have the whole history of our people to date, and that alone will take time to reassemble in order here, but to list all the history of others, we will need far more people than we currently have." Bridget shook her head, her violet eyes burned with wisdom.

"We can only grow as a people, and there will be no shortage of new young scholars, we have many ambassadors already at work within all the realms, we can ask them to document the affairs of those lands and send them back to us. Ariel this is a task that someone must do, the worlds are changing and a record of our times should be made, which is why I want you to go to Avalon when she finally starts to build it."

"What? You cannot be serious? There is far too much to be done here my Queen, I have years of work ahead of me just sorting everything out." Bridget shook her head.

"Ariel that is a task for another, you are wasted sorting scrolls when you have so many other gifts that you could use. I am going to let Bade organise this place, for you are as a daughter to me, in whom I have complete trust. I want you in this new realm to record her progress, and keep the balance of peace between the two lines of Fae. It is the most important task I can give to any, and I do not offer it to any other than yourself." Ariel felt a huge disappointment building inside her, Bridget turned to her and her voice was soft.

"I know I ask a great deal of you, but who else can I trust in this task? Ariel, you know of the comments I made to Rhiannon and why I chose to make them. You and you alone understand my thoughts on this; no other could honestly act in my place. Rhiannon and you have such great knowledge of both our people; but most importantly, you have grown up beside me and understand all I have done. I feel you could even give her better advice than I could. Please, I know I ask a lot, but do this for our people and the love and trust I hold for you."

It was impossible for her to refuse, as much as she wanted to stay here in the new world being built for her people, she knew no other held the confidence of the queen as she did, and with a heavy heart she smiled and gave a nod.

"You know there is nothing I would not do for the peace of our people, and so I will accept your offer and do the best I can." Bridget gave a smile.

"Fear not we have time before your appointment, I mean let's be honest, it has been over a year and she has not sent her people down. I know her well, and regardless of the words she speaks before the white lord, I know she is not capable of change, for that would hurt her precious pride. If I am right, those she sees as lesser beings will be sent to build her realm, there is no doubt her plans are as elaborate as ever, so it will be some time before she walks in her realm of glory."

Bridget gave a soft giggle, and Ariel could do nothing other than smile. It was not as she had planned, but as she began to think about it, she knew it would be a golden opportunity to really see and understand the workings of Rhiannon and her people.

*I*t was over a year later when finally, Rhiannon opened the realm to others, as her advanced parties of workers cleared specific sites for the building of her largest town, and her new seat from which to rule on earth. Bridget was right, and thousands of members of the Fae Ofmoon descended, and tunnelled under the earth and through the rock to create an elaborate hidden world, below the large lake that flowed into the heart of Avalon. Houses were built, and high above the lake on top of the flat peak where the large round white table had been created by Albanlin, Rhiannon built a huge citadel of white stone, on which she placed the crystal dome and decorated it with silver. From the base of the mountain, a wide road was carved from the floor, and it ran the whole length of the lake to what would become the gate to the realm, and it was named 'The Queen's Road.'

Behind the Mount, the huge wall of rock that housed the citadel, the country ran from the rocks into a series of valleys and meadows, and it was here out of sight that most of the Fae took up residence, and they began to create a thriving industry that was dedicated to the glory of their queen and the peoples of Fae.

To many it looked idyllic, and great hope lay in the creation of this realm, but scratch the surface, and it was clear, that not all in

Rhiannon's kingdom was as would at first appear. Avalonia was the name given to the centre of Avalon, and it contained the mount and the lake and all the land around it. The large town that grew around it was filled with things of great beauty, as the Fae laboured hard to carve a place of great wonder out of the rock. It was seen as the jewel of the Fae, for everything within it was to the highest of standards, and gave the impression of great power and affluence.

It was in this ideal that Bridget had seen how Rhiannon's mind had worked previously, and this had been the cause of the feud that had grown between them. Not only was everything in the town created to look fair and beautiful, so were the people who were invited to reside there.

Bridget had accused Rhiannon of favouring only the people of her kingdom who had fair hair, her accusation implied she exploited those of darker hues of hair, and this had led to the row that had ensued, and the parting of their races. Once again, as Avalon slowly rose from the land in all its glory, it was clear that Rhiannon had not changed in her ways, as all of those with darker hair, were given places to reside that were located in the far off outer reaches of the realm. When Ariel finally arrived to take up her post long before the queen was due to arrive, it was clear that despite the new truce between Bridget and Rhiannon little had changed.

As Ariel stood at the end of the Queen's Road with her bags, she marvelled at the sight before her. All the way up the large white wall that was the sheer cliff face of the Mount, wooden scaffold had been built and was a hive of activity. Thousands of men chiselled away at the rock face, cutting out a huge roadway up to what she knew was a building of great wonder. Below at the base, the large stones that were being cut from the face of the cliff, were lowered on long lines, and used to create buildings of extreme beauty. The noise was deafening as thousands of hammers pounded the stone, and echoed across the lake. To her side a huge fortress had been built, and in front of it she could see another road that led down to the lakeside, where a long bridge was being created to cross the lake.

A young fair haired soldier approached her, and she handed him her papers, he took them and inspected them, she could see the white dust around his shoulders and in his hair, which had fallen from the stone. His face was soft and kind as he smiled.

"Welcome Miss Ariel. If you would care to follow me, I will show you to your new dwelling. You will be residing with one of our researchers by the name of Branna. Seeing as your people do not disturb the earth, we felt it would be better if you resided with her, and not in the apartments below ground."

She gave a nod, and before she could speak, he lifted her bags off the floor, turned, and walked off towards the scaffold. Ariel quickly followed behind him, he occasionally looked back to talk to her. He had to shout above the noise, and she strained her ears to hear his words.

"Don't mind the wall; we have a tunnel of wood as we pass under the work into the tunnels below the mount. You are quite lucky Miss, you will be on the other side of the mount, I hear it is very lovely over that side and has a lot of green life, which is another reason you have been placed there, our queen felt it would be more to your liking." She gave a polite nod, as she hurried to keep pace with his long strides.

The noise appeared to dull as she walked under the wooden bridge below the scaffold, and then into the tunnels of white walls. It felt eerie at first, the walls were bright and glistened with millions of tiny crystals, and her footsteps echoed off the smooth floor. For her, a Fae of Earth, it felt very unnatural, and she shuddered, as the guard in front walked briskly on, and she felt her breath shorten as her nervousness rose.

It took over an hour to pass through many tunnels in what she now realised was a labyrinth below the Mount. The guard appeared to know all of them, where as she felt afraid and completely lost, and when she saw the light up ahead, she breathed a sigh of great relief, as the warm air around her changed to a cleaner fresher feel. Walking out in the daylight and feeling the sun again, she felt a great sense of relief, and realised she was damp and clammy all over from her fear.

As she breathed in the clean fresh air, and gasped to recover her composure, she looked up to see the guard had placed her bags on a small cart. Sat up front was a slender young woman with long dark hair, her face was tanned, and yet she looked withdrawn and her eyes carried the lines and dark patches of many nights without sleep. Ariel wiped her face and took another long breath of air; the guard turned and gave her a smile.

"This is Branna Miss, you will be residing with her, and so I will leave you in her good care."

Ariel looked up and Branna smiled and patted the seat beside her, the guard offered his hand, so she walked towards him, and he helped her up onto the seat. Branna leaned back to look at the guard, he gave a slight nod.

"Thanks Bran, I will see you later in the week." He gave her a cheeky wink.

"I will look forward to it." He looked to Ariel. "Goodbye Miss, you are in good hands." Unsure of why she felt relieved, she smiled.

"Thank you." He touched his brow, turned, and headed back towards the tunnel; Branna sat quietly watching him go, and then turned to the horse and flicked the reigns.

"Come on then, let's get away from this awful place and find some peace and quiet, I am Branna by the way, and you are Ariel of Florae I am told?" She nodded.

"I am, it's nice to meet you Branna." She smiled.

"You don't know me yet; you may regret saying that." She gave a chuckle and the cart lurched forward, and Ariel wondered just what exactly she had got herself into.

*T*he journey from the Mount to her new residence took a little over an hour. At first the surroundings were stark and rocky, but as the cart trundled along, and Branna began to talk, the rock opened up revealing a long valley filled with lush trees and plant life. There were many different varieties of tree and shrub growing all over, and many she knew, although some she did not recognise as she looked at the strange shaped leaves and many different colours. It felt like a new world, and one she thought she would enjoy exploring; the one thing that surprised her was the abundance of apple trees.

The further away they got from the Mount, the chattier Branna became, and she started to fill in Ariel on her life and work. Branna was a researcher like herself, her task within the realm of Avalon was to collect data to send back to the queen as to the progress of the outer towns and villages that were springing up due to the influx of mass labour. In her spare time, she had been given permission to do what she saw as the real work, it was her task to research the mysteries of the Merle, the darkness that surrounded all the realms.

Whilst she had been on the realm of the moon it had been her principal work, but being transferred to Avalon, she like so many others had to take on an extra task to ensure the realm was prepared and built in time for the queen's arrival. Branna explained that it was not something any of them were happy about, but being in Avalon gave them freedoms they did not have in the moon realm, which was the principal reason they had travelled to the realm, to be a part of the advanced team.

Ariel found it all very interesting, but she sensed that Branna was resentful of Rhiannon. Ariel looked at her companion as she thought for a moment; Branna had a stern face, which appeared to lighten very quickly when she smiled. She was clearly very pretty, it was difficult to tell at times as her hair which was right down her back, was also a little wild and untamed, and would blow across her features covering parts of her face. She felt she should respond, and asked.

"Were you unhappy in the Realm of the Moon?" Branna gave a snort.

"Happiness is for those of fair hair, the rest of us do not have that luxury." Ariel felt a little taken aback, she knew how Bridget Violet felt about Rhiannon favouring those of fair hair, but to be sat here actually hearing a member of Rhiannon's people state it out loud felt shocking, she lowered her voice.

"I am not sure you should say such things out loud, after all she is your queen, and Rhiannon is renowned for her wisdom." Branna gave a hearty laugh and her face softened.

"I know who you are Ariel, I too am a researcher and knew months ago that you would be lodging with me. I know you have the favour of your queen, and I also know what caused the rift between her and my queen. Do not worry about me being heard, it is not like they do not know what we all think out here, which is the reason we are so far from the queen's gaze. Like you I am Fae, but unlike you I am not an equal in my own race, the rules for the Fae Ofmoon are very different, give it time and you will see. We live out here because here we are ignored by the officials, but we are not unhappy, as here we have something we do not have in our home realm, here we are free to do as we wish as long as it does not cause trouble for our queen."

*B*ranna lived in a house of stone surrounded on one side by large fruit trees, and on the other was a steep slope up the side of a huge white rock face, into which had been cut a small path bordered with a low wall. Branna explained that was where she observed the skies at night with her equipment, and looked deep into the Merle to continue her research.

The house was a nice place, but was very messy, as it was covered in charts and scrolls. Ariel's room was small but neat and clean, the bed was large and soft, and she had two small sets of draws, and a large wooden cupboard to place her belongings in. Across the room was a door that led to a study for her, it contained a desk next to the window and two tall cupboards filled with parchments.

It was all very basic and simple, and yet it appealed to her, and she felt very much at ease as she looked out of her window onto the thick green trees that lined the long valley. Somehow it felt idyllic, and deep down inside she felt a strong feeling of connection to it. She had been so apprehensive about coming here, but a little hope rose within her, maybe Bridget was right, considering her companion who she was to reside with, maybe Bridget had shown great wisdom in picking her for this task, and she gave a sigh of relief. It was quiet and peaceful, and surrounded by the beauty of the realm, yes maybe she would feel happy and content here, as she applied herself to the task she had been given. As she watched Branna walk down to the well in the garden beyond her window, she thought that maybe this slightly odd character, would be the ideal person to teach her all she would need to know about the Queen Rhiannon, and the new realm she was about to rule.

Chapter Two.

Ariel And Branna.

Settling into Avalon took several days for Ariel. The house was very untidy, and so as Branna sat at her desk in her own room, Ariel set about giving the place a good cleaning out, a job that revealed that Branna was a little bit of a slob. The pot cupboards were empty, and yet once all the used plates had been found and washed, there was not enough cupboard space to house them all. Branna confessed she simply purchased more. The weather was warm and sunny, and so Ariel opened all the windows and swept the place clean, and after two long days, the place was unrecognisable.

The one huge benefit of Ariel to Branna was cooking. It appeared Branna was so busy with her daily duties, followed by her evenings and night time observations, for her research into the Merle that she often forgot to eat. Finding a wholesome cooked meal on the table when she finished her daily papers for the administrators of Avalon, was a very welcome surprise. As the days progressed and both of them got into the routine of life, things settled and Branna felt that Ariel was a good companion, and actually pleasant to live with.

Most days there were many visitors, as officials from all over the region arrived with their reports, on the various tasks and duties they were undertaking, in the building of a realm for the queen. Ariel was delighted to find she was in the centre of everything, and simply by helping Branna read through her reports, she found she was given the most accurate snapshot of life within the Fae community during the time of preparations for a queen. By the end of the first month, Ariel had a very accurate report that documented the daily life of Avalon, which she sent back home to Florae for Bridget and the House of Scribes.

The only rule of the house for Ariel was that she must never walk up to the top of the high wall of stone, which formed a long flat peak to the side of their house when Branna was working. Branna was quite adamant that her work at times could be dangerous, and so on those nights when she left the house with her books and equipment, Ariel must not follow her. Ariel tried to question as to what exactly she did up there, but Branna became quite irritable about the whole issue of it, and would snap at her that it was dangerous; Ariel learned very quickly that Branna's moods could change rapidly when talking on the subject of her experiments, and she soon learned to not ask.

Her days were spent dealing with all the reports that came in and helping Branna, and on the slower days she would work in the garden, or take long walks through the woodlands and trees that lined the sides of the long valley below their home. Life felt slow and more relaxed, and Ariel found that she very quickly came to love the place that she felt was filled with life, not unsimilar to Florae. Her evenings would be spent sat in the garden, and on the nights when Branna was not up on her rock working, she would join Ariel, and whilst making her notes they would have long deep conversations about the two similar, yet very different races of the Fae.

One area of concern for Ariel was Branna's opinion of the political class within the Fae Ofmoon, it bothered her that Branna would talk so openly of her dislike for them, and she often cautioned her about it.

"Branna you must not say such things, she is your queen, and if others hear you talk like this, you may find yourself in big trouble." Branna gave a snort as she lifted her glass to drink more wine.

"I do not lie; I believe the truth to be exactly that. Out here in the back of this realm, we are out of sight and believe me Ariel, no one is listening. That would imply that they care, which they do not." Ariel felt a cold shudder run down her arm.

"I just feel it is unwise to talk so freely about your distaste of them, I do think you should lower your voice a little when you talk like that." Branna gave a chuckle.

"Who exactly is going to hear me? Ariel look where we live, we are high up on the valley side with the advantage of seeing every road for miles, no one can get close to this place without us knowing, it is why I picked it." Branna gave a wide smile as she gestured out across the valley, almost spilling her freshly filled glass of wine.

"Why you picked it, you mean you deliberately chose this place to ensure you could have a clear view of what… enemies?" Branna nodded.

"We are a lower class of citizen within the ranks of the Fae Ofmoon, our purpose is to serve and work, we can be replaced or killed at will. I made sure when I chose this spot that if anyone wants to turf me out, I will see them long before they arrive and make sure I am ready for the fight. I hate to say it, but having you stay with me is a little bit of added insurance." The revelation shocked Ariel.

"How am I insurance?" Branna took a long swig of her wine.

"You are an ambassador to the one person who has seen our glorious queen for what she is, blinded by colour, and as such if they attack me for simply having an opposing view, they will have to do it right in front of the one person who is regarded as kin, and reports directly to Queen Bridget Violet. Even my queen will not risk another confrontation between the lines of Fae so close to her arrival, the White Lord would never settle for it. In an odd sort of way, you are my protection, and I might add being with me, you get to report the truth of what it is really like to be a Fae with darker hair, when only those of golden locks are in favour. It benefits us all perfectly." It was a startling thought for Ariel.

"I never realised it could be so bad." Branna stood up and swayed a little.

"I love having you here by the way; at first I just figured it would be a wise move." She took a few rather shaky steps forward. "But I have really enjoyed having you here; I feel I can live a real and free life here."

Her face looked a little solemn as she looked out across the valley, almost as if some terrible memory had passed through her, and her voice softened.

"When I heard about this place, all I wanted was to come here and simply be me, just me, I wanted so badly to be able to live on my terms without the worry of clashes with politics or officials. I am so free inside, and yet up there in that awful place I felt like I was living in a cage, here I can spread my wings and be free of all of it." She turned and gave a smile.

"I am drunk, ignore me, I get like this at times, I think I need a bed." She staggered a little, and Ariel put down her glass and stood up, and took her arm to steady her.

"Come, I will help you to bed."

She gave a giggle, as she suddenly swayed herself, the wine here was far more potent than she realised. Both of them staggered and giggled as they made their way indoors, and across the living space to Branna's room, and her large soft comfy bed. The wine and the cool night air had taken its effect, and their laughter became infectious as they staggered up to the side of the bed. Ariel stood and gave a giggle as Branna struggled with her dress ties; she shook her head as the drunken Fae pulled to no effect.

"Come here you are doing it wrong." Ariel unloosed the ties, and Branna's dress fell to the floor revealing her tanned naked form, Branna gave a smile, and much to Ariel's surprise, she lifted her hands to her face, and pulled her in close and kissed her on the lips.

The shock ran like waves through her as Branna smooched her, and then stood back with a beaming smile. "I have wanted to do that since we met." Branna watched Ariel's bemused face. "What you did not like it?"

Ariel struggled for words as her cheeks began to pink up. "It's not that… It's just… well I mean?" Branna gave a look of almost jubilation.

"Oh lords of all the realms, you have never been kissed before?" Ariel felt her face turn scarlet, Branna gave a chuckle.

"Well, no not really… I mean, well you know, I kissed my mum and dad and stuff but… Well not… Well, you know… Er… not like that?"

Branna leaned forward and kissed her again, but this time Ariel gave a response, and Branna pulled her in closer as their mouths met and lit with passion. The shock followed by surprise coursed through Ariel, and then it began to melt as other feelings she had never known before began to tingle within her.

All of a sudden, a very surprising warmth flowed into her, as the sweet smell of Branna and the softness of her lips on her own, ignited a new feeling that filled her with a strange warmth. She was not sure how it happened, but somewhere in amongst the long and passionate kiss, she ended up on the bed with her dress hiked up, and Branna began to explore her soft white skin, and then it happened. From nowhere deep inside her, everything exploded in one of the most powerful and intense sensations she had ever known, and her entire body shook with almost electric vibrations. As she began to understand what was happening to her. Just for a moment, she thought about ending it now, but her body took over and screamed out in ecstasy, and she surrendered to this new and glorious feeling.

When Ariel woke snuggled within the blankets of Branna's bed, she blinked as the bright light flooded in through the windows, and stretched the aches out of her body. She slid her arm across the empty side of the bed that still felt warm from where Branna had recently risen, and she smiled to herself. She had never made love to anyone before, and had never thought for a moment that her first would be a woman. She knew many couples back on the Violet Isle that shared their lives and beds who were of the same sex; she just had never imagined she too would one day.

The memory of the previous night, and the softness of Branna as she had guided her into the ways of love flooded her mind, and she felt alive inside in a way she had never thought possible. Her mind flooded with the pictures of the caring and loving Branna as she had embraced her with a soft smile, it was a side of her that she had never thought for a moment was possible, and it made her heart beat a little faster. Was this love?

She heard movement and rolled over in the bed, there stood Branna with a smile, two cups of steaming tea in her hands, her long messy hair cast across the sides of her face and over her shoulder, and down onto her naked breasts. She looked happy and beautiful, and Ariel gave a smile and sat up in the bed.

"How long have you been there?" Branna chuckled, and came across the room towards the bed.

"Long enough." She stepped up onto the bed and handed Ariel the mug of the sweet smelling fragrant tea. She strode over her and slid down behind her on the pillows, and Ariel leaned back onto her shoulder. Branna's slender naked frame pressed against her back, Ariel felt the warmth of her body and her life force warmed through her skin into her. She sipped her drink, and gave a happy long sigh; Branna kissed the top of her head.

"How are you this morning?" Ariel snuggled back with a smile.

"I am fine, although my head is pounding." Branna gave a chuckle.

"Yes, me too, that was pretty good stuff we drank last night, I will buy that again. What I really meant Ariel is are you alright with this?" Ariel turned slightly and looked up at her dark eyes, and tanned face surrounded by the mass of tangled dark hair.

"You mean last night?" Branna nodded.

"Yeah, I was pretty drunk and got carried away, I have tried very hard to remain at a distance, as I was not sure how you felt, but I have wanted to do that since you came here." Ariel sipped her drink, and then gave another smile as she turned again, to look at the face of this woman who not only had seduced her, but she had responded back.

"It was my first time you know that? I mean ever, with a man or woman?" Branna gave a swallow as she sipped at her own tea.

"Yeah, I realise that now, did I go too far?" Ariel gave a small giggle.

"It was pretty surprising at first, but I did not stop you, no you did not go too far, it was beautiful and I am glad you did it. I suppose the question is now, what is this, and where do we go from here?" Branna stared out of the window for a few moments, her voice was soft and reflective.

"I want this, I want you, I want something real that is open and free, I love living here with you, I have wanted something like this for so long, and yes I want it to be here with you."

Ariel could see that look on her face, the one that was longing for something she had dreamed about, and she understood more than ever the person deep inside her. In many ways her work for her people had taken up all of her life to date. She had never contemplated a life shared with anyone, and had no idea of the feelings sharing a life like she had for the past year with Branna, could stir deep within her as it had. Sat there snuggled up in blankets and pressed into the naked body of this remarkable woman, Ariel felt something deep within her stirring, and it felt right and natural. She slipped her arm over to the small cabinet beside the bed and put her tea down, then she turned slightly on her side snuggling into her soft warm flesh and wrapped her arm around the side of Branna.

"I want this too; I have never really understood until now how lonely I have been in the past working in dusty rooms filled with nothing but papers. Since I came here, I have felt more alive than ever before, I think you have been very good for me."

Branna put down her tea and then slid down under the blankets and cuddled into Ariel. Warm and snug they faced each other and stared into each other's eyes. Branna smiled and leaned forward to kiss her.

"It is still very early; we have plenty of time before the work day starts." Ariel smiled and leaned in to complete the kiss.

"Let's make this moment last forever."

*T*hat day felt like the first day of a new life, there were fewer visitors than normal, and as the work day finished and the sun burned brightly in the sky, Ariel and Branna walked hand in hand through the vast woodland surrounding their home. They bathed together in the cool river and washed each other as they laughed and giggled together. Branna missed her usual night of research as they made love on the grassy bank of the river and then walked naked back to their home. That evening they sat in bed and shared a meal, and drank more wine, and they folded into each other's arms, and made love until the dawn, before falling into a sweating and exhausted happy sleep.

It became the pattern of life, and over the days and weeks that grew into months they shared their bed and their life, and Branna who had changed so much over the time they had lived together, smiled more and hummed tunes as she worked, and became the focus of Ariel's life. They shared everything, and Branna opened up about more and more of the life lived by the Fae in the realm of Ofmoon to such an extent that Ariel learned everything about her counter parts within the Fae lifestyle.

One afternoon as the sun reached its hottest, Branna took Ariel by the hand and walked her up the steep incline to the top of the white rock where a small wooden shelter had been constructed, and she showed Ariel all of her work and equipment for observing the Merle. On the table below the beating sunlight, she unrolled her charts and notes, and talked of a life force within the darkness that had a conscious state and understood other life forms. She also hinted at the malice in the furthest reaches of the darkness. As she finished showing Ariel the charts, she looked up with dark hopeful eyes.

"Don't you see Ariel, what this proves is that this darkness contains life, it is a life that understands us, it is conscious and has its own will, it is not the inanimate blackness we thought it was. I am not completely sure, but I think this dark life form has powers, and maybe if we can understand them, they can be siphoned off and added to the forces the Fae already control. It appears to be some sort of energy, and if we can tap into it, well it will change everything we have ever accomplished." Ariel was lost for words, and she sat on her chair.

"Bran this is big you know?" Branna gave a huge excited smile.

"I know." Ariel thought about it for a second.

"You need to show this to the queen when she arrives, this is massively important Bran." Branna looked at her with a serious look.

"I am not sure Ariel; she has little time for us out here." Ariel shook her head and stood up; she pulled Branna into a close embrace.

"Bran you fool, do you not see? This changes everything; this shows every one the talents of all of you lost here out of sight. Rhiannon will have no choice but to listen to you, she cannot ignore this as it changes everything we have ever known about the darkness that surrounds us. You must send a request to meet with her as soon as possible. Oh, Bran my love, this is recognition for you and proof that all of your lines are equal regardless of your hair colour." Branna looked at her with hope in her eyes.

"Do you think so?" Ariel pulled her into a long passionate kiss. She withdrew with a huge smile.

"This means everything, this my love is your freedom guaranteed forever, this proves beyond a doubt that you are equal to all of them. I mean let's be honest, all of her golden haired researchers have never even come close to understanding what you have discovered. Oh, my love I am so happy for you."

*I*t was an astounding piece of research that Branna deserved a great deal of credit for, and in that moment as their passions and love for each other soared in happiness, Branna had not fully understood the smallest of errors in her judgement. The Merle was alive, in that she was right, but the powerful force that existed on the outer limits of the darkness was not one that could be tapped like water, for it was corrupt and evil.

Her love for Ariel was strong and pure, and without really understanding things properly, it was the only thing that was protecting her, for the darkness feared the purity of it. Branna had miscalculated and without realising she had connected herself to the Merle, and already deep within her tiny fragments of her were being seduced by the darkness. The purity of her love would protect her, but not forever, as the Merle learned constantly, and over great time it would overcome her completely.

Chapter Three.

Proven Right.

The building of Avalon had taken two years, but as the days passed it was clear that the arrival of Rhiannon was coming closer. For Branna and Ariel it had been two years of living happily, and to a degree separated from everything else that was happening around the realms. In Florae under the rule of Bridget Violet, the realm had come together quickly, as Bridget invited all of her Fae lines to come to her and join the effort, to build a realm of great beauty. The realm which consisted of nine mountainous islands surrounded by sea and covered with green life, was indeed very beautiful. It had been decided very early on that it would be built in harmony with the surroundings, and after two years of intense hard work, the houses and official buildings were constructed of natural products within the trees and plants that surrounded them. As a result, Florae grew fast, and yet the islands changed little as each home was nestled amongst the trees, and decorated to reflect the wonders of nature.

Just over eighteen months into the building a strange melancholy like illness swept through the realm. People residing there felt ill and withdrew for a time, and were struck with a deep sadness, and it was soon brought to the attention of Bridget. She spent a great deal of her time visiting each of those with the strange new illness, and many were amazed at her ability to take time out for each of them. Most of the herbalists and healers were unable to state what the illness was or even how to cure it, but miraculously, after each visit by Bridget Violet they appeared to recover. What at first brought panic, soon subsided into calm, as the Queen of her realm appeared to single handily aide all of her sick people.

No queen was loved as much as Bridget, her efforts to save her people as she brought them out of Erin, and then resettle them on the Violet Isle, followed by her negotiations to create a single realm dedicated to the Fae of Earth, won her massive support and adoration from her people. The wave of illness passed, and the realm developed further, and for a time all appeared settled and moving as planned, but behind the scenes a different story was developing.

In private Malcolm, Bridget's husband had a growing concern. Bridget had started to experience very bad night terrors, and would wake in a frenzy of fear, shaking violently as she rambled incoherently. It had started as an occasional bad dream, but had increased to a point where Malcolm was very concerned as it seemed to be draining her of her energy. The healers were called in and for a time she appeared to stabilise, but the effect was noticeable as Bridget began to lock herself away in the House of Scribes. She spent day's endlessly reading through documents that dated back to the times when the Fae were new to the world. Bridget's granddaughter Gwendolyn, who was extremely close to her grandmother, was briefed about everything, but as Bridget locked herself away, she appeared to push Gwendolyn away from her, and to Malcolm it appeared that she was trying to avoid her. Malcolm and his son Ninian had many meetings with the council of elders, but no one could explain the strange behaviour of their queen.

Bridget talked endlessly about her need to protect her people, she had always been the sort of queen who placed her people as her biggest priority, and yet now it appeared as if it had grown to become her biggest obsession. Ninian and Bade consulted regularly to try and understand what had befallen, that would make the queen so insistent on her obsessive behaviour and rhetoric over her people. Finally Malcom wrote to the only person he thought could help, he wrote to Ariel, and sent a messenger to Avalon. Ariel wrote back, but Bridget demanded she stay in Avalon, and so what then began was a series of correspondence between Ariel and Bridget, of which no one else was privy to. The arrival of letters from Ariel appeared to do the trick, and Bridget appeared to recover a little much to the relief of Malcolm, Ninian, and Gwendolyn. Life slowly over several months appeared to return to normal, as the realm approached completion.

*I*n Avalon things had picked up pace, as the final preparations for the coming of Queen Rhiannon drew closer, and in the small house on the side of the valley, after a hectic time, things began to slow down a little as most of the major building work came to an end. Branna found herself with more and more time to work on her research, and spend valuable time with her lover Ariel. Branna was happier and more relaxed than Ariel had ever seen her; she sat up at night in bed talking with Ariel, and had an optimistic air to her comments and views.

Ariel had seen such a huge change in her over the last six months, and her love for this somewhat different and at times irreverent woman, had grown to a deep and caring bond between them. On the nights when she was alone, she thought about her life before she came to Avalon, and in truth, she found it hard to remember the detail of what had been a mundane way of life. The simple truth was, she could no longer remember what life was like before Branna.

*O*ne evening after it had been announced via a message that Rhiannon would be arriving at the bottom of the Queen's Road on the rising of the fourth moon, Branna left Ariel alone, and walked to the top of her high plateaux to continue her work. The sky was clear and the stars shone in their millions against the darkest backdrop Branna had seen to date. With all her instruments set up, and her black bound note book open on the table, she prepared a tall rod of copper and ensured it was secure and fitted into the hole in the stone floor that she had spent two months slowly grinding out. Returning to her table she checked her notes and charts to ensure the timing was perfect, and gave a smile as she swept her long tatty hair back from her face. On the table to her left was a large heavy glass jar with a tightly fitted lid, she turned and connected a long copper coil through a small hole in it, and sealed it with a thick paste. Branna then began to unwind the other end, and walked slowly backwards to the tall rod. It took a few moments to connect the two, and then she walked back to the table to check her note book, on which was an elaborately drawn diagram of what appeared to be an orbiting mass. Branna looked back to the heavens.

"All I need now is to wait, I cannot be wrong; I know I will see it tonight."

In the darkness of the night with just her flickering burning torch, she stood transfixed and watched the sky. The sands in the hour glass passed through the small gap and fell to the bottom, but she did not move, her gaze fixed on one point in the sky. As she watched, she felt her heart deep inside slowly start to increase its beating. The time was almost upon her, and her breath slowed as she watched what at first appeared to be nothing but a dark patch of sky. To any observer it was, but Branna who could sense it, noted it as it slowly moved across the sky, slowly blotting out the stars it passed in front of. The air all around the huge rock top felt electric, and oppressive, and Branna watched with a faint smile on her lips, if she was right, tonight all her work would come to fruition.

Her head never moved, but the air around her seemed to darken and become more and more oppressive. Stood as still as a statue next to the tall pole, which looked like it reached into the stars in the darkness, Branna focused and began to concentrate her Fae powers within herself. It was almost as if the darkness noticed her, and it slowed down surrounding the area just above her. As she concentrated on the one single spot in the sky, her hand slid out from her sleeve and lightly touched the pole for the slightest fraction of a second. There was a small spark, like the lighting of a flint, a faint blue flash shot up the pole like a line of fine thread. It rocketed up the pole, and then shot from the very end into the heavens above, and with a gasp, Branna gave a smile as there was a faint wail above her.

"Got you!"

In the air above her, across the darkness, long lines of fine blue flashed across the sky, and then suddenly from nowhere, there was an almighty blinding flash of blue. Ariel sat up in bed with a start.

"What in all the realms was that?"

The resounding crack that filled the night air gave another brilliant flash of light, and then rumbled, Ariel flopped back on her bed. "Thunder." She pulled her blankets up to her face and nestled back into her soft pillows that carried the scent of Branna.

*B*ranna sat up several yards away from her table. Her head slightly spun and she felt the cool trickle on her temple where she had cut her head from the heavy fall that had thrown her clear of the pole. Her elbow hurt and she rubbed it as somewhat dazed, she lifted herself back to her feet. She had no time to concern herself with any injuries, she had to know if it had been a success, and quickly she staggered to the table and peered at the large glass jar, and her heart soared.

There inside the bottom of the jar was what looked like a small dark cloud the size of a small coin purse, it was not very transparent, and appeared to pulsate like a small cowering creature would in a trap. Her heart raced as she snatched a taper out of a stone pot and moved quickly to the flickering torch, she pulled a small brass lantern towards her containing a tallow candle, and then held up the taper to light it from the torch. The taper flickered violently for a second, and she used her other hand to shield the flame as she manoeuvred it into the open door of the lantern, and lit the tallow candle within. Branna gave a long gasp and breathed deeply in as she closed the door, and then lifted the lantern up to fully inspect the contents of her jar. What she saw almost made her heart stop, and she took another sharp intake of breath.

The cloud like entity within the jar slid across the bottom of the jar away from the light, and pressed itself flat against the high round wall of the other side of the jar as if in fear. Branna moved the lantern to one side and it moved again as if afraid of the light, she gave a giggle knowing it had reacted this way, and at that moment she realised everything she had ever speculated over from her years of research were true. Whatever this darkness was, if it reacted to light, it was indeed a living.

There on her table sealed within the glass jar was a small part of what she and everyone else knew as the Merle, and it was alive. Staring at it with her dark eyes fixed on it, she could not believe she had done it, but there was her proof, she stepped back a little and slid the lantern a few feet away from the side of the jar, the object inside looked like it relaxed and slid down the side of the jar back to the base. Branna turned slightly in front of her note book and then sat with a bump, her eyes never leaving the jar. Part of her wanted to cry, the other part of her wanted to scream with joy, but she could not make a sound as she watched the strange dense smoke like thing surrounded by the glass walls.

Thousands of questions ran through her mind. What was it made of? Did this thing need to be fed? How intelligent was it? If it was afraid of the light, what would she do in the day time? Would it die in the light? I cannot wait to show it to Ariel. The questions spilled into her mind as her thoughts ran wild, and then somewhere in the midst of all of them, she heard a voice that she knew did not belong there.

"You cannot tell her." Her thoughts crashed to a halt as she stared at the jar and then blinked as if snapping out of her head and back to reality.

"Huh?" The voice was there again.

"You cannot tell her." Branna swallowed for a moment and blinked again, was she dreaming?

"You are very much awake, yes you are right, but deep down you

have always known that haven't you?" Branna stared intently at the jar.

"Are you talking to me, or have I finally gone mad?"

"You know who we are." She gave a nod in response; the voice within her mind was too coarse and deep for it to be anything to do with her thoughts. The mass within the jar was quite still.

"Cover the light, it hurts us." Without even thinking, she turned and lifted her red shawl off the back of the chair and quickly wrapped it around the sides of the lantern.

"Is that better? Sorry I was not thinking."

"Much better." She gave a smile.

"I am…"

"We know who you are, we have been watching for some time."

"You have?"

"We see and understand everything." She gave a gasp; it was far more intelligent than she had realised it would be.

"How old are you and how can you talk to me like this?" There was no response. Branna waited for a few moments. She leaned in closer her eyes fixed on the mass at the base of the jar. "Do you not understand me?"

"We understand, we just do not know this concept you call old, we are trying to work it out… Dawn is coming." Branna glanced up and gave a nod.

"I know, but my day is free, I am not in a hurry."

"The light will come." She suddenly realised what it meant.

"Oh yeah right… Sorry, yeah I will have to hide you away from it." She looked round the top of the high stone plateaux and all her assembled belongings for her work. "Will you be alright in a box for the day?"

"Is it shielded from the light?"

"It will be with the lid on, and I can pack it to make sure it's free of all small light beams."

"Do it and hurry, and move us away from the edge, here your light is brightest." Branna gave a nod.

"There are rocks over there that are shaded for most of the afternoon, it will be cooler as well."

"We do not fear your heat."

Branna quickly moved away from the table, and lifted the larger crate off the floor. Once empty it was quite light, so she hurriedly walked away from her work station towards what was a rocky outcrop, which she knew contained several places where she could place the crate to keep it as shaded as was possible this high up.

"Hurry the light."

She quickly found a good spot and set the crate down then made her way at a good pace back to the table, she undid the wire connected to the top of the jar and lifted it containing her piece of the Merle, and hurried back towards her hiding place and the crate. Once the jar was placed inside the centre, she slid off her long black coat, and packed it into the crate around the jar to ensure no light would permeate the jar during the daylight, as she reached for the wooden lid for the crate she stopped.

"Will you be alright here; do you feed or need anything? I mean you are going to be alright in here, aren't you?"

"We have fed, you will find you will feel tired around us to begin with, leave us here and return when the light fades, and tell none about us." Branna gave a nod.

"No." She lifted the lid.

"Especially the other one, she will not understand us, she lives to defeat us." Branna gave a frown.

"What Ariel? No, you must be wrong; she is full of nothing but love."

"You cannot tell her; she will destroy us." Branna gave a soft nod, although she was not sure why they would say such things, Ariel was the love of her life, and she knew that she could not harm anything.

"Have no fear, I will tell no one of you; I must admit I have a million questions to ask you."

"You need to rest, leave us and return later." She felt a little disappointed, and placed the lid on the top of the crate.

"See you later."

*B*ranna felt the excitement grow inside her as she lifted several large rocks onto the top of the crate to ensure it remained sealed. She rushed back to the table and gathered together her things, and dropped them into her bag, and then as the first rays of light came over the horizon, she slung her bag on her shoulder and hurried to the path that would take her down and back to her home and Ariel.

By the time she reached the house she felt drained, and even with her enthusiasm coursing through her body, she still felt the weariness of her body, and knew that she needed sleep. Once inside the house she slipped quietly into her room, slipped off her clothes and slid into the bed beside Ariel. She snuggled in tightly and felt the warm soft skin of Ariel press back into her, but as quick as the warmth flowed from Ariel into her, she fell into a deep and exhausted sleep.

*T*hat night as Branna faced the dark fragment of the Merle, far away in the realm of Florae, Bridget Violet woke with a start in her bed. Her eyes burned with violet light, and the sweat ran rapidly from her matted damp hair down her face. Sat alone in her bed as she hugged the blankets, she felt something deep inside her stir, and it frightened her more than she ever told any.

For months she had secretly looked at anything related to the documentation of the birth of the Fae, and as she sat alone in her bed her suspicions began to feel more like truth. Her instincts had told her that there was a sickness within the Fae, something she could not explain, and of which there was no history of it written in any parchments. It was impossible to prove or verify, but she knew she was right. Her people had fallen ill with a strange melancholy that would build into an anger she had never before witnessed, for months now she had visited every member of her people who had suffered this strange illness, and using the power of her people, she had taken the core of the sickness within her. It would be many years before someone realised what she was doing, and she understood that by the time they realised, it would be too late for her.

Bridget planned to free her people completely of this sickness, by carrying its cause alone inside her own body, as queen she knew she had the power to subdue it, and on her death, she planned to take this core of what she could only describe as an evil within, into the heavens out of all the realms and destroy it forever. Alone that night and filled with fear as she struggled to contain the growing force of darkness inside herself, Bridget's biggest fear was realised, this was no longer a sickness of the Fae of Earth. She gave a gasp as she summoned the powers within her to once more push back the darkness as it fought her, and then as she stared out of the window into the night she quietly whispered.

"I knew it, I have known all along my friend and sister, you have it too, and it has escaped into your people. The Fae of Moon has a battle to come, for I am too weak to fight beside you."

Chapter Four.

Protection From The Past.

For most of the next day, Branna appeared impatient, Ariel looked up from her desk on the other side of the room, as Branna once more scribbled her notes, then got up and walked up to the window to check the sky.

"You are restless today, whatever is the matter?" Branna gave a long sigh and returned to her seat.

"I have much to do; I need the day to move faster so I can get back." Ariel nodded.

"You worked late last night; I take it all went well?"

"What?" Branna looked shaken for a moment, as her eyes watched Ariel writing a report.

"Yes… Well, you know there is a lot to do before she arrives; I want to make this the best opportunity just in case." Ariel put down her quill and smiled.

"Bran my love you worry too much, when the queen arrives, she will be pleased with your work. I really do think after that you will be given the grace to continue here." Branna flicked her eyes to the window and then back towards Ariel.

"You see the good in everyone, I am not as naïve and I know how she thinks, and if she sees merit in my work, she may well hand it over to her golden haired minions to finish. It is a good job my notes are all written in code, those idiots will not have a clue how to read them." Ariel felt a little surprised.

"You write them in code?"

She had often seen Branna's heavy black note book, but she had never actually seen her notes, as she sat at her desk it made her realise something, and she remembered how on every occasion over the last two years when she had approached Branna whilst writing, she closed the book as she approached and looked up at her. Branna watched her intently across the room.

"I have to, you still after all this time do not fully understand the way of the queen, everyone on this side of the white rock has to protect themselves, if not we will be walked over and all our efforts will be taken and the credit claimed by those in her golden haired inner circle." Ariel shook her head.

"You are hopeless, you need to relax a little you are safe here." She smiled but Branna did not smile back, she stared out of the window her mind lost in her thoughts, and her voice sounded distant as if she was voicing her inner thoughts.

"I wish that was true Ariel, sadly it is not. I am only as safe for as long as your visit, things will change when you leave here, trust me, once she is queen and the realm hidden beneath her veil, there will be many changes to Avalon, and a lot more than you know will go unseen, the Fae Ofmoon hide their secrets well."

Ariel watched as Branna stiffened a little, a few moments later the sound of hooves could be heard on the road below heading their way at speed. Ariel stood at the same time as Branna turned, both of them reached the window side by side to see a rider in blue, it was a marshal of the Fae.

"This cannot be good, why does she send a soldier here?" Ariel felt the apprehension build inside Branna, she touched her hand.

"Relax it is one marshal, there must be important news for us."

She left Branna stood by the window, and walked into the living area and across to the open door, she stood and waited for the rider to slide to a halt, and then dismount. He was tall with long golden hair; she had not seen him before in this part of the land. He walked briskly down the stone path between the beds of growing vegetables and smiled as he approached. Ariel had felt a little tense, but relaxed as she saw the smile.

"Good afternoon, Marshal, can I be of service?" He came to a halt, and gave a slight bow.

"You are the Lady Ambassador to Florae I take it?" Ariel gave a nod.

"I am." He gave another smile and reached into his pocket.

"I have an important despatch for you My Lady, and I have been instructed to wait for your response." He handed over the folded sheet of paper bearing the seal of Gwendolyn. It came as a slight surprise as she saw it, Branna who had heard the conversation walked up to her side.

"It must be important if it is from the granddaughter and not the queen. Open it and see." Ariel fumbled on the seal and broke it unfolding the letter and began to read, Branna leaned in as the marshal stood waiting.

'Dear Ariel.

I have a meeting in an official capacity on behalf of my mother in Avalon, and I would care to speak with you face to face when it is concluded. It is important we meet and speak as I have concerns about home. I know of the close bond you share with my grandmother and would seek your advice as soon as possible. Please instruct my messenger if you will attend.

Gwendolyn.'

Ariel turned to Branna who gave a shrug. "You know she has been ill, maybe Gwen wants to talk to you and fill you in on more detail, I say go see her." Ariel gave a soft nod and then looked to the Marshal.

"When will the Princess Gwendolyn be here?"

"She is already here My Lady; she is the guest of Merlin in his newly built house on the far side of the river. She told me she will be free for a few days if you could find time to visit." Branna looked to the trees.

"You should go now, I will saddle a horse for you, this feels important." She looked at the Marshal. "Can you take her back with you?" He gave a respectful bow which made Branna smile.

"The Princess was hoping the very same thing, and I have instructions to accompany the ambassador if she requires it." Branna turned to Ariel.

"Pack a bag, I will sort the horse." Ariel turned and hurried into the house, and Branna walked across the garden towards the trees, and the small fenced off pen where the horses stood. The marshal stood where he was and waited patiently.

It did not take very long for Ariel to pack, and within the hour she had left Branna with a kiss and a long hug, and set off with the marshal. Branna, who was feeling more and more impatient, sat back at her desk to finish her notes. It felt like forever before the sun passed over the sky, and began to slowly drift down towards the horizon and mark the start of the night. As the light faded, she grabbed her things and almost ran up the steep path, and back to the pile of rocks that hid the old crate beneath. As the sunlight faded into darkness she opened the lid, and then lifted out the Jar from its padded place of safety, and carefully carried it to the table beneath her wooden shelter. She sat in her seat with her eyes level with the jar on the table.

"Are you awake?" The black mass in the bottom of the jar was motionless.

"We can hear you."

Her excitement bubbled inside her, for a moment she had wondered if she had fallen asleep the previous night and dreamt everything. Branna took a deep breath.

"How are we talking, I hear no words out loud, yet I can hear you in my head, do you understand the ways of the Fae." The gruff voice echoed in her mind.

"We know more than you all realise about all things, for we have studied everything for many of your years here. We need you to help us for we will not survive long in your world in this form, we need a garment to hide within and protect us, you must get one."

It took a few moments for Branna to fully understand what the dark mass in the jar was requesting.

"Oh, you need a body." She thought for a moment. "What sort of body? We do not make these easily."

"Bring us a life form, for we can share it." It puzzled her a little.

"Share it, you mean live inside another, if that is so take mine."

"We need you, and we need something smaller and powerful with speed. We cannot use you; you have been touched by the woman of light and for now it is too powerful for us to bear."

Branna had to think, her brain was slow as she was so excited to actually be able to communicate with the darkness that her thoughts were racing inside her head. She took a small moment to try and process what was being said to her, it took a few minutes before she fully understood what they meant by the woman of light, it suddenly became apparent.

"Oh, you mean Ariel, she is Fae of Earth, she is lovely, isn't she?"

"We do not trust her line; find us a life to take on."

Branna gave the moment more thought, something small and fast, yet powerful. Her problem was that she did not know what other life forms lived in the valley, she had seen Rabbits and the birds, but there were few other animals visible apart from the abundant horses that lived in the wilds. The darkness seemed to understand her before she could even speak.

"These birds in your mind, tell us about them." There was little to tell.

"Birds are small things that fly in the sky, apart from eating the odd ones, that is all I know, although don't eat the Ravens, they are a bit tough and leathery when you cook them."

"Tell us more of these Ravens creatures?" Branna thought for a second.

"Well, they are bigger than most the other birds round here, the older ones say they are birds of ill omen, for they are intelligent and cunning. The old myths say they carry the souls of the dead to the evil realms, and they are known to be able to possess the souls of those dead and return to create fear. I sort of like them, I have a few who come down from the trees and I feed them stale seed and stuff. They do kill other birds and eat them too, so I throw them out scraps of meat at times. That is pretty much all I know, Ariel is sort of more into nature and that kind of stuff, so she would probably know more."

"Bring us one alive. Put us back and leave this place, and do not return until you have one." Branna felt the disappointment flow into her.

"What I have to go already, but I have so many questions?"

"WE SAID BRING US ONE, NOW GO!" The voice screeched through her head, and she felt a coldness seep into her, it frightened her, and she jumped back from her seat.

"Alright there was no need to shout, I will get you a Raven."

She carried the jar back to the crate, but her mind remained clear and empty, the darkness meant what it said and spoke no more. Once she had placed the jar back and placed the rocks on top of the crate, she walked back to the house in the darkness feeling disappointed.

*T*he journey from the house to the cottage of Merlin was fast, Ariel found it hard to keep up with the marshal, but he pushed her on hard, and she could not quite understand the urgency. It became apparent as the sun began to fall in the sky; he wanted to get her there safely whilst they could still see the path. The road they took was a long winding one that took them over the large central mountain

range of the back of Avalon, and then down to marshes. It had been
a hot road over the summit, but as they descended in the failing light
to the marshes, and rode over many wooden bridges across the mire,
Ariel took great joy from the cool damp air. As darkness fell, they
made it onto the road, and after a short time at a gallop, she saw a
newly built white stone cottage surrounded by long grass and tangled
scrub ahead.

When they finally came to a halt outside the cottage of stone,
Gwendolyn was waiting at the door, she gave a smile as Ariel
dismounted, and Ariel noted how much she had grown and changed
since she had left Florae. Ariel gave a courteous bow.

"Princess Gwendolyn, I came as fast as I could."

Behind her the marshal took the horse and walked round the side
of the house, Ariel lifted her eyes and noted the differences in her
future queen. She was taller, and her hair was much longer and wavy
than she remembered. Gwendolyn's face was soft and kind like her
mother's, and her eyes although blue shone bright. Gwendolyn walked
up to her and held out her hands to embrace her.

"Ariel, you have been a part of my family for so long, there is no
need for ceremony between us."

"It would not be right, for your future is as the ruler of our people, I
could not be so disrespectful, and I will also add, I stand on ceremony
always with your grandmother, even though she is like a mother to
me. Tell me how is she, her letters do not dwell on detail and I cannot
help but feel there is more to this than she writes?" Gwendolyn
looked around, and Ariel felt her caution, she turned.

"Come inside, we can talk more openly, this house has protections
even the Queen of Fae cannot penetrate."

*G*wendolyn pushed open the door, it was a strange phrase and
Ariel could not at first understand. She lifted her bag, and followed
the young princess through the door, and down a long corridor,
which turned to the right and entered a large open space, with a big
fire place in which the stacked logs burned brightly. Ariel looked at
the sparsely furnished room; it was bare, even compared with the
home she lived in with Branna. There were a few carved chairs, and a
newly built wooden table on which a large earthen dish contained five
burning candles to light the room. The walls and floor were bare and
yet with the glow of the fire it felt warm and cosy.

Gwendolyn sat in one of the chairs situated by the side of the fire, and gestured for Ariel to sit in the other; she dropped her bag on the floor beside it and sat down. Gwendolyn smiled.

"Things have changed in Florae, and a great deal of what I tell you is known only to my grandfather, myself, Gwynfor and my father. Bade has some knowledge but not all." Her tone was soft, but Ariel could read the urgency in her words.

"You know that I will not divulge anything I hear, I would protect your grandmother with my life such is my love for her."

It felt odd, Gwendolyn had been such a young girl filled with life and always giggling, before she had left Florae. Sat here in the dim light of the cottage, it was clear how much Gwendolyn had grown up, and Ariel marvelled to see just how much like her grandmother she had become. Gwendolyn reached into a canvass bag at the side of her chair and drew out a small circular plaque of wood; Ariel recognised it immediately as a charm plaque that all the Fae hung above their doors to add protections to their homes. Gwendolyn leant forward and handed it to her.

"Tell me what you know of this symbol?" Ariel took the small wooden disk of dark pitch pine and looked down at it; it was smooth and highly polished plain dark wood. "Turn it over, and tell me what you see, I know you more than any of our line have studied the symbolism of our past."

Ariel turned it over in her hands to reveal a symbol. The second she saw the bright red five pointed star within a white circle, she felt a shiver run down her spine, and she gave a slight gasp. She looked up to see the concerned blue eyes of Gwendolyn watching her every move, she looked so young, and yet Ariel sensed a greater wisdom behind the eyes. She looked back to the symbol on the small circular plaque.

"This is a symbol I have not seen since my youth of nearly 200 years past, my mother wrote this symbol many years ago for Tideguyde, and placed it on the moon realm in hope she would return one day to collect it." Gwendolyn gave a slight nod.

"Can you explain what it means?"

Just to see it and hold it in her hands felt painful, it had been on her mother's return she had been struck down with a great illness and melancholy which ended up in her taking her own life. Ariel felt the surge of pain in her chest that had been a frequent part of her solitude; a tear welled in her eye and ran onto her cheek. Gwendolyn leant forward in her seat.

"I know the meaning this has for you, so please tell me as I think my grandmother fears something none of us know of." Ariel gave a sniffle and wiped the tears from her eyes, she swallowed hard to compose herself.

"My mother was not just a Seer, she was also a caster of runes for our people, she held a power of protection that rivalled everyone. She felt something no other could and created this to protect Tideguyde, but she never returned to collect it, as far as I know it now protects Rhiannon. I watched her as a small child create this, it is the power of the earth blended in the circle of the White Circle, it is a very powerful symbol that gives protection from the unseen enemies. The points of the five tips of the star represent the elements of life on earth. Earth, air, fire, water and spirit, they are coloured to the power of the spirit of Eve who gave us life, the white circle you know is as you and your father are named such, is the light of our race that brings balance and wisdom to create peace." She looked up from the symbol to Gwendolyn. "My mother said wherever this was placed, darkness could not enter. What does this have to do with your grandmother?"

The fire crackled in the hearth as Gwendolyn sat back for a second and thought, her words were soft. "What indeed?" She looked at Ariel and pointed to the plaque.

"This I will share only with you for no one else must find out the truth. After the setting of the last moon, when Grandmother had visited every home in Florae and cured those with the sickness of melancholy, she moved from her apartments in the House of Scribes, to a spare room at the far end of the house. That symbol is painted on the floor of the room with her bed directly over it, she also has one on her ceiling and on every wall, she has even placed it on every window."

"What?" Gwendolyn shook her head.

"I have no knowledge of why, I just remember being shown it by my mother as a child, but Ariel that is not all, she has demanded that every house in Florae bears that symbol, and I mean demanded, she is obsessed with it, we now fear for her mind."

The news was startling, and Ariel was unsure just how to deal with it. Deep within her she felt a huge wave of fear pass through her, as the memory of her mother doing the exact same flooded into her thoughts. Everyone at the time had said the very same of her mother, her hands began to tremble and her voice stuck in her throat.

"It is the same as my mother, she died and your grandmother took me into her home and cared for and treated me as a daughter." Ariel felt her voice quake. "Do you think they are the same?" Gwendolyn gave a faint smile as if understanding that Ariel was coming to a similar conclusion as herself.

"All I know is your mother feared something so great she took her own life. My grandmother is the most powerful member of our line, far more powerful than your mother, but what I need to know is why your mother created that symbol? Ariel if you know anything that will aide her you must now say so." Tears filled her eyes again.

"I know nothing more, I was just a young child, and my mother pushed me away, she told me I had to be protected, she sent me to your grandmother, and days later she was gone. If I could tell you anything more I would, for your grandmother is in every way a mother to me and in every sense my family. You know this Gwendolyn, you were raised and educated by both of us, I have always and still do consider you to be like a daughter to myself." Her tears rolled down her cheeks and dripped onto the floor. Gwendolyn gave her a gentle nod.

"I know, and I see you as kin too, but I am so afraid to lose her. Ariel, I am not ready to be a queen, I have so much more to learn from her before my time comes to carry the mantle of our people. Ariel if you can think of anything at all that will help save her, I would owe you my life."

Tears welled in Gwendolyn's eyes, and Ariel saw the fear that was hidden deep within her. How could she allow this young girl who was destined to be a queen one day, suffer the same painful fate as herself?

"Gwendolyn, I have asked your grandmother and she has refused, you must convince her to allow me to come home to Florae, and send a replacement for me here."

"I have tried believe me, it is the reason I have come here to see you in person, it was Merlin who suggested it, he knew here of all places with the runes cast over the place, no one would be able to hear any words spoken. There is a truce between the two lines of Fae but it is held in a delicate balance, my grandmother still holds her objections to Rhiannon's rule, she has called all Fae back to Florae, and demands they are met in person by herself before she admits them. I do not understand her thinking Ariel, but you know her as well as I do, and you know she has powers and wisdom that go beyond us both. If she is afraid or wary of anything, I have learned throughout all my life to heed her warnings."

Ariel gave a reassuring nod. "You have deep wisdom, I too agree, if she fears something, we too should be wary."

*I*t was a strange night sat together in the newly built house of Merlin. Gwendolyn prepared food, and they sat at the table and ate a good meal, before Gwendolyn showed her the room, she could rest in. They talked until late into the night of many things. Gwendolyn gave her a far deeper briefing on life back in Florae of how her father Ninian and brother Gwynfor were working so hard on the buildings across all of the islands of the realm. Gwynfor was becoming quite the man, and was well loved as his skills with wood excelled, and brought a greater beauty to everything he was involved with. The House of Scribes was almost finished, as Bade had managed to train over one hundred new scribes, and had them organise the large rooms of the history of their people, and now they had fifty of those scribes organising a new library of all the histories of the other races. The last two years had been very busy, but they were reaching a point where Bridget's plans for the new realm were coming to fruition.

*A*riel slept little that night, as she lay in her bed, her mind was filled with the painful memories of her past as she watched and relived the decline of her mother in her dreams. She woke with a start to find it was morning; the sun streamed in through the little windows, and outside the air was filled with the chattering of birds. Ariel rose and dressed and wandered into the living room which was empty, from a door to the side of the large fireplace came the sounds of pots rattling. Ariel sat in the chair next to the last few smouldering ashes of what had been a roaring fire last night and rubbed her eyes. Footsteps on the wooden floor announced the presence of someone entering. Ariel turned and looked up through slightly blurred eyes, to see a figure slowly clear of a man, she had expected it to be Gwendolyn, he was holding a steaming cup.

"Good morning."

He smiled. He was young with long semi golden hair and a goatee that stretched from his chin to his shirt. His eyes were soft and gentle of the deepest green, and yet held a sparkle of life brighter than any she had ever seen. She reached for the mug unsure of who this stranger was exactly.

"Good morning, where is the princess?" He continued to smile and gave a nod of understanding.

"Gwen sends her apologies; she has had to return home." He turned and pointed with his other hand as Ariel took the cup. "She has left you a note." Ariel lifted the cup as she nodded. He gave another smile.

"I am Merlin by the way."

"What?"

The cup lifted slightly with her jump of surprise, and Merlin reacted quicker than lightning as it left her hand and caught it. Ariel shot straight up with flushed cheeks, and gave a regal bow.

"My Lord Whiteline please excuse my rudeness; I am Ariel of Erin and at your service for the people of Fae of Earth." She stared at the floor as her face burned red with embarrassment. Merlin gave out a mighty guffaw and bellowed with laughter.

"My dear lady of Fae, you are in my home, we do not stand on ceremony within these walls, did Gwen not you tell this?"

Ariel who was still bent over looked up her face quite red as the young lord bellowed with laughter, his eyes danced as he reached his hand to lift her back up straight.

"I see your queen has taught you immense manners and respect, I am honoured by such a tribute, but please treat me as any other in my house. Goodness, all this bending and bowing will wear you out." Ariel smiled, still feeling embarrassed and stood upright.

It was surprising to see this young man who only looked like his mid thirties, who she knew was older than her race. He was greatly revered by all the races as the guardian of the Whiteline, and the apprentice trained by the great White Lord Albanlin. Merlin handed back the cup of tea, and in her mind, it felt like a treasured gift, he had made this for her, her mind spun, the Guardian of the Whitelines had made her tea, the legend himself had actually made her tea and she was standing in his house… Alone! Her voice was frozen in her constricting throat.

"Thankyou… sorry… forgive my clumsiness." He simply giggled and pointed to the table where she saw the plaque and a folded piece of parchment.

"I believe I was informing you of her note."

She nodded like an idiot, and moved closer holding her cup, which shook slightly in her hand. Merlin lifted the note and passed it to her; she took it and placed the cup on the table at the side of the plaque containing the symbol of her mother's. Ariel unfolded the sheet and read the neat hand writing.

'I trust my grandmother, you should too. Protect yourself."

Ariel glanced from the note to the table, and turned to see Merlin watching her, he smiled and shrugged.

"It's sound advice; listen to her she will be a mighty queen one day."

Chapter Five.

Roack.

*T*he day had felt longer than usual, when Ariel finally arrived home. She had risen to find Gwendolyn had left early, and was alone in the house with Merlin, which had been a massive surprise. It had taken some time, just to get use to the fact that she was actually talking to him like he was an ordinary person, which he was in many ways, even though he was also a hero of all the Fae. He had suggested they walk their horses round the lake in the morning sun, and so for the next four hours Ariel enjoyed walking and talking about what was hoped for the new realm, as Merlin pointed out some of the more important landmarks of Avalon. She had not realised the Forest of Time that bordered the realm was in fact as close as it was, and just knowing she was walking along the border of what was the home of Eve and Hearne was so exciting, she had for some time been lost for words.

The tour of the realm ended with her once again walking along the long white Queen's Road, and up to the base of Citadel Mount, something she had taken a great deal of joy to actually see on this occasion, as the sky was crystal clear and it was not obscured from view by the low clouds. So much had changed since her arrival, and the whole face of the Mount was now free of the scaffold and was a brilliant white. The town at its base was almost complete, as long rows of white buildings with neatly thatched rooftops were prepared for their new inhabitants, and as she stood with Merlin and took in the sights, she felt a growing feeling deep inside that reminded her of Branna.

She had not mentioned many of her findings whilst living with Branna to Merlin, but as she gazed on the completed town which was filled with dark haired craftsmen, all adding the finishing touches to windows, doors, and signs; she wondered just how many of these workers would actually get to live here. It was almost as if she heard

Branna's voice in her head answer her.

"You think anyone not of golden hair will live there? It is not their sweat that has carved out this realm Ariel, it is the sweat of my kind, but we can only dream of the joy of one day being equal enough to call that town home." It sent a cold shiver down her spine.

Her mind wandered to a moment in the previous summer, when they had bathed in the river and were both lay together on the soft grass as they dried of in the sun. She had turned to watch Branna as she spoke of her people, and once again her voice was soft in her mind.

"The truth is people talk of the two lines of Fae, but believe me Ariel it is really three, for although I am Ofmoon, I will never be seen as a full member of the Fae. Everyone who is not golden is yet another line; you must never forget that; we are very separate."

Merlin took her down the road to the completed bridge across the lake, and here he said his goodbyes and handed her back to the tall Marshall to guide her home. His parting words stuck with her all the way home.

"Never forget the wisdom of Bridget, for I consider her to be the greatest of the Fae and a trusted friend. She chose you above all others for this task, it is your duty to document the truth of all you have seen to place on record forever in your House of Scribes. Every word you write will be the future of all people here and across all the realms, and one day those words will have wisdom that could save a great many. Write from the heart my fair member of your line; be true to yourself, and to those who surround you."

She was not completely sure what he had fully meant, but as she set off back to her home under the guide of the Marshal, she pulled out her note book and wrote down his words line for line, and then spent the rest of the long journey back home in deep thought.

*W*hen she arrived home, there was no sign of Branna and the house looked a complete mess. She busied herself cleaning up, and then set a pan of stew on the fire to cook. Whilst she let the stew cook, she went into her room and unpacked her bag where she found the small plaque given her by Gwendolyn. It felt very precious to her, as it was also a strong symbol of her mother, and she smiled to herself, and then walked out of the room to the outer door. Standing on a chair she took three small brass pins and using them to hold the plaque against the wall, she secured it by knocking them in with a flat stone from the garden. Standing back, she quietly spoke the charm of protection over the house, bowed, and stood back and admired it positioned just above the centre of the door, she said the second small charm, taught her by her mother quietly to herself, and blessed the house and asked for protection from all that would harm her.

Branna arrived a few hours later carrying a small cage of fine wooden strips, and a large woven net, she came through the gate and saw Ariel sat in a chair in the sun next to the carrot bed. She looked hot and a little angry, Ariel smiled.

"What in this realm have you been doing?" She was about to giggle when Branna snapped at her.

"NOTHING…WHY?" It surprised her, she had been really looking forward to seeing her, and had thought Branna would have felt the same.

"Sorry, I missed you and just wondered."

"WELL DON'T!" She threw the net on the floor and kicked it. Ariel stood up and walked quickly over to her.

"Bran my love what has happened to get you so upset?"

Branna stomped across the garden and through the door into the house; Ariel quickly followed her and caught up with her in her room.

"Bran wait, please tell me, can I help?" Branna turned and smiled as she came level with her, and lifted her arms and pulled her into a kiss, Ariel felt lost for words. She stepped back and looked at Branna, her voice was soft. "What was all that about?" Branna looked confused.

"We kissed I missed you." Ariel did not understand, and she shook her head.

"Not the kiss, before that out in the garden, you shouted at me." Branna looked confused.

"Did I?" Ariel nodded.

"Yes, you did, you came stomping back through the gate angry with a net and shouted at me." Branna looked confused.

"Did I? Sorry I have been out trying to catch a raven, I want one for an experiment, but they will not come near me. I have been out all day trying to get one."

It sounded like an odd thing to do, but knowing Branna as well has she now did, Ariel accepted it, but her sudden change of attitude and the fact she could not remember just a few moments ago bothered her. She made light of it, and went with the flow.

"Ravens are cunning and very intelligent; you know this Bran. You have got no chance trying to catch one with a net, you need to charm them. Bran it is basic Fae magic, you should know that." A look of understanding crossed Branna's face.

"Yeah, your Fae not mine, do not forget we are indeed both Fae but we both have different abilities. Hmm, I should have realised it is an earth thing, your people are good with animals and the like." She gave a big smile and leaned in and gave her another kiss. "Could you talk one into getting in the cage?" It was a strange request even for Branna who had some very peculiar ways at times.

"You are not going to hurt it are you?" Branna looked really surprised.

"NO… Ariel I have never hurt anything, why would I do that?" Ariel had been unsure after Branna's outburst.

"Just checking, you know it is against my creed to harm any living thing unnecessarily?"

"Yeah, I know that, Ariel I am not going to harm it, I just need to watch its reaction to an experiment I need to do for my research, honestly it is nothing sinister." Ariel gave a nod and smiled.

"Alright if it is that important come with me, but you must promise it must be set free when you are finished, I think there is nothing sadder and more unnatural as a caged bird." Branna gave a smile and nodded.

"If I can, I hope I can train it to stay with me up there as I work, you know sit on my shoulder and stuff?" It all felt very odd to Ariel, but there again Branna was not the most normal member of the Fae that she knew. She turned and walked outside, she stopped at the low wall.

"Hold up the cage with the door open."

Ariel closed her eyes for a moment and summoned her powers, she opened her eyes and they shone slightly, as she scanned the trees around the house for any sign of a Raven. There was a large one sat on a branch high up in one of the apple trees, she focused on it and it gave a twitch. Ariel connected with the bird and closed her eyes; she could see herself stood with Branna holding up the cage with the door open. As Ariel focused her thoughts the bird swept wide its wings and glided out of the tree, and down towards Branna. It landed on the open door of the cage and walked inside, Branna closed the door behind it with a smile.

"That was really something to watch, you have got to show me how to do that, wow Ariel that is really special magic." Ariel gave a smile as she saw what looked like a sense of relief on Branna's face.

"She is called Roack, treat her well." Branna smiled a huge smile.

"Hi Roack, we are going to be good friends and work together. Thanks Ariel, I love you."

"No problem, come on it's almost time to eat." She walked indoors and the smiling Branna followed holding her new companion in its cage.

Inside the house Branna was filled with joy, and before they could get a chance to eat, she pulled Ariel into an embrace and kissed her with passion. Before Ariel knew what was happening, they were undressed and in bed as Branna made love to her with a passion like she had never experienced before. After what felt like an age of the most mind shattering love making in the whole time, she had known Branna, they finally parted and lay naked on top of the bed gasping for breath and covered in sweat. Branna looked up at the ceiling her face painted with a happy smile.

"I missed you." Ariel took a deep breath; her body was still responding to the touch of Branna.

"I have noticed… I missed you to." Branna rolled over on to her side to face her.

"I love you more than you will ever realise, you know that don't you?" Ariel gave another gasp followed by a giggle.

"If that was anything to go by, I think I am reassured." She lifted a hand to stroke back the wild dark hair so she could see Branna's dark sparkling eyes. "You are the love of my life too, I cannot tell you how happy I am here with you Bran, and this has without a doubt been the best part of my life."

She smiled and leaned over to kiss her softly on the lips. Ariel felt in total bliss, she had missed her whilst she had been gone, even though it had only been for a short time, she too had realised that being here in Avalon alone with Branna had changed everything about her, and she had finally found a place after so many long years where she felt she truly belonged.

Branna jumped up on the bed and giggled, she slapped Ariel on the buttock.

"Come on let's go for a quick swim before we eat." She bounced off the bed, and ran out of the door. Ariel jumped up and shouted after her.

"BRAN YOU FORGOT YOUR CLOTHES!" But she had run giggling out of the house. Ariel jumped up, and ran as fast as she could to catch her up, and Branna looked back and saw her, and ran laughing and screaming down the path and into the trees towards the deeper part of the river.

*I*t had felt like the happiest day ever as Ariel kissed Branna, and she carried her caged bird with her bag of notes off to continue her work. She felt a warmth within her she had not experienced before, as she watched Branna turn on the path, and head for the high wall of rock, and the path up to her work station. As the light faded, she sat by the window at her own desk and filled in her journal of her thoughts and feelings about her meeting with Gwendolyn, and her arrival home with Branna. It was not long before the exhaustion of the long day took its toll, and she closed her book and placed it on the top shelf of her cupboard, before locking it, and walked into Branna's room to snuggle into their bed. The pillows smelt of her, and she gave a contented smile as she relaxed, and within minutes was fast asleep.

High up above her on the rock, Branna carried the jar to her table where she had also placed the cage containing Roack the raven. The bird watched her with small dark eyes as she looked into the jar.

"I have brought you what you wished for." The dark mass swirled up within the jar.

"You have done well." Branna looked at the bird, which had pressed itself back against the bars of the cage, and had fear in its eyes.

"It's a raven, and she is called Roack."

Before she could finish her sentence, the bird went wild and began to screech and scream in its cage. It flapped its wings violently to a point where the cage began to rock on the table. Branna grabbed the cage, but as she steadied it, to her surprise the dark mass passed right through the side of the jar, and flowed through the air into the cage. It rose to match the height of the screeching bird and then expanded out to form the shape of a raven.

Branna felt panic flood into her as she saw the bird's reaction, but it was too late, the mass was free of the jar and forming into a perfect copy of the Raven. It rippled and shuddered as it took shape, and then as the raven gave an almighty screech, it slid inside the raven and disappeared. The raven stopped flapping and went silent, and began to twitch. It gave Branna a sick feeling to her stomach, but she knew there was nothing she could do to stop it, she had thought she had trapped the dark mass in the large jar, but as she had seen, she had been fooled as the mass had just passed through the glass as if it was not there. The raven stiffened in the cage and then relaxed.

"This will be perfect, thank you we were very hungry." Branna shuddered.

"Hungry… What did you eat?" She could see the bird was still completely intact.

"It's spirit, we believe you call this a soul, is that right?" Branna swallowed hard and shuddered again.

"You ate its soul, no offence but that is a little bit creepy, what are you really?"

"We believe you call us Merle, but now we are Roack. We are many and we are one, we live here all around you, you can see us as you have part of us within you, as do many of your line."

The sudden horror of the moment hit Branna, and she felt the hairs lift on the back of her neck.

"You are in me?" There was silence for a few moments.

"Fear not for you are safe. Open the cage and we shall talk."

Branna felt unable to move for a moment, and then found the strength to lift her hand which was trembling up to the latch. She lifted it and the door swung open, and out walked the bird, and stretched out its large wings.

"This is good, these ravens can fly, and it will serve us well."

"Is the bird dead?" Her voice was soft and shaky. "It's just that I promised Ariel it would not be harmed." A crude laugh echoed in her thoughts, and made her shudder.

"It is now but an empty vessel for us to control, but it will serve a great purpose for you and us, and its life will be longer than any other in these realms."

The Raven walked along the table and stretched its wings out wide, and then turned to face Branna.

"You have done well child of the moon, in this form we can take what we need to maintain this body, and it will be very useful to us as we can watch again from above. You will need rest to recover what we

borrowed, but your strength will grow in time, and you will find the power within you will grow stronger with each day, for we are now connected as one."

Branna felt empty and weak, her mind raced as she tried to fully understand what was being said, but such was her exhaustion she slipped back into the chair and her eyelids flickered. As Branna drifted into a deep sleep below her small shelter, the Raven flapped its wings and lifted into the sky, high above it the clouds swirled and lightening streaked into the air. All over Avalon the heavens opened, and the rain thundered down with force. Roack flapped vigorously, and screeched into the dark sky as if it was shouting out in joy to the rest of the night.

Ariel sat up in her bed and shivered with the coldness flowing through her. The air outside exploded, and lightening streaked down hitting a tree close to the house. It flashed with white light, and then split down its trunk as flames erupted.

"BRANNA!"

Without thinking, she jumped out of bed and grabbed her dress. As she crossed the house, she fumbled awkwardly into it. She raced out of the door and into the pouring rain, and ran for the path that led up the side of the steep rock towards where Branna had gone. Her heart pounded in her chest, as the rain pelted into her eyes, and she gasped for breath, her legs running for all they were worth. It felt like the hardest fight of her life as she forced her slender body forward against the pressure of the driving rain. Half blinded by the water and gasping for air, she staggered to the top of the path and onto the flat summit. Trying her best in the total darkness; as she shielded her eyes with her hand to hold back the rain from her pale grey eyes.

"BRANNA... BRANNA WHERE ARE YOU?" She screamed for all she was worth.

The lightening flashed high above her. For the briefest moment she thought she saw a slumped figure on the floor below her shelter. Ariel ran in the general direction hoping the lightening would guide her to the right place, it did and she realised she had almost stepped on her. Ariel fell to her knees below the broken shelter at the side of Branna, as her ears exploded with the noise of the crack of thunder.

She dragged the soaked limp body of Branna into her arms and held her tight as she wailed with fear, hoping she was not dead. Branna was ice cold, and she pulled her as close as she could to let her own warmth flow into her, and leaned forward to shield her face from the driving rain. The skies lit up again, but Ariel was too busy looking down at the pale face of the woman she loved, to see the huge figure of a black bird outlined in the clouds above her.

Branna moved and gave a slight moan, and Ariel's tears exploded from her eyes with relief as she snuggled into her and held her close. All she could do for the moment was hold her tight and cradle her and protect her with her love, Branna's cold white hand came up to her face.

"Ariel?" Her voice sounded weak, and Ariel squeezed her as hard, as she could and wept.

"I am here my love, I have you, you are safe."

Somewhere in the distance of Branna's mind a voice croaked in a vile tone, and her eyes snapped wide open.

"Get rid of her, she needs to leave."

For a moment Branna felt dazed, but then her mind cleared and she twisted on the floor and lifted herself up, and was instantly snatched back into Ariel's embrace. Branna slipped her arms around the weeping figure in the darkness.

"Ariel it is not safe here, we need to leave." Ariel just hung on tight and wept. "We must go Ariel it is not safe for us here."

Branna struggled free and tried to stand, her legs felt weak and she wobbled, Ariel was up in a flash and grabbed her and pulled her close. She pulled Branna's arm around her shoulder, and then taking her weight she lifted her slightly.

"I thought I had lost you, never scare me like that again." Branna could feel the fear in Ariel's shaking body, and pulled her tighter.

"I am sorry, I never expected this."

*T*ogether in the driving rain, they began to slowly make their way towards the path that would take them down the side of the rock. The lightening continued, and the thunder roared, as they staggered down the path towards their home. As they approached the doorway Branna noticed the plaque, and suddenly she felt a huge wave of fear pass through her. Ariel staggered for a moment and Branna tried to stop and not pass under the door, the fear coursed through her body, but she was just too weak, and the strength of Ariel had appeared to increase as she approached the door. Her body began to shake and spasm, but she could not prevent Ariel dragging her over the threshold and into the house.

Just for an instant she thought she heard a terrible scream in her thoughts, then Ariel and herself collapsed through the doorway, and fell sprawling onto the wooden floor, and she felt a wave of peace flow through her. Branna lay still for a moment feeling a little strength seeping into her body, she had not realised that she was gasping for air, and as she breathed in deeply, her head turned to see the soaked form of Ariel lay on her back at her side gasping for air. She watched as Ariel lifted her left foot and kicked out at the door, and it swung at speed into the frame and banged closed. Ariel turned her head to see Branna watching, and she felt a huge wave of relief wash over her, she took a long breath in and let her lungs fill with oxygen.

"Please tell me you did not cause that Bran?"

Chapter Six.

The Fateful Day.

When Ariel awoke the following morning, the sky had cleared and the sun was bright in the sky. It was far later than she normally woke, and as she stirred, she felt the heat radiating across the bed from Branna. Ariel lifted her head out of the pillow, to see the wet matted hair of Branna. Her face was bright red and the sweat was rapidly running down her face. She stiffened to see her love in what appeared to be a violent fever, sitting up fast, she swept her hand towards Branna's temple, and her thoughts were confirmed. Ariel gave her a gentle nudge, but Branna did not stir, her eyelids flickered as if in some form of delirium, and a coldness swept rapidly through Ariel, this was a fever she had seen many years ago when she was only a small girl.

Without even thinking she was out of bed, and ran through the house tearing the door open, as she raced to the well. She grabbed the bucket and flung it into the small circular hole, and let the rope run through her fingers down into the dark depths towards the cool water. Everything felt like it was running at high speed in her mind, such was her panic. With a bucket filled, she pulled furiously at the rope, raising the cool clear water to her with all her might, as she desperately knew that she had to quell the fire burning within her lover. Minutes later, she was back at the side of the bed as she tore away the sheets, revealing Branna's tanned slender naked form. Dragging the sheets from the bed, she tore at them, ripping them into wide squares that she plunged into the bucket of ice cold water, and then without ringing them she lifted them out and spread them onto Branna's burning body.

With her eyes closed she quietly focused her powers, and chanted the charms of the Fae healers. It was well over an hour before the colour faded a little and the red burning flesh felt a little cooler. Keeping her covered in the damp torn sheets, Ariel left the bed and opened the window to allow the cool breeze to flow into the room and over the bed. As she felt she was starting to gain a little control, she left Branna in the midst of her fever and headed to the stove, where she placed a pan on to boil and stocked up the fire with timber. In her room in the bottom drawer of her small cabinet, she retrieved her bag of small glass tubes; each sealed with a cork stopper, and carried them to the kitchen. Ariel mixed up an herbal potion, and added it to the pan to boil.

*F*or the rest of the day, she sat on the bed and pulled Branna into a sitting position, and alternated between trying to feed her small amounts of the potion, and damping her burning flesh down in order to break the fever. By evening Branna had cooled a great deal, but was still lost in her fever driven dreams, and muttered words Ariel had never heard before, but Ariel felt a little relief that Branna was starting to cool, even if it was taking much longer than normal. Throughout the rest of the night, with every window in the house open and the cold air of the dark night flowing in, wrapped in a shawl, Ariel sat beside her and nursed her through the worst of the fever.

*I*t was four days later when Branna woke shivering on the top of the bed. Her body was still warmer than normal, even if it was shaking, and her mind felt clouded and groggy, she opened her eyes to see the smiling face of Ariel.

"Welcome back." Branna tried to sit, but her body ached and felt very weak.

"What happened?" Ariel handed her a cup of sweet smelling liquid.

"Drink this. You have been in a fever for five days, don't try to get up, you have been quite sick, save your strength." Ariel leaned over as she handed her the cup, and then pulled the pillows up behind her to help her sit. "Do you not remember the storm?"

Branna tried to think, but her mind felt weak and strained, and she shook her head. "No… Why what happened?"

"There was a really violent storm and you were injured up on your rock, you would probably be dead if I had not come looking for you, and brought you back here." Branna tried to remember, but just could not. She lifted the cup and drank a small amount of the liquid, which quenched a thirst she had not even realised she had.

"Thank you." Ariel stood up.

"What in all the realms were you playing at up there?" Her voice held the concern and worry she felt, but was also very stern.

"Branna you could have died, who is so stupid they would point a rod of tall copper at a lightning storm?" Tears flowed into her eyes and she sobbed. "Branna, I thought the lightning had killed you, I thought I had lost you." She fell on her knees at the side of the bed and flung her arms around her, plunging her face into her chest as she wept. Branna felt a deep pang of guilt as she saw the distress in Ariel; she brought her arm round her and pulled her closer.

"I am so sorry." What else could she say, her mind was fuzzy and she could not remember the detail of the night? "Please don't cry, I am still here. I told you, I get so carried away I do not always think, please Ariel I hate to see you cry."

It was some time before Ariel was calm enough to talk. She curled on the bed next to Branna and explained what had happened, and slowly Branna began to remember small parts of the night. Ariel talked slowly and softly of finding her under the smashed shelter, and how she had half carried, half dragged her back to the house, and how for a moment she had appeared to resist coming in through the door. Branna listened carefully and then suddenly remembered something.

"My notes?" Ariel gave a sigh.

"They are safe, once your fever started to ease, I went back and got your bag, they appear to be safe, they were under the table so avoided most of the rain. I hung your bag on the door over there see." Branna gave a long breath as if greatly relieved.

"That is my whole life; to lose that would be the end of me." Ariel gave a smile,

"They are in better shape than your shelter, it appears the Fae Ofmoon may be good at tunnels, but your skills at carpentry are much to be desired."

"Is it that bad?"

"It's damaged beyond repair, but fear not, every Fae of Earth has had some experience with wood, I can help you build a stronger one if you intend to go back up there." Branna looked a little apologetic.

"I have too. I am sorry, but it is the reason I am here, and I need to finish before the queen arrives." Ariel had figured she would, although having seen some of the danger she was not keen, but she understood. She got up from the bed.

"You need to recover your strength; I will make you some broth.

Old William from the house at the other end of the road sent you some beef when he heard, I will prepare it, you need to rest up until you are back to full strength again." Ariel walked to the door and Branna watched her, she turned as she passed the frame. "Although I was relieved to see Roack was unharmed." Branna looked a little surprised.

"The bird was unharmed?" Ariel smiled.

"You must have made an impact; it's been sat out there in the tree watching you all the time you have been asleep. I told her to come in and sit on the bed, but I think I scared her, she seems to be wary of me. See I told you ravens are intelligent, she probably thinks I am going to put her back in a cage."

Branna turned and looked out through the window, high up in the apple tree across the garden, she saw the large black raven watching her, she was not sure why, but an icy shiver ran down her spine.

For the next few days, Branna much to her annoyance was confined to bed. Her strength returned but she slept a great deal more than ever before. During her sleep piece by piece her memory returned in the form of her dreams, and each time she woke in a cold sweat, she understood more of what had transpired. After three days she remembered every detail, and decided that she could no longer lie in bed, she got up and began to slowly get back into her routine.

*T*he arrival of the queen was drawing closer, and so the number of visitors each day declined, as each task was finished in preparation for Rhiannon's arrival. Most days as Branna sat at her desk writing the few reports of the day, unbeknown to her Ariel carried the tools up to the rock, and rebuilt her shelter, which was far more solid and weather resistant. In Ariel's mind she thought if she built it, she would feel more at ease if the weather turned bad again overnight whilst she was at home, and Branna was alone up there.

Eventually the time arrived, and Branna made her lonely trek up the rock to her work post, and within minutes the raven appeared and landed on the table. For a moment it had felt like a bad dream, but as Branna sat, and Roack told her of her flights across the realm to learn as much as she could of the inhabitants around them, and of the things she had seen, Branna began to understand that the darkness had far more intelligence than even she had realised. It was also clear that to try and control them would be a very difficult task. From that day onward she understood that their relationship would be more like a partnership of understanding, as both of them still had many questions to ask. One thing was very clear; Roack did not like Ariel, and referred to her as the woman of light.

The weeks passed slowly, and considering that Branna had always insisted that Ariel stay away from the rock, as the work for the realm slowed to a halt, Branna would spend many afternoons up on the rock finishing off parts of her study. The days heated up, and on the occasional hot afternoons, Ariel would climb the steep path and bring Branna cool drinks and small parcels of food.

The view of the realm from the high vantage point was vast, and Ariel would spend her time sat on the edge of the rock watching the world below or adding to her journal. Branna mainly sat below her shelter writing her coded entries in her note book, but occasionally she would join her and talk of the realm below and all the masses of workers scattered in every part of the area. It was valuable information that gave Ariel a better understanding of the Fae who laboured for Rhiannon. There was gossip all over that Bridget was sick again, and Branna told Ariel of the rumours, and although she did not want to face it, somehow it felt like things were heading towards sadness and endings. Slowly the fateful day approached, until one afternoon as Ariel worked in her kitchen a messenger arrived from the main town of Avalonia.

*I*n many ways she knew before she opened the sealed letter, she was to be called back to Florae to report on her finding to the House of Scribes, and would be gone for at least a month. It was with a heavy heart and few tears she made her way onto the path that would take her to see Branna. It felt like a difficult walk, her heart was heavy before the letter came, Branna had been quieter over the last week, and had spent much more time working on her research than normal. Ariel had felt a little left out and isolated, and in many ways, she wondered if going back to Florae would maybe help ease the tension between them.

Branna had been in her mind, working too hard and not sleeping enough. Her face was paler than normal, and under her eyes black lines were clearly visible. She had on a few occasions mentioned it to her, only to find Branna got very angry and shouted. It was hard, but she did understand the pressure as each day came closer to Rhiannon's arrival in Avalonia, and the pressure on Branna intensified.

Ariel reached the summit and started to walk across the wide plain on the top of the rock, the sun was scorching hot on her shoulders and face. Branna stood lost in thought as she read from her endless notes. Ariel called out to her, and her eyes lifted to see the small slender figure of Ariel dressed in deep burgundy, walking smiling towards her. She lowered the parchment to the table as she smiled, and slipped it into the large open black book, and then closed the cover to hide it. The approaching figure of Ariel waved, and Branna lifted a hand to wave back.

In the few minutes it took for Ariel to walk the distance to the shelter, Branna packed her large black book into her bag, and poured out two large silver goblets of wine. Ariel gave a pant as she came under the shelter, and Branna embraced her.

"I saw the marshal this morning, and I am sorry to hear about Bridget Violet, it appears the word is out on her health. She is a good queen, how is she, is there nothing that can be done to cure her melancholy? Her presence is missed in all the realms." Ariel gave a sad smile, and took the goblet to quench her thirst from the walk in the hot sun.

"She is unchanged, we fear for her now, and I think it is likely that Gwendolyn will soon take her place, but thank you. I have been ordered back to Florae, hopefully not for too long, but it is a least a month. They are sending a marshal shortly and I wanted to say goodbye before I left. I will miss you and your wild ways my love." Her soft grey eyes held the sadness of the moment, yet Branna smiled.

"It is probably better; I have been thinking a great deal, and I think I too will be leaving here." Ariel looked surprised; her heart began to beat rapidly deep within her.

"When… How… I mean your work is here, isn't it?" Branna walked back to the chair beside the table.

"It is finished for this place, for what good it has done me." She sat down and took a sip from her goblet; Ariel walked over and sat in the chair in front of her. Branna looked drained and tired.

"I have done all I can here, but it matters little, Rhiannon has refused all of my requests for an audience, she is so wound up with Sequana, I fear my studies will never see the light of day." Ariel shook her head.

"You cannot give up; not after one hundred years of study, you have learned things here that we all should know about the darkness and what it contains." She leaned forward and took Branna's hands in hers.

"Do not give up, stay here for soon the queen will descend and take up guardianship of this realm, it will be a new beginning where both lines of Fae unite for the first time in this new realm. The council will then have more time and have great need of what you have learned. Branna you must wait and then present your findings, wait for my return and let me help you, I know I can get you influence." Branna slipped her hands out from Ariel's and sat back in her chair, her voice was stern and harsh.

"You know the queen has no tolerance for me or my kind, even now after years of hard work, I am seen as inferior because I carry the mark of dark hair. I have told you so many times, she is short sighted and will not listen to the wisdom of a Fae she deems unworthy. So, I have decided to leave and take what I have learned with me, she will regret her favouring of those with lighter hair one day, and see it for what it is, her weakness."

Ariel felt uncomfortable and she looked around, her voice lowered to a cautious tone. "Please, I have told you before, you must not say such things, she is your queen." Branna scoffed.

"She is their queen not mine, remember the line of the Fae Ofmoon runs golden, and there is little tolerance for us sent down here on this Earth to build a realm for her. When she comes down here, most of us will be shipped back to the Moon Realm, or we will remain here in the outer reaches of Avalon hidden from view so as not to offend her, you know it is true, we are a race apart Ariel. I will not be caged like my parents, or brother, not after this, not after the freedom I have felt living with you, it has been the happiest time of my life, and I cannot go back. Bridget is warm and welcoming to all in Florae, and I would imagine Gwendolyn one day will be the same. You are so lucky Ariel, your brown hair is not a curse to the Fae of Earth as it is to us here, all we are fit for is the toil of working underground out of sight, or out here in nowhere so our darker hair does not offend the eyes of our blind queen." Ariel felt a pulse of fear run through her, the thought of losing her after all their time together was simply too painful to even contemplate.

"Then come with me, I realise things look bleak for Bridget Violet, but I am sure when Gwendolyn is crowned, she will be fascinated in what you have learned. Branna please, you must travel back with me, and present your findings to the House of Elders in Florae." She smiled but shook her head.

"No my love, I have thought a great deal of late, I want to see this world around us, I aim to travel and find a place where I belong, and I am not seen as lesser because of my hair colour. Many of my race have travelled into the realm of men and found happiness, I too will follow that path, for I feel there are many things out there to interest and please me." Ariel thought her heart would break, and became very upset as her eyes filled with tears.

"I cannot bear the thought of us losing touch, I don't want you to leave, Bran please I beg of you, return with me and live in my house as I have yours, my heart will break if I lose you." Branna smiled, her love for Ariel was also strong, but she knew this was the only way.

"Ariel, you know of the love I hold for you, but I aim to do this. I have given this a lot of thought and you know as well as I do that I do not belong here. We have both known always that my spirit is wilder than most others; I am marked by my hair and have a freedom of thoughts and actions that the others of my line do not have. It is time for me to break free, and walk out into the world to find out where my destiny lies. Fear not for as soon as I find a place, I will send word to you in Florae and you can come to me, I will not be parted from you for long I promise." Tears spilled onto Ariel's cheeks and a sob grew out of her throat.

"The world of men is still fierce and dark. I shall fear for you until I hear word from you." Branna rose from her seat and knelt before Ariel; she pulled her into a deep embrace and kissed her. Her dark eyes glistened with tears, as she smiled.

"Let me do this, let me fly free, and I shall return to you, for you are a part of who I have become, and I will not have us parted for long. I am hardly defenceless now, am I? I have many skills and powers not given to the lines of men; I shall thrive as my fellow Fae have out there. Think of all you have taught me, not only will I survive, I can be of use to the lines of men." Ariel held her tightly in her arms and kissed her again as she wept.

Both of them held each close for a long time, it was heart breaking for both of them as they hugged and kissed, but as the time approached Branna took Ariel by the hand, and talked quietly of being brave and facing what would be the next chapter of their lives, and a reunion to come at a later date. Together they walked back down to the house where Ariel gathered her things. When the marshal arrived to escort her to the gate so she could travel to Florae, Ariel broke down and sobbed bitterly as she said her goodbyes, and Branna tried her hardest to be brave, and hugged and kissed her farewell.

Finally, Ariel mounted her horse and set off, and Branna stood at the gate and watched as she disappeared out of view sobbing. Branna ran inside and threw herself on her bed, grabbed the sheets that still carried the scent of Ariel, and wept bitterly until she was exhausted and fell into a tearful sleep. Across the patch of rough grass from the house, Roack the large raven sat in the top of the apple tree watching, and within herself she talked.

"Finally, the woman of white has gone, and now is the time to awaken you my sister of darkness, for we have much to do together. Cry your tears for they are the last you will ever shed, remember them well, for they will become nothing than a mere memory, and you too will rise to be a raven of power to rule your own land. Destiny waits, for this our child of the Fae will be the destiny we set for you many years ago. It is time to leave the house of that retched star of light, for soon it will not be able to influence you and control your powers as it has. Now is the moment when we will take you from this land and unlock the true darkness within you."

*I*n the great scheme of things, it all appeared to be an irrelevant moment of the separation of two lovers, but it was so much more than that. Here in the centre of nowhere on the outskirts of Avalon, the day moved on and the fate of everything began to take a direction that was unseen, and would remain so for a very long time. Before this day became of interest, many things would occur, and as a result the symbol of the raven would rise to bring great fear to all the realms.

Chapter Seven.

Dark Fae.

Whilst Branna drifted into an exhausted sleep, Ariel was taken through Avalonia and down the long white Queen's Road. Close to the gate that would take her out of the realm, the Fae guards from Florae who had been sent to escort her approached her, and as she smiled at the face of Cullen, a guard she knew well from home, he stepped up and clamped a bracelet onto her wrist.

"I am sorry about this my friend, but it is the order of the queen."

Ariel looked at the bracelet and knew instantly, it was a charmed object that would prevent her from turning and flying home. She looked back to the sad face of her escort.

"Am I under arrest, what is the charge?" He shook his head.

"This is not my doing Ariel; this is a direct order from the queen for everyone entering the land of Florae. It is not my place to question, and as much as I know you and have watched you grow up, I must obey the orders of my queen." She understood, but it did not remove the fear she felt.

Cullen escorted her to the gate, and then with a wave of his arm, the gate flashed blue, and he gently pulled her by the arm into the pulsating light. Within a moment, Ariel was stood on the path that led to the large House of Scribes, and just for a second, she caught her breath. So much had changed since she had left the basin that formed the large open area that was the heart of Florae, it had been transformed into a city within the trees.

As the high walls that began the base of the mountains formed a huge horseshoe covered with trees, below in the base of the valley houses and tall buildings had sprung up everywhere. The slanted slope that led up to the base of the mountains were filled with an elaborate labyrinth of paths, all of which had triangular shaped houses, of highly carved wood, which nestled perfectly between the trees.

At the end of the path, and in the very centre of everything, the tall House of Scribes rose up in many triangular tiers, to its left stood the Royal Lodge, which housed the apartments of the Queen and Council of Fae. The House of Scribes was elaborately decorated, and housed many artefacts, as well as the large archive that recorded the entire history of the Fae. Ariel walked slowly taking in the beauty of both buildings side by side, all framed with the large high peak of Mt Kivi behind it, and the two smaller twin peaks of Petra and Mt Bridge either side.

Cullen walked a few paces ahead, with the second escort walking slightly behind her, and slowly they walked the long road flanked with pastures and farm land towards the dominating centre of Florae, and the steps up into the official offices of the Fae of Earth.

"Tell me Cullen, am I to walk into my home a prisoner disgraced before the people I have served over my life time?" He turned back; his look was one of guilt.

"I have been ordered to take you into the House, I cannot release you until you are before the elders, believe me, this is not my choice. I have known you a long time, and I can assure you, I am as uncomfortable with this as you are." Ariel gave a soft smile and nodded to him; it was clear in his eyes that this was not something he wanted to do.

As they came to the steps and the building towered high above her, Ariel felt her heart beating deep within her and for a moment she felt the pangs of fear, and wished she could be back in Avalon curled up with Branna under the safety of their blankets. Her feet met the polished wood, and she took her first steps up towards the building she had talked so often with Bridget about as she designed it. Now seeing it built, instead of feeling the joy and excitement of entering it, her thoughts turned to her fears, and she tried to think of what crime she could have possibly committed to deserve such a homecoming.

As the huge doors drew back, her heart skipped several beats, as the cool air rushed out to meet her filled with the scent of timber and parchment. Ariel felt the smile on her lips, it was impossible to do anything else, this was her dream, and she had taken her first steps into a building she had designed and planned with Bridget Violet for many years of her life. She walked into a gigantic foyer, beyond which she saw the doors that led into the Council of Elders chamber, and she knew above that was the central tower, filled with floors, all with fine rails of carved wood on which in long lines of shelved pigeon holes, thousands of scrolls would sit for eternity. Her heart beat faster as it came into view, and as she saw the wonder of it, tears filled her eyes, finally her dream had become a reality and it was stunningly beautiful.

She stood frozen in awe as she looked up, completely unaware of the twelve silver haired members of the council of elders who watched her. The elders sat on their highly carved chairs, slightly raised above all the other seats in the room in a wide semicircle. Ariel had been led into the centre of the room, where she stood looking up at the archive; her attention was suddenly brought back to her situation, as a loud bang echoed in the room. She looked down and at the elders for the first time, on the floor level stood the blonde haired figure of Bade holding a long golden pole, he lifted it up and banged again on the floor, and his voice rang out deep all around the room and up into the tall tower above her.

"Clear the room, the council is seated!"

Ariel turned to look behind her to see all the guards and scribes exiting through the large doors, which swung closed behind them sealing her in and alone with the council and Bade. He rested the pole on an ornate stand and walked across the polished floor towards her, she smiled recognising her friend, although his features did not change, and his face remained stern. Bade came up to her side and turned to face the council, as he did so, he breathed out a barely audible whisper.

"Sorry to welcome you this way, some things have changed in your absence."

She was not sure why, but she felt a sudden sense of relief, and breathed out a long slow breath, but felt her knees quivering as she stood before the council and waited for one of them to move or speak. The elder in the centre gave a nod, and Bade spoke.

"My Lords, I present Ariel of Erin, Ambassador to Avalon, as requested under the new ordinance of arrival issued by Queen Bridget Violet."

The old silver haired man appeared to recognise the name and gave another nod; several of the council moved in their seats and sat up straight. He lifted his hand covered in golden rings and beckoned her to move towards them.

"Come forth and be seated."

Bade escorted her towards a table with two chairs directly in front of the centre of the council. Her feet felt a little unsteady, and she shivered with nervousness. Bade held her arm softly as he guided her, they reached the table, and the old elder waved his hand again.

"You can be seated."

Feeling the seat on her behind, and the pressure taken from her legs felt like a relief, the old man looked down at her, now sat just ten feet in front of her, he stared with slightly sparkling eyes of a deep green.

"Do you know why you have been summoned here this day Ariel of Erin?" Her throat suddenly felt very dry, and her nervous words stumbled on her lips.

"No My Lords, I was told I had to report to the house, I was not aware it was the council in person." He gave a nod as she saw all of the twelve ancient members staring down at her, which just added to the intense feelings of nervousness that was coursing through her. The old man gave another nod.

"I am Elgin, head of the council of Fae of the Earth and advisor to our Queen; I am instructed to interview everyone who arrives from realms deemed dangerous to this realm." Ariel felt a jolt run through her stomach.

"Dangerous My Lord? I have returned from Avalon our sister nation on the realm of men."

"Indeed, a realm that has no ruler present, and is so regarded as dangerous by our noble highness, I take it you are not aware of this new law passed in the last month due to your absence?" She shook her head.

"No My Lord, I am not." Bade moved forward in his seat.

"If it pleases My Lord, we have not instructed our ambassadors of the new ordinance, due to the nature of its sensitivity, the Queen wished news from this realm censored for the protection of all our people outside of Florae." Elgin waved his hand impatiently.

"Yes, yes Lord Bade we are well briefed… Ambassador, tell me, what role exactly have you played in your time at this new realm for Queen Rhiannon?" It felt an odd question, after all, the Fae had many ambassadors in every realm, Ariel turned to Bade, he gave her a small nod and, she turned back to the council.

"My Lord's, I was sent at the express wish of the Queen, she requested I made reports on the daily life of all members of the Fae there, and report them directly back to the House. I have tendered weekly reports since my placement there." Bade gave a nod to the council.

"The reports were received and filed after they were inspected by the Queen herself My Lords." He considered the point for a few moments and they gave another nod.

"I see, and where are these reports filed, for it appears they are absent from this archive?" Ariel looked confused and turned to Bade.

"They are... Why?" Bade looked a little uncomfortable.

"My Lords it is the Queen's command that they are kept in her personal archive." This was a great surprise to Ariel.

"But why, they are just the day to day reports of life within the Fae of Avalon, why would the Queen keep them there, they belong here as the start of the archive for Avalon?" Bade shook his head.

"It is not my place to question the actions of our Queen, I do as she wishes." Ariel simply could not understand, she turned to look at the council.

"My Lords this makes no sense at all, they are just reports on life, such as how the work is progressing, the type of architecture they use, their eating habits and working skills etc... There is nothing within them that does not show the simple life of all who live there." As she spoke some of the others began to mumble and murmur, it all felt very unnerving. Lord Elgin spoke in a clear and loud voice to raise it higher than the sudden outbreak of sound from the others.

"Whether it makes sense to you or not is irrelevant, we do not question as to why the queen chooses such actions, and you should bear that in mind if you wish to continue in your position." Ariel realised her mistake, and lowered her head.

"Forgive me My Lord's, I spoke at liberty and meant no offence to my Queen, whom I may add is also someone I regard as family, for she raised and educated me." The grumblings and murmurs of the others settled down, and Lord Elgin spoke with a softer tone.

"I can excuse your lack of knowledge of certain aspects of this realm, as much has changed in your absence, but be aware Ambassador, as much as I am aware of your familiarity with our queen in the past, to question her actions is not tolerated. I will excuse your comments this time, but please control your emotions in this chamber and stick to the facts. Now tell me, what have you learned of Dark Fae?"

"What?" The question completely surprised her. "My Lord, I have no understanding of the term, there are no dark Fae… Are there?" Her response surprised Elgin and he straightened in his seat.

"I believe I am right to assume you alone were picked for this task in the confidence of our queen to investigate dark members of the Fae, were you not?" Ariel was baffled.

"My Lord's, my task was to watch every aspect of life in Avalon, and report back to the House of Scribes, at the time when Queen Rhiannon arrived on the completion of the building, I was to play the role of advisor to her if she so wished on the ways of our people. I know nothing of reporting dark members of the Fae Ofmoon, unless of course you mean those who have dark hair? It is no secret there is unrest in Avalon as those individuals feel they are not represented equally by their queen. But My Lord, if you are implying there are members who contain darkness in the form of evil, I am sorry to say I have no knowledge of these creatures. I believe the Fae of both lines are a force for good, and so I have not encountered any that I know to be evil or dark as you put it." He sat back in his seat and looked very surprised.

Ariel looked at Bade, and then back to the council who all looked equally as surprised at her statement. Lord Elgin fidgeted in his seat for a moment.

"So, you are reporting no suspicious activity in Avalon at all?" Ariel really did not know what to say, she was as equally surprised as all of them.

"My Lord I have nothing to add, everyone I have encountered in all of the realm have been very nice to me. I really do not know what else I can add. I have always believed the Fae to be from the light, I know of no one who may have been touched by the darkness."

It was obviously an unexpected revelation, and it was clear the council had expected something else; Elgin lifted his hand and flicked his fingers towards her.

"If that is the case then there is much we must debate, go to your quarters, although until we are satisfied, you will remain there and speak to no other until such time as our investigation is taken to its full conclusion. Bade take her away." His chair slid back and he stood up, his voice again was very low.

"Stand up, follow me, say nothing." He looked at the council and gave a bow.

"As you wish My Lord's." Ariel rose to her feet and gave a bow, she turned quickly and felt Bade take her arm and hurry her towards the doors. She followed his lead saying nothing, until they had both passed through the doors and they swung shut behind them, and then she turned shaking her arm free of his grip.

"Bade what in all the realms is going on?" His head did not move as he stared towards the outer doors.

"Not here, say nothing until we are in a more private setting."

*B*ade strode off towards the doors, and Ariel had to run to keep up with his long strides. He walked out of the doors and turned left onto the wide balcony that ran the whole length of the building, and she quickly turned to follow his lead. As they moved at a fast pace along the balcony filled with many members of the Scribes who politely nodded as they recognised her, Bade kept his mouth shut, but as she caught up she could see the concern on his face. She said nothing until he turned three quarters of the way down into a doorway, she swerved and ended up in a room filled with all her possessions, Bade closed the door and walked into the room behind her. His voice was low and soft.

"This is your new quarters; you will have to remain here until the council are satisfied and release you." Her head was spinning as she fought to understand what had just happened, and make so sort of sense of it all.

"What in Albanlin's name is happening, and why am I being treated this way, I have led this house at your side since it began?" He gave a long sigh.

"Sit down Ariel, things have been difficult of late, I will do my best to fill you in on what I know, but even I do not know the full story."

His response somehow just did not feel enough, and rather than sit, Ariel paced what was actually quite a nice room, it had not become apparent yet that this was actually her home when in Florae, and it had actually been gifted to her by the Queen. She spun on her heel.

"Sit down… is that it? You calmly lead me here and ask me to simply sit down after that, what in all the realms is wrong with you? We are supposed to be friends, what just happened, and when did the Council start to question every ambassador who returns home?" She drew a long laboured breath to refill her lungs.

"And what in all the realms are Dark Fae, and why would anyone even for one moment think I knew them?"

Suddenly she felt exhausted, the whole entire episode of her arrival home after having to leave Branna just collided with her, and as her breath ran out, so did her energy and she flopped down onto the chair in front of Bade.

Bade watched in his normal calm and collected manner just as he always had been in the past, which in itself was quite annoying, she looked at his cool eyes and gave a frustrated sigh, he smiled and leaned over to pat her on the knee.

"It's nice to have you home." He sat back in his seat and crossed his legs and placed his hands on his lap, something she had seen him do a million times, and so she relaxed a little and knew he would bring her up to date now that she had calmed down.

"Are you feeling better? Firstly, I am sorry I could not be there to meet you and warn you, I did want to, but I was called by the members of the council, so for that I am indeed very sorry."

Ariel knew him well enough to understand that his loyalty to the queen was such that his duty would obviously be a priority; she gave a nod of acknowledgement. He understood and proceeded as intended.

"Ariel much has changed in your time away, I know you have spoken to Princess Gwendolyn, and I also know the queen herself has sent you correspondence, so I can only assume you have some knowledge of the night terrors the queen has suffered of late." She gave a nod.

"Yes, I am aware of her dreams and the concerns it has raised." He shuffled a little in his seat.

"Ariel I cannot say I know the whole story, but you know how information leaks in places like this, and so I will give you my impression of what is happening as I see it, based on the facts that I know are true."

"Alright, what are these facts you know to be true?" He smiled; he knew her well enough to know that she played her cards close to her chest.

"Shortly after you left here for your new position in Avalon, a strange illness swept across Florae. Now at this point I have to confess that I use the word illness as there really is no other way I can describe it, except to say that the result of it left members of the community feeling at a low ebb. It was a strange melancholic, almost oppressive feeling that infected those who contracted it, and in three particular cases it was so bad, that those affected killed themselves."

"What?" He gave her a very reassuring nod.

"I know, it is unheard of in our race, as you probably can understand such news alarmed the queen greatly, so much so that she felt obliged to visit each person who suffered and personally attend to them. As we both know, she is very powerful and very skilled in the arts of our people. Anyhow to cut a long story short, she was very successful, and after a few days of staying with each member, they appeared at her side cured, it was to say the least miraculous, as every other healer here could not figure out what the illness was, or how she alone was able to cure it. I will add that I too was perplexed by the whole affair, but considering her success and the fact she is the most powerful member of this line, who am I to question the results?" Ariel smiled.

"But you did?" He gave a long sigh.

"Ariel this was like nothing any of us have ever seen before. I jest not when I say, people just went to bed and stopped everything, they did not eat or drink, and they did not care for the realm or the duties of their work, call me old fashioned but in this realm that is simply unheard of." She agreed.

"I must admit when Gwendolyn came to see me, she told me of this, and yet I too could not fathom it, do you know how she cured it?" He shook his head.

"No, I do not, although I do have my theories, although I will say this. You know that it was her dreams that created the rift with Rhiannon, and I suspect that was the reason behind you going to Avalon? The queen felt something was not right with Rhiannon's rule, and she commented on it which was what caused the argument they had. I know you know the full truth of this, although I will not ask you to divulge something our queen told you in confidence. What I will say is this, I think the two were related, as her dreams became more intense after she healed our people, and over the last year in particular she has become, how should I say this?"

"Withdrawn?"

"Yes… Ariel she spends hours alone in her room not seeing anyone, she talks to very few, but from the small amount I have been able to get from Malcolm or Ninian she has talked of an evil infecting the Fae." Ariel frowned.

"An evil?" He gave a long sigh and nodded.

"I get the impression she is a little obsessed with it." She was starting to understand.

"Well, that explains the strange interview, and it makes more sense now, so that was the reason for their question of Dark Fae. Which I have to ask, are there even such things as Dark Fae?" He shrugged his shoulders.

"We are all as surprised as you were when we first heard it. It is the queens command that everyone is interviewed when they arrive back from which ever realm they have been in. Although I will add, this is known to only a few of us, Malcom has decreed that it not be known in the general population to avoid panic."

"So how many know, and how is Bridget now, I mean is she alright, can I go and see her?" For a moment his face clouded over.

"I am sorry, you are confined here until the council release you, so for now your only visitor can be myself. I know how close you two are, I also know how much she has missed you, but as long as you wear that bracelet, you will not be allowed out of your apartment." She felt a pang deep within herself.

"Well, how long is that going to be?" He stood up.

"Honestly, I have no idea, you will have to wait until the council are satisfied with your answers. I can assure you they will be discussing everything you told them as we speak."

"Bade this is ridiculous, they cannot seriously think after dedicating my life to the House, I would do anything at all to risk Bridget or our people?" He smiled.

"I know you better than any, and I know how much you have sacrificed to see the house built, but for now you must remember, the council act on the queen's command. I have vouched for you and it has been accepted, so for now be patient and hopefully soon you will be able to go and see her, she does know you were called back, so stay hopeful she will grant you an audience."

There really was little Ariel could do, for now she had to accept that she was to be confined to her new quarters, and as Bade left her, she had no other option than to accept her fate. The day was drawing to an end, and so she sorted through all of her possessions, and tried to make the best of her situation. Ariel tried to keep busy as the evening wore on, and she made her bed and placed her clothes in the cupboard in the corner. The sight of her bed sitting empty drew her mind back to Avalon and Branna. Her feelings rose up within her and she sat on the end of her bed and wept, she was alone and imprisoned

and she needed comfort, and yet the only person who could give
her that was in another realm, and it felt like worlds away. Her tears
clouded her eyes and she felt very much alone, and she lay back on the
bed and cried into her clean pillows.

*I*n Avalon, it had been very much the same for Branna. She had
come to the realm and lived alone and been happy, but with the
arrival of Ariel, she had not really understood what had happened,
and as she lay in her bed for most of the day, she felt the pangs of
separation and understood how strong her feelings for Ariel truly
were. It was late afternoon when a messenger arrived with a note for
her from the commanders at Avalonia, but apart from getting off the
bed to sign for the note she had not read it, and had simply cast it onto
the small table in her living area. Roack the black bird, had sat outside
for the whole day watching her lay on her bed weeping. The raven was
frustrated that when Branna was inside the house that the connection
between them was cut, although the dark bird knew it had something
to do with the symbol of protection Ariel had placed above the door.
The bird sat in the old apple tree, and had no choice but to wait for
Branna to step outside the house, and so as the day progressed, it
hatched out the plan to find a way to remove the love that consumed
Branna, for in doing so, it knew then would be the time to truly open
her up to the power of the Merle.

Without really knowing why, it was clear time was running out,
for Roack had gleaned a lot of information of late flying around and
listening in to private conversations, and the bird knew that the letter
that lay unopened on the table in the middle of the room, was in fact
the orders sent to Branna to pack up her things, and return to her old
life back in the realm of Ofmoon.

*R*hiannon was no fool, Branna's request for an audience
combined with a recommendation from Ariel had caused her to look
in the direction of the pair of them, and she was not pleased to see
that a relationship had developed between the two women. She had
deliberately placed Ariel well out of the way of Avalonia, as she had
suspected that Bridget had sent Ariel there to confirm her suspicions
over her favouring of the fair haired members of her race. Ariel had
become involved with Branna, and so whilst she had Ariel out of the
realm, she planned to pull Branna to a place where no member of the

Fae of Earth could reach her.

Time was running out, and Roack knew that something had to be done soon whilst the white fairy was out of the picture, and before the guards of Rhiannon came to take Branna back. As Branna lay on her bed with her mind drifting in her sadness, Roack swooped from the tree and flew straight into the window. It was a brutal collision, and the raven reeled backwards in pain flapping on the floor. Branna jumped up on her bed and stared at the empty window not sure as to what had just happened, she slowly slid off the bed and pulled on the latch to open the window. As she looked out, she saw and heard the bird flapping wildly on the floor and looked at it puzzled.

"What the hell are you doing, you scared the life out of me?"

The bird squawked on the floor slightly dazed, finally the seal had been broken as Branna leaned out of the window and the connection was made again.

"You must leave; they are coming to take you back. Pack your things and meet me up on the rock, time is short now go."

"What… How… I mean how do you know?" The bird lifted up into the air somewhat shakily.

"The message, read it, I was there when they wrote it, they are taking you back to her realm, you have to leave or you will be a prisoner forever, now stop talking and go, hurry the time is short."

There was shock, some disbelief, and then anger as Branna turned back into the room. She grabbed her big canvass bag and stuffed her notes and clothes into it. She knew it, she knew Rhiannon would not keep her word, after all they had done, she knew it. Branna moved like lightening, grabbing anything that she thought she would need and cramming it into her bag as she went round the house like a whirlwind. As she reached the door to leave, she stopped just for a second and looked back, the place was a mess, she had knocked a few things over in her rush, yet there at the back of the house was the open door to Ariel's room, where everything was as it had been all neat and tidy and organised. Just for a moment her emotions swelled in her throat and she swallowed hard.

"Goodbye my love for now, this is not over we will meet again, I love you."

*L*ike a flash of light, and wiping the tears from her eyes, she whipped through the door banging it closed behind her and locked it, and was off towards the path that led to the top of the high rock. She had no idea where she would go or what she would do, she just knew that she was not going back to the realm of Rhiannon.

Branna wanted to be free of the oppression, and she meant to make sure she was, for now her trust was in the bird, it had the answers to her research and her search that had lasted for most of her life, and in her mind no one, not even a queen would stop her finding out the answers. Life within the Fae was over, she would run to the world of men, and with Roack to help her, she would finally delve into the true secrets of what the Merle contained, and then she would destroy the Queen of the realm Ofmoon.

This was the start of a journey, and she had no idea of where it would lead, all she knew was her path now ran towards freedom, and she was taking it to get as far away from the prisons of Ofmoon as possible. As she ran for the path up the slope her mind came sharply into focus, no matter what she had to do to escape, she could not allow them to take her back, and she would fight to the death to stop them.

Chapter Eight.

Whispers Of The Powerful.

Branna gasped for air as she bent forward, the raven flapped on the table, and inside Branna's head, she heard the coarse voice of the Merle.

"Destroy everything; you must not leave them anything to work out what you have done, leave nothing connected to your research intact, now hurry, your time here is short."

There were a few things too precious to smash, so Branna collected her viewing scope, knife, and her herb powders from the table, and then began to throw her glass jars and containers at the floor to shatter them. She bent and twisted her long copper poles, and kicked over the table, stamping on anything she thought could be of use. Finally, her task was done, and as the sweat ran down the side of her face, the old raven gave a croak, and flapped its wings lifting it into the air.

"The soldiers are on the road, time is gone, follow us."

Branna lifted her bag onto her shoulder, slipping her arms through the strap so it hung down her back, and then as the bird flew low over the surface of the rock, she ran after it, making her way across the flat rock towards a path she had never taken before. As the sun headed towards the west, and the soldiers arrived to escort her to Avalonia, Branna was already moving at great speed along a mountain path that would take her up to the summit of the neighbouring rock, and then down the other side towards the marshes and the thick scrub covered with a deep mist. As she ran, the raven instructed her to use the veil, a spell known only to the Fae Ofmoon, and hide herself where no prying eyes could follow her.

The soldiers broke the lock and entered the house to find it empty, and the unopened message on the table, and after searching each room and the surrounding woodland, as the darkness fell, they came to her workstation high on the top of the flat rock plain, and discovered the damaged and smashed table and the last of Branna's belongings. It was clear that she had been tipped off and fled, but the darkness was falling fast, and any chances of a search would have to be called off until dawn. The senior Marshal was furious; he kicked out at the table in temper.

"She must not get away; FIND HER, THE QUEEN DEMANDS IT!"

A few of the soldiers who actually knew Branna, shrugged their shoulders; it was already too dark to find a trace of her, although they feigned a search of the area. One of the marshals who was new to the unit, found the broken twigs at the side of the path and the crushed ferns that Branna had trampled down in her panic.

"Sir she went this way." The Senior Marshal turned and viewed the fresh faced member of his unit.

"What is your name?"

"Frazer Sir." The Marshal nodded.

"Can you find her trail in this darkness?" He looked up the path that led up to the next summit and gave a nod.

"It will not be easy, but yes I think I can pick up her trail further on." The Senior Marshal gave a nod of approval and lifted his arm to point.

"Go then, and if you catch her, it's fifty golden crowns to you, hurry boy, she must not leave Avalon." The young marshal gave a fast nod and turned on the trail, and within seconds had disappeared into the darkness.

*T*he light was falling fast as Branna ran at speed gasping and panting. Her heart was beating so hard she could hear it inside her head. Her legs pushed on the rough ground, as she jumped and wove past obstacles she could not see, and all the time Roack the raven flew above her watching the path ahead. Her head felt light, yet it was filled with thoughts, and in the midst of her own thinking the rough croak of Roack's voice could be heard giving her directions. Branna tried to clear her mind, in the darkness shapes loomed and she somehow avoided them, although considering her pace and speed she really had no idea how she was doing it. Her own voice talked constantly to her in her head to reassure her.

"This is it, don't stop, there is no going back now girl, this is the dream you have waited for, you must keep going, you must not stop. Run... Run until you are out of this realm, once you are outside, they will never find you, so push Branna, push yourself as hard as you ever have, you can do this now run and run hard. Never again will that queen rule you, never again will you be trapped and forced to do anything, this is your time now, it's your chance, there are no rules and there are no laws, you are Fae and you are free, so run and run like the wind."

Like all things, the disappearance of Branna became food for the gossips. It was clear to those who knew her that she had escaped, and many envied her as they were rounded up and taken into the town of Avalonia for relocation back to the realm of the moon.

Within the ranks of the Marshals, there were a few who would talk discreetly about how Branna's escape had angered those surrounding the queen, some even said a high profile member of the queen's household had been despatched to Florae to question Ariel, as to where Branna had gone. The one thing that was never truly known was whether or not Rhiannon had known all along of the work Branna had done.

Alone in Florae, Bridget Violet suspected that Rhiannon knew more about the Merle than she had ever admitted, and there was far more to the story than anyone could ever suspect, but even Bridget was not aware of the full truth, and like many things, the secrets of that time would pass from knowledge into history.

The only one to truly know the full truth was now a fugitive, Branna had spent most of the night stumbling, and clawing her way through the thick tufted grasses and low bushes of the marshes. As dawn arrived, she found herself sat in dense woodland as she collapsed exhausted and unable to move another foot. The raven sat above her in the tree watching as Branna closed her eyes just for a moment, and found herself slipping into a deep exhausted sleep. She had no idea where she was, or where she would go, her only certainty now was that she had to keep moving and stay clear of any Fae on her road. Her dreams were dark and she disturbed many times, and whilst she was not fully aware of it, all the time she slept, deep in the centre of her thoughts, the mind of the raven was still connected and talking to her, and it spoke of magic known only to a few of the elite members of her race, and yet as she slept, the black bird that had been possessed by the power of the Merle, began to educate her on the charms and spells she would need to hide forever.

Ariel paced within her room, her dreams the night before had been very vivid and she was filled with unrest. She had organised her rooms a hundred times the previous day. Her morning was spent pacing followed by bouts of sitting by the window, watching the growing central city of Florae, as the people of her race constructed new houses and stores from the base of the House of Scribes, all the way down the long road that led to the open sea of the Island.

Her mind was turning over everything that had happened since her arrival, and she felt the ache inside her as she realised that she would remain a prisoner in her own home, and that she would not get back to Avalon as quickly as she had promised. She missed Branna, and just wanted to flee back to her, but the bracelet on her wrist prevented her from taking her true fairy form and jumping back to Avalon.

The few hours she sat waiting felt like an eternity, until finally she heard a voice she knew at her door, it opened and in walked the tall figure of Bade. He smiled as she jumped up from her seat.

"Can I go now? Can I see Bridget, you know she will see me and put this nonsense to rest?" Bade placed a package on the table.

"There is food here for you." He walked round the small table and sat down on a polished chair; his eyes looked tired.

"It is not that simple Ariel; things are changing all the time as new information has arrived." She felt his concern in his tone of voice, and sat back on her padded chair.

"What news?" Bade shook his head.

"I have only limited opportunities to gain what I can, so I cannot tell you everything that is being discussed, but early this day, a new ambassador arrived from Avalon, it is Luminaria." Ariel had not heard the name before, and gave a shrug; it meant nothing to her so as to its importance she could not tell.

"I know nothing of this person, who is she?" Bade lifted his eyes.

"She is a member of the inner circle of Rhiannon, she is the daughter of the seer of the Fae there." He paused for a second and stared at her, she knew the look and she had seen it many times in the past when they had been planning the building of the House of Scribes, and had encountered problems. She leaned forward her eyes fixed on his.

"What is it Bade, why do you second guess everything before you speak, are we not friends, can you not be open with me as we have always been?" He gave a long sigh.

"Ariel, I have known you all my life, but things are happening I have no understanding of, and I need to know that you are being completely open and honest with me." It surprised her and she sat back with a gasp.

"What! How could you even say that? I have always been truthful to you and everyone else, how could you even suggest such a thing? I have never lied to anyone; you know me better than to think I would not be honest to you or any other member of the Fae." He smiled and gave a nod.

"That is as I thought, and believe me I trust you beyond many, but the news we are getting is conflicting and we are simply trying to establish just what is happening in Avalon."

"Avalon, I thought this was about Bridget?" He gave a sigh.

"It is and it isn't. Things are happening and have happened in Avalon that the council think have had an effect on our queen. Somehow, and I am not sure at the moment how, but all of this is related."

"All of what? Bade you are telling me nothing, yet you seek my advice. Please you must tell me just what is happening, if it is affecting the queen let me help." Bade stood up and walked slowly round the room as if thinking, he stopped and looked at Ariel, then he gave a sigh and walked over towards the windows and stood for a moment staring out into the sunlight. After a few moments he spoke with a soft voice.

"I fear for the Queen, things of late have not been good, she has taken to staying in her chamber, she hardly sees anyone, and has painted a huge symbol of protection on the floor of her quarters which she seldom leaves." He turned slowly and his eyes fixed on Ariel's soft grey. "It is your mother's symbol of ultimate protection, the red star within the white circle." He shook his head and turned from the window, and before Ariel could respond he shook his head.

"It makes no sense Ariel, why would she need such a powerful symbol?" She understood his concern; she had felt something similar when Gwendolyn had shown up at Avalon with one on a small plaque to place above her door. Ariel reached out and took his hand in hers.

"Come sit, we must use this time wisely, and you must tell me everything, we both lead the house here, and so if there is some unseen danger, it must be us who know the most about our line that find it and destroy it for the sake of our queen, and the protection of all our people. Sit and tell me everything, leave no detail unsaid, for that is the only way we shall uncover the truth."

*B*ade sat and began to recount everything that he had heard or had been told, he told Ariel of the dreams of Bridget and how at first, they had just been the occasional dreams, which no one appeared concerned about, yet Bridget took them very seriously. He talked of the strange illness and how she had been alarmed by it, and had gone to each and every member and healed them when none of the other healers had been able to do so. It was after that time the dreams had become more frequent, and Bridget had begun to slowly withdraw from many of her duties. Then one night she had horrendous night terrors, and her screams of fear could be heard throughout all the Royal Lodge and the House of Scribes. He had run to her apartments to find out what was going on to help, and Bridget was locked in her room with Malcom and would not allow anyone else in there, she had even banned Ninian, Erin, Gwendolyn and Gwynfor from the Royal Lodge.

Reports came in a day later that at the time of her night terrors, there had been a terrible storm in Avalon that had caused a great deal of concern for Rhiannon as it blocked out all connection with the realm of the moon, and it was only contained within the area of Avalon. There had been nothing in the upper atmosphere, so Rhiannon had suspected that a member of the Fae had unleashed a great power there. The problem was, almost as soon as it had been felt, it disappeared and was untraceable. Bade believed the two were connected. It was shortly after that time Bridget drew the symbols of protection in her room and placed five golden ornate stands containing the five violet stones on each point of the red star, and she spent the next two weeks chanting words of containment and protection from within the circle.

"She has given no explanation as to why; she simply demanded every house and building within all the islands of Florae placed a red star of a white circle above their doors to protect all within. She made it a royal decree, and we have had workshops working night and day to create and distribute one to every building and dwelling. Bridget has become more and more reclusive, and her health has suffered greatly as a result." Bade gave a long sigh.

The council had met to investigate, and it is their conclusion that a race of darker Fae has come to the earth, which he did not believe as there really was no accurate evidence to prove it. Things of late altered their view, and they had become obsessed, and they sent an envoy to Avalon to investigate with Queen Rhiannon. At this point he stopped for a moment and he looked both saddened and afraid, his voice trembled a little as he spoke.

"Ariel, Rhiannon named you as the culprit; she has suggested you made a pact with your lover there, and have unleased evil into the lines of Fae."

"WHAT?" He shook his head and looked at the floor.

"It is insanity I know, but it is the reason you are being detained, Ariel I know you, and so does our queen, and the only reason you are here in your quarters is because both myself and the queen have spoken for you, but the council is blinded by Rhiannon at the moment, and so for now the only thing we can do to keep you safe is to hold you here with the bracelet until we resolve this matter."

Ariel was reeling with the shock; she could not find the words, as she looked at her greatest friend who trembled with fear. Her throat was dry and her head felt hot, as she struggled to understand everything; Bade looked up at her with sad eyes.

"Rhiannon believes your mother was seduced by the Merle and she passed it on to you after she visited the realm of Tideguyde, which was why she wrote the symbol of protection there, and Rhiannon has accused you of infecting and corrupting your lover, and any other Fae you have been in close contact with."

Ariel's head exploded with a million thoughts, but all she could muster with her shocked and somewhat muffled voice was.

"How could anyone think such things? Bade this is not true, I have done nothing wrong, all I did in Avalon was help Bran with her reports, which in turn allowed me to get the detail on how Avalon was structured and operated. I was sent there to paint an accurate picture of the Fae of Moon under Rhiannon's rule, and that is all I have been doing." He gave her a smile and leaned over to pat her hand.

"We know Ariel, and believe me Bridget has made it very clear that you have nothing but light within you, and I think the council saw that when they interviewed you. I must admit though, the official papers say nothing of you reporting an accurate picture of the Fae in Avalon, your orders were simply to assist and give council to those helping Rhiannon, although I think I see some sense now."

"You do, where?" He gave a light chuckle, probably the first she had heard since arriving back.

"I know a little of your real task, I know that Bridget suspected something, which was why she had the row with Rhiannon, maybe that is why Rhiannon has struck out at you, maybe she wants to tarnish you to prevent the truth of Avalon coming out. Ariel you are the adopted child of Bridget Violet, Queen of all the Fae of Earth, Rhiannon fears Bridget as she has pointed out things about her rule, she must quash to maintain face. Think about it, what better way could you use to discredit Bridget than name a child she raised as dark? It makes perfect sense, except of course, Bridget is not the only one who has noticed certain injustices within the ranks of those at Avalon."

Ariel felt a little hopeful, she knew that Bade was highly respected and did to a degree wield a great deal of power within the ranks of the Fae at Florae, the problem was, did he have enough to swing the views of the council. He sat back in his seat watching her carefully.

"Tell me of this Branna, with whom you have become involved."

"Like what?"

"Well… I don't know her, so tell me what she is like; after all you have been quite taken by her." Ariel thought for a second.

"She is funny and sweet; she can be a little wild and outspoken at times. I know she was very unhappy in the Realm of the Moon, and was really happy to be chosen for Avalon. Her research was the sky around us and the darkness surrounding the moon, she felt that there was more to it than we first believed, and wanted to discover what. Her task was to look into the darkness and report her findings which she did with great detail, she submitted many reports and made several requests to present her full findings to Rhiannon, which were all turned down and frustrated her. Bade I love her, I have never met anyone like her, she is kind and very loving to me and we are very happy, I cannot wait to get back to her, I miss her."

He gave a nod as she spoke and then brought his fingers to his mouth as he thought, Ariel felt the burst of happiness inside her as she spoke and smiled at the same time, Bade listened attentively and then sat forward.

"So, you want to go back, even after all this, you want to go back and continue living with her?" It confused her.

"Well yes… That is what I have been telling you, Bade I love her, I want to be with her, I just want to get all this over with so we can be together again." He nodded.

"So, you will be surprised to hear she has disappeared then?"

"WHAT?" Ariel was up on her feet. "What do you mean disappeared?" He gave a nod. "But where is she, is she in trouble, is she hurt, what have they done with her?" Bade seemed a little surprised that Ariel had not been told.

"They sent for her last night, but when they arrived, she was gone, to date they have not been able to locate her, it does appear like she is not in Avalon, which is why Luminaria has come here, they simply thought she had run away to be with you." Ariel sat down with a bump.

"No, I have not heard from her since I left, we said goodbye for now, I told her I would be as fast as I could, then came straight here, and well you know what has happened here?" Tears welled in her eyes. "She once said she wanted to leave, but I never for a moment thought she would, she was happy, we were happy living in our home on the outskirts of Avalonia. Bade please you must help them find her and make sure she is safe." Her tears ran down her cheeks and dripped onto her lap; Bade leant forward and took her hands in his.

"I will, I promise, I will do everything I can to track her down for you. Don't worry she will turn up and when she does, we will try and get her here for you." Ariel gave a sniffle.

"Protect her for me." He smiled and squeezed her hands.

"I will, I promise."

*B*ranna walked with the raven sat on her shoulder, they had been up for several hours walking and her legs were starting to tire a little.

"Where are we?" She spoke her words out loud, and the bird replied deep inside her thoughts.

"It will please you to know you are no longer in the realm of your people, you are now free of the ties that have bound you. It is the time to let go of all that has held you captive, it is time to unlearn everything and prepare for the teachings of a new way of being." Branna frowned.

"New way of being, what does that mean?"

"You cannot hide your thoughts as you flee, I heard everything. You have lived for a long time under the rules of your kind; but now you are a magical being in a world of men. You are now free to become

what you have always desired, for in this realm none can oppose you, we too have great power, and in time you will be able to wield it, and rule any land you wish too. The dominance of your queen has no play here, this is a land just waiting for one such as you to take anything you desire, and you too will rule with great power and one day become the equal of your queen." Branna smiled.

"The power of a queen, I like the sound of that." Her pace quickened on the dirty path, and she forgot the pain of her legs and picked up her pace, the further away from Avalon she was, the happier she knew she was going to be.

Chapter Nine.

The Raven.

Although Branna and Roack had made it across the border and out of the realm of Avalon, they were not as free as they first thought. The young marshal of Fae, Frazer, had managed to pick his way through the darkness on the trail of Branna. He was somewhat far behind her, as his going was slow and hampered by the failing light, and the obstructions he had to manoeuvre past in the darkness. Branna did not really understand that Roack had been in control of her movements as she fled, and had flown above her to help guide her at a greater speed, past the many obstacles she had encountered. For Frazer it had been a much harder task, but by dawn, he sat just inside the outer reaches of the marshes of Avalon.

Back at the house that had been shared by Branna and Ariel, the Marshals gathered as much of her broken equipment as possible, and packed it into crates to be sent to Avalonia for inspection. They searched the house and went through all the papers, but found nothing to connect Branna with the Merle. None of the marshals really understood why they had to conduct the search, a lot of them knew Branna well, and they saw her as a fun and friendly person, one or two of them had even been involved in some of her sexual encounters. It made little sense to them, but the queen's aides had been very specific that everything must be collected and labelled and delivered to them in Avalonia.

Branna was exhausted, apart from the short rest she had taken, the events of the night had taken its toll, and as she staggered and stumbled through the woodland on her tired limbs, Roack flew on ahead to find a place she could rest up in safety. Roack was aware the connection between them had drained a lot of her strength, but also knew that until she was as far away as possible from Avalon, she would not be completely safe.

Branna reached a small stream; she dropped to her knees on the damp sand and pebbles at its edge. Her face was dirty and had small cuts where she had caught it on brambles, and she was red and sweaty. Her hair hung knotted and lank, and with great relief she bent over and scooped the cold clear water into her hands. Her throat was dry and burning, and the ice cold water felt like nectar, as she swallowed hard and felt it extinguish the fire in her throat. She closed her eyes and just enjoyed the moment of relief, as the water ran down her chin, and dripped back into the stream. Roack flew down and landed on a stone by her side.

"You need to find somewhere to rest, I have found a hole in the rock not too far from here, it is small, but big enough for you to rest in, come you will be safe there."

Branna looked at the bird.

"I thought I was free, why do I need to be safe, this spot has water and wood for a fire, can I not rest here?"

"Your Queen has sent a man to track you, I fear she will not release you easily, soon others may come. We need time to rest and plan, go to the hole which is well hidden and sleep, we shall take care of those who try to follow."

It was a chilling feeling knowing that even though she was outside of the realm, Rhiannon intended to follow her still, she thought for a moment, and understood that without the bird she would not have made it this far.

"Okay show me this cave, but how can you take care of those who follow, you are just a bird?"

"We are more than just a bird, trust us and you will stay free."

There was something in the manner of which Roack spoke that made Branna shiver, and she felt it better not to question. She followed the path, and soon found herself walking into a small ravine filled with trees. The stream she had followed merged with others, and as she entered the ravine and climbed down some of the small rocks, the waters fell into a wide shallow river. Roack took the lead flying just ahead, and Branna followed as she wove into the thick shrub and bushes that grew at the base of the rock wall. There hidden from sight of the path was a small cave, it was not very high, but it ran back a little way, and she stooped to enter and squatted down. The floor was dry and sandy, and it felt cool compared to the warmth of the day.

Sitting down she realised how exhausted she was, she slid off her bag, loosened her jacket and slipped it off her shoulders and pulled it off her. She then pushed her bag against the wall, and arranged it for comfort, and then lent back onto it and pulled her jacket over her. The raven watched as her eye lids fluttered, and then closed, she looked weak and very drawn, and Roack knew that now the big sleep would come and she would rest.

Quite far back behind her on the very edge of the border between Avalon and the world of men, the young soldier Frazer waited patiently. He had been joined by two more marshals from the squad, and they stood slightly up front of him as he sat in the grass and observed while they debated their next move. The squat fat sergeant looked to his well seasoned counterpart.

"You have been out there in the world of men many times, what do you think, should we follow or call it quits?" The tall and muscular marshal spat on the floor.

"Well to be honest Smithe, it seems she is pretty angry and wants this Branna pretty badly. I mean you heard the lieutenant; he got his arse kicked good and fried because she got away at the house. The young'un back there says she must have run for most of the night, so even though we may be a ways behind her, she is going to have to stop and rest at some point. With that in mind, I think we should push on and try and nab her, I mean you heard the lieutenant, not sure I fancy going back empty handed if you catch my meaning." He looked back at the young marshal sat in the grass.

"Looks to me like this lad has some talent for tracking, I mean, he kept her trail all night in the dark, so with his abilities it cannot be that long before we catch up, although I do not know this side of the realm so I cannot say what type of territory we will be covering, or even if there is any kind of settlements round here."

Smithe gave a nod and considered the point for a moment, he glanced back to look at the young recruit sat in the grass.

"The young'un has skill and no mistake, what say you lad, do you think you can keep on her trail long enough for us to catch up with her?" Frazer gave a nod.

"That won't be a problem Sarg, she bolted like a wild horse and has left a trail a blind man could follow. She cannot run at that pace forever; I would say give or take an hour we could have her in the next four." The Sergeant loosened his cloak and folded it up, before pushing it into the flap of his pack.

"Well, I must admit, I would rather carry a corpse back than come back empty, right then, I say we go at the double and try to catch her as quick as we can, I mean let's be honest its one girl, how hard can it be?"

The three marshals shouldered their packs, and started off down the trail through the thick trees, the sun was almost at full height and it was turning into a hot day. They trudged on with Frazer leading as he read the signs at double pace, none of them were completely sure if they were still in Avalon or actually in the realm of men. Most of the other entrances had curtains of light, but here in the wilds the realms overlapped in a seamless plain of grass and trees, and so they pushed on at speed in hope of finding Branna somewhere in the not too distant wildlands.

Roack flew into the trees leaving Branna who for the last two hours had been in a dead sleep. High up in the branches the bird could see for miles, and it did not take long before the large black bird had spotted the three marshals dressed in the well recognisable and distinct blue uniforms, of the Marshals of the Fae in the distance. The marshals had found Branna's first rest place, and fresh tracks, and they knew that they were getting much closer than they had expected this early in the chase. With renewed vigour they pushed hard to catch up to her, and as they approached the small falls where the stream dropped into the start of the ravine, Roack knew that something had to be done. The sergeant slowed as he saw the pools of cool clear water.

"Hold up lads, and let's take a break."

He was red in the face and puffing hard, it had been quite a few years since he had been forced to move at such a pace. He came up to the water's edge, and knelt down to fill his water skin, behind the two others halted and took in more air, as they rested their hands on their knees, and bent over gasping. The birds above them fell silent, and then suddenly took flight scattering in every direction, Frazer looked up at the water's edge. He watched uncertain at first, and he saw the black shape of a bird swoop out of the air and drop like stone to the surface of the water. He stood up not certain of what he had seen, and as he watched his eyes widened in terror.

Roack swooped across the surface of the water and lifted up in front of the Sergeant who had also noticed the strange behaviour of the bird. As Roack lifted up in front of its target, the bird expanded out in size and the outstretched wings came flapping round and snatched the sergeant clean off his feet and into the air. Frazer watched in horror.

"What in the name of all the gods is that?"

There was a blood curdling scream, and as Frazer watched the gigantic bird rise into the sky, a black mist exploded out of its wings and they opened wide again, as the bird swerved to the right dropping its prey. Frazer's eyes watched as the mass surrounded in black mist came hurtling back to earth, and smashed into the grass a few feet in front of them and the mist disappeared. Frazer tried to scream but nothing came out of his throat, as he saw the putrid smoking remains of a blackened skeleton covered in black and red slime, which had formerly been his Sergeant. His head snapped back to his comrade as panic flooded into him and he pointed at the putrid corpse.

"She said nothing of that!" He staggered backwards and began to whimper. "This was just supposed to be a tracking job, they told us nothing of friggin huge black demon birds that suck your skin off and eat it…. Screw bloody this!"

Roack swooped again, Frazer turned and bolted. He ran for his life back into the trees screaming and wailing in panic, as he saw the large bird cruise across the water at speed towards his companion who had drawn out his sword. He ran blindly wailing in terror, tripping and sliding on the stones and rough surface between the trees. His heart felt like it was going to explode, as branches lashed into his face, cutting and biting at his soft young skin.

Gasping for air he would look back, as he blindly ran to make sure the bird was not chasing him. There was no scream and no wails, so he wondered if his companion had slain the bird, but he was far too afraid to stop and find out, as his feet slid and slipped on the rough floor of roots and stones. All the time he ran and babbled to himself.

"This was not what I signed up for, I am a tracker for helping the hunters, I am not supposed to be the bloody hunted, I came here for a break, I did not come here to fight frigging huge birds that suck off your face."

He broke the trees into long grass and felt his pace quicken. His breath was straining in his throat as his lungs screamed for more air, he had no idea of where he was or where he was going, he just knew it was as far away from the huge bird as possible. He stumbled on across the open space blindly, and then he felt the huge pressure on his back, as something smashed into him, and he reeled forward and stumbled, his hands thrust out to save him as he hit the ground hard at speed, and went twisting and sprawling into the earth.

His head spun out of control, and his wide terrified eyes came face to face with the slimy red and blackened remains of what he knew was his sword wielding companion. Face to face with such a terrifying ghastly image, he opened his mouth and screamed for all his might, as he frantically tried to right himself, and push himself away from the putrid steaming body. He rolled backwards on to his back and felt his pack wedge into the floor, and as he looked up, he saw the red glaring eyes of the huge bird as it walked forward and stood over him.

It took less than a millisecond to understand his life was over, his body shook, and his voice trembled and croaked in fear.

"Please I did not know… they just said follow the girl, that's all I did, I meant you no harm, I thought you were just a girl, I did not know… please you must believe me I did not know." Roack's wings opened to full width with a snap.

"Arrrghhhhhhhhhhhhhhhh!!!......................."

*T*he woodland fell silent; it was as if the voice of the world had been momentarily robbed. Bridget Violet sat up in her bed in Florae, and screamed with terror.

Ariel was sat in her chair reading her notebook and remembering her time alone with Branna. She had an uneasy feeling, but she just passed it off as feeling homesick for the small house in Avalon, and missing her wild dark scruffy haired love. The scream of her queen came out of nowhere, and her heart almost exploded in terror, as it echoed through the whole of the Florae basin. Startled, she jumped to her feet, and ran to the window, outside scribes and people had fallen to their knees in fear.

She pressed her face to the glass of the window, but could see little except for the wide walkways and the centre of Florae before her. Heavy feet pounded down the decks outside, and suddenly she saw the shadows of figures at her door. Ariel felt panic, and backed slowly across the room away from the door and windows, the lock rattled, and then the door burst open scaring her half to death, as she jumped back another foot. Bade entered in a hurry, he looked white as a ghost and terrified.

"Are you alright?" His voice was panicked, and he shook with fear. "Ariel are you unharmed?"

For a few moments the look of his terrified face had caught her off guard, she gave a nod momentarily unable to voice the words, she swallowed hard and her faint voice came forth.

"Yes… Yes, I am fine, nothing has harmed me." Her hands were shaking holding the note book, but she was not that aware of it, Bade gave a sigh of relief.

"Thank all the lords of Fae, I thought it would have come for you." It was an odd statement, and one she was not sure how to answer, her legs felt weak and she flopped backwards into her chair.

"What had come for me?" Bade took a long breath and relaxed.

"I just thought…"

It felt like a meaningless statement to Ariel, and yet from nowhere she felt her anger begin to rise. She trusted him, he was one of her oldest friends, and yet just for a moment he had questioned everything she had told him, almost as if he did not believe her. Her rage suddenly erupted as her voice rose, and she stared at Bade as he stood helpless and pale.

"What did you think…? What Bade, you thought the phantom dark Fae had come back to claim me?" Her voice rose to a shout, as her fear and anger mixed. "You think that was the work of Bran, is that really what you thought, my lover had come to take me back?" She burst into tears. "SHE IS NOT DARK, SHE IS THE LOVE OF MY LIFE, AND THE MOST GENTLE SOUL I HAVE EVER KNOWN!" He put his head down, as Ariel lifted her hands to her face with her feelings of loss and fear and wept. Bade fidgeted for a moment and took a step forward.

"Look Ariel you have to understand…." She snapped at him again in anger.

"NO, I DON'T…" Ariel lifted her head. "You are just like all the rest. None of you have an idea of who she is, her queen snaps her fingers and all of you just jump to the same conclusion, you just assume that miles and miles away across the realm, Bran is the cause of everything we here have suffered, because of what?" She stood up.

"WHAT BADE?" He shook his head.

"It's not like that at all." Ariel gave a sniffle and lowered her voice.

"Oh, but it is… The mighty Rhiannon clicks her fingers and you have all jumped to the same conclusion as her. I have seen how

Rhiannon rules, I have spent two years in the heart of her precious realm watching good people slave and toil for what Bade?" He shrugged looking hurt and apologetic, but also unable to answer.

"I will tell you exactly what will happen in Avalon when her mighty royal highness arrives." Her anger felt like it had taken over, and even though she knew it was wrong to voice such discontent, she no longer cared.

"She will arrive with all her precious faired haired folk in Avalonia, which I might add is something beyond the dreams of everyone, it is a sight to behold, you should visit it. What you won't see though is how all the workers, the real Fae of skill, will be rounded up and hidden in the outer reaches of the realm so as not to offend her precious grey eyes. It's so easy to place all the blame on Bran and the thousands of others, who I have watched work themselves into the ground to create such a dazzling place of glory and wonder. As she sits her privileged fat ass on her silken padded seat, every one of those workers will be shipped out of the realm and taken back to the moon realm. They are destined never to live in the homes that they built, and do you know why Bade, do you even care? Let me tell you, it's for no other reason than they were born with dark hair like me, and unlike our own queen, who is the personification of pure goodness, Rhiannon is a misguided bigot."

*B*ade smirked, and Ariel who felt such strong anger gave a long sigh, movement by the door caught her eyes, and there set back from the frame stood a tall woman dressed in all pale blue, with long golden hair, at her side stood Elgin the leader of the council. The tall woman looked furious as she turned to Elgin.

"Is this how you allow your ambassadors to speak in public? You allow them to bad mouth the most intelligent and wise queen of all the Fae, it is disgraceful." Ariel felt the defiance rise up in her as the tall woman turned back to say something, her eyes met with those of Luminaria and her voice was soft but held every ounce of her anger.

"Tell me I am wrong?" Luminaria looked like she was about to explode, she gave a huff of anger, turned, and stormed away yelling at her personal guards to catch up, Elgin watched Ariel and gave a gentle nod to her, his old voice was soft.

"Meet with me tomorrow, I shall send for you and you alone, we will talk."

Chapter Ten.

A Step Towards Darkness.

*B*ranna woke as the light streamed through the trees into the cave. She slid her hand across the sand, and stirred slightly.

"Ariel?"

She groaned on the floor as she came slowly round, and as she realised the stiffness of her joints. She was used to a soft bed, not a sand covered floor, and a bag filled with lumpy objects for a pillow. It took her several minutes to fully wake up, and in that time, she began to remember all that had happened and where she was. Branna turned to the cave entrance protected by the thick lining of shrubs and trees, through which the sun cast dappled shade across the floor. Several large rocks lay on the floor at the opening to the cave, and as her eyes focused, she noticed a large lump of what looked like meat, but there was no sign of Roack.

Slowly she tried to stand, but her aches and pains left her stiff and awkward. She really wanted to stretch out the pains, but the cave was not high enough, so she bent forward and slowly got to her feet, making sure to avoid banging her head on the rough jagged ceiling of rock. Her feet were sluggish as she walked forward, and as she approached the entrance, she blinked as her eyes got used to the bright light outside. It looked like late afternoon, the air felt warm, but it was hard to tell by the angle she was at just where exactly the sun was in the sky.

Branna stopped at the entrance, and looked down at the large lump of what looked like half cooked meat, her stomach suddenly awoke and gave a long whine, and it must have been almost a day since she had last eaten. Branna picked up the meat, it was covered in sand.

"Bloody bird has no sense of hygiene; I wonder where it is?"

Her mind felt clearer as she stepped out of the cave holding the meat, and walked into the trees, she had no sense of Roack at all, but with the sudden second whine of her stomach, she felt it was not worth the worry, and walked through the trees towards the sound of water. It took a few minutes to reach the shallow river, so as she walked, she stretched and tensed her body to try and relieve the stiffness of her limbs, as the sound of the water grew louder, she licked her lips and felt the off taste in her mouth, she was parched and dry, and just the thought of clean water to drink hurried her steps.

*T*he river was wide, but shallow. The banks broke in places to create small patches of sand scattered with small rocks. Branna knelt at the edge and placed the sandy meat on one of the rocks, and then leaned forward and placed her lips to the fast flowing surface of the water. After a few hurried gulps of the icy liquid, she just pushed her entire face into the river and felt the rapid water enclose her face and run over the back of her neck. Her head came quickly up as she gasped with the coldness, and she shook her long tangled main of hair spraying the water all over the surrounding dry stones. It was icy, and yet it served its purpose as she gasped with shock, and suddenly felt wide awake. She plunged her hands into the water and rubbed them together, she noticed the cuts and scratches from her long run through rough blade grasses and brambles. They stung slightly but it was nothing she could not bear, and just having clean hands made her feel so much cleaner and less groggy than she had been.

Feeling a little more revived, she took the lump of partially blackened meat and washed it free of the sand and grime, it puzzled her as to where a raven could acquire such a large lump, it was still raw in parts and her mind turned to cooking it, her eyes cast round the bank to see what was available. It was not long before she noticed the familiar grey of flint stone, and she sorted through one or two looking for the right pieces.

Once selected, she picked up the drying clean lump of meat and walked to the bank in search of moss and sticks. Collecting what she needed took only a short time, after all Ariel and her had made it part of their daily routine to collect wood each morning for the fire, so it was not long before she had the means and was kneeling on the floor, as she struck the stones together to create a spark to ignite the moss. Within minutes she was lay low blowing on the embers, as the moss ignited and the small sticks, she had prepared caught the flames. Several minutes later her little fire was crackling away, as she skewered her meat to a long stick that she angled above the fire to cook fully.

By the time Roack swooped out of the sky to land on a rock close to her, Branna was licking her fingers, and had devoured two thirds of the meat. She gazed at the bird and smiled.

"Thanks for the meat I was starving, I am not certain of this taste though what is it?" The bird bobbed on the rock.

"It's the marshals that tracked you; they will no longer be following you." Branna gave a happy nod and tore another piece off the dwindling lump attached to the stick.

"Great, you got rid of them, clever of you, I mean I am grateful, and really happy you brought their food. What about you, have you eaten?" The rough voice croaked in her mind.

"We have eaten more than what we need, our strength has grown a great deal. We will need it for future days."

Branna chewed another lump of the succulent meat happily, Roack was unsure of her, did she realise she was actually eating the marshal? The bird felt it best not to concern itself; after all she had been weakened and needed food. Branna swallowed and licked her fingers.

"What time is it?" She looked at the sun. "I have lost my bearings a little so not so sure if its morning or afternoon."

"We do not understand your markers of moments, since you slept, the light has fallen into darkness and appeared again, and now it has crossed the sky over half the distance it should do." Branna stopped for a moment startled.

"You mean I have slept longer than a day, so it is now late afternoon?"

"If that is how you name it… Yes, your body was weak from the travel, it needed rest." Branna swallowed the last chunk of meat, and lay back on the grass.

"I was tired, I was also afraid." She turned her head to look at the bird. "Thanks Roack, I would not have escaped without you."

"We need each other, we like your world, but there are dangers for both of us here, we must prepare and find what we need to move faster, and then we shall have what we desire." She sat up and rested on her arms.

"You know I never thought to ask, but why me? I mean why did you come down here to me and help me escape from Avalon? I am sure there are many others who wanted to escape." The Bird flapped its wings and settled back on the stone.

"You came to us, you reached out to us and we responded, we saw the desires inside you, we understand the fear of those who control the light powers, and want also to be free of them, we also were here first, it was those with the light that pushed us out to create this world, they did not ask, they took, we would have shared it, but they did not ask. You asked to meet us and we came."

Branna listened to the voice inside her head and thought, she found the bird strangely fascinating, although she knew Roack was not a bird, but all the same, whatever it was inside the bird that was now controlling it, appeared to be far more intelligent than anything anyone had ever thought.

"You said you were here first, then there must be many of you, because you always say we and not I. So have you all been there all the time watching and learning from us?"

"All that has been done has been seen; we have watched and learned many things from your strange world. Your power and forms are different, we have seen much in your making and we want to share that with you, we were never asked, but we waited as we knew that we would be asked one day." Branna's words were quiet as she thought, and she spoke more of her thoughts out loud than think them.

"All this time watching, you have spent a whole age watching us grow and learning, wow you are a very patient lot."

"We do not understand that. Your spirits are like ours, and they are nourished by the form you are contained in, we wanted to see if we too could be contained and protected from the light." It was a simple statement, and yet it surprised Branna.

"You are all spirits, but you have no bodies, yeah I understand now. Eve took the land and created us from it, she took the spirit of all of us and blew us into it, it makes perfect sense if you were watching that you too would want to do the same, so you all want a life, you want to live here among us as people or beings, is that what you want?"

"We want the same." Branna gave a nod, it did make perfect sense, the Merle simply wanted bodies of their own to live in.

*F*or most of the day Ariel paced up and down in her room, just the thought of getting out into the air was more than enough to drive her crazy, and it felt like the longer she waited, the harder it was to bear the strain of waiting. Shortly after noon, Bade arrived with food, he sat with her as she ate and apologised.

"I was very frightened, and I am sorry, it was not as you thought though, I did not for a second believe it was your Bran. I did not know what it was, until I was informed it was Bridget." Ariel gave a nod.

"Is she alright, it was a terrifying scream?" He gave a nod.

"I spoke to Ninian this morning, Malcolm stayed with her all last night, and she had a good rest that was dream free afterwards. You see what I mean though; everyone is talking about it, whatever these night terrors are they terrify her, and she is a very powerful person, it scares me just to think of it, I mean think about it, if it terrifies her so much, what the hell is it?"

It was a sobering thought, and not one Ariel wanted to consider, she remembered the fear inside her mother, even now after all these years she remembered the fear in her mother's eyes.

"My mother never spoke of what she encountered; I just know it really frightened her. I am sorry Bade, but I cannot believe that whatever it was she witnessed has come down to here. If something that is powerful enough to frighten my mother and Bridget is here within us, the news would spread rapidly and Hearne and Eve would be here to fight it with us, nothing that frightening could live amongst us." Bade gave a reassuring nod.

"This is what I have said all along, and yet Rhiannon insists that whatever it is living up there has infected a member of the Fae."

"Well, whatever it is, I can tell you now, it is not in Bran."

*I*n some ways Ariel was right, it was not inside her, but it was beside her. What had caused such a stir was that the entrance into this world had been detected, but what no one realised, including the white lord, was that the Merle was far more intelligent than anyone realised.

The Merle had watched from the moment of creation, and learned of everything that had been done. It could sense the powers of the council and the Fae, and it knew that they would destroy it if ever they crossed it. The Merle had watched for a long time, and it had taken many ages for it to realise the one thing that everyone had missed. If it came on mass, it would be found and destroyed, but due to its nature of connection, all it needed to do was allow a small part to infect a host, and then from the world of men, it could communicate without being seen to the rest of the Merle. Roack was simply a small and minor connection to the full host. Branna had no idea of the power connected to the bird, and her life's obsession was clouding her judgement.

The garment of Tideguyde had tiny particles of the Merle within it, and these had been passed on into other members of the Fae. Bridget was not completely right, but she had been wise enough to understand that because of her great power, she could absorb the tiny particles into herself, freeing her people from any contamination and holding back the connection to the rest of the Merle.

Rhiannon was blinded by her greed and obsession with Avalon, it was her pride that had in fact stopped her from understanding what was living within the darkness that surrounded the Realm Ofmoon. In her arrogance she had never thought that Branna whom she saw as a lesser being had the talent or the skill to contact the Merle. The tiny particle that she had attracted to herself, had been drawn so fast into Branna's world it was undetectable, and so as Rhiannon looked for ways to hide her incompetence by blaming an adopted relative of Bridget's, Branna walked out of Avalon with a direct link to a source of power that could bring chaos to the world.

Branna had the tiny particle of the Merle within her from birth, and that was the beacon the Merle had connected with, but it could not take her over because she felt something that was actually more powerful than the Merle, she was in love with Ariel. Her love for Ariel was so powerful in the powers of the white light, all the Merle within Roack could do was connect to her thoughts and feelings, and for as long as Branna loved Ariel she was safe, but Roack had other plans for her.

*H*aving had a good sleep followed by a meal most of the day had been lost, and by the time Branna collected her things from the cave and set off, the day had slid towards late afternoon. Knowing that no one was following her, or at least for now, lifted her spirits, and she walked with a good pace along the side of the river following the trail towards a new future. Roack appeared to be talkative and she asked as many questions as possible, especially about where they should go. The raven sat on her shoulder and spoke to her using her mind.

"We must leave this land, we have watched for a long time, and the land of your queen has many openings to this realm. You must cross the water to other lands for there are places we know of that you can

live out of sight from your own people."

It did make sense, but Branna who had always been a little carefree was not too worried, she knew that the veil she had cast over herself would stop Rhiannon from seeing her wherever she was, it was one of the main reasons why the Fae used it, for even though they were connected to the Fae of Earth, they still had many rituals and secrets that they did not share, and kept all of them well hidden.

Being tracked by a member of the marshals was an entirely different thing, but she knew that the longer it took for them to send another, the further away she would be and the trail would eventually become cold, leaving her free from any chance of capture. Branna felt a sense of warning and came out of her thoughts, the raven stiffened on her shoulder and then swept into the air.

"Beware, I smell the red light."

Branna smiled, it amused her how anything that emitted light like fire, was given a name that described it rather than actually used the common name for it. She slowed her pace a little and tried sniffing the air but could smell nothing. Roack was high in the sky just ahead of her and she watched the bird turn and sweep back towards her.

"There is a man alone with the red light, go to him, he has the things you will need."

*B*ranna kept on walking in the direction that Roack led her in, and soon the river turned and the banks were covered with large green fine needled trees. Just a little way up the bank, she saw a figure huddled down beside a fire eating. Rather than slow her pace, she continued and then deliberately turned her head towards him, she could see he had already noticed her and was watching. Branna smiled and changed her course towards him.

"Greetings Friend."

He was larger than her, and a little thicker round the waist, his clothes were tatty and dirty, his hair hung lank and matted, and his face was hidden behind a thick beard of brown matted hair, he rose as she approached and she could see the twinkle in his eyes, his voice was somewhat higher than she expected, but she put that down to his surprise.

"Greeting's stranger, I see few in these parts, but never a woman alone."

Branna noted the thick leather belt and long knife attached to it, against the tree behind him was a sheath of arrows and some snares, and five rabbits hung from a branch, she smiled again.

"Likewise friend, I expected to meet none on my trail, until I smelled the fire, what brings you so far out into the wilds?"

She could see he was a little confused, she was not aware that it was her clothing that had raised his suspicions, after all they were well tailored, and unlike the women of the man's world, she wore pants.

"I hunt for furs, what brings you here stranger, for I see from your garments, you are not of these parts?" Branna stood a little ways off and looked at the pot that bubbled on his fire; he still held the bowl in his hand, which was almost empty from his meal.

"I am passing this way on my travels, but the day is warm and my pace is slow." He gave a nod and looked at the pot.

"I have food if you need to eat, the day has been kind, although I am leaving these parts for there is ill omens in this land, I would advise you eat and do likewise." Branna gave a nod and another large smile. She took a few paces towards the fire as the man bent down to his pack to lift out another small wooden bowl.

"That is mighty kind of you, I would be grateful to sit a while and share a meal thank you. I am Bran." He nodded.

"Halbrand."

He filled the bowl from the pan using a carved wooden spoon, and Branna approached and crouched down by the fire to take it. He handed her a piece of what looked like baked pastry and she could smell the herbs within it, she took it with a smile, and he sat back in his spot opposite her. Roack sat close by on the lower branch of a tree, and she spoke into her mind as she watched the stranger lift his bowl, and start to scoop the stew into his mouth with the pastry, and she did likewise. Branna looked round the camp at his things, there were pelts and weapons.

"Are you a hunter?" He gave a nod and lifted a stone jug to drink.

"I am one of the best, I travel here far from my home to trap, and trade what I take in the large settlements. There are few who come this far out, for me it makes a good living and my purse is filled with gold and silver enough for my life." Branna could feel his pride in himself as he passed the jug towards her, Roack croaked in her mind.

"He has what we need, his gold could help us, we need supplies and he has many, I feel the liquid in the jug clouding his mind." She tried to ignore Roack.

"So, you are one of these rich traders I hear so much about? I must say you have a good stock of furs; your house must be large and comfy." He gave a sly grin.

"I have many comforts and my needs are taken care of." Branna gave a giggle.

"I would think the women of your tribe prize you highly?" Halbrand smiled as Branna passed him back the jug having not drank from it.

"I have known a few women in my time." She gave a small laugh.

"Yes, I would think so." Roack spoke in her thoughts.

"This man has thoughts that make his insides race, he does not intend you peace or goodwill, he wants to do the things you did with the woman of light in Avalon."

Branna chewed the food and talked back to Roack in her head.

"He is dirty and smells, I have no wish for sex with this man."

Branna sensed the change in Roack's mood.

"I do not think this man will ask, I feel his thoughts, and he wants to take, be ready." She scratched her stomach as she held the bowl, and made sure her jacket was open just enough to reach the knife that she had attached to her belt underneath it. Branna smiled as she ate.

"This is good, again I am grateful to you Halbrand."

He gave a nod as he lifted his bowl and drained it, it was clear to Branna his stature had changed a little, and even though she played along as being innocent, even she could notice the subtle signs as he watched her eat. Halbrand lowered his empty bowl to the floor and wiped his mouth on his sleeve, she could see him wiping his tongue around inside his mouth. She felt this was him deciding if he had a taste for what he intended. She reached the last of the stew which was mainly the broth, and gently lifted the bowl to her lips to drink it. Roack croaked inside her mind.

"The time is close, be ready."

As she lifted the bowl with one hand to her mouth she prepared, he had no idea who he was dealing with, and she tensed ready as her Fae senses alerted her to the sudden change in the air around her. As the bowl came level with her eyes, she sensed the moment, Halbrand had sank back on his heels, and the twigs under his heels cracked as he did so, Branna was ready and it was all the warning she needed.

Halbrand sprang forward over the camp fire, and as he did so, Branna who was holding the bowl in her left hand, brought up her right arm with her palm out flat. As Halbrand pounced towards her, his forehead collided right into her upcoming right hand, the flesh made contact and there was an almighty blue flash of light. Halbrand bounced with a yell backwards across the fire, and collided with great force into the tree, his hands came up to his face and covered his eyes and he wailed in pain. Branna was up on her feet, and came round the fire towards him; Roack swooped out of the tree and landed on her bag which was set to one side of the fire.

Halbrand rolled around in pain on the floor his body jerking with spasms as he kept his face covered with his hands, Roack appeared impressed.

"You hide your talents well, he was very startled, and we feel the pain he feels inside his head." Branna looked down at him on the floor and then back to Roack.

"He will not follow us for some time, come on let's get out of here." She moved towards Roack and her bag, but the bird remained still sat on top of it.

"No… End him." She felt a jolt in her stomach as she looked at Roack.

"What… No… I cannot do that; I have never killed anything; I am Fae we do not do that."

"You must, now end him, we are but a small creature, we cannot do it, he cannot live as others will come looking, he must be silenced now end him." Branna panicked slightly.

"You cannot be serious, I am unharmed, he was never a match for a member of the Fae. Roack you ask too much."

"You want freedom, don't you?"

Her hands were shaking, and she stepped back a little away from Halbrand, who was still rolling around in agony. He screamed out at her.

"You friggin witch, I am blind, I should have known when I saw them three yesterday morn, I should have known it would be you, only a witch could do such things that defile all the gods of the land. Just you wait… Just you friggin wait you whore, I will find you and I will rip out your black evil heart and burn it." Panic flooded into her, he rolled around and kicked out all around him, what should she do? Roack appeared right and she did not know what to do, but Roack knew.

"End him, take the rock and smash his head in, he will talk, and he

will tell everyone about you, not only will the marshals look for you, his people will hunt you, now end this now… Take the Rock!"

Branna felt the sweat on her face; she had no idea how to do this. He was shouting at her and calling her names she did not understand, his foot caught the fire and the flames erupted into the air, and she jumped back as Roack flew into the air to get away from the red light. Her heart was pounding in her chest and she was finding it hard to breathe, she could see the large rock on the floor a few feet away, but she really did not want to use it, Roack was getting louder in her head and sounded angry.

"DO IT, KILL HIM!"

She knew Roack was right, she just wanted to be free, but this was not what she wanted, but she knew that he would come after her. Roack continued to talk, filling her head with her croaky voice, and clouding her thoughts even more.

"You must, you must kill him and take the things he has, you need to leave this land and his furs will fetch a good trade. Kill him and take what is his and use it to escape, now do it, end him, take the rock and end him."

She had not even realised that she had moved round the fire closer to the rock. The rock was just a foot away, it was round and rugged, and she knew that it would be enough. Roack continued to shout in her head, and Halbrand screamed all sorts of words she did not understand at the top of his voice, as he kicked and lashed out on the floor. It was all becoming too much for her to handle, and she felt her own panicked temper rising within her, without even thinking she screamed out at the top of her lungs, and then snatched the rock off the floor and lifted it up into the air above her head, she screamed from the depths of her being at both of them.

"FOR THE LOVE OF THE GODS BE QUIET!" Crunch!

*H*er eyes were wide, as she suddenly realised what she had done, she was breathless and panting, her chest moving in and out at speed. At her blood stained feet, the rock sat where she had thrown it down with all her might. Halbrand's head was covered with it, and bits of bone and mush were slowly slipping out from the underneath, and mixing with the red stream that flowed into the dirt. His body jerked and wriggled in strange sorts of spasms, and all around her was total silence, as if her world had suddenly stopped.

Branna stood frozen her eyes locked on the red liquid as it drained out and soaked into the leaves and dirt, her insides felt dead and hollow, as if every emotion she had ever felt had been stolen. The only thing she felt was the strange feeling in the pit of her stomach, and she stood frozen and stared lost inside herself, she felt it build at the base of her stomach and then suddenly rush upwards at speed.

Branna felt the convulsion, turned towards the fire and leaned over and vomited. The hot burning liquid came at force and speed, straining her windpipe, and then exploded out onto the remains of the fire that hissed and spat as it contacted it. Her stomach lurched again, as the putrid smell of her vomit hitting the hot coals entered her nose, and she retched and then vomited again. She gasped in for air feeling helpless as her stomach contracted and then lurched again, and this time she stepped back away from the dead Halbrand and the fire, and her left arm came up and made contact with the tree for support, she just had time to gasp before everything she had eaten that day ejected out of her mouth, and splashed onto the floor of dead needles and leaves. It took her several long moments to regain her composure and wipe her mouth.

Roack watched from the trees feeling satisfied, without understanding Branna had taken her first step away from love and into darkness, she had broken her most sacred vow of the Fae, and taken the life of another. Roack watched as she wiped her mouth and started to weep, she muttered to herself quietly, but she had forgotten that the bird could feel and hear everything.

"What have I done? Why did I listen, this is so wrong and this is not who I am, Ariel will never forgive me?" Roack flew down from the tree, and landed on the blood coated stone on Halbrand's head.

"Why do you weep, this is not the land of your queen with rules, this is his realm, where you take what you want. Dry your eyes, you act like a child."

Branna stood up and turned to look at the bird, she saw the still body in the pool of blood, and Roack sat on the rock implanted in Halbrand's head, it turned her stomach.

"How would you know? This is not who I am, I do not kill." Roack stiffened and pecked a small piece of flesh off the rock and ate it.

"But you do, look at what you have done. This is the real world, this is what you desire, to be free is it not?" She shook her head.

"Not through the death of the innocent." The bird gave a squawk almost as if it was laughing.

"He was not innocent, he wanted your body, and then he would have taken your life and left you to rot, I could see what was in his mind. Look at him, look at what you are capable of. You tell me this is not you, and yet I watched as you took the life he held and threw it away. This is you; this is the freedom you desire; this is the choice you made when you ran from your queen. This is why I came to you."

"What?" Branna shook her head and took a step back. "I did not ask for this." Roack stared her.

"You did not say the words, but I am connected to you, I can feel everything, I feel your powers and they are very strong, I feel your desires to prove yourself worthy to a queen who deems you as secondary. Look at what you are capable of Branna of the Fae, look how easily you broke the golden rule of your kind. Feel your power, and look at your work and feel the freedom. Tell me, what has happened in breaking your golden rules of your line, are you dead, did your queen appear and take you away to be punished forever?"

She stammered feeling a little afraid of Roack's words.

"What… What do you mean?"

"Nothing has happened, has it? You are here alive and well. You used the power of who you are and nothing has happened. Branna you are free of that life, you are in a new world with great powers and no one here can stop you, here you can rule and not be ruled. In this world you can do as you please and take what you want, can you see the power you hold?" She stared at the bird unable to fully comprehend it. Roack could see that she was starting to understand, but it would take a little time.

"Come we must leave here, gather his things for he has clothes and weapons. Take his furs and food, for you will have good need of them, we must move away before the darkness comes."

She wanted to leave, but she knew the bird was right, she snapped out of her daze, and tried not to look at the body, as she quickly moved round the camp. She pushed her bag into his larger pack, and grabbed his bow and quiver. She tied the rabbits to the pack and as quick as she could she hurried back down the bank to the path beside the river. Before they moved, she quickly stepped into the water and washed her boots and hands and cleaned the vomit off her face. She took a long drink, and filled Halbrand's water skin.

Within thirty minutes she was packed, clean, and off down the pathway at the side of the river moving as quick as she could. Roack took to the sky and flew in front of her to look for a safe route away from any settlements.

Walking alone she had a lot to think about, and as the hours past and the darkness headed towards the end of the day, Branna began to understand what Roack had said. She was now free of the Fae, and that did mean their rules, for now they no longer applied and she was in a completely different world that was less advanced than hers. Roack was right, here she could go where she wished and do as she pleased, there was nothing and no one who could match her Fae powers, she could rule anywhere should she choose to, everything had changed.

She had spent so many years trapped and wishing to be free, and now she suddenly realised she was free, and she really did not require any rules at all. This was her life now, and for the first time she understood this was actually her own life and her own fate.

Roack had been right, she did have powers that outmatched everyone in this world, there really was nothing she could not do. She had taken a life in her own hands and robbed another of it, there was no other power greater than that, was this the power that Rhiannon held above all of them? Her feet moved quickly and a faint smile crossed her lips, she knew now what she wanted to do, she would build her own empire and she would rule her own piece of her world, and when everything was in place, she would send for Ariel and they would be able to live and rule together. There really was no light or darkness, all there was out here in the free world was power, and she now knew she had that and could use it.

That night, neither Ariel nor Branna slept very well. Ariel moved a chair closer to the window, and with the shutters opened wide, she stared into the night sky above Florae. Miles away across the realms, Branna lay on her back rolled up in a blanket, and looked up at the same stars. Neither of them realised that they were completely synchronised as they watched the sky, and felt the love they held for each other, and missed being close.

Ariel thought of her conversation with Bade, and Branna considered all that Roack had told her. Little did they understand that at that very same moment in time, they both were stood on the verge of change. This was the turning point, as both of them accepted that they would one day be together again, but before that, both of them had to move forward in the tasks they were about to choose for themselves.

Ariel had no idea where Branna was, and so as Bade advised, she decided she would take the time to readjust to all the new ways that her people were developing in their new world. For Branna the choice was simple, she had to escape, and then find a way to rise to the challenge of showing the world how her queen had betrayed so many of her race to preserve and protect herself. Branna had sworn revenge for her people, and in her mind that meant she had to follow the path of the raven, and build an empire to match the realm of the moon.

Chapter Eleven.

Truths Of Light And Darkness.

It was late afternoon and the sun was radiant across the land of Florae. Between the tall houses that lined the incline from the centre of the main town, all the way up the steep slopes the songs of thousands of birds twittered in the high branches. The air was filled with the scents of a million plants and fresh growing herbs, and the sense in the air was one of calm after the previous evening's sudden and terrifying scream, from the queen in her night terrors.

After a very long and impatient day, Ariel was finally outside her apartment, and walking beside an escort who had been sent to take her to the meeting with the leader of the council. It felt like such a huge relief to finally be outside the four walls of her living space, and at the slow pace, from the balcony rails of the long House of Scribes, Ariel got to see a little more detail of the changes that had occurred in Florae during her absence.

This was Ariel's first chance to see how what would one day be her home again was growing. She looked out from the steps of the House of Scribes at the long road that stretched from the steps of the house all the way down to the edge of the sea in one long straight line. Along its edge were orchards, community gardens, and fields, where the food for the Fae was grown.

Around the edges of what was a huge natural basin surrounded by mountains, the steep sides were filled with trees, in which all of the houses and workshops were built, all of them roughly the same design of a large pent roof on stilts into which the floors balconies and windows were fitted. Every single one was decorated in a different way, making all of them look completely unique from each other. It had changed so much, and there were so many new faces, it was clear that Bridget had done as she planned, and had brought most of her people together in one spot for the very first time in their history. Ariel felt in awe of it all, and deep within her she felt a great happiness in knowing how much Bridget had wanted this.

At the far end of the long walkway, on the north western side of the House of Scribes, a large private garden had been built. The whole area was surrounded by a trellis wall, and within it long heavy planters made of intricately carved wood, were filled with shrubs and flowers of great beauty. There were pockets of spaces into which benches and tables had been arranged for meetings or for moments of quiet contemplation, and it was here that Ariel was led to her meeting with Counsellor Elgin.

He looked restful as she approached sat back in his seat before a table laid out with fresh fruits, meats and breads. He noticed her arrival and stirred in his seat, he stood up and offered a hand as if to welcome her to his table, Ariel gave a smile and approached him, and as she arrived, he took her hands in his in greeting, and escorted her to a seat.

"Thank you for coming, please take a seat and feel free to join me and share a meal with me."

Out here in the sunlight and surrounded by plants and the beautiful scents of the flowers, the old man with his white hair and his long robes of deep emerald green, appeared friendly and kind, and not quite as fearful as he had first appeared on her arrival. Ariel took a seat in front of the lavish table, whilst Elgin filled her goblet with a rich red wine.

"Thank you, My Lord Counsellor." He smiled and his eyes twinkled.

"This is a garden of great relaxation, here I am Elgin only, I hope you like it here, it is my contribution to this new land of our people, designed with a calmer more relaxed approach to things in mind." She smiled and admired the simple beauty of the place.

"It is beautiful and a very welcome addition I feel."

Elgin returned to his seat and lifted his goblet; he took a small drink and then began to move items of the food to his plate. Ariel joined him and began selecting pieces of fruit, he lifted his eyes and they appeared happy and bright, and he smiled as he sat back in his seat.

"You are probably not aware of this, but your mother and I were great friends and worked together many times back in our old lands on Erin. I have watched you grow from a child into a worthy and dedicated member of this community, you have done well to overcome much and achieve as much as you have, it is indeed a mark of your good character." Ariel felt very calm and relaxed and she gave a little giggle.

"I am not convinced Rhiannon would agree with you." He smiled and nodded his head.

"She is somewhat irritable of late." He lifted some cheese and laid it on a slice of brown wholesome bread, and took a bite. He chewed for a moment in thought as Ariel followed suit.

"I find Rhiannon far too rash in her judgement; she is renowned for her wisdom, and she is certainly a woman of immense power, but I feel she still lacks the wisdom of her age, and can trip over her pride in her rush to judgement." He lifted his goblet to drink. "You were right to stand your ground in front of Luminaria, you defended our queen's position, you showed great respect for Bridget, and I may add loyalty." Ariel was a little taken a back.

"I thought I was in trouble for showing disrespect to a fellow ambassador." He gave a wide smile.

"She is very demanding and not at all like her brother, I find him to be more thoughtful in his approach to his dealings with people, he is a remarkable craftsman, but that is by the by. It was your actions yesterday that have led me to great thought about the current scenario, which is why I wish to talk with you alone." Ariel understood, but she was not aware how long exactly he had been observing her conversation with Bade.

"I feel I should apologise to Luminaria, but I also am quite angry that both Bran and myself have been accused of such evil dealings, when I know that the truth of the matter is simply the fact that a member of Rhiannon's people, whom she deems as unworthy, has outshone all of her advisors." He gave a nod of his head.

"I am aware of your companions work; I have recently read all of your reports." She was surprised.

"You have, how?" He smiled.

"I simply asked the queen, and she gave her permission, it is where I have been for the last few days. Your reports were thorough and very detailed. I can now understand why you were made ambassador to the place, and not retained here to continue your work in the house, although I must confess, I feel it is unlikely that you will return." Ariel agreed.

"Yes, I have thought about it now, after yesterday I cannot think Luminaria will recommend I return, it is why I feel I must see her and apologise."

"Well sadly it is too late for that now, she left almost immediately, and I would imagine by now she has made her report to Rhiannon, so I fear for now you are probably not a very welcome guest in her realm." Ariel felt a tinge of regret, although deep down inside she knew she was protecting Branna, and as hard as it was to accept, she felt her loyalty to Bran was worth far more.

"What about my things? I still have many possessions at the house, I was led to believe I would only be here a short time, so did not fully pack?"

"For now, your home there is sealed to all, it will not be possible to retrieve anything until this matter is settled to its fullest with Rhiannon." She understood and thought that maybe that would never happen, and so she had to accept that there was the possibility her things were gone forever.

"So, what will happen to me now?" He gave her a smile.

"It has been suggested that you remain within the confines of Florae for a time, although I will add more out of protection. I have spoken with the council and for now they feel you should not be involved with the house, although I disagree but I am but one of twelve. However, I have also discussed this with Bade, and he as you are aware has vouched for you, so I would suggest you continue to live in your apartment and if he should require assistance, well you have a place where you can talk privately. It is the best of a bad situation for the moment, but it is for now as much as I can do for you. Take some time Ariel, get to know Florae and walk in its wonder, I am sure you will find there are many tasks to offer help and support with."

She felt downhearted, she could not return to the one place she regarded as home, and she had no idea where Bran was, her only solace would have been returning to organise the house, but even that had been taken from her. Ariel gave a nod of her head and agreed she really had no other choice.

"Will I be allowed to see the Queen? She is like a mother to me and I consider her family, can I not go to visit her?" The old counsellor smiled.

"I have personally informed the Queen of your plight, she will send for you when she is ready, but I would suggest that considering your liberties, it would not be unreasonable for you to see the rest of your family, adopted or otherwise." He smiled and she gave a warm smile back.

"Thank you I would like that."

"Now I feel we are wasting a beautiful day, and a rather handsome feast, so let us relax and talk of more pleasant things."

*F*or the rest of the afternoon, Ariel shared a very pleasant time, being a scribe to the house she had often seen him and knew who he was, but had never really worked or spoken enough to him to form an opinion. Elgin was far more relaxed and friendly than she had ever thought, he told her of his days in Erin with her mother, which she found fascinating as it revealed things about her, she had never known.

They spoke of the House of Scribes and her planning of it when she had been living on the Violet Isle, he expressed how remarkable her design skills had been, and recommended she spoke with Ninian and Gwynfor, for he felt her design skills would play a huge part in helping them with some of the smaller islands of Florae. It was as the sun began to fade and they had laughed and eaten their fill that as both of them sat together, Ariel plucked up the courage to ask the one question no one had answered since her arrival.

"Can I ask honestly; do you really think that a member of any of the Fae peoples could be dark? You see I just cannot believe that any of us could turn on our line and act against the rest of us."

Elgin was sat relaxed in his seat holding his goblet, in the fading light his hair and beard appeared whiter, and in many ways to Ariel, he appeared to be possibly one of the wisest members of the council. Elgin thought for a few moments and then his dark eyes fixed on her, he could see clearly how eager she was to hear his thoughts.

"Hmm my dear Ariel, that is a question on many lips and in many thoughts at this time. I would suppose I would consider the meaning of dark, would that mean corrupted, and if so, would that suggest Arrogance, greed, political ambition could be viewed as dark traits?" She listened intently as she watched him ponder the thought.

"If I am honest, I would find it hard to believe that any member of Fae could be so dark as they would place at risk their own people. Dark is a word coined by Rhiannon to describe certain actions that she has accused others of, but as to any actuality of the possibility of a line of Fae being born in such a way, I am not altogether certain. I suppose the real question to ask would be could a member of the Fae be corrupted by true evil?"

"Corrupted, as in convinced to be a certain evil way?" He shook his head.

"I would say more like an infection, some means by which a member of our lines could contract an evil intent and then use it against its enemies and its own people, you see I do not believe any Fae is born dark. I have watched the race of men who I may add are a weaker breed with shorter lives than ourselves, and I have seen man turn on man, were they dark at heart? I am not sure, were they corrupted? I feel that could be possible, but we are a line of people who contain the power to do good in these worlds, so I am still unsure as to whether or not it would be possible." He made a great deal of sense; she paused for a second before asking.

"I know the Lord Albanlin had suggested that what lives above us is very dark and evil, so I suppose what I am thinking is that if Rhiannon is right, she is suggesting that this entity we call the Merle has come down to this world and actually inhabited a member of the Fae. I mean if it is up there and we are down here, how could any Fae be born dark? The other thing also is, surely if this Merle can drop down here and take over one of us, would that person not be changed so much that they would not be themselves anymore? I would have thought if the Merle really could do that, whoever it chose would fight it to regain their own control." He gave an agreeable nod.

"You make a valid argument, but that is why I use the term corrupted; I honestly do not believe any member of either Fae would choose to harm others, but if they were corrupted, then I would speculate that it would be that member of the Fae that chose to willingly allow this Merle to control its actions. I have to confess that is where I am trapped, because like you I do not believe that any member of the Fae would willingly make such a choice, and it would be a choice, everything in life is about choice and making the right ones. No Fae would choose to hurt its own kind; man, I believe is a different matter entirely."

"I have read a great many things over the years that have been said by the Lord Albanlin, and if I am right then he has never actually specified just what this Merle is, to be honest we have no idea what it is, let alone what it can do, that is why Bran's work was so important, I feel Rhiannon has acted irresponsibly." He gave a nod.

"I feel you are right, and yes I must admit we really do not know enough of this thing, it could be spirit or have a body, it could be some form of entity we have no knowledge of and have never encountered anything like it before. The simple truth is, we really know absolutely nothing about it. I may also add, we still have no idea if this thing really has come to this world, or if this is not just an elaborate smokescreen created by Rhiannon to hide the fact that she has been seen to be lacking in wisdom. These are the questions we will ask at the council in days to come, and so for now I suppose all we can do is wait and see what becomes of it all."

"But I am still trapped here instead of out there trying to find Bran." He gave a chuckle and rose from his seat.

"If this Bran of yours is anything like what I think she is from your reports, I feel that like you she will find a way to contact you. I would say fear not my young scribe, if I know anything of the power of love, this is not the end and you will hear from her when she surfaces. Never forget the one secret that escaped the high ranks of the Fae Ofmoon was the veil, they must have kicked themselves to discover that young Opal secretly stole their secrets, and then shared them with all of us. Your Bran is safe and under a veil somewhere, she will pop up when least expected for you." He gave her a small bow.

"It has been a most fascinating and rewarding day, but alas I feel the tiredness of my limbs and have made a promise to my granddaughters to read to them before bed, so I shall excuse myself, you must come by and meet them some time, Isolde and Filomena are delightful, I am sure they would love to listen to your stories of building this house. Fear not Ariel things will turn out for the good you will see, and you will find when you return to your apartments, a guard will remove that bracelet of yours and you are free to wander the realm. Enjoy your time and stay out of more trouble." He gave a chuckle. "Good night." She stood and returned the bow.

"Good night My Lord Elgin and thank you for your wisdom and kindness, and yes, I would love to meet with your grandchildren one day."

With a fond smile he walked off through the garden towards the House of Scribes, and as he turned at the entrance, he lifted his hand and waved, Ariel gave a happy smile, and waved back, and then he was gone and she was alone with no guard for the first time since returning back to Florae.

*S*omewhere in the world of men, Branna had been quiet for the rest of the day as she walked through endless woodland, fields, and along the side of small lakes. She had no idea in which direction she was going, she simply followed Roack who flew in front watching their path to ensure they stayed away from settlements and other people.

As she walked, she gathered fruit from the plants and trees and also firewood, which she bundled up onto the back of her pack. Her mind was still in turmoil as the vision of the dead man haunted her thoughts. At the start of her journey away from that fateful scene, Roack had talked in her mind constantly and told her of her courage and bravery and her skill for killing. It had driven her mad as she felt sick to her stomach, and eventually her thoughts had crossed to Ariel.

Branna knew how terribly upset she would be to find out what she had done, and she felt worse knowing of how Ariel loved all life as sacred. Branna missed her and just wanted to run to her, but she now knew that she was being looked for by Rhiannon, and she knew that to go to her would place Ariel in danger. Branna had not realised that Roack had gone quiet in her mind; her thoughts had just increased as all the happy moments she had shared flooded into her thoughts.

Long hours had passed silently between her and Roack, when finally, she realised it was getting very late and the sun had already set. She looked from the path hardly able to see Roack or where she was going. She looked around her to see if there was a place to stop but it appeared useless.

"Roack where are you, I cannot see you?" The bird croaked into her mind.

"We are here sat on your pack."

"Oh… It's very dark I think we should stop for the night." She felt the bird increase in her mind.

"Walk a little more there is a sheltered place under the trees ahead of you." Branna walked a lot slower, now she had her senses it was difficult walking, she continued until she saw the darker outline of something large before her.

"Is this it?"

"Yes, stop here."

Branna came to a halt and slid the long bow off her shoulder; she dropped it to the floor and then slid the heavy pack off her back. Her shoulders felt the immediate relief as it thumped to the floor, and she groaned as she stretched her arms to try and release the aching. She was not sure where the bird had gone, but she still felt the connection to Roack so knew they would not be far from her.

Dropping to her knees she felt around for the wood she had collected and dragged it towards her. The two flint rocks she had found by the pool were in her pocket, as was a small amount of rough fabric lint she had found in Halbrand's pack. Working blindly in the dark she shredded the lint the best she could, and then using the rock she struck a spark from the flint. It took a while for her to gain her bearings and actually hit the lint with the spark, but after some time, she had the ember she needed and began to softly blow, as she placed the finer twigs on it to burn.

One hour later, Branna sat at the fire feeling its warmth as she prepared rabbit and hung it from the stick to cook, Roack who was not keen on the red light sat in the tree above her. Her thoughts had wandered a great deal over the day, and so as she sat there waiting for the rabbit to cook, she thought of Roack and the connection to the Merle. She felt hesitant at first, but thought that maybe through the connection the bird already knew, she still asked the question.

"Was that really me, or did you make me do it?" The croak of the bird in her head almost sounded like it was insulted.

"We do not have that power over you, it was all your doing, you have the power and the abilities to do far more than you realise, we knew you could do it, and told you to do so. If you had not, he would have killed you, we saw that in his heart."

Branna was quiet for a second.

"It is against what I want."

"It was necessary, you are not in Fae world now, in this world you kill or you get killed."

"So, you cannot control me, I am still free to do my own thing and make my own decisions?"

"You can go and do whatever you want; we do not have the power to stop you." She was not sure which was worse; in the back of her mind, she had thought that Roack had forced her to kill Halbrand, realising that it was her made her feel worse.

"If you do not have the power to control me, then what is this connection you speak of?"

"We can hear your thoughts and feel your feelings, nothing more. We told you what he meant to do and we were right, it was good you understood we know these things and saved yourself."

"I am not sure I want you to hear all my thoughts, I mean I do want some privacy at times."

"We understand that, we do not like the woman of light, and we let you go when you think of her. Your people can talk to each other like this, we know that, and we know you can block them out if you do not want to speak, you can do that too with us as we do with you."

"You blocked me out?"

"Yes… We told you, we do not like the woman of light."

"But why? Ariel was sweet and kind, she could never hurt anything."

"She lies."

"What?"

"You heard us; she lies. It was her blood that came to us and when we ran to greet her, they killed many of us with the star of life and death."

Branna felt shocked, as she realised that Roack was talking about Ariel's mother.

"You remember that? It was two hundred years ago; it was not Ariel's fault she was just a little girl."

"Her blood was sent to kill us and many parts of us died. The woman of light and her kin are our enemy, in this day many are trapped by her blood and held in a white space where they suffer, we hate the blood of the woman of light. When you think of her and feel for her, we leave you alone."

Branna felt shocked, it took her several long moments before she finally began to understand what Roack was talking about.

"The sickness, of all the lords I never realised until now, you do not just mean Ariel's mother, you mean all the Fae of Earth, the sickness is an infection of your beings, you are the Merle, you really are and you are alive and living and thinking as I have always thought. When you talk of trapped you are talking of Bridget, she has taken you all from those who were sick to save them, and now she has all of that trapped inside her, Bridget is cleansing the Fae of Earth."

"We know this, and we thought you did too." Branna shook her head in front of the fire.

"No, I had not realised it until now, but now it all makes sense."

Branna felt her spirits lift slightly; everything she had thought during her research was true, suddenly a thought rushed into her mind, and she was not sure if it was Roack, or just the natural process of understanding.

"Rhiannon knows, doesn't she?"

"We cannot see into her thoughts." There was something about the way Roack appeared in her thoughts that made her think Roack was hiding something.

"Have you ever spoken to her?" Roack was quiet for a few long moments.

"Why does it matter?" Branna snorted.

"It matters because if you did, then she knows you talk to the Fae, and that matters a lot, because at this point in time there is no one else in the realm of men that knows that, which means she has hidden this from everyone."

"You know now." Branna gave a nod in the dark.

"Yes, I do… Oh yes I do indeed."

"We cannot talk to all of your people; some of them cannot hear us."

"What do you mean?"

"We told you, some of them are light, we cannot talk to the light."

The moment hit her like a bolt of lightning, the Merle could not communicate with those of fair hair, it was like a massive hand had slapped Branna across the face, and she was stunned for words. Her head almost spun out of control as her thoughts raced, Roack understood and took off from the branch to go look for food, and left Branna alone to fully understand the implication of what she had been told. Branna stared at the rabbit dripping over the fire, her words hardly heard as her thoughts spilled quietly.

"She knew… She has known all along that the powers we hold can connect, so she has pushed us away and made us her slaves, and she surrounds herself with the idiot's incapable of communicating. All of this time, all of the misery and suffering on the Realm Ofmoon was because she wanted to protect herself, and was afraid one of us would realise and challenge her. I will never forgive you Rhiannon, Queen of the fair haired, just you wait and see, one day I will rise to meet you as an equal, and then my dear queen, you will fall and fall hard."

Chapter Twelve.

Fae No More.

Over the days and weeks that followed, Ariel took to walking around the realm, usually with a bag filled with parchment and charcoals. It became a normal event to see her sat back from the crowd sketching the progress of the building of Florae. In truth it helped her to calm her mind, and the feelings of loss she felt not being in Avalon. She was also frustrated that even though the council had decided that there were no Dark Fae, she was still not allowed to join in the work inside the House of Scribes, setting up the new libraries that would concern the other races observed by the Fae.

Branna travelled on foot for many days with Roack flying before her ever vigilant. She was skilled with a bow and would shoot large birds or rabbits for food, of which it had become customary to give some of the insides and raw meat to Roack. It turned Branna's stomach to watch the bird devour it, but the bird had a strong liking for it, and she cooked her meat, so it worked out well for both of them. Roack suggested she lose her clothes and wear something more in line with the lines of man, and so after some effort as she was not that good at sewing to begin with, she fashioned new clothing out of the things she had collected belonging to Halbrand. Using her knife, she cut away her long matted hair, which changed her appearance a great deal, and she felt more at ease, as she passed through settlements looking more like she belonged to a Celtic tribe than the lines of Fae.

Rhiannon arrived in all her splendour in Avalon and took up her new seat of power, Gwendolyn had visited in her grandmother's absence and been cordially welcomed, but it was clear that there was still a strain between the two lines of Fae who were polite to each other in public, but avoided each other in private. Rhiannon was kept very busy, but she had not forgotten Branna, and Luminaria was still in charge of the several scouting parties that had been sent in search of her in secret.

Gwendolyn's requests to have the belongings of Ariel taken from the house on the outskirts of Avalon and returned to Florae were denied, and in secret a marshal who had been very fond of Branna, informed her that the house was sealed and guarded night and day, just in case Branna returned. There was little chance she would return, having made her decision, Branna was slowly adapting to life in the world of men, and enjoying the freedom she now felt.

*O*ne day whilst travelling through one of the settlements on the coast, Branna noticed a woman sat in her doorway weeping whilst clinging to a child; she slowed her pace as she watched most of the villagers passing by and ignoring the weeping woman. Branna approached her as she sat rocking the child whilst her tears fell.

"What is the matter, is the child sick?" The woman looked up with a dirty tear streaked face, revealing an infant no more than two summers old.

"She is dying, nothing more can be done, and soon the gods will arrive to take her." It was clear from the redness of the child it had a fever of some form, Branna crouched down to view the child more closely. She offered her arms out.

"May I see her, I have seen an illness like this before, and if she is strong, there may be no reason for your gods to visit just yet." She gestured to the child. "Please… let me help."

The woman was nervous, but she had nothing to lose and handed the child over, Branna cradled the child in her arms and looked upon its face, this was a normal thing in the outskirts of Avalon. She smiled as she looked at the woman.

"Show me where the child sleeps."

Still uncertain, the woman stood and beckoned Branna inside. The room was very dimly lit, it was a large round room, with a dirt floor and central fire pit, the windows were small and she had to strain her eyes to see properly. Around the room there were patches of straw, on which roughly woven blankets were thrown, these were the beds all of them used. Branna turned with a smile.

"I will need water boiling, and a new cloth twice the size of the child, and where is the child's father; I will have need of him. If you do as I say this child will live."

The woman fell to her knees and wailed something Branna hardly understood, as she gripped her long dress and thanked her over and over. Branna gripped her shoulder hard.

"You have no need to thank me, make haste for we have little time, go and bring the father to me now… Go!"

Branna knelt with the child in her arms and slipped off her pack, she tugged at her own blanket and pulled it free of the top of her pack. Cradling the child in one arm, she made a rough nest like bed on the floor with the blanket then laid the child carefully in it. The child was like most of the others in the settlement quite dirty, so she pulled the clothes over the child's head to actually reveal it was a little boy. His body was red and clammy, the fever had a good hold, but she had seen cases far worse, and knew she could make a difference. Outside there was a commotion as Roack landed on the roof of the house, to many the Raven was a bird of ill omen and they feared it.

Branna worked quickly pulling her own bag open, deep within the pack she had taken from Halbrand. Inside she knew she had some of Ariel's medicines and ointments, it made her smile, in all of her panic whilst racing round the house to gather her things, she had seen the small box and roll of herbs, and just grabbed them, she still was not sure if it was because she thought she may need them, or simply because they belonged to Ariel and she had used them to save her life once.

Branna moved quickly checking all over the naked body of the child, and her suspicions were confirmed when she discovered many small red swollen marks. As she finished her examination the woman arrived with her husband. Both of them entered and it was clear he had some doubts, but Branna had no time to banter with the pride of a man.

"You, are you the father?" Her voice was stern and he was a little surprised.

"I am, and I am not happy the bird of death follows you, what is your business with the lad, leave here now and take your evil with you." Branna's head snapped back to him from the child, and her voice became deeper.

"Do as I say or the bird will take the boy now." He looked shocked, his wife pulled at his tunic and pleaded with him.

"Let her try Brig, I beg thee, let her try where the others have failed." She turned to Branna.

"His name is Brig and he will do as you say if it keeps us our boy, I am Moll, now tell me what should we do?"

Branna smiled at both of them, more because they were very afraid, but also because even with the fear they held, they were trusting her due to the love of their child. Branna lowered her tone of voice.

"Moll I need water, a lot of it, set water to boil in other huts if you can, the child has been bitten by infected fleas many times, and we need to clean the child and brew a tea that will help him fight the fever." The woman gave a nod and reacted in seconds, jumping to her feet to arrange the water. Branna looked up at Brig who was stood motionless watching nervously.

"You? Take all the bedding out and burn it, you have to kill everything living on it. The floor must be swept, and boiling water needs to be splashed all over it. Tell the others to cut fresh hay and bring it here, but before they bring in this house, it must be dipped in boiling water and then set to dry outside off the floor in the sun." He did not really understand why, but he agreed, and then went out through the door to arrange others to help.

Moll returned quickly with a large cauldron of boiling water, she set it down and then built up the fire under her pot to boil. Branna mixed some of Ariel's herbs in the bottom of a wooden goblet and then added some of the boiling water, then set it to cool. Whilst it cooled, she rummaged around in her bag and lifted a block of thick green soap. She dragged a bowl over to her and added more hot water, and then rubbing the soap on her hands to create a lather, she went to work washing the child thoroughly all over. When she had done and noticed there was no clean cloth in the whole place, she dried the child with her own blanket. Once the child was thoroughly clean, she checked all the swollen spots. As she checked each one, she took a small jar of thick white paste out of her bag and smeared a little of it on each spot, and when she was done, she handed the child back to Mol.

"Take him outside and let him sip this slowly." She lifted the cooling tea, and handed it to her.

Moll looked hopeful as Brig returned with two other men, they gathered up all the hay and straw and took it out doors where a fire burned in the centre of the settlement, the three of them cast it on to the fire and the flames roared up. Branna came to the doorway as they returned.

"Use as much boiling water and scald the floor, it will kill anything living, and then bring me two stout poles the size of the child, and two poles a little longer." Brig looked confused, and she smiled. "You do not have time to question; trust me it will aid the child to live."

It was clear that he did not take to being ordered around by a woman, but he followed her instructions, as Branna walked over to where several other women gathered to watch Moll get the child to drink her tea. She heard them mumbling as she approached.

"There is nothing to fear here, the tea is nothing more than Nettle and Calendula, and the paste is from Witch Hazel, these plants grow here I know I have seen them, and yet you do not use them for the safety of your children. Fear not Moll the bites will subside and the tea will break the fever, your child will live."

Branna turned and looked behind her to the house where the large black raven sat watching, she lifted her arms in its direction. "BE GONE BIRD OF DEATH, THERE IS NOTHING HERE FOR YOU THIS DAY!"

To the surprise of all the gathering, the raven gave a deep squawk and flew off, and the voices around the whole settlement murmured, whilst Branna turned back to the child and smiled.

Brig arrived with the poles and scalded the floor, and then Branna showed him how to make a hammock to sling the child in above the ground, explaining that being on the flea infested floor, his child had been bitten so many times that the infection which most people will normally fight off, had increased and threatened his life. Brig was very grateful as was Moll, and they invited Branna to stay for a while, but she knew that the people would talk, and any that followed behind her would know of the Fae cure that had not yet made it into the hands of the world of men.

In gratitude, Brig slaughtered a hog and traded half of it for new blankets with the weaver, one of which he gave to Branna as repayment for hers which had been soiled, she took it with gratitude and left.

*T*hat night she made camp a few miles up the coast feeling good about herself, she walked down to the beach, and made a fire close to the cliff and watched the waves on the shore. Roack returned as she cooked a large slice of pork from Brig's hog, and ate the small parts she had left raw on a rock, it felt good to have saved a life, and in many ways, she felt it repaid the life she had taken, she knew Ariel would be proud of her for the swift action she took. She looked at the bird as it ate.

"Thanks for understanding what I meant, when I told you to be off, where did you go to?" The bird swallowed its food.

"We flew back along the water checking our trail to see if others like you follow, then we came back high in the sky to see if you were safe, and moved on past this place to see what lies ahead." Roack took another piece of meat into his beak and swallowed it.

"You are no longer safe, this world of men does not know of the cures you bring, others like you will know it was you and come looking, the world of men talk too much, you should have let the child die. This place is now dangerous for you."

Branna brought up her knees and leaned her head onto them as she stared at the sea, she felt a strange calming feeling in rhythm with the waves that seemed to talk to the core of who she was.

"It is called Tintagel."

"What is?" Her eyes moved to look at the bird.

"This place, or that place with the child, it is called Tintagel."

"Safe or not, I like it."

"A name means nothing, it is still dangerous for you here now, we must go, we must make haste and leave this place. They have things that ride the water, you must go to them and take one, and we shall leave this place or others will come and take you back to her." Branna smiled.

"You are wrong Roack, a name means everything, it is possibly the most important thing you can have, as it gives you an identity, your history and a sense of being." She lifted her head and looked at the bird watching her.

"You always answer when I call out your name, and yet you say we all the time, when you should say I."

"It matters not we have heard both, your people say we the Fae, or we the marshals, and we the men. They never say I the Fae, we are happy with our ways." She gave a giggle.

"To me you are Roack the Raven, you should recognise that and say I. We no longer belong to anyone Roack; we are simply two lost souls who are homeless, and searching for our way to a new life. I am Branna the individual no longer of Fae, and you are Roack the Raven, neither of us are in our homeland, we are both wanderers in a new world, together we are we, but as individuals we should refer to ourselves as I. You should say I am Roack, for that is the name you were given when your body came from the egg."

"We only use the stupid name because you use it." She gave a loud giggle.

"Never the less my friend, it is still the name given to the body you took, and in that you should use it as your own."

"We might."

Branna shook her head and gave up with a smile, her mind drifted back to the sea and her thoughts of who she was and where she was heading. She had run away from her roots, and also the people she had lived with, all those faces of her time in Avalon flitted through her mind, all of them like her, suffering for no other reason than the fears of their queen. She felt she had in some strange way betrayed them all by leaving and denying she was a part of them, what was she going to do now she had thrown herself out of the land that had been hers for all the generations that had come before her?

For the shortest of times, she had lived with hope, the hope that with Ariel she could somehow start all over again and start a line that was free from oppression, but she had realised too late that it was just a dream, as Rhiannon had even robbed her of that. Branna felt her anger inside, Rhiannon had done this to her, it was the queen who held the lives of her people in her hand, but she now knew that she could do that too.

Halbrand had proved that she had equal power over others, and she could use that to further her goals. In many ways this had to be the best chance she had ever had at starting over, and she pondered the point as her eyes gazed into the rolling waves. This was a good chance, for now she was free, and in many ways it made good sense now, to deny the Fae heritage as she had, and build something new, but what? What could she say if asked by others?

Her gaze turned back to the bird; somehow, she understood the bird was inside her head curious as to just what the two of them could say when questioned. Branna gave a slight smile and breathed out a long breath as if this was the last time Branna of the Fae was real, her next breath would be as someone different, her words were quiet and reflective, and yet for her they held more meaning than anything else she would ever say.

"Maybe I too should be called raven. The Raven Branna, for I too am an ill omen to many of my race, we shall both adopt the term of Raven as our new identity, and then we can be, we Ravens. Show me this place tomorrow where we can get a boat, as much as I like this place, I do not want to be caught just yet. Together we need to start a new way of being, and from that point we will build a life that will be long remembered, and one day I will return here, and when I do, the Fae Ofmoon will fall, what say you my raven companion?"

"We says you are free, and can do as you please, call yourself Raven and live by that if you want to. If it lets you cast off the people of light, we agrees."

Branna gave a chuckle, and stared out across the rolling waves, and allowed her mind to wander.

Chapter Thirteen.

Understanding Everything.

The story of the curious woman curing a child at Tintagel did eventually make it back to Luminaria at Avalon, but by the time it did, the story was months old and the trail cold. Luminaria was confused as to why there was no sign at all of Branna, she had her spies in Florae, but all they reported was that Ariel had become a little bit of a loner, who travelled round the nine islands drawing and talking to those who have moved there. Luminaria did not understand why Branna had made no attempts at all to contact Ariel.

Bridget's night terrors appeared to subside, and after several months she made an appearance in front of her people, and she looked rested and well, so much so she resumed many of her duties. Malcolm worked hard to help with the building of the realm of Florae, but with nine islands to work on it was a mammoth task, as the Fae built bridges, roads and housing for their people. He was devoted to the project working with his son Ninian, as they trained Gwynfor, there were some that said it aged him, and even though he always wore a smile, his appearance did change as his hair grew white at a much quicker rate than was normal for a man of Fae.

As the months passed by into a year, any onlooker would say things simply slipped back to normal, although one thing that Bade accidently disclosed to Ariel during one of their many long conversations, was the fact, that on what were now referred to as rest days for Bridget, were actually days when she left the realm to work on something she wouldn't divulge the nature of. Ariel did find this strange, and it concerned her as they had met and spoken many times since her release form the bracelet, and yet Bridget had never mentioned anything at all about her hidden project. The time may have passed, but Ariel had not forgotten Branna, she hid her emotions, and in secret she had times where she wept and worried that maybe Rhiannon had got her and secretly killed her, although she knew that could never be confirmed.

Avalon rose to a great power as it opened its doors to trade with many of the other realms created by Hearne and Eve. It became the place of fashion that set many trends, and the world of men prospered to have it set in the heart of their realm. Life moved on, and the gossip of the time slipped in to tales for drunken nights, and in many cases became something of myth, as those who were new to the realm talked of Branna as if she never existed, and was made up by those dragged back to the realm Ofmoon, as a symbol of hope for the many that remained enslaved there. The people forgot and new stories arose, but Luminaria was as vigilant as ever, and apart from her duties to the Marshals, where she was second in command to Rayne of Moon, most days her desk would contain many parchments of strange goings on across the realm of men.

In truth the stop over at Tintagel, had played a large part in making Branna understand her new position. Roack had spent many hours lecturing her on the danger she posed to herself by standing out. The following night after a whole day of thought, Branna agreed and stole a boat with the help of Roack, and sailed in a slightly difficult fashion to Britany.

Once on a different continent and wearing the veil constantly, Branna travelled round the coast to the sacred site at Carnac, and then south down the coast where she could avoid contact with others as much as possible. It was during her travels that she began to enhance her magic with the aid of Roack, who told her she would need to increase her abilities, and then she would be able to tap into the true powers of the Merle. Branna started to call herself Raven when in public, and with her Fae communication abilities, she could speak any language and accent as good as any of the locals, something that removed any suspicion from those she met.

Branna never really understood her true power, although Roack did, and she had no real understanding of actually how powerful she was, or how powerful she would become. She had vowed at Tintagel to deny her Fae roots and become something new, and she very quickly realised that once she ignored her vows to her line, she truly was free to do as she pleased. It was an important discovery for Branna, and from that moment on her attitude changed, especially under the guiding influence of Roack.

Whereas in her time at Avalon her moods had lessoned and she had relaxed more around Ariel, under the guidance of Roack the opposite happened. Roack actively encouraged her to enjoy life to the full, which from the point of view of the bird, meant sexual encounters of every kind, and long days fuelled by alcohol. There were many occasions where she slept with a man or a woman and it created trouble from the spouses, and so she had to pack up and leave quickly. All of this played nicely into the thoughts of Roack, who knew that the less she remembered of Ariel, the less likely it would be that the strength of her love would prevent the Merle from growing within her, and to a degree it was a very successful plan, as subtly the Merle began to grow and influence her judgement.

Branna travelled further away from Avalon, trading medicines and herbal cures, and she also used her very feminine talents to con a great deal of men out of their wealth, and as a result the cart she bought and travelled in, contained a hidden bounty of wealth in the form of gems and gold. Just over a year after leaving Avalon, Branna found herself on the coast of southern Spain, or Galicia, as the locals called it. She took a small shack off the white beach and enjoyed the quiet solitude, and for a time, she found some peace and extra time to work on her spells and practice. It was during this time her thoughts returned to Rhiannon, and for the whole summer she gave a great deal of thought to just exactly how she would find a way to make her pay for her bad treatment of her people.

*I*n Florae, for Ariel life was slow, calm and quiet. She missed working in the House of Scribes, but her time alone combined with her time in Avalon taught her how much of her life she had dedicated to the work of a scribe. Her life now was mainly made up of free time to do as she pleased, although most days she would sit with Bade in the gardens and discuss the progress of the archives. What had become her temporary life had grown over the year into a passion for drawing and meeting the people moving back to the new homeland, and she found great contentment in the liberty it brought her.

Ariel sat on the steps of the House of Scribes, sketching on her parchment, she was lost in thought as her hand moved softly across the paper, as she outlined the soft lower curls of Branna's hair. Her mind was filled with the picture of the moment, where they had been sat together on the grass below the apple tree. It was a warm day and Ariel was lost in her moment, when a shadow crossed the parchment.

"It is a good likeness, you have talent."

She looked up to see the royal blue of a Fae Ofmoon Marshals uniform, and the long flowing curls of Luminaria. Ariel turned the picture over and slipped her charcoal back into her box.

"Go away; I have nothing to say to you." Luminaria gave a chuckle and remained where she was; she looked out over the town below.

"I see you still harbour ill will towards us; can you not see that I like you have a job to do? If you think about it, the reports you gave on Avalon were not pleasant in their bias towards the queen. You judge me, and yet I still am here offering a hand of goodwill." Ariel scoffed.

"Good will, you are just looking for more information on Branna." She stood up. "I really have nothing to say, and even though I know nothing new, if I did, I still would not give it to you."

"You still love her I realise that, but you must understand Ariel, she poses a threat to everyone, even you must be able to understand why she cannot run free, and bring darkness to the lines of Fae." Ariel could not believe her ears, she stared Luminaria in the eyes.

"How can you even talk of love; do you even know what love is? There is not and never was any darkness in Branna, she worked herself to death in the cause of the queen, and how did she get treated? You all looked down on her and treated her like a second class citizen to do your bidding until the realm was finished, and then what, ship her back to her cage in the realm of the moon like you did all the others? I don't blame her for running; she is probably a lot happier without the likes of you oppressing her." Luminaria gave a smile.

"I admire your loyalty, and just for the record I understand love, I have a husband and two children, but I also have a responsibility to my queen and her people. The work Branna did revealed great dangers for everyone, and whether you agree or not, I will find her and question her as to what she unleashed into our realm." Ariel shook her head.

"You are so blind; the truth is before you and you cannot see it."

"Really? Please elaborate." Ariel could feel the anger within her growing.

"Branna's sole function was to continue her study on behalf of the queen, you must have read her many requests for an audience, she found things out there no one else had found, and she reported all of it back to Rhiannon. You all knew of her work; she never hid it; she was open about everything she did. There is no darkness in Branna, what she has is an understanding of the injustice of her treatment. I mean honestly can you really not blame her for fleeing? You would have imprisoned her again, all she ever wanted was to live in her house, do her work and be happy, and even out there miles away from the gaze of your precious queen, you could not just leave her alone. Honestly what crime did she ever really commit, apart of course from being born with the wrong colour of hair?" Luminaria shook her head.

"There is far more to it than that, and you do not understand the implications of this matter, you were in over your head and had no understanding of the dangers around you."

"Danger… What Danger? I was protected for my whole time in Avalon by something far more powerful than your Queen." The comment surprised Luminaria and Ariel could see the effect of her statement, she smiled.

"Yes, that is something you did not know, you should study harder Luminaria, your queen with all her wisdom missed the one thing that would have proved to her there was no Merle in Avalon, I had the means to ensure it could never enter there and I used it." Luminaria's eyes widened.

"What is this you speak of, what could be more powerful than the Queen of Fae?" Ariel gave a cheeky smile.

"Do yourself a favour Luminaria; instead of chasing innocent girls around, go read a parchment or two, you may actually learn something of your people." Ariel turned on the steps and began to walk up them, Luminaria turned quickly.

"No wait, you cannot walk away, tell me of this power you know of that is more powerful than a queen." Ariel gave a scoff, and continued to walk away up the steps.

"I told you, I have nothing more to say to you."

As she reached the top step, she noticed Elgin standing there, she smiled and walked past him as Luminaria came bolting up the steps, Elgin put out his hand to stop her.

"You are wasting your time Luminaria, you have angered her, did I not warn you to leave her alone? Ariel is possibly one of the greatest scribes we have ever known, her entire life has been devoted to the study of our people. I warned you did I not? You will have to study for a very long time to outwit her, and if I am honest, even then you shall fail." Luminaria looked panicked.

"But I need to know, I have to find out what this power is that is greater than a queen." Elgin laughed and she looked very annoyed.

"Lumina, the answer is all around you, all you have to do is open your eyes for once, and look through your eyes, not your queens to the houses of Fae."

"What? I do not understand."

Her eyes lifted to the doorway of the House of Scribes and the carvings above it, and there before her was the red star set within a white circle, she turned and looked towards Ariel as she walked to her apartments, and there above every door was the same symbol. Elgin gave a nod of recognition knowing Luminaria had worked it out.

"Her mother created that symbol for Tideguyde to protect her if she ever returned; I believe your queen has one above her seat in the house of crystal in your home realm?" Luminaria watched Ariel walkaway.

"No that cannot be possible, are you telling me her mother was Enaria, the great mystic, and teacher of my mother Sequana?" She turned to look back at Elgin, her voice contained her amazement. "I did not know; I honestly had no idea." Elgin gave a broad smile.

"I have watched her grow under the protection of the queen; I do believe she is more and more like her mother with each passing year." He took her by the hand and turned towards the house. "Come I shall walk with you a while, and let you hear my thinking." Luminaria stopped and pulled free her arm.

"That symbol is above the door of the house in Avalon." Elgin finally knew Ariel had proved her point. "That means on the night of the storm, no one in that house could have communed with the Merle, that symbol would never of allowed it." He gave a gentle nod.

"It was above the door long before anyone detected anything suspicious in Avalon, and I do believe that Ariel and her companion were living together as a union of two Fae." Luminaria swallowed hard.

"But it makes no sense, we know something was there, but if they were together in the house that bore that protection?" Elgin gave a smile.

"I think it is safe to assume nothing dark entered the house that night." Luminaria could not comprehend its meaning; she shook her head.

"No… No this is not right, it had to have been, there is no other possible answer, Branna had to be the one, it had to be her, because the Queen…" Elgin smiled.

"Told you so?" Luminaria stepped back from Elgin and shook her head again.

"No this cannot be right, all the evidence points to that house, it is not possible, Rhiannon was absolutely certain. The soldiers we sent after her, how do you explain their disappearance, we have found no traces of them, it had to be her?" Elgin shrugged his shoulders.

"I know the power of that symbol and so does your queen, it is impossible, nothing sinister could pass that symbol, as it would have protected everything in that house. As for your missing men, you have no idea of their fate. You sent them into a hostile land in the world of men, you cannot say with any accuracy that Branna played a part in their demise. For all you know, they too felt discontent and are out there now living a free life, or they died at the hands of the tribes of men. I think maybe you should return to Avalon and recheck your steps; for I believe you are right, there has been a grave mistake somewhere." Luminaria was lost momentarily for words; she looked to the large symbol above the door of the House of Scribes.

"It is Branna, it has to be, we have spent well over a year trailing her to try and flush her out, she has to be the one, why would she run otherwise?"

"To be honest, if Rhiannon was after me, even with my wisdom and powers, I think I would run too." It was just too much for Luminaria, and Elgin could see the doubts within her.

"Branna has to be guilty, she has to be, it was her, I feel it and I know I am not wrong; I am not. Lord Elgin please I beg of you, tell me I am not wrong on this?" The old man gave a sigh, and his voice dropped.

"Go home Luminaria, go home and look deep within yourself, there I think you know where the truth sits."

Ariel returned home to her apartment, she hurried through the door and closed it, leaning back on it and resting for a moment as she gasped her breath back, her eyes sparkled from her tears and they ran slowly down her cheeks. It took her a few moments to compose herself, and then she turned and slipped the bolts into the door frame. Quickly she grabbed her bag and crossed the room, going through the opposite door into her bedroom. She dropped to her knees and lifted the blanket that hung down below her soft bedding. Ariel gripped a handle and pulled, and out slipped a heavy wooden strong box, she placed her hand below her neck and into her top, and gripped the long chain which she pulled up and out of her top, on which was a silver key.

Hurriedly using the key to unlock the box, she lifted open the lid and there within was her note books and a pile of parchments all containing pictures of Branna. Every sketch she had done in Avalon and everything she had done since was stored safe and sound. She took the parchment drawing out of her bag and added it to the growing pile within the box, and then she dropped the lid, locked the box and slid it back under her bed.

Ariel stood and hurried back to her front door where she slipped the bolts back to ensure the door was open again. Her heart still beat a little faster than normal, but it was nowhere as fast as it had been confronting Luminaria. She crossed to her chair by the window and sat down, she needed a moment to calm herself, and then she would head off to meet Bade.

For Ariel, everything had rested on those last few moments they shared up on the high rock. Branna had told her she would leave, and then find her way to establish herself a place, at which point she would send for her. Ariel endured the loneliness and the separation simply because she believed in Branna, and she knew that at some point she would receive the message. The days, weeks and months dragged through one year then two, but Ariel did not lose hope.

Branna had lived in Hispania for over a year, swimming naked in the sea, walking on the white beach and practicing her craft in a cave that Roack had found that was lined with a thick band of crystal.

Branna was changing, she grew herbs and aromatic flowers in the garden, and mixed up potions, which she took into the small town at the weekends to sell or barter to those who needed cures. She always returned with three or four people, and would spend the rest of her time drunk and cavorting naked on the beach with them all. Everyone saw her as the person to go to for fun, and her sexual desires fuelled by the Merle became more and more outrageous and depraved.

She had decided, she wanted to live the ultimate life of freedom, and so around Branna, unlike the lands of Fae, there were no rules to govern those who came to her house. Out of sight on the outskirts of town, she dabbled in pleasure and pain of every type of combination imaginable, it was almost as if she was looking for something that would fulfil her, and she was unable to find it. In a world ruled at the time by men, this was one corner of the realm where Branna ruled, and it was never a case of them seducing her, she was the one on the hunt for an even bigger thrill than the week before. It was almost as if those around her were nothing other than toys, she had no feelings or emotions for these people; she just wanted the pleasure of her seducing them in the search for the ultimate form of ecstasy.

Roack would fly off and leave her for the day when she entertained, the bird was happy that Branna was pushing every feeling she had ever felt for Ariel out of her system, and with each passing day, it was clear that it was working and the Merle was gaining more and more influence on the power possessed by Branna.

Feeling satisfied with the way things were going, Roack knew that her time in Hispania was coming to an end, the time for her to leave and seek out a place where they could build something more permanent and safer together was almost upon them, as Branna's powers combined with the dark edge that they had taken on were almost ready. Roack needed somewhere remote, a place not many would wander to, a place that was secluded and out of sight, and more importantly, away from the prying eyes of the Fae. Over the period of a year they had searched, but found nothing remotely fitting, and as the third year from their running away came and went, the Raven flew further and further afield in search of the perfect spot.

Roack still needed more time to prepare Branna, and so on each journey they flew, they went a little further watching the contours of the land, and listening to the travellers who told tales of their travels. Roack was not aware, but at that time a new and powerful warrior was about to be selected to lead a tribe of warriors from their village in the northern reaches of Saxony, Grembald was his name, and it would be his brutality that would shape the hopes and dreams of a young Saxon of the Varisci tribe who was but twenty summers of age.

Grembald would be brutal, but his second in command would go through a trial that would strengthen his resolve and in an act of twisted fate, he would be cast into the path of Branna. Even Roack could not see or predict what would come of the meeting of Branna and Berengar, but when it happened, it would be almost as if they had been born to meet, and bring chaos down on everything.

Chapter Fourteen.

The Warrior.

As the years passed by, Ariel had grown content with her life around her people. Being free of the House of Scribes, had in many ways finally allowed her to live a more relaxed and free life. Most days she would talk to Bade, and he would give her his thoughts on the house, but she found she was more and more distracted with her life, wandering around Florae meeting the residents, and watching the land develop as she sketched each new building that was erected. At night she would write in her journals, and lock them in the box with her precious drawings and sketches.

Luminaria returned to Avalon, and it appeared as though she had discontinued her investigation into Branna, and so everything suggested that things had returned to normal. It all slipped into the past as a simple misunderstanding to be swallowed into time and forgotten. Branna was enjoying her freedom, but Roack felt ill at ease, and the mind of the black bird was turning towards moving on, for they had been settled for far longer than the bird had expected.

Miles away in another country in a region known as Sachsen, an ill wind was blowing as a young warrior returned home, after many days away from the settlement high in the rough mountains. He was tired and weary, as he made his way across the loose stone towards his parent's long house. His frame was thick set to match his tallness, his eyes as dark as jet, and around his waist hung a sword of highly sharpened precision steel. The afternoon's pale sunlight glinted off his smooth shaven head, and ran down the side of his chiselled face towards his chin, sporting a long fine plaited beard of brown hair.

As he approached the door, he slipped off his long grey coat of wolf pelt, revealing the might and thickness of his heavy arms, which bore the scars of many nicks and cuts from his fights to defend his people. He pushed back the door lined with pelts, and walked into the long dim room, lit only by the fire that burned in a stone pit towards the centre of the house. Further up a woman turned and gave a smile, she dropped the knife and the kale she was chopping, and ran down the room.

"Beren my son, you have returned to us, praise the gods they have kept you safe." His stone like stare softened as he embraced his mother.

"I told you before, I need no gods to watch me, I have a sword and the will to use it." She slipped back smiling and turned to look up the room to a table and seat, where an older man sat with long grey hair.

"Look who has returned to us Vulgan, it is our boy." The older grey haired figure, lifted a wooden goblet in salute, although from where Berengar stood, he could see his father had not mellowed much.

"Father I have many skins, and fresh meat." The old man rose up from his seat and took a pace forward, it was clear his leg was stiff, caused by an old wound that he had taken during a long defence of raiders many winters back. His face bore the long healed scar, of a fight at close quarters, and his eyes were stern. He was a tall man like his son, and it was clear he was Berengar's father, as there was a great likeness between them, yet Vulgan carried with him a mantle of authority, and for many years he had been a great defender and advisor of his people.

"Tell me boy, how did you come by this meat and pelts, were they taken from an honest arrow, or are they your payment from that demon you follow?" Berengar's mother turned sharply.

"Please not again, did we not say far too much before our son left? Please I beg you, do not do this." The old man stared at his wife.

"Stay out of this Filiberta, he is my son and as such answers to his father." His gaze lifted to his son. "I asked you a question, will you not answer?" Berengar gave a long sigh.

"I am weary from the march; I do not wish to fight."

"Since when does addressing your father who has asked an honest question be seen as a fight? If I meant to fight you boy, I would have drawn out my sword." Berengar looked at his father's stern face.

"Do I not provide for you well? What matter is it as to where the meat is from, as long as you have a full belly and furs to keep you warm when the snow comes?" Vulgan limped towards his son.

"It matters to me, I was the one that raised you, it was I that taught you to hunt, and gave you value as a man. So yes, it matters that you took out your bow and fired true for the sake of this family. I

did not teach you to sneak and steal like your so called leader does."
Berengar's voice rose a little, it was clear he was irritated.

"I do not sneak, I have fought with the honour of my tribe always in
my heart, but fear not father, I stalked the deer and he gave me his life
with the kiss of my arrow." Vulgan gave a nod, and opened his arms.

"Then we shall set the table for when your brother's return, and
tonight we shall feast with wine and celebrate your return in victory
in the true style of the Varisci." Berengar turned.

"I cannot, I sit at the table of victors tonight with Grembald, I shall
bring in the pelts and meat, and leave you to it." He was about to walk
away, when he heard his father's quiet angry voice.

"How can you turn from your family to sit with that demon, have
you no shame at all?" Berengar had known it would come and had
wanted to leave before it erupted, his head snapped back and his eyes
took on a similar glow to his father's.

"That demon as you call him is the leader of this tribe. I am duty
bound to serve him as I would have served you if you had been able
to lead. There is no shame being second to the man who leads us and
defends us. All of you should be grateful that we shall never have
invaders as we did the night you were taken down, no one would dare
to walk into this camp in day or night now because of the strength of
this tribes' warriors."

His father's face began to redden, his voice rose and growled deeply
with his anger. As his lips parted within his thick grey and brown
beard, his spittle leapt from his mouth as his words tumbled out.

"There is no honour serving at the beck and call of that butcher,
how in all of the names of the gods can you stand below my roof
and pretend there is honour in the rape and butchery of innocents?
Do you think we do not hear the stories; do you think that people
we encounter do not tremble and quake with the fear for their lives,
knowing we are part of the Varisci, a tribe once revered for its
honour?" Berengar's voice rose to a shout.

"He is our leader; I serve him and the tribe. He rules as he sees fit,
I am not one to question as I would never have questioned you if you
had led our people, but you could not, could you? It was your folly
that took this tribe into an ambush, had it not been for Grembald,
none of us would be here now living as we do."

Vulgan almost shook with anger, as his face turned redder and
redder. Filiberta fled up the house back to her table, she knew better

than to anger her husband more, although her eyes sought Berengar's in a silent plea to ask him not to enrage his father more. Vulgan lifted his arm filled with golden bracelets, and pointed at the door.

"GET OUT!! You walk into my home and insult me, and praise that demon you serve? Go to your precious leader, eat with him, get drunk and sleep with those you captured. I am ashamed of you, take your face from mine and insult me no longer."

There was little to say, and as it had been the case many times in the past year, Berengar lifted his cloak and cast it across his broad shoulder and walked to the door. He paused briefly turning to look at his mother, and his voice was softer.

"I will get Otto and Vlad to bring you the meat and furs." She gave a gentle nod of recognition, and Berengar turned back to the door and left. Vulgan turned, and limped back to the table, his eyes cast across the long house to his wife.

"Say nothing, I will not hear it." She kept her head down, and did not speak as Vulgan limped to the table and poured a drink.

"He is a fool and knows better, Grembald has turned the whole valley against us, and years of good ties with them lay slaughtered on the fields. The man is possessed of greed and it will be our ruin you will see, and then your son will not return home." She paused and turned back to her husband.

"What are these words you are saying, he is your son and first born to you?" Vulgan shook his head.

"I have lost him to that butcher. Grembald has filled his head with gold and lust, he is blind to the hate his own people feel towards their leader. I no longer have any influence; his pride will be his downfall and the wedge between us. Only when the tribe turns will he understand what I have tried to teach him, but by then it will be too late." He lifted his goblet and took a long drink.

"Who am I fooling, I am nothing but an old warrior with a bad leg, he feels the pull of a man of action, sadly Grembald is not the man he could have been, and Beren will have to learn that in his own time. Let's hope he does not take too long, that last demand for a bigger tribute to Grembald has got everyone riled up."

*I*t was true there were few who could defeat Berengar in combat, but Grembald could be taken by the right men. He had been shrewd to pick Berengar as his second, as it prevented any of the others rising up to challenge him, the drawback was that as Grembald became more and more greedy, and demanded bigger tributes not just from the surrounding tribes but also his own, mutterings of discord had begun to move throughout the whole tribe.

Berengar had been raised as a man of the Varisci; he was in his heart a loyal servant of the tribe and warrior of great honour. His father had trained him from an early age, and he had once looked up to him and felt nothing but admiration and respect for him. In the year of his sixteenth summer, he had proven beyond doubt that he was a powerful warrior, by winning all of the trials of combat within the tribe, and as a prize and reward, he was allowed to join the forward guards of the town.

This was a time long before the coming of those who carried a crucifix, and times were hard, life was always a struggle against the forces of nature and other tribes for fertile hunting grounds, and the Varisci had proven to be mighty opponents, as they watched the lands they ruled over. Vulgan was seen as a fair and powerful warrior and had been tipped to become the next leader of the tribe, but when a passing Bohemian trader had come through and reported a gathering of tribesmen in the lower valley pastures, Vulgan as leader of the guard acted without thinking. He took a large party including his son down to the valley floor to meet and challenge the gathering.

The gathering was far bigger than Vulgan had been led to believe, and they were not on the valley floor, they were half way up the valley side lay in wait. Vulgan led his men right into an ambush and the fight that ensured was brutal and bloody. Most of them were killed before they saw off their enemy, and Berengar returned carrying the limp half dead, and badly wounded Vulgan.

Grembald had missed the fight as he had been off sleeping with the daughter of one of the other tribe's leaders. He saw his chance, and gathered the remaining warriors and took them off on the trail of the retreating attackers. Berengar joined him, and eventually they caught up with the injured warriors who had fled before they were killed, and slaughtered them. They learned the names of all their villages, and then Grembald took full control. Rather than return victorious, he took the Varisci to every village and burned it to the ground slaughtering all the inhabitants after raping the women.

Not a village was left standing for thirty miles, and even though many had begged for their lives, stating they had not been party to any attack on Vulgan, yet, he slaughtered them and took their lands for the tribe. On his return the leader of the village, an old seasoned warrior named Vox chastised Grembald for his lack of honour. As had always been the tradition of the tribe, Grembald saw his chance knowing Vulgan was injured and challenged Vox to judge his honour. Vox was no match for the younger Grembald, and the fight which Vox fought with great skill for his age did not last very long, and Grembald killed him in the centre of the village, and declared himself the new leader.

Berengar was still very young, and when he was named second, something Grembald did deliberately to stamp on any plans a recovered Vulgan may have, no one in the village challenged him. From that day onward Grembald focused on his dreams to rule and rule with power, and the way of life of the Varisci changed forever.

Gone were the days of sticking to their lands, and hunting in peace, Grembald knew the power of his tribe and wanted far more than he had, and so began five years of brutality, murder, rape and drunken outbursts. Following a leader backed up by one of the most skilled fighters of the tribe, the once proud warriors had no choice but to follow Grembald, and Berengar was witness to horrors and scenes that over a period of years changed him from the kind natured boy to a silent brooding and at times intimidating figure, so much so, Grembald remained safe in his role of leader.

The Varisci were now feared for over a hundred miles as news of their brutality rapidly swept from valley to valley. Grembald felt secure in his leadership, and revelled in his rapidly growing wealth, but that was just the start of the tale of Grembald and Berengar, for like all things under a dictatorship, history would prove that those who saw the unfairness would slowly over time work on a plan to set them free.

As Berengar reached twenty one summers old, he left his father's house to seek out his brothers and attend the meal with his victorious leader, the sands of time were already running to make big changes in the lives of all of them.

*F*ar away across the hills and valleys towards the sea, a black raven possessed by the power of the Merle, had got wind of the Varisci, and it would not be long before the news reached the ears of a member of the Fae who had fled her land, to find freedom and power for her own. Branna of Moon who was currently masquerading as Raven, would soon be forced to leave the home she lived in by the shore of the lands of Galicia, and when she did, her travels would lead her towards Bohemia, passing through the southern border of Sachsen, and when she did her fate would join with a member of the Varisci and change forever.

Branna lay on the beach under the hot sun; her naked skin was now a deep golden bronze colour. She was tired having spent the last four days drinking wine, and having sex with the party of eight men and two women that had left her earlier that morning. Her head ached and her thoughts were cloudy, and all she wanted to do was lie in the soft sand and listen to the waves as they crashed up the beach behind her. Roack swept out of the sky and landed on the sand in front of her.

"The house you prize so much is smashed and littered with foul smelling things." Branna gave a moan.

"Leave me alone for a while, I am tired."

"You sated your appetites we see; this is good but have you studied the charms we left you with?"

Branna moved her head and tried to look at the bird, but the sun was too bright and her eyes couldn't handle the brightness.

"Let me sleep, can we not talk later?"

"NO!" The rough croak echoed in her brain, and she instinctively jumped and pulled her hands to her ears.

"HAVE YOU DONE AS ASKED?" Branna sat up quickly

"YES!"

"And have you mastered them?" Her head hung with her eyes closed, as her annoyance started to surface.

"They are done; now leave me alone." The bird rocked on its feet.

"This is good; we fear you will have need of them sooner than we thought."

Her head turned to the Raven as her eyes grew a little more accustomed to the bright light.

"What do you mean…Sooner?"

Roack pecked at the sand plucking a thick fat worm into its beak, he gave it a tug and flipped it into the air and caught it in its beak, and swallowed it. Branna gave a shudder.

"I do wish you would not eat those things in front of me." The Raven gave a satisfied nod as it enjoyed the morsel.

"It will be time soon to leave, we stopped at the village on the way back, there are people complaining about you and your life here, it appears that they have tolerated you for the medicines you have

supplied, but they do not approve of your appetites and lifestyle."

"Don't tell me the women are complaining that their men are sneaking off here instead of taking care of them?"

"Something like that, the details bore us, we just take what is relevant to us and report it back to you. Trouble will come soon, and now is not the time, it would be unwise to stay here for much longer, and their leader is under great pressure to throw you off this land." Branna gave a snort.

"Last week he was not so keen as he pounded my hips into this very spot, he appeared more than eager to have me stay a while, according to him I service him in ways his wife has never thought of, especially with my mouth." She gave a slight chuckle. "Maybe I should service his wife too."

"It is irrelevant, as the pressure grows you draw attention to yourself, and as much as we know you have enjoyed being in this place, it would be wise to move onto new pastures. You cannot risk staying anywhere for too long, you have tarried here for long enough, you are forgetting why you are here and that could be dangerous. She has not stopped looking for you, and so until we find a place to claim, you should use your power of wisdom and move on." Branna gazed out at the ocean.

"I suppose so, I have thought the same at times, although it has been nice to be a little settled and have a house for a while. I needed this time Roack, I needed the quiet and the peace of mind to work out what I really want to do, not all of this has been about the pleasure, although I have enjoyed tasting the freedoms of this life in a way none of my line ever have before."

"You have increased your powers through it, we feel the strength within you, and with each conquest you have grown, we are happy to lead you onto new roads and more conquests, it does appear this world of men has no shortage of amusements for you." Branna gave a slight chuckle.

"They are certainly more than willing, but no you are right, I have thought much of late, Rhiannon will be firmly placed in her new seat, I think it is time I sought out mine."

"This is good news; we ravens need to begin to seek out our place. Gather your things and destroy anything that might reveal who you are here, and in a few days we shall leave this place."

Roack flew off, and Branna sat on the beach with her knees drawn up to her chest as she watched the waves roll onto the sand a few yards in front of her. Apart from her pounding head, she did feel better rested and stronger than she had ever been. She rested her chin on her knees and lifted her arms round her legs, and stared with dark clear eyes at the horizon.

"You would love it here Ariel, I wish I had brought you with me." She gave a long wistful sigh. "Rhiannon has taken everything I care about away, my home, my parents, my brother and you too my love, she has to pay."

The waves crashed onto the beach, and Branna sat watching as she thought about everything that had happened in her life, she blinked and sat up straight.

"I have been lazy and forgotten why I am here, I need to move onward and find a place that is my own again, out of her gaze where I can prepare."

Branna slid her legs away from her face and stood up; she turned to see the small wooden house on the dunes and gave a soft smile.

"It has been nice, but this is not enough, I will not rest until I spill the blood of their precious queen and take back what is rightfully mine, only then will I feel the happiness I long for."

Chapter Fifteen.

Dangers Of The Trail.

For three days, Branna worked to sort through everything she had acquired on her journey. It was surprising how many possessions she had managed to gain, since her time with just the pack of blankets and supplies that she had taken from the dead body of Halbrand. Across from the house, close to the beach, her cart with a hooped canvas top slowly filled, as she made up a bed inside it, and stored her clothes and the few possessions she wanted to keep within it.

Soon the time was ready and her wooden slatted house was almost empty, apart from the few pieces of broken furniture that remained from some of her more exuberant evenings. In a way it felt strange, her house in Avalon was so much more advanced than the primitive ways of the world of men, and yet this place had become very much a small haven for her over the past year, she felt a strong bond of fondness to it. Roack flew in and out as the days moved on, as the black bird watched events a mile away in the village where there was growing pressure on the leader to act. So, as Branna climbed up onto the seat of her cart, and took hold of the leather straps to pull the horse round and leave, Roack flew down with relief to report that a mob was forming against the wishes of the village leader, and Branna's departure was not a moment too soon.

Branna departed along the worn rough track across the top of the headland, moving east away from the village, the soft breeze softly stroked through her hair, and the sounds of the sea crashing into the beach in her ears to her right. Behind her in the distance the wisps of smoke rose into the sky, where the mob arrived at her former home to seek revenge only to find the place deserted, and in their anger, they set light to everything and burned the place to the ground.

In a way for Branna, it felt like a fitting end to her days of peace and rest, she knew now if others from Avalon came looking, there would be nothing left to even show she had been there. All that remained would be the stories of a woman who seduced everyone who she met, not at all the sort of tales Luminaria would be looking for, and even though to many she had given up her search, in secret she still kept a few parchments in her office in Avalon that spoke of a woman with talented gifts for herb lore and strange habits.

The days began to blend into one as Branna journeyed across the Galicia coast and turned inland back towards Gaul. The roads became less sandy and more earth, which were muddy and hard going in the long days of rain. Roack would perch on the top of the canvass hoop over the cart, as Branna sat wrapped in a cloak holding the reins, and urging the horse on through the slippery mud. On those days were the rain pounded so hard it made the roads impossible, she would pull her cart up under whatever tree cover she could find, and light a fire close to the cart under the protection of a wide sheet for warmth and shelter. It was during these times that Branna would talk to Roack, and gain whatever information she could about the true power of the Merle.

Roack was satisfied that under their corrupting influence, the effects of Ariel had diminished, although there were still times where Branna would reminisce about her. As Branna had embraced her freedoms, Roack had seen how very slowly the influence of the Merle had grown to influence her, as her wild sexual conquests and alcohol fuelled nights in Galicia, had lowered her defences and slowly the corruption of the Merle had increased in its power, something that was also aided by Branna's very inquisitive curiosity.

Branna had been intrigued by the powers of the darkness all her life, and although she still saw herself as a reasonably good person, the damage done by investigations was far deeper than she even realised, something Roack could plainly see. As her transformation from Fae Ofmoon to free individual progressed, Roack began to tell her more and more of the Merle and the powers contained within it, which they knew would lead to the very natural conclusion of Branna wanting to use it and control it even more. It was a subtle plan, but it was one that appeared to be working very well indeed, her greatest weakness was the act of killing, something Roack knew would speed up the process much faster than her current position, but as much as Roack tried to convince her it was necessary, Branna resisted.

*F*or four days it had rained and Branna had taken refuge under the canopy of six wide elm trees. As the day progressed, finally the rains stopped and the sun came out towards the early evening. Her supplies had run low and she cooked the last of a salted boar she had caught weeks ago, in a pot with a few meagre vegetables and roots. Roack flew down from his latest excursion to check where they were and landed on a large root at the base of one of the trees, Branna looked up from the pot as she stirred.

"I have no fresh meat… Sorry." She knew the bird did not like the salty preserved meat, so had not saved any.

"We have eaten." She nodded as she threw in some more herbs and continued to stir.

"Are we safe?"

The bird settled down on the root, its dark eyes watching her. It had been agreed that in order to put time and space between the events in Galicia, they would avoid as much of the human population as possible, so for the last few weeks they had made it a point to avoid any settlements or travellers on their road.

"We are safe, no feet walk these lands."

"Good."

"You miss them?" Branna looked up.

"Who?" The bird eyed her carefully.

"Men, you have not companioned with one for some length of your time, we feel you miss them." She gave a slight smile.

"I enjoy the feelings it gives me, although towards the end in Galicia, I found it less satisfying." She looked up at the bird. "I know you do not fully understand, but I want something more real, the men back there were fun, but although they were good at explaining their prowess, I found them lacking in abilities."

"You found the women better?" Branna gave a giggle.

"A woman knows better the ways of a woman; they touch me in ways men never could." Roack did not fully understand her, but the feelings they felt inside her as she spoke as she remembered one or two of the women she had bedded, gave them a better understanding of the way in which it made Branna feel.

"You need a man who can touch you the same, one day you must bring forth a new person."

"What?" Branna spluttered slightly and dropped her spoon.

"What are you talking about? Do you think I want to bring a child into this kind of a life, you are mad?" The bird moved to gain better comfort on the root.

"Now is not the time, but a day will come when it will be right to bring forth a new person to continue what we start. You will need a man who can please you to do this."

It was something Branna could honestly say she had never ever thought about. Back in Avalon her life had improved greatly with the freedom the house brought her compared to the Realm Ofmoon, but she had never for one moment considered starting a family. She spooned out her food into a wooden bowl and sat back against the wheel of her cart and started to think as she ate.

*H*er life alone in the house with Ariel had felt perfect. Ariel had made no demands of her and accepted her for whom she was, and their life together had been simple and easy, and it had felt very natural. In her mind Ariel was perfect, her eyes, her hair, her small soft breasts and smooth pale skin, everything about her had been a delight, and Branna knew that it would be hard to find anyone who would have suited her as well as Ariel.

The Bird gave a shudder and flew off, and Branna sat lost in her memories of her moments alone curled around the strange person who had walked into her life, and turned everything into a dream of desire and love. The pictures flowed into her mind of her soft white skin as she traced her lips along it, the coarse hard voiced screamed into her mind.

"FORGET HER!" Branna jumped out of her dream startled, and looked to the empty root where the bird had moments ago been sat.

"WHAT?" She looked round at the empty area, and blinked back into reality. "Roack… Roack where are you?" Their voice came back into her mind from nowhere, she turned looking round but could not see them.

"You must forget her, she is light, she will hurt us." Branna understood, she had promised to warn the bird so it could break the connection.

"Sorry I got lost for a moment, I didn't mean to." The bird flew down from high up in the canopy.

"You cannot trust those feelings, they lie to you of things you can never have, let them go or you will never have what we can give you." She gave a long sigh.

"I said sorry, it was just a moment of lost thought that's all." The bird looked uneasy.

"Her light will one day come looking for you, and when it does, she will kill you." Branna shook her head.

"You are wrong Roack, Ariel could never hurt anyone, especially me, her line do not kill unless they have to, I will always be safe with her." The bird bobbed nervously, and then stabbed at the ground and pulled at a long red worm and swallowed it whole.

"If we give you our power, she will become your enemy, her line has tried to kill us before, they hate us, they will hate you too, for you will grow to challenge their queen, they will have to kill you or lose to you, which will be a choice for you one day."

Branna shook her head slowly.

"That maybe so, but when the time comes it will not be Ariel… It will be Rhiannon who tries not her."

"It matters not, if you kill their queen, she will see you as an enemy, there is no future with her, you need a man, his seed is your future, she has no seed."

Deep down inside Branna knew that Roack was right, but what if she could unite with Ariel and convince her to join with them, that would solve all her problems. She felt the sudden lack of connection and knew that Roack had decided to leave her to her own thoughts. She pulled the blanket round her and settled again in front of the fire, and knowing the bird would fly off to find something else to do, she snuggled down and closed her eyes, and there in her mind was Ariel lay in her bed waiting for her. Her hand slid down under the blankets, and as her mind filled with her memory of that precious moment, she drifted into her fantasy free of everything and feeling the power of her lust and feelings for her love of her fairy of light.

*M*any miles away in Florae, Ariel disturbed in her sleep, the sweat dampened her forehead as she rolled in her bed moaning loudly. She woke with a start, her hand pushed hard between her legs.

"OH Bran!"

She gave a gasp and sat up with a jerk, her breath coming in fits and starts. For a moment she was still trapped in her dream, and as she came to her senses, she realised what she was doing to herself. Her hand moved quickly up above the covers, as she understood where she was and what she had been doing. Her body still tingled, and she felt a strong and overwhelming sense of Branna all around her, but as her mind cleared the feeling began to subside.

The moment began to pass as she realised, she was in her bed at home in Florae and it was just a dream. She gave a long sigh and felt the bitter pain build in the pit of her stomach, once again the loneliness crept into her, and she pulled her knees up to her chin and rested her head as the tears filled her eyes. Her voice was soft and filled with her loneliness.

"Where are you, why have you left me here all alone? You promised… You promised you would come for me." Her tears flowed, and with her head pushed into her knees, for the millionth time since coming back to Florae, she wept alone in the darkness.

High in the sky, not too far on the trail on which Branna had travelled two figures cloaked in long dark blue cloaks, waved on the side of the track as a wooden caravan came to a halt. Roack noted it and swooped down to take a closer look and landed silently in the semi darkness on the green roof. The two men dressed in dark blue looked up at the driver, a broad man with a well clipped beard and a soft cloth cap.

"Hail traveller." The traveller pulled on his brake and steadied the horse.

"Greetings friends, if you need a ride, I have room for two up front." The taller of the two men dressed in dark blue, walked closer to the caravan and into the light from the candle that was flickering inside the metal lamp attached to the side.

"All is well my friend; we have shelter in the village over yonder." He slid a piece of parchment out from inside of her cloak. "We have stopped you to make enquires as to if you have come across a traveller like yourself." He handed the parchment up to the driver, who leaned over and took it.

Roack moved along the top of the roof, and slowly edged closer to its edge to look over at the driver and the parchment. The driver held the parchment in the light to gaze upon the image, Roack noted the likeness to Branna drawn on it in charcoal.

"We seek this woman; she is believed to be travelling on this route." The driver stared at it in the failing light under the lamp and shook his head.

"She is a looker, I have seen no one like this on my journey, why what has she done?" He handed the parchment back to the taller figure, who rolled it up and slid it into his cloak.

"She is wanted by us, she is a run away from the land of Avalon, our queen seeks her whereabouts and return." Roack slipped back on to the safety of the roof out of sight, the driver gave a sniffle.

"I see Fae folk; I have heard of your kind. I would say a woman as good looking as that would draw a lot of attention, I know for sure I would not forget her, but alas on these trails, women that good looking are scarce, all we see is old hags and women wore out from the toil of the fields." The tall traveller gave a nod.

"If you do see her, there is a good reward for knowledge of her whereabouts or her capture, we are moving north towards the border and expect to be there for several days, so if you hear of her or see her, come find us and let us know, and you shall be well rewarded." Roack watched as they stepped back from the caravan, and the driver gave the reins a snap.

"Well, if a see her I am heading that way, so I will look you up, especially if there is gold or silver in it for me." The Fae marshals gave a nod and a wave.

"Travel safe routes and thank you."

As the caravan moved off, the two travellers turned and walked towards a side road, quietly talking they made their way along it, and as Roack lifted into the air, he could see faint lights off in the distance. For some time, their keen eyes watched as the two walked quietly along the track towards the village in the distance. It would be an easy kill, but that would raise too much suspicion, so Roack kept high in the sky their black feathers almost invisible as the sun sank, and the clouds blotted out the bright moon.

After a long walk, the two travellers arrived at a dwelling, and entered in the centre of the village. Roack silently glided down and landed in a tree across from it. Watching the silhouettes through the thin woven fabric that covered the windows, cast against the candle light within, the two figures spoke at length to another, and then settled down to eat a meal. Roack sat patiently in the tree for a long time, but finally one of the figures appeared at the door having eaten to take the air, and the moment they stepped out Roack could see the golden hair and the blue of the uniform and recognised it right away. The years had passed, and yet it was very clear, Rhiannon had not given up her search for Branna.

After watching for some time in hope of learning more, the large black bird turned and lifted up into the sky, and flew back towards the sleeping figure of Branna. It was more than clear that Rhiannon had no intention of giving up her search, and she was a lot closer to them than Roack had realised. Branna was in danger, and she had to get as far from here as possible. Crossing the border further north was now out of the question, they would have to change their course and head onto the roads heading towards Bohemia, avoiding the lands of the northern Germanic people.

Flying as fast as was possible, Roack swooped with speed over the fields and trees, the dark bright eyes ever vigilant in case there were more Fae on the roads. Through the darkness the black bird, zig zagged as it avoided trees and small shelters built for the livestock, its mind set on getting to Branna as quickly as possible. Soon the group of elm trees on the hillside came into view, and Roack lifted up into the air and headed straight towards it. It was completely dark, but the clear dark eyes of the bird had no problems picking out the small soft glow of the fire, but all was not as it was when they left, and as the large black bird got closer, the faint outline of a second cart came into view, and Roack lifted higher in the air and looked to the tops of the trees.

Branna sat by the fire pouring out herbal tea, as Roack arrived back and landed in the uppermost branches of one of the Elm trees. Far below, Branna gave a slight giggle as she placed the pot back at the side of the fire. Roack had no connection to her as they had broken it earlier whilst she dreamt of the woman of light, but through the canopy, the roof of green of a traveller's caravan could be plainly seen. The man who had been questioned sat by the fire and laughed as he spoke to Branna, she was in great danger but not even aware of it.

Roack rested onto the branch to watch, and deep within the thought was simple, he had to go, he would give Branna up to the Fae. Already, Roack could feel how his heart was growing with the excitement of a reward, he would have to go there was no doubt. As Roack watched, it became quite clear, this time it would have to be Branna who took the life, that way the corruption of her being would be increased, and she would be closer on her journey towards the darkness than she had been for some time.

Chapter Sixteen.

The Seduction.

Dawn brought with it a thick mist, which hugged the floor and drifted through the trees surrounding both of the carts. High above in the large finely twigged Elm trees; Roack was as ever vigilant, watching the land below for signs of movement coming from the direction of the small village on the distant horizon, where the Marshals of the Fae slept peacefully.

Below there was a light thump, and the bird looked down, Branna had pushed open the door of her companion's caravan, and holding her skirt and top close to her naked breast, she quietly made her way down the small steps, and shuddered in the cool morning mist. Quickly she dressed, and then made her way across the camp to her cart; she leaned into the back and pulled on a long heavy shawl, which she quickly wrapped around her shoulders as she shivered.

After a few minutes on her knees blowing into the embers of the night before, the fire gave a crackle as the new wood ignited, and it was not much longer before she had built up the fire to a good blaze, and sat warming her cold bare feet, as the pan bubbled filled with herbal tea. Sensing the man in his cart was still asleep, Roack swooped down and landed close to her, the mist parting as they glided softly to the root in front of her. Branna looked up and her eyes met Roack, and the connection between them was made.

"Where have you been, I could not feel you last night?" The black bird shifted on the root in front of her.

"We watch, we always watch, and we learn everything." Branna gave a scowl.

"What does that mean?"

"We watch, and we learn, and we see everything, and what we see protects you." Branna gave a slight scoff.

"So, what is so important that makes you feel I need protecting?" She could sense some feeling within the bird that was almost smug.

"We see who your companion talks to, and we hear what they say, and we know why he is here with you." Her brow wrinkled.

"I am tired Roack, I have no use of your games, if you know something say it, or don't it's up to you."

"He knows who you are, the men of light told him, your queen still seeks you out."

Branna was unsure if it was just the early morning cold, but an ice cold trickle ran sharply down her back, for a moment she was lost for words, and Roack sensed it within her.

"This man seeks a reward for your capture, you are in great danger, and you must act quickly or you will be taken back to her."

Branna's words finally found their way into her mouth. "After all this time, it's been years, she cannot still be looking?" The Bird straightened up on the root.

"Time is wasting, she seeks you still, and he who sleeps knows who you are, he has seen a likeness scribed on parchment. When he wakes, he will take you to her, and take the shiny metal as payment." She shook her head.

"No… We must leave now… We have to get away before he wakes."

"It would be better if he never wakes."

"What?" The black bird stretched out its wings.

"You know what to do… He has a good cart and things you can use. Cast the spell to make the dark around you thicker, and then take care of him. It is time you learned more of our power and learned how to use it fully, you have trained long enough. Take his life and join with us always, and we shall be free of her kind, and any who use the light to harm you, embrace us, and use us, for now is the time to begin your rise to the power of a queen."

I t felt as if the mist was seeping into her soul, something in the voice of the bird within her mind had changed, was it crueller or colder she was not sure? Branna stared into the dark eyes of the raven sat on the root before her, and her mind wandered feeling the fear that was building inside her, her head shook slowly and her thoughts which were meant only for herself, leaked out into the mind of the raven.

"I cannot take life, I swore an oath to the Fae, it is against our creed and must only be when our own life is at threat. I swore I would never take another and work to save lives." The cold voice echoed in her mind.

"Your life is in danger; do you think your queen will let you live when she finds you?" Her mind reeled as her gazed fixed on the dark eyes of the bird and the cold voice within her head.

"He wants the shiny metal and will barter you to them, they will take you dead or alive, when he wakes will you have the power to kill him, are you big enough or strong enough, now is the time to act." Her head shook slowly.

"I swore an oath to Fae."

"You are no longer Fae, that is the past, you are now the Raven, have you forgotten your own words?"

She blinked; her voice was soft as she spoke the words in her thoughts.

"I have not forgotten, there is not a day passes that I think of those days of fear and the freedom I took when I ran from her gaze."

"Then do it, act while you still have the time, strike now and remain forever free to join with us fully."

"Roack, I am afraid."

"The first step is always the hardest and made with fear, take it, and you will be free of her forever. Come to us and be the Raven, walk into the power we offer, take his life and join with us, and you will have our protection for this life and many more. The time is now, you are ready."

The black bird flew to the roof of the covered caravan like cart, and landed without a sound, it turned to see Branna stood wrapped tightly in her shawl by the fire staring back at them. Roack could sense the apprehension within her.

"Do the spell, close your eyes as we have taught you and call the darkness to help you."

Reluctantly Branna closed her eyes; her knees trembled as she felt the power of the bird within her increase. Her mind wandered a little as she tried to find her focus, and remember the words that for almost a year the bird had told her to recite in her head. She struggled as she searched again for the words she had up until this moment been able to simply recall.

Her mind filled with the pictures of the bloody rock and the red stained grass from her first days of freedom; even now she found it hard to hide her revulsion at what she had done. Suddenly in her mind two large dark and reddened eyes appeared, and the gruff voice of Roack echoed within her head.

"Focus… Relax and draw the power within you. Feel its strength; embrace the power of a future queen. Think of her on her white seat yearning to take you and destroy you, think of all she has done in your life to hurt you and those you love, and harness your hate and take the power we offer you."

The mention of Rhiannon focused her mind as her hate of a queen who had mistreated half of her race flowed into her. It felt almost like sliding through a soft curtain of silk, as something cool trickled over her head and down her face, and raced over her body filling it with both a sense of coolness and fire.

Roack watched with delight as Branna's face, which had been heavily tanned from her days on the beach appeared to blanch and pale, it was almost as if the colour just ran like milk across her features, and in the early morning light it looked almost as if it had begun to shine with a pale radiance. Outwardly Branna did not look like she was filling with life, she looked quite the opposite, almost as if she had died. Her lips darkened, and around her a cloudy fine fog appeared, the veil was becoming visible, and yet all around them as the veil appeared surrounding the whole of the camp site, the view of everything beyond the camp, slowly faded from sight as the blackness of the veil deepened. Roack was very pleased.

"That is it our Raven of Fae, absorb us, take us within you deep, and feel the strength of what we offer you, for you will be the one to bring more to us, and we shall grow to rule stronger than your queens of light."

*S*everal miles away in the small village where the Marshals of the Fae still slept off the ale of the previous night, the sun in the early morning sky faded into the clouds that rolled across the sky. What had begun as a bright morning quickly fell into a heavy oppressive darkness, as thick black clouds drifted in from the east. Labourers who attended their fields looked to the sky and felt the oppression floating above them, they threw down their tools and ran for cover, as the clouds parted and white forks streaked to the floor in a flash of dazzling bright light. The rumble that followed was deafening, as the thunder tore through the sky and into the ears of the villagers, who threw themselves to the ground in fear.

The first drops of water on the floor were large and round, and then almost like flicking a switch, the rain came cascading down with great force and pounded everything. Children in their shelters and homes of stones and timber, cried with the ferocity of the storm as it thundered onto the rooves of every dwelling. Crops crumpled under the sheer volume of the rain, and all over the village the few who had remained sleeping jumped from their beds in fear, for none had ever witnessed a storm as fierce.

Within the large dark circle created by Branna, all was as silent as the grave and calm. Branna was still frozen in her place with her eyes closed, as the power of the Merle flowed into her soul and through her veins. Roack watched from the top of the caravan, feeling a sense of great achievement, for several years they had trained Branna for this very moment. As the power flowed out of the storm and into Branna, it was clear that this had been her destiny from birth. Even though she was slender and at times frail looking, her Fae body was perfect as a container for the powers that she was receiving. The Raven stood up and stretched out its wings as it grew in size, filling itself with the power that flowed freely out of the storm, and feeling stronger than ever before.

Below the birds' feet inside the caravan came the sounds of feet as they thumped onto the wooden floor. All around the camp was dim in the faded light, as the sound of a large man moving within the caravan, flowed out as he dressed. Four loud thumps came as he approached the door at the rear of the caravan, yet Branna remained as still as stone.

The door swung open and the large traveller walked out and down the few steps to the ground, looking around to try and understand why it was still so dark. He turned at the foot of the steps to face the camp and the cart with a cover of hoops and canvas which belonged to Branna. Then he spotted her stood near the fire, her face looked almost translucent in the light, her long black hair wafted in a gentle breeze behind her. His face began to break into a slight smile as he noted she was still here. A slight movement from the corner of his right eye caught something, and turned and looked up.

His heart almost froze with fear as his mouth gaped open and widened; there on the roof of his caravan was a giant bird of black that stood as tall as two men with wings outstretched. Its eyes were a deep violent red, and they stared right through him and into the depth of his soul. He took a step back as fear filled every fibre of his being, and inside his head he heard what sounded like a course and rasping version of Branna. Slowly in his frozen face his eyes shifted from the bird to the white faced figure by the fire, her eyes were open but they were not hers, her bright sparkling eyes that danced had gone, there were no whites just two sockets filled with a dull blackness that froze his soul, and paralysed his heart, as a cold cruel soft voice echoed around the camp.

"You would sell me for gold and silver to that bitch?"

He wanted desperately to deny it, but he could not move, his throat was as dry as parchment, and his body locked with terror. She turned and moved slowly as the mist swirled around her feet, giving an appearance that made her look like she was floating within it. His eyes grew even wider, but as much as he wanted to scream and run, he was frozen to the spot as she slowly advanced. He wanted so desperately to close his eyes, her face was smooth and as white as death itself, and he did not want to see her close up, but was held prisoner to the fear within him.

Branna advanced coming right up to his face so he felt her cold breath wash across his cheeks. Inside his head her cold cruel voice continued.

"Feel my power and know that your greed and lust is the reason you will die this day. Feel the breath fill your lungs, for that will be your last."

His eyes blinked and he gasped a long hard breath to fill his lungs, and all through his body he slowly began to feel the tremors of his fear as they shook his limbs, and he felt the warmth of the fluid that leaked and ran down his legs.

The ghostly face of Branna gave a sinister smile and her lips blackened. In the centre of his chest, he felt a burning as if his lungs had set on fire, he gave a twitch, and as he began to exhale Branna lifted something up in front of his face and took a bite out of it. The realisation as her lips sucked and her teeth tore, she was holding his fresh warm heart and eating it was his last thought, and as he was released from the tight grip that held him, he tried to scream, his throat gurgled as the blood filled it, and he fell limp to the floor and into darkness.

As the body hit the floor and Branna chewed, Roack shrank back to their normal size on the roof of the caravan. Branna walked back to the fire and tore a piece of the heart off and cast it over her shoulder towards the bird. Roack opened their wings and swooped off the roof and down catching the chunk of meat, and glided to the ground where it was torn up and devoured. The bird looked up to Branna.

"Move your possessions to his cart, and burn everything else."

*T*he cold swept through Ariel and everyone as they started their day and the horrendous scream echoed all across Florae. She looked at the frightened face of Bade as he stared up the long road towards the Royal Lodge.

"Oh no not again, it's been so long, how can this be?" He shook his head slowly.

"I have no words, it has been well over a year, I thought we had finally seen the end of it."

It had been just one long scream, but Ariel knew well the fear it cast across the people of her race. Bridget had been fine when she had spoken to her only a week ago, it made no sense to her that she would have such a terrible dream now after so much time.

"I must go to her." Ariel felt the tight grip of Bade's hand on her arm.

"Wait, this is not for you, she will not allow any but Malcom close to her, you know this Ariel. If the dreams are starting again, she will push everyone close to her away. She always says the same thing, I will always protect my family, and then heads to her room of symbols, you will serve no purpose going to her, she will see none now." Bade released her arm.

"I will go to the Royal Lodge and see what can be learned from Malcolm. You must continue as normal, even though I know in your heart you feel the same desperate despair I do, but we must be seen to continue on for the sake of everyone here, it is Malcolm's wish. When Gwendolyn returns from Avalon, I will ask her to come to you." Ariel felt a little surprise.

"She is in Avalon again?" He gave a nod.

"Her duties are greatly increased as her role now is to replace the queen who will not leave this realm. She has done well for her age; I feel one day she will serve our people very well indeed. Go about your day and act as normal as is possible, I will send word of her to you as soon as I know anything."

Bade walked off up the long road towards the Royal Lodge, and Ariel was filled with a thousand thoughts. It seemed impossible to know if Bridget would ever overcome her affliction of night terrors, and she simply could not accept the thought of losing the one person who had saved her at an early age, and raised her as her mother would have done.

Her stomach ached and twisted at any thought of losing Bridget, and she felt a cold tingle run down her spine. All these years and still no one knew of the cause, and Bridget would not speak of it to any, not even her husband. It felt wrong and unjust, she wanted so desperately to help her, and yet she knew that like every attempt she had made with each meeting with her, Bridget would not allow any talk of the cause of her terrors. Ariel knew deep down inside that she could help, if only Bridget would allow it, but it was hopeless to try, and she knew it.

Movement caught her eye, and she turned slightly to see all the workers staring at her, and for that moment she knew she had to snap out of her deep worry and focus on Bridget's dream, this realm meant everything and it was so close to completion. She took a long deep breath and clapped her hands.

"Come on the Queen will be fine, we have a lot to do, so let's focus and make this realm the beauty of all realms for our beloved queen." Movement began, and slowly everyone collected their tools and returned back to their day of labour.

Chapter Seventeen.

The Fourteen Stars.

It had been a long night for Ariel, like most of her city, she had sat up in thought after the screams that had echoed throughout Florae the previous day. The night terrors of Bridget had appeared to have eased, so hearing her screams across the land during the hours of daylight had unsettled her. Her request to go to the queen had been rejected, and Bade had not returned to give her any word as to the queen's wellbeing, the frustration of the day had sat with her all night, and she hardly slept a wink.

With the rising of the sun, and the prospect of a long hot day, her spirits had not risen much as she ate the grains that were her morning meal sat by her window. As much as she wanted to face the day with a positive attitude, deep down inside her emotions reeled. When a quiet tap came to her door, her heart sunk more expecting yet another dispatch to inform her she could not meet with Bridget.

As the door opened and the light flooded in temporarily blinding her, the relief she felt at the outlined sight of Bade gave her hope to her heart. He looked pale and tired, as he stepped in with his usual faint smile.

"I am sorry, I know I said I would get right back to you, but it has been a busy night, but fear not, she is safe and will speak with you now."

Bade looked somewhat shocked as Ariel grabbed him and pulled him close, he gave a smile as he relaxed and rested for a moment on her shoulder. Her night had also been a long one of worry but with his pale face at the door and gentle words, suddenly she felt the relief wash into her, and a slight excitement overtook the feelings of apprehension she had been feeling.

"Oh thank you… When can I see her?" Bade gave a small chuckle as he was released from her hug and stood back, his smile widened.

"It is why I am finally here; she has requested you go to her." The happiness rose quickly within her and her soft grey eyes sparkled.

"When, where, ooh I must brush my hair and change my clothes." She spun on the spot and hurried into her room; Bade gave a smirk and turned to look out of the still open door while he waited for her.

*I*t was forty minutes later when Ariel escorted by Bade, walked up the steps and through the large oak doors, carved with the two mighty figures of Bridget and Malcolm of the House of Scribes. Since returning after its completion, Ariel had seen the house several times, and yet she still got a massive thrill as she walked inside into the large room filled with blue light from the windows. To her left she saw the seats of the council, and directly in front were the two large carved and impressive chairs that served as the thrones for Bridget and Malcom. The Thrones had been brought from the Violet Isle once the House of Scribes had been completed, and it was on the seats that Bridget held court with her council.

Ariel had expected to walk past the thrones towards the royal apartments, which were located at the back of the House of Scribes, but she was surprised as Bade took her arm and gave a gentle pull.

"Not that way today." Ariel glanced up at his twinkling green eyes, and she felt a jolt of excitement in her stomach.

"No way… Its finished?" He gave a very cheeky smile.

"It is, and she wants you to see it with her." Ariel almost exploded with excitement.

Since their arrival on the island, Rhiannon had promised an offering of peace between her and Bridget. Outside in the centre of the city, at a point where all the streams flowing from the mountains converged, the water poured into a huge depression, onto a large pillar of stone, and as they fell into the deep depression, they made a faint almost whispering sound.

*T*he falls had been named Whispering Falls, and Rhiannon had heard about them, and so offered her services as she knew the Fae of Earth did not like to dig more than one foot below the surface of the soil as a mark of respect for the land. The Fae of Moon were skilled workers of stone, and so she sent a crew of talented men, to carve away the pillar below, creating a table of stone onto which the water would fall, before cascading down the side into the deeper rivers that ran through underground tunnels and towards the sea. When the land of Florae had been given to Bridget, Albanlin had visited the place and placed a charm upon the falls with Eve and Hearne. Bridget herself had joined in the ritual and used a charm of her old friend Enaria, and the waters that ran into the cave below created a place of special powers, for here many of the works and deeds of the Fae could be retrieved in private by the queen from the many records of the scribes.

The waters above flowed down creating a wall of falling water around the floor upon which a seat would be placed for use of the Queen of the Fae alone. Rhiannon's workers had been working none stop since the arrival of Bridget, and now after years of skilled work, the tunnels below the ground had been widened and extended to create an extra labyrinth of storage for the house of scribes. Here many very secret and private documents would be stored for the use of future queens of Fae. Ariel had been dying to see it finished, and she could not believe her luck to be one of the first invited, as she knew well, few of the Fae would ever walk these chambers.

*T*hey passed through a new wooden doorway and onto a flight of wooden steps that descended deep below the halls above. Bade led the way and Ariel felt her nervousness growing with her excitement.

"So, what does it look like?" Bade was his usual calm self.

"No idea, I have not had the privilege, doubt I ever will." Ariel stopped and tugged at his arm.

"What… You mean I am the first?" His voice sounded droller in the cave below ground.

"You are. There is a long tunnel leading to a small covered bridge that crosses the water into the stone circular room, I have not made it past the bridge, the work done by Rhiannon's people has been very secret. Bridget wanted to visit alone to bless the room, she gave strict orders that no one but you must approach after she is finished, and so here I am doing my duty as requested by my Queen." Ariel could feel his disappointment.

"I am really sorry, you have done so much here, you should have been first." He gave a small sigh.

"I serve Fae with honour, honestly I see my life here as privileged, I am not that concerned Ariel. You have done equally as much, but of late you have been prevented for no other reason than you have been wrongfully accused. I feel you more than any deserve this honour."

There was a tone to his voice inside the cave that showed his concern and affection for her, Ariel was unsure how to respond, he stopped at the end of a side passage.

"This is it, follow the path and Bridget awaits you." It surprised her.

"What, are you not coming down to the bridge?" He smiled in the torch light.

"I have seen the bridge; my instruction was to leave you here, and return to ensure no other disturbs you." He lifted his hand to the side of her face. "You two have not had anywhere near enough time of late, go to her and enjoy this." She gave a nod.

"Thanks."

With a cheeky wink, he turned back in the tunnel, and returned to his duties leaving her alone at the end of the passage. Ariel watched him leave and then feeling a little apprehensive, but also filled with excitement, she walked into the passage that would lead her to the most sacred place in the Fae kingdom.

At the end of the tunnel was a hall cut from the stone. It was at least twelve feet high and Ariel considered it to be at least twenty feet wide, the walls were a smooth highly polished grey, lit by the many torches that burned from brackets of iron bolted to the wall. At the far end of the room, she saw the wooden platform with a pointed roof that separated the water and gave her the first glimpse of the finished room beyond. Bridget stood there in the centre, her back to her, and Ariel thought that maybe she was deep in thought. Millions of gallons of water appeared to be flowing across what she knew was a table of stone, and streaming off the edge and down into a deep ravine below, creating a perfect ring of a glistening, shimmering water like curtain around the whole room.

Ariel walked slowly down the tunnel, her heart beating fast within her, she approached the wooden bridge and watched Bridget carefully, she felt unsure as to enter or wait for Bridget to welcome her. It was a surreal moment, millions of gallons of water thundered down the sides of the circle of stone, and yet it felt surprisingly quiet, as only moments earlier, the water had thundered past and made her ears ring. She gave a loud cough, which appeared to bring Bridget out of whatever thought she was in, and she turned and smiled as she saw Ariel; stood waiting at the edge of the wooden bridge.

"Come… Come and have a look, I know how much you wanted to

see this complete."

Ariel gave a smile of great relief, Bridget looked her normal self, she was a little paler than she had been, and she had dark rings below her eyes, but her smile and the sparkle in her eyes was its powerful usual self, and she gave a large sigh of relief to see her as she had always known her. Ariel stepped onto the bridge and walked the few feet across the deep ravine that surrounded the circle of stone, and stepped onto the floor within the chamber, and she felt awe as she looked around. The wooden bridge slipped backward, and the wall of shimmering water was complete, and Ariel marvelled at the absolute silence that fell within the sealed room. Bridget looked very happy indeed.

"It's wonderful, isn't it?"

Ariel was lost for words as she looked up at the huge stone smooth roof above her, held up by four tall intricately carved pillars, Bridget walked over to her side.

"Considering her behaviour of late, I think Rhiannon has done a wonderful job don't you?" Ariel gave a wide smile.

"Her workers are skilled indeed, I doubt Rhiannon really cares much, but I think she will make sure everyone knows of her generosity." Bridget chuckled.

"You are possibly right." She walked to one of the pillars. "It is more beautiful than I thought it would be, and once the stone seat is brought down here, this will become the centre of everything in this Fae world. I already feel the power here, this will be a very important place for both of us." Ariel looked confused.

"Both of us?" Bridget turned to face her, her violet eyes shining.

"Well yes, both of us, Ariel you are the daughter of one of the most important mystics of our line, you may not see it, but you have many of her talents, one day it will be you who reveals the whole history of our people to the rest of the world." Ariel still felt very confused.

"How, I don't understand?"

"You have been the most important member of the scribes here; every word you have written will be seen and heard from this place by every queen of the Fae that follows on after me. Ariel do you not see, this place is the living embodiment of the House of Scribes, very soon every document we hold will be available to the queen of this line with just one simple request? They will ask, and the falls will whisper back the answers." She smiled as she watched the curtain of water bouncing light all around the room like millions of small crystal lanterns.

"Whispering Water, I like the idea of that."

Bridget walked round the large empty circle surrounded by cascading water, as she circled the room, her violet eyes would lift to look at Ariel and twinkle, it was almost as if she was deciding something. Ariel stayed silent hoping that maybe Bridget was finally going to explain what was happening to her. Bridget stopped and looked right into Ariel's soft grey eyes.

"All your mother's secret work will be added to this place, I am the only living soul who has read it, and a day will come when you shall be required to come to this place and translate it for a new Queen of this realm." Her voice was soft, almost a whisper, and yet Ariel sensed she was being told something of great importance.

"Why will I have to do it, there are many in this realm who can read the elder codes of the Fae, not just me?" Bridget smiled.

"In this you are as always correct my trusted child, but even to those of us who can fully translate them, there is little meaning if the translator is not an accomplished mystic, and you are her daughter." Ariel shook her head.

"But only a Scribe, she did not live long enough to pass on her gifts to me, you know that." Bridget walked forward.

"You are wrong, at our last meeting before she left for the realm of the Moon, she told me she had already passed them to you, but they would only surface when the time of need was upon you." Ariel frowned.

"Time of need, what does that really mean? Our whole race's survival has been a time of need, and considering some of the things that you have encountered of late, tell me is this not a time of need for you?" Bridget gave a soft giggle, and her eyes sparkled.

"My dearest Ariel, you are so like her… My time is almost over, Gwendolyn will take my place and she will be stronger than I because of the things I have done. The story is too long a tale to tell, and there will be a day when you will come here and the whole truth will be revealed to you. For now, accept that what I have told you is true, and that you my dearest child, will one day be the reason these fair people thrive." Ariel felt a lurch in her stomach, and it felt like it was tying itself in knots.

"What are you saying, what is this foolishness? You are our queen and the most loved of all the Fae, you have years of time ahead of you." The tears filled her eyes. "You cannot leave us, you must not leave us, you are the most powerful member of all the Fae lines. You are needed here, you are needed in Avalon, you are the only person who can bring Rhiannon to book, you know this, so why do you say such things?" Bridget came forward and wrapped her arms around her, Ariel mumbled.

"You are all I have, when my mother died, I would not have survived if you had not taken me in, I have lost Bran, I cannot lose you too." Bridget squeezed her hard.

"Hush my child, I still have time here, and you have never been alone, Enaria was closer to me than a sister, and I know she is within you and has always watched over you. Oh Ariel my child, she loved you so deeply, she did not leave you alone, have you not seen that?" Ariel lifted her head and gave a sniffle.

"Since that day I have not felt her presence, I have always been alone." Bridget shook her head slowly.

"No child, you were never alone, I have felt her within you always, and I know the gifts she bestowed upon you, they have been the ones that have guided you always onto the right path. I knew she was there; it is why I have trusted you so much across the years, it is why I sent you to Avalon." It felt like a surprise to Ariel, and she wiped her eyes.

"It is why you sent me? I do not understand."

"Ariel, whether you believe me or not, you have her powers, and they guide you. I knew that you and you alone would not be swayed by Rhiannon; I also knew that the truth of your mother was ingrained within you, and it is fierce and strong. Very few could cut through the politics of Avalon and the Fae of Moon for they are skilled in their words, I knew that you and you alone would see right through them and report only the truth, that is why all your reports remain unseen by many eyes and are kept hidden within the chamber of my private scrolls. I was right to send you, for you did uncover a greater amount of the truth of the realm of Rhiannon than any other could." Ariel felt surprised, she had done little in her time there, just report the mundane life of those building the realm, and she felt there was little to learn from such scrolls.

"The life of those who work in Avalon is dull, I wrote nothing of great importance, I really do not understand?" Bridget gave a smile.

"A time will come when you do, and it is at that time that you will return here and the full truth of everything will be revealed." Bridget placed her hand into the pocket of her long blue robe. "Do you remember the long white box?"

Ariel felt a shudder run through her, it was a memory from a very long time ago, and a vague picture grew in her mind, as she stood aged thirteen moons old before her mother who was holding a long white box. Her mother smiled and opened the box to reveal fourteen stars, twelve of gold, one of red, and one of black. Her soft voice echoed from the past through the haze of Ariel's memory.

"Do you like them my darling? These are the stars of the mystic earth, they are the stars of life and death, and the protection of our race, your father made them, and I wrote the charms that filled them. One day it will be your duty to hand them to a new queen. Remember this moment, hold it in your mind how I showed you, and when the darkness comes, think of them." Ariel gave a nod.

"I remember the box, why is it important?"

"It is important Ariel because one day they will fill the table of a queen of Fae, or at least twelve of them will. Those twelve will bring protections few will understand." She thought for a moment and then looked into the eyes of Bridget.

"What of the other two?" Bridget smiled.

"The red will fill a table of white, and wield immense power." She gave a nod of understanding.

"And what of the black one?"

"That will be seen by few, but according to your mother, the fourteenth star will weaken the darkness and allow the light to pass through." She gave a frown.

"That is a bit cryptic." Bridget laughed.

"It is indeed, but you will work it out eventually. Your mother was a very powerful and clever woman, and when my time comes, I will pass from this realm confident in the knowledge that she alone is the saviour of this race." It made little sense to Ariel, but she knew that there was no way Bridget would give her a clearer explanation. Bridget turned and across the wide floor of grey stone on the opposite side to them, the cascading water parted and the long wooden bridge came through into sight.

"You must leave me now Ariel, for there are things to be done here known only to myself. I have informed the elders that you are to be admitted to all the records of the house, but I do not wish you to return to your duties of old. Take this time Ariel to find the answers to the questions that have long been inside you, read to your heart's desire, and gather your understanding of all your mother told you in those early years. Your destiny is close, go forth and prepare to meet it." Ariel gave Bridget a long hug.

"I love you Bridget, thank you for this, and yes I will love returning to read again, I have missed it so."

"Go my child and walk the realms of learning with a happy heart."

After a long embrace, Ariel made her way towards the bridge out of the room of the Whispering Waters, stopping for a moment to look back and smile. Bridget gave a soft wave, Ariel departed, and the bridge slid through the water and disappeared, leaving Bridget once again alone in the newly finished chamber. Her eyes stared at the water where the small wooden bridge had disappeared.

"Protect her for me Enaria." The waters gave a slight shimmer as they flowed down from the edges of the roof into the floor and a soft voice whispered back

"I always have and I always will, she was always my true hope, of this you know my dearest of friends." Bridget gave a smile and nodded.

"I know."

*I*t felt like a long walk back through the tunnels to the heart of the House of Scribes for Ariel. Bridget had been more cryptic than she had ever really known her to be. There was a different feeling around her, and yet Ariel could not quite put her finger on what it was. Her mind searched for answers, but she now found she had too many questions to really focus and understand what was actually happening to her beloved queen.

Suddenly and quite unexpectedly she had yet another role to play, and she was unsure as to just what exactly that was, her mind processed the endless possibilities of Bridget's words, and without even realising, lost in thought, she found herself stood outside the House of Scribes in the radiant sunlight at the top of the main steps.

Bade was at her side speaking and she had not even been aware of him, for a moment her mind jumbled as she shook her thoughts free and turned to him.

"What… Sorry I was lost in thought, what did you say?" He gave a slight chuckle.

"The world moves ever onward and yet never really changes. As always, I am talking and you are so lost in your thoughts that once again you do not hear me, feels like things are back to normal, doesn't it?" She gave a soft smile.

"Nothing here appears normal to me at the moment." He gave a nod.

"It has certainly been a testing time my friend, but look on the bright side, you are back indoors with us all again. I cannot wait to give you the tour I should have done when you first arrived back."

She felt the happiness slightly warm her with the sunlight through the large windows, it was nice to know that she would finally be able to work in the building that had been planned by her for many years, but something inside her told her it was never going to be as it had been. Things had changed within her forever, and she was not sure exactly just what, but deep down inside Ariel knew she had changed much since she had left for Avalon. The scribe that she had been was no longer there, but something was, she was just uncertain as to what.

*D*eep down inside the chamber of the Whispering Water Bridget stood silent as she focused her powers, and in her mind a picture formed of a figure dressed in a long black tattered garment. His voice was soft and caring.

"Greetings little violet eyes, I take it you still intend to go through with this?"

"I do, you promised there would be a circle of pure light."

"I did and it shall be if you wish it."

"Then make the circle and take the red star, build her the means to protect everything. Gwendolyn must have every tool she will ever require; I trust you to understand this."

"I understand what you wish for, I simply do not understand why the urgency, will you not share what you so cleverly hide from me?"

"I will My Lord in time; please you must trust that what I ask is for the sake of everyone."

"If that is how you wish it, then my Queen it will be done, fear not for when her time comes, I will guide her in all things."

"Thank you, My Lord, her future will be in your hands, but I will be happy in the knowledge that she is protected within the White Circle."

"It is no easy task that you request, when the red star is placed, then there will be a white star surplus, what would you have me do with that."

"Save it, for a time will come when Ariel calls out to her mother, and when she does, deliver her the power of the Fae to aid her and pass on the star."

"The Daughter of someone so enlightened as Enaria should have no need of a white star, but if this is your request, I shall as promised honour it. Be at peace Queen of the Fae, for it shall be done as you request."

"Thank you My Lord of White, I will be forever grateful for the protection you bestow upon us."

"It is done, I shall prepare the way for you."

Bridget opened her eyes, and the violet light within them flashed off the water pouring silently through the chamber. She dropped to her knees and gave a long gasp, as the exhaustion overcame her, and for a few long minutes she gathered her breath, and rested to restore her composure.

Chapter Eighteen.

Betrayal And Salvation.

High up the mountain paths in the remote wilderness of Sachsen, the Varisci tribe had been called together and informed that trouble was brewing, and other tribes had despatched a raiding party to take down the village in revenge for the attacks by Grembald and his men. Berengar had been about to leave for a hunt, when he was called back to join the party that would head down into the valley and meet the oncoming raiders. Once again, his father tried to stop him and begged him not to go, but Berengar grew angry, he had a duty to his tribe and its leader, and even though he did not want to go against his father's wishes, he knew he had to play his part, as he was honour bound to the tribe. His father cursed him, calling him stupid and disloyal to his family, and yet again, filled with anger Berengar left the camp with the others, filled with a heart of conflict.

It had been almost four months since the killing of the traveller by Branna under the forces of the darkness, it had taken a lot of her strength, but her recovery had been quicker than even Roack had expected. With a new caravan as a travelling home, she had more comfort than ever before, and had taken the advice of her Raven companion, and turned away from the roads towards northern Brittany, and made her way across country towards the southern borders of Sachsen. Along the way she picked up a traveller from Bohemia, who was making his way home, whose name was Boris, although judging by the feelings she felt when she first asked him, she doubted that was his real name.

Boris was tall and strong, and not unattractive, and on their first night of camp she took him into her caravan and spent the night seducing him. He was not as skilled with the ladies as he had first suggested, but that was not a real concern for Branna, she knew what she wanted and how to get it, and after a great deal of suggestions and dominance, Boris soon learned many things that would impress the ladies back home.

Knowing that the Marshals from Avalon had come close in their search for her, Branna felt a companion would serve as a good cover for her, and seeing as Boris had offered to pay with food that she felt he had probably stolen, she accepted his offer and allowed him to drive the caravan, which although unsaid, did suggest to passers by that they were a couple. Branna knew that the marshals were looking for a single travelling, woman, so for now it suited her purpose.

Boris was not the most conversational person, but he liked to talk about his homeland, and although his language was broken at times, she managed to learn a great deal about Bohemia and the simple life style of its people. Boris painted an idyllic picture of his family life growing up, and it struck a deep chord with Branna, as she remembered some of her own youth back in the realm Ofmoon, and many of the dreams that had shaped who she had become when she finally escaped, and was sent to Avalon.

Travelling along the dirt track, she found she would drift into her thoughts with the gentle rocking of the wagon and day dream of times past, but it would result in her feeling a strong and violent anger boiling up inside her. It bothered Branna, as she had never known such rage before, yes, she felt bitter and angry in the past at the way Rhiannon had treated her family and friends, but never like this.

Roack knew well the anger inside her, for unbeknown to Branna, on the night she had killed the traveller for his caravan, the Merle had connected far deeper to her than even she had realised, and deep within her as the day's past, it was starting to gain more and more control of her.

The time separated from Ariel had finally started to wear away her feelings, and the Merle as it gained strength began to supress her love for Ariel, controlling it and forcing it deeper inside her, but Branna was not aware of the struggle that was going on deep within her core. Roack's seduction of Branna had been slow and strategic, and as the bird flew high in the sky above her, the Merle within her communicated in secret, and followed each and every command given it by the cold and callous black bird.

Branna had many flash backs in her day dreams, moments that flashed into her mind of a man stood with a hole in his chest, the silhouette of a bird larger than any man, a feeling of floating on the mist, panic as she ran round a site and grabbed her belongings, but as soon as they appeared in her mind, Roack ensured they were pushed deep down inside her and out of her mind. The days slipped by and the memories faded along with everything else, as anger boiled up more and more deep inside Branna, controlled by the large black Raven that never let her out of their gaze for a second.

Berengar had the lead as he headed towards the valley floor, where the raiding party had been spotted. The Varisci moved with great speed and ability, through the trees and scrub towards their intended target. Berengar was at the front leading the way, accompanied by Elric, one of the older and more season warriors of the group. Berengar was several paces up front, when Elric called to him and he slowed his pace for his companion to catch up.

"What is with the pace, we know where they are?" Berengar stopped and wiped his face on his sleeve, his hairless head tanned and glistening in the sunlight.

"I want to get this over with." Elric caught up and patted his shoulder.

"Save your anger for them, not your father." Berengar scowled at him and he gave a slight laugh. "You are not the first to have his ears clipped by your father, I too have suffered his wrath. Let it go Beren, he has his way and Grembald has his, let them argue it out, it will serve you no purpose to be stuck in the middle." Berengar gave a nod, but he could not help the anger he felt.

"He has no understanding of my place, he sees me as a child, but I have grown far stronger and seen more combat than many my age, he should show me equally as much respect as he does the others." Elric gave a nod of agreement.

"You are not wrong my friend, and yes you have a duty to all of us at the command of our leader. Beren you also have to understand his place, he should have rightfully been the leader, all of us thought that one day he would take charge and lead the village. He is a proud man too, and yet his injuries have taken a great deal of his pride. Do not judge him harshly, he will come round at some point, remember this is between him and Grembald, neither of them agrees with each other on how to lead us. Let them fight it out or yell it out, because it will happen eventually." Berengar took a sip from his water sack.

"I know you are right, I just… I just wish he would see that I have my orders just like the rest of you, and I am honour bound to them." Elrick gave a shrug.

"A man like your father uses strength to support pacts and treaties for a peaceful existence, Grembald is not a man of words, he is more a man of swords and death. There are many within the tribe that agree with your father, but also others who back Grembald, a day will come when you must choose, but until that day why worry?" Berengar cleaned out his mouth and spat on the floor.

"My duty is to the one who leads, he taught me that, and yet even now he prevents my brothers from joining us and disgraces them by it. Vlad and Otto should be here at my side, not sat in a lodge listening to the bitterness of a fallen warrior." He turned to look at Elrick, and the anger in his eyes was evident.

"Whether we agree or not, Grembald's iron hand has taken more land and brought more wealth to this tribe, and we have all shared the benefits. My father has done little but yell and complain, my sword is Grembald's until such time as another replaces him."

Berengar looked from Elric down the steep bank towards the river path to ensure it was still clear. "I am saddened to hear that Beren, I really do like you."

"What?"

The coldness took a few seconds to catch up with the reality, Berengar looked down at his side to see the five inches of steel glinting where it had not been blood stained, but it was too late as the left leg of his pants turned red, and he suddenly realised what had happened. The steel withdrew sharply, but this time he felt the pain as it tore back through his side. His left leg was already starting to go numb as he tried to turn to Elric, realising what he had done to him. Shouts and screams came through the trees as his head turned to see Grembald on the floor, and Halbreck lift his axe as the others yelled and jeered.

His eyes felt strange and his arm refused to move as he stared at the axe as it came down with a thud, cleaving Grembald's head clean off. It felt like a daze as everything slowed down, the voice of Elric appeared deeper and slower, as his head slowly turned back to face him, and saw him still holding the bloody sword.

"I am sorry Beren, but it is your father's wish that if you will not support him above Grembald, you too must pay the price."

He felt dizzy and sick, as the coldness ran through the rest of his body; this was his father's wish? His father had betrayed him. Elric's foot came up and hit him in the waist, but he did not feel it, his eyes filled with the sky, the trees, the sky, the earth and then the darkness came. Berengar bounced down the hillside smashing into trees and crushing the bushes, he felt nothing but the cold and the darkness, as his ears filled with the distant sounds of a celebrating tribe and trickling water, and then there was utter silence.

*T*he sun was high and the road dusty, as Branna drifted in and out of her thoughts, staring ahead at the long road before her. Boris was sat slumped and snoring quietly, when she became aware of the soft thump of Roack as they landed on the roof of the caravan. She came out of her thoughts and waited for the bird to speak in her mind, it had been several days since they had last spoken, the bird found Boris irritating, and had taken to staying high in the trees out of sight to avoid Boris's constant whining about Branna and her love of a bird of ill omen.

Branna gave a smile to herself, it amused her how much it irritated Roack, there came the familiar soft tap on the roof of the birds' claws, as it made its way forward, and peeped over the canopy to see the scruffy form of Boris sat beside Branna.

"Your pig sleeps more than the stones on the roadside, there are things about your kind I will never understand. Why not just slit his throat and be free of him?" Her dark eyes lifted towards the bird.

"I have told you; he provides me with a good cover should I be stopped, whilst he sits up front and sleeps, it looks like we are a couple to those who pass by." She felt the bird's irritation.

"His presence is inconvenient, there is still much we must do, he is always in the way of our progress, you have grown far more powerful and learned much these last months of your time, but if you are to build a place of great power to challenge those of your line, we must do more to prepare. I feel the destiny you crave move closer to our grasp."

"We have time Roack, we are close to the borderlands and he will leave for his home, and I will rest for a while in a sheltered place. There we can take our time and perfect all we need to achieve the start of building something of value." The birds head appeared to bob up and down, and it shuffled its feet on the roof.

"You have gained a great deal, but you are far too relaxed in your ways still, you must find a place that is secret where we can begin. You

must put in more effort to learn of these lands, for it is here I sense you should create a place to build a seat from which you can rule."

There was a rough tone to the voice Branna had heard many times, she understood the impatience of the bird, but her time on the realm of the moon taught her to bide her time, and wait for the perfect moment? It had been that skill that had won her the favour to be sent to Avalon, and deep down inside she knew that when the moment arose her inner senses would tell her that this was the moment.

"You have waited many spans of time for this Roack, a little longer is nothing compared to that time, relax and enjoy the moment. Maybe the vessel you have occupied is in need of some way to ease its frustrations, after all even though you occupy its insides; it is still a physical being, have you considered allowing its natural urges to be quenched?" The bird physically shuddered and disappeared out of view.

"We have no need of your kind of physical pleasures, I understand the feelings it brings to your body from feeling your pleasures, but this vessel has no need of those types of feelings, it is a basic primitive creature that contains a higher life form."

There was a sense of indignation to the tone of Roack's voice in her mind that made her give a small laugh, and Boris grunted and stirred a little before settling back in his seat. Branna felt the amusement within her.

"You should not dismiss primitive instincts, there is a reason they are so strong, and the body requires them. Never underestimate the power of pleasure and the liberty it brings you Roack, for it may surprise you how allowing for natural urges can benefit all life forms, including the one you are currently being hosted by." The bird lifted off the roof into the air.

"I cannot speak to you when you are like this, you should think more of your goals than your basic urges with that pig."

Branna gave a slight titter as Roack climbed high into the trees, and she glanced over at Boris and the lump contained below his belt. She laughed to herself, he was in many ways a pig, he certainly needed to bathe, but for all his moodiness and his odd ways, he had proven to be a reasonably satisfying lover to date.

The sound of the river grew louder and she saw the trees thicken ahead, Boris had told her to watch for where the road narrowed as it made its way into the start of the valley. Branna slowed the horses a little and viewed the road ahead, there was plenty of room on the road for the caravan, all she had to do was watch the road, and look for a place to pull in so she could fill the barrels on the side of the van with fresh water.

As she entered the valley, the banks grew steadily steeper as they ran along the side of the rapidly flowing river. To her right, the bank climbed high, with trees sitting on heavy stone outcrops. On her left, the road fell away down a gentle incline to the sandy side of the fast river, Branna watched for a place where she could easily access a calmer part of the river to fill the water cans.

The caravan rocked from side to side at a gentle pace, as she made her way slowly watching for the right spot, and her mind wandered casually as she gathered her thoughts. Maybe Roack was right, she had not meant to have taken so long in her search for a place, but the years had passed by so quickly in this world of man. She had hardly understood what she was doing, before she realised that her days in Avalon were now years in her past. A glint on the water's edge caught her eye, and she came out of her thoughts for a moment as her understanding quickly caught up as to what it was, she was seeing.

"Is that a man?" Her soft whisper was unheard amongst the rushing sound of the water of the river.

She pulled on the reins and the horses slowed, as she pushed on the brake and the caravan shuddered to a halt. Boris jerked in his seat; he was woken with a start.

"What is it?" Branna pointed to where the bank of the road fell away towards the river.

"There is a man lay face down in the mud, I think he is hurt."

She jumped down from her seat onto the road, as Boris leaned over to try and see. Branna walked carefully down the bank towards the still figure, there was blood on the grass as she carefully approached trying not to slip on the wet stones. Boris stood up as she bent down and pulled back the cloak lined with the thick matted fur, of what looked like wolf pelt. Branna seeing that he was face down gripped at the green garment on the shoulder, and gave a mighty pull; he was big and heavy set, and she had to yank him hard before he rolled over revealing his shaved head and long plaited beard of soft brown.

This man was obviously a warrior of high standing, his belt and adornments were high quality gold, his sword was still in its scabbard and was of the highest quality, and yet it made no sense that he would be here alone, surely whoever had attacked him would have robbed him? Boris looked on as she moved across his body looking for the source of his wound, it was in his side, and it was clear it was deep and he had lost a lot of blood. She looked back to Boris, who she had heard grunt with disapproval, he was stood at the top of the bank and he spat on the floor.

"Varisci scum, leave him to rot and let's get going, this road is not safe." Branna did not understand.

"Boris he is wounded, I cannot leave him here to die." Boris scowled.

"That is no man, he is the dog of all men, leave him to rot and do all of us a favour." He spat on the floor and turned back to the caravan. She felt her anger grow inside her, how could he just leave a man to die like this?

"I care not who he is, look at his clothes, he is a man of wealth, I cannot leave him to die in the road, he may show us great gratitude and reward, now help me." Boris turned reluctantly.

"I will not." She felt her temper rising.

"You ride with me you help me." He pulled himself back up to the seat.

"I paid to ride with a beautiful woman for companionship, not to lift dogs off the road. The Varisci are devils hated by all the gods, why help him? He will not thank you; he will slit your throat and steal everything you have. I will not help any of that murderous thieving bastard's kind, if you want to save him, do it alone."

Boris sat back and watched as Branna struggled. The man was heavy, so she tried to roll his heavy frame onto his back and his thick cloak. Taking a firm grip of the cloak, she pulled with all her might, and slowly she dragged him inch by inch out of the water.

*I*t took her almost an hour for her to drag him up the bank, and onto the road behind the caravan. She unfolded the wooden step, and unlocked the door and opened it wide, then using a fresh shawl wrapped under his arms like a rope, she dragged the body off the road and up into her small living space. She felt exhausted once she had managed to lift him up and onto the bed at the rear of her caravan. Once she was on board and not really caring, Boris flicked the reins, and drove the horses onwards leaving Branna alone with the heavy warrior to tend to his wounds.

Panting for breath, she leaned against her cupboard doors to rest for a moment, wiping her face and brow with the used shawl. Once she got her breath back, and recovered a little, she examined this wounded stranger who had been the source of her exhaustion. He was dirty, and she could see the fever that burned on his brow, Branna pulled the jug of water across to her, and reached for a cloth and the vials of herbs she had collected near her old beach home. She stripped him down stopping as she looked at his naked muscle set body; she was impressed especially as she noted his manhood.

"Wow I am sorry you are not awake, never have I seen such equipment."

She giggled to herself, as she cleaned his wound, and pulled her sewing kit towards her. His face burned bright red and beads of sweat rolled off his head, and she knew the struggle between life and death was to be his own. Once she had tended his wound, and tried to get him to drink the little of her potions as she could, which was not an easy task with a heavy, delirious, and almost unconscious man, the day had almost passed, and it was growing dark. Boris had pulled in for the night, and was building a fire to cook.

Branna covered him up after binding his wound and left him to his fight for life, from what she had seen of him, she knew he was strong, but only he could conquer his darkness alone now, and so she came out of the caravan and down the steps where Boris was sat by the fire eating, she was not happy with his attitude, but she was intrigued.

"Tell me of these Varisci." He scowled as he looked up at her.

"I told you, they are murderous bastards, you can heal him and lay with him, if he does not rape you first, but he will still rob you and slit your throat. They are scum, demons in men's skins, they are hated by everyone." She looked back to her caravan and smiled.

"You can only rape what does not want to be taken; I would enjoy feeling him take me." She looked back to Boris who looked upset and she laughed. "Don't worry; it will take a long while before he is healed to full strength."

She pulled at the ties on her dress, and it fell to the floor revealing her naked body, he gave a smile as she came towards him, and he pulled at his shirt to pull it over his head. She smiled as she knelt down, and began to undo the threads of his pants.

"I have lots of time, and I have not finished with you just yet."

Chapter Nineteen.

Not Quite Knowing.

Boris lay curled in his blanket by the fire, Branna was sticky and needed to wash between her legs, she stood up in the darkness, and walked towards the barrel on the side of the caravan, her eyes looking in through the small doorway at the dark lump of Berengar as he fought against the darkness of his inner demons lost to this world but not yet in the next.

Taking the small ladle, she lifted the cool water out and sloshed it on her privates, rubbing away the sticky ooze of Boris, and rinsing herself off to feel clean again. Pulling a rag that hung on a line on the side of the barrel she patted herself dry, as she walked back round to the rear of the caravan towards the small doorway. Branna stepped up into the small room of her living space, very little light came inside, but she could still see the beads of sweat as they glistened on the warrior's face, and ran down towards the softly padded sack that served as his pillow.

Roack flew down and landed on the door step, he looked inside and then fluttered up to a drawer unit just inside the doorway.

"His path is dark and his fight is fierce." Branna turned hardly noticing the dark bird sat only a couple of feet in front of her.

"I have no idea as to why, but this is the man I seek, I feel it strongly within my core." The dark eyes of the bird shone in the darkness as he watched each of her movements and mannerisms.

"We feel it too within you, we feel that this is the sign you have searched for, but his fight will be one of dark terrors, there is no way to know if he has the power to face it and come through back to this side." Branna understood, and gave a gentle nod of her head.

"He will, I know it. I will use what I learned from Ariel and I will fight beside him, I feel a great injustice growing within him. There is hatred growing for those who did this to him, that will give him a greater power than he knows, he will defeat this darkness Roack, I feel it."

It was a defining moment as Roack observed her in the darkness, all the frustrations that she had created for them contained within the black bird appeared to fall away, and they knew that this was the moment they had been waiting for. It had taken much longer than expected, but Roack could see how the powers of darkness swirled and mixed within the Fae powers of Branna. Finally, after years of waiting, they watched as everything they had showed her fell into place. She was finally ready to accept the full power of their gifts to her, for it was now clear to them that through her will, others would soon be able to walk this earth contained within the life forms of another, the first stage of their plan was about to finally be complete. The raven sat motionless observing her.

"You must find us a secret place before he gains his health, you need to complete the circle with us and then be ready to embrace him unto us."

Branna nodded in the dark, her eyes fixed on the wounded warrior, as he fought his inner demons, her words were more to herself than Roack.

"I know, I am already looking."

*H*er meeting with Bridget in the room of the Whispering Falls had set alight something deep in Ariel, and she returned at last to the sacred halls of the Scribes to work on a new project. To her surprise she found that Bridget Violet had arranged for her to work in her own special room, which was adjoined to the private halls of Bridget, which contained a large stone table of power. Ariel leaned on the door frame and looked into the large room and the stone table that she had heard so many things about in her youth, but had like most Fae of Earth been kept from seeing.

The table was stone, and had been lifted from the earth in the centre of the land of Erin, and was then shipped across the hostile sea to the Violet Isle, before being moved to Florae where it was given to her people by Eve and Hearne. The table was edged in a natural circle of white crystal, which overlapped the edges, and formed a large white ring around the upper surface of the smooth table; the centre was filled with a deep violet.

"It is beautiful, isn't it?" Ariel jumped.

"What?" She turned to see Gwendolyn smiling behind her.

"Sorry I was lost in thought; I did not hear you enter. You are back then?"

Gwendolyn gave a nod, somehow, she looked much older and more mature than she had on her last meeting. There was a radiance to her, almost an air of authority, and yet her smile radiated the warmth of the young loving girl Ariel had watched grow into a woman. Gwendolyn came forward and up to her side.

"I heard they had finally let you return to the house, it's about time, your talents are wasted walking round and drawing pictures. Still, it is good that the council have finally seen reason, do you want to go in and have a closer look?" Ariel felt her heart flutter.

"What, no… it's not my place. That is a royal chamber, I would never be allowed in there." Gwendolyn gave a giggle.

"What are you talking about, you are considered family to all of us, I mean Ariel you are almost like a second mother, such is the role you have played in mine and Gwynfor's life. You have more right to walk in that hall than any who bear the seal of this family line, was your mother not the greatest aide to my grandmother and queen in the first days of the Fae of Earth?" She felt a little awkward.

"Well yes, but blood is blood Gwen, I am not of your blood line, and that does make a huge different, plus… Well, it is a little disrespectful to take liberties with the family who raised me, for which I am eternally grateful to, but I know my place in the scheme of things." Gwendolyn gave a large smile.

"You can be silly at times, are we not all the children of the first moon goddess in one form or another? No matter how you look at it, we are all related as we come from her line."

"Well yes I know that, but this is different, there are rules and laws, and well if I am honest, I have had my fill of problems with the rules of this house. I am happy just to be left alone to study my mother's work." Gwendolyn looked surprised.

"You are studying your mother's work? Wow my grandmother has finally seen the light, well I must admit that it is about time." Ariel was now surprised to hear Gwendolyn talk this way; it was not like her to even hint at any disagreements with her grandmother.

"How do you mean about time?" Gwendolyn leant on the door frame opposite and her voice lowered.

"Ariel there are things in those manuscripts no one understands, not even the mighty queen of this realm, your mother was a prolific writer of many things, she saw all sorts of things in the worlds that no one really understands. I always told my grandmother that she used blood runes, but she would not hear of it." For a second Ariel did not quite understand Gwendolyn's point.

"Blood runes, I have never heard of them, what exactly are they?"

"They are the runes of pure love; your father discovered the means to write them and taught your mother. I have talked with Merlin, and he also agrees, that your mother was skilled beyond all the scholars of the Fae, he too agrees that your mother used these runes to write things that only her daughter would be able to transcribe back into Fae for the people of this land, it was one of her gifts did you not know that?"

"I had no idea, but just to be clear we are talking of runes written for a future blood line, not actually written in blood?" Gwendolyn gave a giggle.

"Yes, a blood line, not blood ink. I am surprised you have not come across them in other text, some of the scribes of old knew about them, although they were so dedicated to their positions, they never married and had children, so very few used them. They say your mother wrote many things using them, so those documents must be for your eyes only, and you will only be able to read them at the right moment in time." Ariel leaned off the frame.

"I have never come across them before, although I have not really begun to read the notes of my mother, so I suppose I will not know until I begin. Although, thinking about it, it makes more sense to me now. I thought your grandmother was being a bit cryptic with me the other day, it makes sense she was in a way telling me that the documents would tell me things no other knows."

"We can all be a bit cryptic at times, not sure why, maybe that is something to do with our blood." She gave a slight laugh. "Have you had the tour yet, after all you designed most of this place, it is only right you finally get to see it?" Ariel shook her head.

"Not yet, Bade was supposed to be meeting me to take me round." Gwendolyn gave a sigh.

"If you wait for him, you will wait all year, he is probably debating something very stuffy with the council, he usually is, and time passes without him noticing. There is another one who will never use blood runes." She gave a mischievous chuckle. "Come on I will take you round, it has been ages since we had a long chat, I can fill you in on things as we walk."

*F*or the rest of the day, Gwendolyn gave the full tour of the entire house to Ariel. Most of it came as no surprise as she had designed most of it, but actually seeing it all finished and completed was indeed a great thrill. Gwendolyn has changed so much since Ariel had arrived back, much of it she put down to her time with Merlin. He was a renowned scholar, and it was clear that Bridget had sent Gwendolyn to Avalon for two reasons, the first being to get her out of Florae where she was better protected, the second being the wisdom that Merlin could teach to a future Queen of the Fae.

Gwendolyn was taller, and more mature. The childishness that Ariel remembered in the young girl who ran round the early days of Florae was gone, and in its place was a more thoughtful and serious nature, that gave her a much more authoritative stature. The girlishness of her appearance had faded, and it was clear that Gwendolyn was maturing into a highly attractive woman. Her hair which had been a little past her shoulders when Ariel had first left for Avalon, was now a long mane that flowed down to her waist, and her eyes that shone with bright blue, now sparkled with intelligence and depth, it was clear to see that Gwendolyn now thought on a much deeper level, she was becoming more and more like Bridget.

As they came down the staircase towards the royal apartments as the tour ended, Gwendolyn turned to Ariel.

"I am happy you have been given the role of working on your mother's journal and writings. I am not sure you are aware, but a request has been made from Avalon that you return to continue as Ambassador." Ariel stopped at her side, slightly wrong footed by the sudden remark.

"How can that be?" Gwendolyn gave a smile.

"Rhiannon is no fool Ariel, and neither is Luminaria. Think about it, here they have no control over what you say or write, in Avalon they control everything." Ariel was still trying hard to even comprehend the idea of returning, or even being allowed to return.

"To even consider such a prospect is madness, how could they think I would return after all they have done to destroy Branna?" Gwendolyn gave a smile and shook her head.

"You have to admit, as blatant as their intentions are, the fact they requested you, just goes to show how much they want to stifle whatever it is they think you know?"

"But that is the point, there really is nothing to know, all I did was write reports of the daily goings on there. All of it was common knowledge to everyone in Avalon." Gwendolyn gave a shrug.

"Well, they must think you saw or heard something Ariel, otherwise why would they be so keen for you to return? Rhiannon obviously fears something, and I must admit, as much as I like Rhiannon, for she can be extremely welcoming, I have often wondered why she has tried so hard to control what is allowed from your writings to be seen. I find it all somewhat fascinating, although there is absolutely no hope of our queen ever allowing you back there unprotected, she has made it more than clear, that your future lies here in this realm working on your mother's life's work."

Ariel felt a great sense of relief, for a moment her heartbeat had increased tenfold at just the thought of being there alone without Branna to watch over her.

"I am glad to hear that, I never want to walk there again." Gwendolyn gave a happy nod.

"You have no need to fear, you won't." At the end of the long hallway, Bade appeared, he smiled and waved and then began to walk towards them. Gwendolyn took hold gently of Ariel's arm to hold her back a moment.

"Ariel, now you are back, you will have access to everything you wrote in Avalon. Take my advice and read through it all again, and see if anything you wrote would concern Rhiannon, you know, just to be sure."

There was a look on her face that made Ariel feel a momentary cold shudder run down her spine, but she did not fully understand why Gwendolyn would ask such a thing.

"I can do that, why, do you really think Rhiannon has something other than her treatment of her people like Bran to hide?" Gwendolyn watched as Bade drew closer.

"I have no idea, but when push comes to shove, I trust my grandmother's instincts. No one really understood why she sent you to Avalon, most of us were surprised at her choice of a simple Scribe, and not a political debater. I feel you should remember this Ariel; it was you, an historian out of all the worthy candidates here, you above all others, a simple living Fae with little knowledge of the politics of both races. She had a reason for her choice, and whatever it was that made her chose you, I trust that and that alone. I have given great thought to it, and I think that maybe historians see more of the bigger picture, because they are trained to look deeper than politicians." Bade was ten feet away, Gwendolyn gave a smile.

"Today was nice, I am happy to see you back where you belong, enjoy your time here." She turned on the stair, and began to walk away back up the steps.

"It was fun, and nice to talk, I have missed it." Gwendolyn raised a hand to softly wave.

"We shall talk a lot more, so until then." Bade reached the bottom of the steps as Ariel watched Gwendolyn leave, she then turned and smiled at him.

"Don't tell me, you had a meeting." He looked a little guilty.

"I am sorry, these things come up. I promise I shall make it up to you." Ariel walked down the last few steps.

"It's alright; Gwendolyn accompanied me round the place to give me her view of how things have gone." He looked disappointed and she gave a giggle.

"It is the position, I have to be available at a moment's notice, and you know how it is?" Ariel slipped her arm in his and linked it.

"I most certainly do, come on I am starving, let's go out to the gardens and eat and talk in the daylight."

Chapter Twenty.

Awaiting Fate.

The death of Berengar and Grembald was gratefully received back at the village. The party returned jubilant, and the feeling soon ran rife round the village. Elric led his men to the front of Grembald's long house, and planted a spear into the floor, on which he stuck the blood soaked head of Grembald for all to see. Vulgan limped up to the severed head and smiled to himself, he looked to Elric who bore a grim face.

"You followed your orders without question?" The crowd went silent; Elric swallowed hard in front of Vulgan and gave a soft nod.

"I did." Behind them somewhere in the crowd, came the deep sob of a woman, Elric's eyes moved momentarily onto the crowd where he knew the woman sobbing was Filiberta, the mother of Berengar.

"Berengar fell on the valley edge, near the rapid river." Murmurs rose in the crowd. Vulgan gave a nod to the warriors, and then faced the crowd, his voice clear in the afternoon air.

"Grembald is no more, a new leader will be selected, nominate your choices to Elric, and let the process begin." With no more to say, Vulgan limped back through the crowd towards his house to face his sobbing wife.

Vulgan had hardly entered the house when he was confronted by his two other sons. Vladimir came storming down the house as Otto comforted his weeping mother, Vlad looked angry and red in the face, his long blonde hair flowing behind him like a lion's mane.

"You had him killed? HE WAS YOUR ELDEST SON!" Vulgan was not in the mood.

"HE GAVE ME NO CHOICE!" Vlad looked startled and then exploded.

"NO CHOICE… HOW CAN YOU EVEN SAY THAT, HE WAS LOYAL TO THE TRIBE, HE PROVIDED FOR US WELL ENOUGH, WHAT CHOICE DID YOU GIVE HIM? YOU NEVER EVER GAVE HIM A

CHANCE." Vulgan stared defiantly as he lifted a flagon off the table to pour a goblet with wine.

"I gave him many chances, he was stubborn and chose not to listen, what else could we do, Grembald was taking everything and the tribe were suffering?" Vlad lifted his arms in disbelief.

"Suffering… HOW? We had everything, for the first time in our lives we were safe in our village, our bellies were full and our fields filled with abundance. Look at us father… We want for nothing, our bellies are full and stores are straining, never have we known times of such bounty." Vulgan swallowed his wine and slammed the goblet down on the table.

"Grembald was taking all of it; do you think that was ours?" He shook his head. "That was Grembald's stores; they were his bounty from the levies he asked of all of us. His demands were getting bigger and bigger, and there was nothing else we could give. What else could we do, your brother was his protector, he would not listen to me or any of the others? He had to be stopped." Vlad dropped his arms and his voice lowered.

"By killing your eldest, your heir, and the reason we have such a privileged position in this tribe, am I next because I disagree with you, is that what will happen father, you will kill me then Otto?" Vulgan poured another drink.

"You are being ridiculous; do you think I did this with glee? It is the hardest thing I have been asked to do, I feel no honour in any part of this, but it was necessary to the survival of this tribe." Vlad stared at his father with hatred.

"Necessary, for what, to get your hands on the seat you lost to Grembald, is that what this is all about, clearing a way for you to even the score between you, because this does not sound like a good action for this tribes honour? I would say killing our leader and his second is the most dishonourable thing we have ever done." Vulgan dropped his goblet and lunged at Vladimir, he gripped him tightly round the front of his vest.

"Honour… WHAT DO YOU KNOW OF HONOUR? I HAVE GIVEN MY LEG TO THIS TRIBE TO DEFEND ALL OF YOU, HOW DARE YOU SPEAK TO ME OF HONOUR, I HAVE PAID THE PRICE FOR MY STATUS FOR TEN LIFE TIMES, TELL ME, WHAT HAVE YOU DONE?"

He pushed hard flinging Vlad backwards, his leg may have been damaged but he was still a very powerful and forceful warrior. His eyes burned with rage, as he watched his second born son slide backwards on the dusty floor, crashing into the table as pots and food went flying in every direction.

Vlad lifted himself from the floor; he stood up and wiped the trickle of blood that ran down his cheek, from the side of his eye where a shard of pottery had cut him. His face and eyes held the hatred he felt deep inside, he spat on the floor to clear the taste of blood from his mouth, and looked at his father with greater defiance.

"I have remained true to our bonds as my father taught me. I have honoured my mother, protected my brother, hunted to feed my tribe, and stood tall as a man of truth. I am proud to be a Varisci, loyal to what is right for our prosperity. Tell me father can you say the same?" Vlad looked at Otto.

"I am going to seek the body of my brother, and give him the burial of a loyal Varisci, are you coming?" He lifted his pack off the table and walked over to his mother and embraced her.

"Fear not he will be honoured in death; he deserves nothing less for his protection of us all." Filiberta gave another heavy sob and wept into her cloth, and he released her and turned.

"I am coming with you."

Otto grabbed his pack and walked down the centre of the house, Vulgan stood watching lost momentarily for words, as both his sons passed him without a word, and strode out of the house lifting their bows off the wall as they passed. For long after they had gone, Vulgan did nothing but watch the swinging cloth that covered the door, both of his sons had departed through.

*T*he trail through the valley bottom and past the high rocky outcrops that took Branna into the green pastures of Bohemia, was hard and rough. The caravan bumped on the rough track, which was littered with many fallen stones, and at times Boris had walked up front, holding the horses and guiding them, which made each day's journey longer and harder than either of them expected. The path at times was so narrow that they slept under the van, as there were no open spaces to camp.

Berengar's fight for life was a difficult one, filled with delirium and night terrors. Many times, Branna gave up driving the caravan, to sit in the back with him and try to comfort him, although, most of the time it felt like a pointless exercise, and she used a powerful sleeping draft to help ease his tortured sleep. His language was crude and he spoke of many things about his life, including the horrors he had seen during many of the fights and battles he had endured.

After two long and hard weeks, they finally made it over the wide river and onto the lowlands at the base of the valleys of Bohemia. There was an instant change in Boris as he looked upon his homeland. For the past week he had complained about the wounded warrior that Branna had been attending too, and how he would be glad to be far away when he recovered, as he was convinced that as soon as Berengar woke up, he would kill her and take all her possessions. Branna took little of what he said serious and tried to ignore him, but Roack appeared unhappy with him, and warned Branna to be wary, and yet once in the lower lands of Bohemia, Boris changed and filled with good cheer to walk on his native soil.

The sun was high on the morning when Boris returned from the woodlands, he dropped five rabbits on the ground in front of the steps of the caravan, and watched as Branna attended to Berengar. His face carried a look of concern as Branna turned to look at him, he appeared uneasy, and fidgeted with his belt then looked at the floor. He looked up and she smiled.

"I sense this is our moment of parting?" He looked even more uncomfortable as she put down the damp cloth and wiped her hands on her dress, and then came out of the caravan and down the steps, he did not look at her, but stared at the grass below her.

"I am home, and have a great need to return to those who are my kin." Branna gave a soft smile, as big and as crude as he was; she saw an almost childlike innocence in him.

"It is fine Boris, we both knew this time would come, I am grateful to you for all you have done on our long journey, you have been a good companion. It is time for you to leave, and I wish you well in your life from this day forth." He gave a nod, and looked up into the caravan.

"His fever is lifted?" She nodded.

"I feel he has seen the worst, and shall move back to this side now." Suddenly Boris reached forward and took her hand.

"I have seen men like this many times, you must leave him, there is a town not far from here, take him there and get away from him, he will not thank your kindness." She gave a smile and rested her hand on his.

"Boris, I know what I am doing, I am not powerless you know, I have many things to aide me in this life." He shook his head.

"I have seen the darkness and the light inside you, but this man is all darkness, he has walked with death in his mind for too long. He may have a mama and papa like us all who see him as a son, and love and care for him thinking he is still the boy they love, but you must listen to me when I say he is a devil from the dark path." She gave a small laugh, but also felt his concern, and in a strange way she could see he meant well for her.

He was dirty and unshaven, and this close even she detected his foul odour from weeks on the road with little water, and yet she also saw the kindness in his heart. For all his foul mannerisms and habits which she had endured, she saw that he had a gentleness to his soul.

"I will be fine Boris, and yes I understand the death that surrounds him, but you also forget that I have known many lands and many customs in this world, and I understand the ways of a warrior more than you know. Trust me, this man owes me a life, he will not kill that which he owes, for it will rob him of his honour." Boris rubbed his stubbly chin looking worried.

"I know Varisci, they have no honour, and they are devils in man's skins. I have seen your ways on the road. I know not from where you come, and the strange wild ways they have there, and you may think this dog can be tamed, but you are wrong. Even with your strange ways to me, I know this man will take your life, and it will be a waste to know you walk in the grass no more." Branna lifted her arms and embraced him.

"I will be fine you must trust me in this, now go to your kin and worry no more. He will wake soon, and then he will understand the power I hold within me. He will not take this life as easily as he has others, of this I give you my word." She released him and felt sorry for the wretched look on his face. Finally, he gave a nod.

"I shall think of you often, you are a flower in the world of struggle to me, I will ask the lady who walks the trees to watch over you." She gave a smile.

"Go with a happy heart my friend, and take tidings of me to your kin for I wish them all well in this life." Reluctantly he stepped back towards his rolled up pack. His smile was genuine and he gave a nod, then lifted his pack onto his shoulder. He walked several paces and then turned.

"The darkness surrounds men like that, so be watchful, and stay walking in the light." She gave a small wave.

"I will."

In many ways she had grown accustomed to being around him, it felt like this had been her longest relationship since leaving Avalon, and she had not realised how fond she had grown towards him. Roack flew down from the tree and landed with a thump on the roof of the caravan behind her.

"He cannot be trusted, he will tell many of you, it is dangerous to let him live." Branna stood watching the figure of Boris as he crossed the meadow slowly disappearing into the green that grew into the hillside.

"Leave him alone, he lives because that is what I choose. I was once Fae and we walked in the light as he does. You take me for a fool Roack, I know the path that you have put me on, and I know the darkness into which it will lead me. I chose this path, and soon that man in there will win his fight with death and return to this land, so I will not walk alone on the road you are guiding us on. I feel what you have done to me; I feel the Fae that lived so brightly within me die and your darkness creep throughout my being. He will live in tribute to the small amount of light I have left, and he will remember me always with love as a result. Here in this place of wild beauty, I shall walk my last in the coming days, and you shall have the prize you have searched for, for my warrior will rise into your darkness with me and we will unite to destroy all that Rhiannon holds dear. I will build my kingdom and have my revenge, for the loss of the love I found with Ariel in Avalon."

The dark eyes of the raven sat on the roof glinted, they had thought that they had been so clever, and yet Branna revealed her true power, and proved that she had been aware all along, but this was a good thing.

"So, you will embrace us all once and for all, and truly become the raven we desire?"

"We agreed did we not on the road from Avalon that you would open up the Merle and show me the wonder of its power?" The Raven lifted itself up and bobbed its head.

"We did, and we will, with our powers to aide you, you will rise to power and dominate here in this land, but there is much to know before your warrior arises from his talk with death."

Branna turned and looked at the large black bird sat on the roof slightly above the doorway to the caravan.

"We have time, when he wakes, he will still need time to recover, now is your time Roack, it's time to honour your word, and show me the darkness in which you hide your strength."

*I*n many ways, Roack had underestimated Branna, for a long time they had assumed that they were in control, and dictating the terms of which Branna would be seduced by the power of the Merle. They had made the error of not fully understanding the powers of the Fae, especially the casting of the veil. Branna had realised after the death of Halbrand that she had been unable to prevent Roack from making her kill him, and in that moment, she realised that the bird was trying to take control of her.

Branna felt a deep hatred towards Rhiannon; after all she had suffered a great deal, and knew that her parents who were still prisoners on the realm of the moon would continue to suffer. As she walked away from the body of Halbrand and over the coming days, she used the veil to not only shield her from Avalon, but also to shield some of her thoughts from Roack. With her privacy restored, she had time to think about her situation. The power of the Merle was trying to seduce her, but she chose to fight it and not surrender completely to it, as she tried to figure out how she could gain the upper hand and control the force that was growing stronger within her. As a member of the Fae, she was powerful, but she was no fool and understood that she could use the power of the Merle to enhance her skills, and make herself far more powerful than anyone would ever suspect.

During her time in Hispanica as she learned more and more of the power of the Merle, she used her Fae power to gain control over the invading darkness, and through her control of the darkness, she was able to balance out the powers and stay in control of everything. Roack had no idea, and she was not about to fill the bird in. Branna knew that her destiny lay further ahead, and all she needed was the opportunity to present itself, which it did the day she dragged Berengar out of the water.

Up until that moment she had thought that maybe her best chance would have been to try and corrupt Ariel to join her, and then together they would build an empire to match that of Rhiannon, but the sight of Berengar changed all that. Here was a man tortured by betrayal, something she understood better than any, this was her chance, as he appeared to be a man of great power, and he was also from the race of men, something she knew she would if required be able to control. In the week alone in the caravan as she nursed him back to life, Branna knew her moment to rise had arrived, all she needed now was to get this warrior to full health, and learn as much as she could of the power contained within the Merle, and then finally she would have the means to strike at the heart of Avalon.

Chapter Twenty One.

Pact In Darkness.

*E*ven back in the oldest times, Bohemia was rural, and travelling through it, there was a feeling it would change little as the years progressed. The people were kind, gentle, and simple living; they worked the land and crafted all they would ever require from the world that surrounded them.

The country was beautiful, filled with valleys of lush green pastures and forests of evergreen mixed with deciduous trees. Wild flowers decorated every corner, and ran alongside the lanes and in deep drifts across fields, and for Branna, who had travelled far since she had left Avalon, it came across as being paradise, and she felt a stirring within her to linger and enjoy the ease of pace.

It was late spring, and Berengar had fought through his fever and was finally awake after burning with delirium for almost two weeks. Branna pulled in on the edge of a large village, into a pasture near by a fast flowing river. There was a plentiful supply of wood for the stove, and she found an abundance of rabbits and wild fruits and leaves she could stew for food.

Roack appeared pleased with the place, as there was an abundance of small creatures that could be caught and devoured. Branna hunted daily for fresh meat, which she would stew in her large pot and then strain off the herb laden meaty gravy and try to get her wounded warrior to drink. It was never an easy task as he was so heavy, even if he had not had a solid meal in weeks, she washed his wound and treated it with a thick paste of herbs to help speed up the healing, and even though he still slept in his state of darkness, it was clear his body was recovering, albeit at a slow pace.

To Branna it was clear that he had to fight from within his soul, and that was clouded by darkness, which was the reason his healing was not as fast as it could be. She could sense deep within him the rage that burned, and for a warrior of his size, she knew that it would be the fight that lived inside him that brought him back from death into a new world that she was going to create for him.

Deep inside at the heart of Branna, she also knew that her fight to conquer the Merle and control the force with Fae powers had won. She did feel stronger and more powerful, and in the long wait for Berengar to recover, she began to play with her thoughts as to how she could achieve her goals and build an empire that she would rule. Roack watched one afternoon as she sat outside the caravan and focused her mind on a rock that was lay in the grass. The bird was impressed as it observed Branna make the rock move and vibrate with her mind, its gruff voice echoed in her mind.

"We have not seen this power of your people before." Branna stared at the stone as it vibrated and then the edges crumbled away forming a perfectly square block, she turned to see the raven sat on the roof of the caravan.

"My father worked the mines, he taught us this as children as a sort of game. I was always better at it than my brother, it is a skill of our people and is the reason we can tunnel and mine better than any other race." The raven bobbed on the spot.

"It is good you keep yourself amused, but it has little use for our coming task." Branna gave a chuckle.

"It has far greater use than you realise, but I am glad my games have amused you, when the time is right, then you shall see why this skill of my line will be of great aide." The black bird still appeared unimpressed.

"You can play with the earth until your warrior awakens; we feel he will come back to this side soon." Branna looked to the open door of the caravan, where inside Berengar still fought for his life.

"I feel he is winning his fight also." She got up off the grass. "It is good to see him grow stronger, I will have need of his knowledge and the source of his hatred, if we are to win him over and use him for our needs."

Roack was right, and a few days later his temperature dropped and his sleep eased away from the night terrors and became more restful. Branna knew it would not be long before his fight was over and he returned back to the land of the living, and so she stayed closer to the caravan each day as her expectations rose.

Berengar was at first startled as he woke, but as he tried to sit, the searing pain from his insides soon convinced him to stay as he was and lie back and relax. He spoke Sachsen, and yet one of the gifts of the Fae Ofmoon was to understand all tongues, and so soon Branna sat and offered him a meal, and told him of how she discovered him lying half dead by the river, and had dragged him up to the caravan, and given him the aid he would need to recover.

Berengar had no choice but to respectfully thank her, under the rule of his tribe, he owed his life to her, and it was a debt he could only pay off by saving hers. Branna was a skilled warrior, as he saw by the weapons she carried, and he knew that for now, he belonged to her until such time as he could recover the strength to find a way to pay back the life he owed her.

"I owe you a life Branna, your kindness and care will not be without reward, I am in your debt, and shall see it repaid." Branna smiled as she handed him yet another bowl of the broth she had made.

"I need no payment; I have all I need right here." He looked down at the wound that was bandaged heavily.

"Did you use sorcery to heal me; I have known many that have died from such wounds?"

"I have talents you will not find in others from these parts, for I am not from this place. I have my own reasons for lifting you off the side of the road. I feel your apprehension, but you have no need to fear the unknown of how you were cured, in time you will see that."

*A*s the weeks moved forward, what began as mistrust grew into dependence. The wound took a long time to heal, and as frustrated as Berengar felt, he had no choice but to accept his fate as he slowly recovered his strength. over the time of his healing, he grew a fondness for the straight talking, hard edged member of the Fae.

One night as he sat in front of the caravan next to the fire, having eaten a good solid meal and drunk a few large tankards of ale, something Branna had traded in the village for medicines, he slowly began to feel a sense of trust.

Finally, after many weeks of silence, he told Branna his story of how he had been betrayed by his own people and left for dead. Branna listened quietly, and when he had finished, she took a long taste of her ale and thought for a moment, before lifting her head to meet the fixed stare of Berengar.

"The way I see it, you must return and recover the strength you once held by making an example of all of those in the town that betrayed you. Grembald was leader, and you were a loyal warrior in his service, but you were also in service to the people of the town whom you protected. They betrayed you my friend, they must pay for their lack of trust in you. I would say grow to full strength and return, and take your anger out on those who deserve it." Berengar shook his head.

"It is of no use, I am but one man against a whole tribe, I can best most men, but alone against the Varisci, I will not prevail." Branna gave a smile.

"But you are not alone you have me." Berengar gave the first mighty laugh he had since he had awoken in the caravan, he slapped hard at his thigh as his bald head shone in the firelight, and his cheeks lifted to reveal the whiteness of his teeth. Branna did not at first understand the joke.

"You are a mightily fine woman Branna, such as I have never met before, but forgive me, for as much as I have learned about you, I fear that even for a woman of such skill with a sword and long bow, we would not last long against the tribesmen of my region. I truly am grateful for your kindness and offer of assistance."

He smiled and she felt his attraction, for there was a glee mixed in with the formidable intensity of the fighter that radiated out, and she found it very alluring. Branna leaned forward and crawled slowly across to the sitting figure of the warrior.

"It appears amusing, and that is a good thing, for neither you nor your people are aware of the things I have learned in my life. None know of the powers I hold, and terrors I can unleash, for there in that plain looking caravan I have the means to wipe out all the Varisci and their enemies at once." She lifted a hand and touched his cheek, her dark eyes twinkling with malice as his stared deep into hers.

"Berengar if you swear here to me now that you will give me your loyalty, I can assure you that with me at your side, the tribe will fall to their knees and beg for your pardon. From that moment you shall rule as no king ever has. Give yourself to me, and the world of men will kneel at your feet and whimper like the wounded animals they are." His smile faded as he looked into the depths of her dark black eyes.

"Do not mock me woman, for you know I would hand over my soul for such a thing." She smiled.

"Then join your soul to mine, and I will show you how to do it."

Roack watched from high in the trees and felt a pulse ripple through the darkness, almost as if Branna had meant for the raven to pay more attention, and her soft voice echoed into the mind of the bird.

"It is time."

*F*or ten years Branna had travelled and seen as much of the world as she felt she had wanted. Through all of her travels she had delved deeper and deeper into the darkness that surrounded the world, and had been overwhelmed by its power and force. In the process of mastering the force of darkness, she had pushed her body to the limits, and as a result she had grown strong and powerful. Her lust for the excesses of life grew more intense, and although she could best most men in combat and drinking, her one desire was to meet a man who would match her lust and desire for power.

As she rested on her knees before Berengar, she knew she had met the one man who shared the lust that ate at her insides. His eyes betrayed him as she looked deep into his soul, and saw the chaos at the heart of him, his desire for revenge was strong, and within that she knew she could see that finally she had met an equal.

*T*hat night as she lay with him and tore at his skin, bit him, and kissed him, she felt the raw power of this man of the Varisci as he pounded into her, and she knew her search for something powerful, and a place in this world where she was an equal, was within the arms of this powerful warrior. After three hours of passion, as he lay in the grass with sweat on his brow, she summoned the Merle to reach down and touch her, and as it did, she took the tail feather of a mature raven, and plunged it deeply into his chest.

Berengar flinched at the pain as she straddled his groin, and her eyes sparkled like gems in the darkness, slowly she gyrated her hips pressing into his manhood.

"Again…Take me again and join with me." She pulled the feather out of the red flowing wound on his chest as he began to rise slowly inside her, her breath gave a gasp.

"Yesss!"

She leaned forward over his chest as her eyes began to flicker, and above her the clouds began to form and thicken as the stars were snuffed out by them. Berengar felt the power of the moment as she began to slide her hips back and forth, feeling him deep within her, he felt his blood pumping through his body as Branna who was lost to a state of what he thought was pure ecstasy writhed and moaned above him.

She brought down the tip of the feather dipped in blood, and scratched on his chest a runic symbol, and high above the lightning flared across the sky. Berengar felt the power surge through him, and bucked his hips upwards and Branna screamed with delight, as she thrust the feather down again and scribed another symbol on to her, and slammed her hips even harder down onto him. The sky above exploded with light, and within seconds the rumble exploded out of the sky in a deafening roar.

Berengar felt the joy, the pain, the lust and clenched his teeth as his hips and back lifted off the floor slamming into Branna, who screamed with wild abandon and pleasure. Never in his life had he known such a feeling as powerful as the pleasure coursing through his body, he lifted his hands and locked onto her firm white breasts, as he pushed even harder to match the force of her, as she slid onto him again and again with powerful thrusts from her pelvis.

They were thrusting harder and fast, and he felt the power in his body building as Branna looked down at him and screamed at him.

"Give yourself to me, join with me, share the darkness I hold in me and be by me always, and I shall grant you the power of life and death to use as you wish."

The heavens opened with another brilliant and blinding flash of light, and yet more power surged through him, as he bucked and slammed faster and faster gasping for air yet driven by a force of power he had never known. He felt the surge of power growing more and more, and the pressure inside him was building as Branna wailed into the sky with joy and the rain pounded down from the sky onto them. He could hardly see, as the water ran into his eyes and all he could down was wail back to her with ecstasy.

"Take me I am yours, take me, use me for I am yours and my life is yours to use as you will."

There was a massive crack in the sky as Branna's wild hair blew sparkling with rain around her face, she slammed forward as the streak of light came out of the clouds and hit her right in the back, it came through her rain soaked chest, between his hands and hit him square on the forehead, and she wailed with delight and went rigided. A huge jolt lifted his body, and he felt the moment arrive, and exploded inside her as his body went taught and his legs and arms shook with spasms.

Branna leaned right back and wailed with pleasure, as her body matched his and stiffened, and as he looked up, the sky exploded as she jerked in spasm, and lit up revealing the outline of a huge black bird, and then with a wail and a gasp, Branna fell forward with a smile onto his rain covered shoulder, and gave a long satisfied gasp of delight.

"It is done."

*A*cross the lands and far away, Bridget screamed into Malcolm as he held her tight, and Ariel woke with a start her body hot and sweating as she felt a burning tingle that ran from her stomach to her labia. She sat up rapidly as the candle flickered and looked down at her naked body and saw and felt the tingles, revealing the large wet patch on the bed, and gasped.

"What was that, was it a dream?" She looked round realising it was her own bed and took a long breath to calm down as her body tingled and pulsated. Breathing in and out to recover her composure she swung her wobbly legs over the edge of the bed and sat for a moment as she tried to clear her thoughts.

"Was I dreaming again about you Bran?"

She was not sure, the dream was vague in her mind, all she could remember was a storm and rain and the feelings that her body was being touched and pleasured, it felt as real as anything, and that could not be so, as she was alone in Florae. She reached for the small pot cup and took a sip of cool water, as she tried to focus her thoughts and then as she reached back to place the cup on the small table, she noticed a slight movement and looked up.

Her heart almost exploded as just for a second there was Branna, pale and tired looking, but smiling. Her voice felt like it was a million miles away.

"I have not left you, I have not forgotten, be patient the time is coming when we will unite again." Ariel gave a gasp as tears flooded into her eyes.

"Take me now, Bran I miss you."

She blinked and Branna was gone and the room was empty, and

her heart was pounding as she looked to the closed window unable to fully understand what had happened. Ariel sat motionless staring into space across her darkened empty room, and yet deep inside she felt a warmth growing as the seed of hope, which had felt like it had died within her, began to grow again.

Chapter Twenty Two.

Strong Connections.

*B*ranna woke curled around the large muscular frame of
Berengar, she lifted her head and stroked the mass of black hair away
from her face and then screwed up her eyes, as the sun beat down
blinding her. It was almost midday, and they had slept out by the fire
under the blankets. She slipped out from the blankets, and stood up
and looked round the site, there was no sign of Roack, just a quiet
empty camp bathed in glorious sunshine, with the hum of bees, and
the gentle chirps of the other birds in the trees.

Her throat felt dry and sore, as she walked over to the side of the
caravan, and lifted the lid on the barrel attached to its side. She took
the ladle off the hook and dipped it into the cool water, and then lifted
it to her hot dry lips. Berengar was still asleep, and she gave a smile
as she swallowed the cool liquid and watched him, and the memory
of the previous night returned to her mind. No man had ever had the
stamina or means to satisfy her as he had last night, and she knew that
she had made the right choice for her future companion.

Branna felt sticky and looked down to her upper legs, which
bore large red and blue bruises from the power of their copulation,
she scooped another ladle of water and poured it slowly down her
stomach and over her sex, she shuddered with the cold and the
sensitivity, amazed by the feeling that ran through her body. She
had read many books on the sex magic of the Fae, but she had never
thought it would make her feel as alive inside as it did whilst she was
washing herself off.

*T*he following hour was spent naked in the sunlight, as she
busied herself by lighting the fire and boiling a pot for her tea, as she
prepared thin slices of meat to cook for their first meal of this new
day. By the time Berengar woke, she was sat by the fire sipping tea as
the meat sizzled in the pan, he sat up and yawned and then stretched

out his arms loosening his limbs, she smiled.

"Good day, how do you feel?" She handed him a plate filled with the cooked sliced meats and a fork. He took it with a smile.

"I have a hunger." She gave a slight chuckle.

"I would think so after the appetite you worked up last night." He gave a nod as he chewed.

"You are without doubt, a woman of many talents Branna, I have never known a woman who could best me in such a way that I feel so alive." He lifted his tea and took a long swig to wash down his food. "Long have I yearned for a wife who could match me in all that I do." Branna stood up with the empty pitcher to go and fill it.

"I am not your wife Beren, we bonded in a sacred ritual, we share the same path and will walk it side by side, but I have no claim on you or you me. Last night we joined as one soul, for our destiny is paired with the same goal and together we will take everything that is rightfully ours, for we will need each other in order to do that." She walked to the caravan to fill the jug as he sat watching her whilst he ate his food, as she turned, he saw the bruises on her hips and thighs and stopped chewing.

"I hurt you." Branna shook her head as she looked down.

"No…Both of us bear the marks of our union, but there is no pain, the power that now flows between us will heal us both and give us greater strength than we have ever known, just watch how that wound on your side starts to heal faster now you are joined to me." He looked down at the long red scar where Branna had sown his side back.

"I need to gain more strength, if this heals faster that is a good thing, for a day will come when I face those who took my right as a Varisci away, and aim for them to pay for it." She gave a gentle nod as she sat back at the fire and filled the pan for more tea.

"That will come in good time, but first I have preparations to make. Take this time to lift up your weapons again and rebuild your body to the ways of a warrior, the time is coming my lover, be patient for just a little while longer."

Ariel sat staring into space at her desk, a parchment held loosely in her hand, Bade leaned over and looked at her.

"Did you even hear a word I said?" She came out of her thoughts and dropped the parchment back to the table, and turned to him.

"What! Sorry I am finding it hard to concentrate." He gave a slight frown.

"Are you alright, you have hardly heard a word I have spoken today." She sat back and smiled.

"Honestly I am fine, I just have things on my mind today, I don't mean to be rude." Bade knew that expression and that dreamy air, he had seen it many times since her return from Avalon.

"Got Bran on your mind again have you, it seems to me that you go through these phases?"

"I saw her last night in my room." He looked shocked.

"What?" He moved closer, and then looked around as he lowered his voice. "She was here, she came back?" Ariel shook her head.

"No…Honest I am having trouble understanding it…I mean I saw her, but I am not sure if it was a dream or just wishful thinking." He gave a slight sigh of relief.

"So it was a vision?" She looked at him in a curious way.

"How do you mean vision?" He shrugged as he sat back in his seat.

"Well, you know…Considering who you are…I would think it is not really too surprising." Ariel did not quite understand.

"What do you mean considering, and who I am?"

"Well…I think…Look you were very much in love with Bran when you came back here, so the way I see it you have a very deep bond with her, and then if you consider that your mother just happens to be one of the most powerful mystics our race has ever produced, well I just naturally thought that you would have some of her gifts. I am not at all surprised to know you had a vision, to be honest I am a little surprised it has taken so long."

It was actually something Ariel had never in her life considered, she looked at the parchment on the desk that had been written by her mother and lifted it up, her voice was quiet and reflective as she thought about it.

"I always thought I was just good at reading and writing runes like my dad, I have never considered my mother's gifts." Bade watched her expression as she read the runes on the page.

"It probably may sound a little odd, but since you were allowed back into the house, all you have done is work on your mother's writings. I don't suppose you have ever considered that within these pages are the keys to awakening all your talents, you know, like your mother hid them and these words are secretly the key to your powers coming to the surface. I have to admit I have thought about it, and wondered why Bridget felt it was so important for you alone to do this work." Ariel stared at the parchment as she thought, her thoughts slipped out of her lips.

"Mother's writing…Awakening, Bridget did say something about it being important to a future queen, and also that I was the only person who could ever have been ambassador to Avalon, no other could have been as successful as I was." Bade leaned over and gave her a soft pat on the shoulder.

"I think I will leave you to ponder, thanks for having lunch with me, I enjoyed it even if you did not hear a word of it." He smiled as he stood up and gathered his things off the desk.

"I would say I would leave you to your thoughts, but as has been the case for the last hour, I am abundantly aware that you would not hear that either." He chuckled and turned and left her alone to think about things. Ariel stared at the parchment.

"What are you telling me Mother?"

Deep down below the earth in the heart of the newly built Avalon, Rhiannon paced the room as the grey haired mystic Sequana peered into a wide silver basin and watched the foggy pictures flow in the water. Rhiannon gave a sigh as the worried look on her face intensified; her impatience was apparent.

"Well! What do you see?"

Sequana lifted a hand adorned with bright glittering stones, and swept it across the surface of the water, and mists swirled up out of it, her voice was eerie and echoed around the room from her trance like state.

"Darkness swirls hidden from the light, there is brightness like the moon goddess captive at its heart. In the east a light once extinguished is starting to flow again, the lines of the past will return in new faces." Rhiannon looked horrified.

"That is not possible, Enaria is no more." Sequana lifted her head and her eyes that were white rolled and her bright blue pupils reappeared.

"I only report what the basin shows, and it shows the light of the past returning." Rhiannon paced more aggressively.

"If Luminaria had done her job properly, we would not have this problem." She looked at Sequana. "I cannot have her loyalty blinded by those in Florae, I want that scribe here where we can control her words." Sequana sat back in her chair.

"My daughter has a good heart, she is a truth seeker, it is why you instructed her for this task, have no fear she is loyal to you, even if the truth revealed you were wrong to accuse the girl of light, my daughter will not falter in the defence of her queen." Rhiannon stared at Sequana.

"She better not, I have called for her to find out what she has learned of late, after the disturbance we felt last night, I want to know what she is doing about it." Rhiannon turned towards the door.

"Stay focused and watch all that happens, I want every detail as and when it happens." She walked at pace towards the door, marched through and it slammed as she exited, Sequana looked back to her basin.

"My teacher, how is this possible that even though your daughter is bound from her power, somehow you still shine with such radiance from her, what task did you set her upon on that fateful day of your parting with her?"

*B*ranna walked down through the trees with her basket and her pail towards the river, she smiled as she sensed the surroundings.

"You are quiet today, are you not happy with the ritual?" There was no answer, and yet she knew the large black bird was hidden from view and watching her.

"Are you sulking, did something displease you?" The harsh croak echoed into her mind.

"You lied." She gave a chuckle as she reached the water's edge.

"Why, because I made him mine and not yours?"

She bent down and lowered the pail to fill with fresh water to refill the barrel, Roack did not respond. Branna filled the pail and then set it down on the bank, she slipped her long dress over her head and walked out into the water to where it got deeper. The ice cold water tingled over her hot bruised parts, and it felt wonderful.

"I did not think something as powerful as the Merle would sulk like a child." The bird flew down from one of the trees, and landed on the edge of the pail as Branna lowered herself into the deeper water and tilted her head back to wash her hair.

"You promised us more, and yet took him for yourself, we did not agree to that."

Branna gave a giggle, the more time she has spent trying to

understand the ways of this dark force the more she learned, and today she could see how it was capable of acting like a jealous child, and it amused her.

"You want me to gain more power so that I can bring more of you here, and yet the moment I do just that, you sulk like a child. Can you not see how strong I have grown since the ritual? You say you have great understanding, and yet you have failed in all of your observations for years to understand the most basic thing of all our lines, you amuse me."

"Tell us of this basic thing you speak of."

Branna slipped under the cold water and felt her whole body come to life. She came back to the surface and shook her head with a gasp, as the water sprayed out from her long mane of hair rippling the water around her.

"I need companionship of another and I also need extra protection. Like you there are many, for myself, bonding with Beren allows me the security of knowing I have the power to protect not just myself, but also you. This man will serve me with the ultimate loyalty until his end, never will I be vulnerable again alone in the wilds. Even though I have you, there will be times when I want to be satisfied by the touch of just one, I had that remember, but you hated her, well now I have another who is as dark as you and I."

The Raven sat still as it listened to her, then dropped to the floor and pecked at the earth, drawing a long pink worm from the soil, it flicked it up and into its beak and swallowed it.

"How is this joining and rubbing of bodies making you satisfied, you have had many like that, what makes this one so different?" Branna smiled.

"You felt my body last night, you felt the purity of the pleasure, lust and desire, and how it enhanced my inner self, you feel it today as you probe my mind. Sex with this man is different, you never felt what I had with Ariel, and yes there has been many since her, but she touched me inside in a way I never thought was possible until last night with Beren. Sex is powerful, it can enhance the body and the soul, especially with those who reach inside you, and you never know until they touch you just how it will feel. You yearn for it to be that special, and at times it is, but not always, the more I have bedded the greater the understanding of my need has been, and last night I understood what I needed as I joined with him. Believe in me Roack,

I did not lie, I need this man with us, his strength is also mine for the taking now."

"This we now understand, but you should have asked us before you took him from us."

Branna stood up in the water and chuckled, it amused her how easy it was to offend the bird.

"As you take the worm to live, I will take what I need to live, never think I will ask you first, if I need it, I will have it, understand that here and now Roack." The bird bobbed on the bank.

"FINE!!" It opened its wings and lifted into the air, Branna stood waist deep in the water and chuckled.

Chapter Twenty Three.

The Jar Of Branna.

Roack, had realised that Branna had used her Fae powers to slowly mix with the Merle inside her, and as a result she had been able to manipulate and control most of her own will, and had fooled the Merle into thinking it was in control. Taking the man for herself and not offering him to them had irritated them, regardless of her explanation.

Roack was still unhappy and had stayed high in a large tree away from the caravan unable to work out what was to happen next. It was clear Branna was in control and had a plan, and Roack was curious as it looked down on her washing out a large glass bottle and then cutting a wooden bung for the top of it. Roack whispered inside its own mind.

"What is she doing, what does she want from us, now she controls her own power, will she kill us, will she use us, can we fight her?"

Branna continued to work as Berengar, who had been drained of his strength during the ritual was still recovering albeit at a faster rate, was resting inside the caravan out of the heat of the day.

When Branna was happy the bung fitted with an air tight seal, she lifted the jar and walked off into the trees heading in the direction of the river. Roack had to know what was happening, and decided to leave the safety of the tree and fly quietly behind her, muttering inside its head all the time, asking question after question.

It took Branna an hour to find her spot, high up the path next to a tall waterfall, where there was a wide smooth, flat ledge. Placing the large jar down, she looked out on a clear view of the western horizon. Roack swooped in silently behind her and landed higher up the rock face, and looked down on her. Branna stood still watching as the sun began to lower towards the horizon, and smiled.

"I know you are there Roack, I feel you like I never have before since the ritual. Whisper all you like to yourself, or the others, or whatever you are, the oneness of Merle, you cannot undo my powers and control me as your puppet as you thought you were. I control everything now, and it is time you understood that you now serve me. It is time we both understood each other better, and we both stop this battle of wits or else I shall have no other choice but to release you back into the blackness of that empty place in which you exist, and you can seek another to try and control."

Roack's head bobbed; in her mind she felt the feelings of rage in the bird. *"You cheated us; it was not what we agreed."* Branna gave a chuckle.

"Sulk all you like, our agreement was not that you controlled me, we agreed to share the power and exist together, and I have not broken that pact we swore, indeed it is why we are here as the sun falls. I have a request of you." The bird flapped its wings.

"We do not do deals with those who wish to control us." Branna turned and looked up at the bird high up on the rock.

"Neither do I. Roack you communicate with me through thought, but what would you say if I told you my people have a way of bonding with animals, a way which allows you a voice, and a way that would allow you the freedom to think for yourself? I can take your mass and divide it amongst many, and so more and more of you can live a free life and experience the human life style. The Fae Ofmoon have hidden talents known only to themselves, and I am sure even with your long watch, even a power as mighty as the Merle has never seen the truth of those powers. This and only this ritual alone will also give the vehicle you use, be it bird, fox or human, a life ten times longer than any in this realm. The bird you live in will soon die and you will be cast out of that shell, let me make it live again and again to keep you and others here as you are now." Roack flew down to the rock floor and walked about in front of her feet.

"We can be many?"

"Yes, and you will live for far longer than everything else." The bird bobbed around on the floor.

"We would want that, we would have wanted that, but we are one, we cannot be split into many."

Branna looked at the bird, her dark eyes glistening in the last of the sunlight.

"I know how I can take parts of you and make you live as one as I did in Avalon, I can bind your life to mine, and show others how to bind their lives to those we will take for our community. Roack you can be a single entity within all of the Merle." Branna knelt down in front of the bird.

"Roack you will be free and share my life, think of what that would be like, one Roack, just one, a darkened free spirit who chooses the life she lives." The bird stopped moving, and stared at her with dark eyes.

"We would want that."

"Then tie your life to mine, and bind with me as Berengar has, and fulfil the pact we swore to each other in Avalon." The bird tapped its feet on the floor, and then turned and pecked the large glass jar. In her mind Branna felt the distrust of Roack.

"What is this thing for, and why do you want it here? We will not go in another like we did before."

Branna gave a smile, and remembered that first night in Avalon when she managed to capture the black mist that entered the bird that became Roack.

"It is not for you; I want it for your friends."

"We has no friends, we are one." Branna nodded.

"At the moment yes, I want you to join with me, and then we shall draw down more of you and divide it into portions like you did the night you came to me. I will need to store them in this until we reach the place that your kind will inhabit, there will be souls a plenty for you to guide your friends into I promise." The bird shook its wings, and then pecked at the jar again.

"This will not hold us; we can pass through all in this realm." Branna agreed, she had seen with her own eyes, how Roack had slipped through her glass container.

"That is why I need you; you must let the others know to remain inside this, until I can take you to the place where you will all be free to choose your vessels. Roack trust me, this is the only way your kind can live in this realm, I really am trying to help you all. Join with me and let your kind be free and join with others, be Roack the raven, free of the rest to live as one."

"We would want that and agree with you Branna the Raven." Branna gave a smile.

"Good, the night is drawing near and I must prepare."

*R*hiannon sat in her seat as Luminaria walked up the chamber and knelt before her. "You requested my presence My Queen?"

Rhiannon smirked, and looked at all the officials and guards.

"Leave us." Luminaria remained on her knees with her head down as was custom in the chamber of Rhiannon, all the others in the long room of walls that were white with rich violet seams, turned and walked to the nearest door, of which there were many.

After a few moments, Rhiannon rose from her seat and stood on the front of the small platform, and looked down the three steps at her commander of all the Marshals of Avalon.

"Rise to your feet and face me." Luminaria swallowed hard.

"My Queen it is forbidden to stand before the Queen of Fae Ofmoon." Rhiannon smirked.

"Never the less I have given you a command, as is my right as your queen, so stand before me as requested."

"Yes, My Queen." Luminaria stood up, and her gaze saw Rhiannon literally a few feet above her on the step, Rhiannon gazed down with a curious expression on her face, her voice was lower and softer.

"Tell me Luminaria, do you fear me?" Again, Luminaria swallowed hard and felt the tremble in her right leg.

"I do My Queen, for there is no other more powerful, and I am just one of many of your race and lower position." Rhiannon smirked impressed with her honesty.

"Tell me; are you loyal to your queen?" For the first time ever, Luminaria looked up with shock, and her eyes met with Rhiannon's.

"I am My Queen; I have lived my life to serve you in a position of great privilege that I dreamed of as a child. I am grateful every day that you alone gave me the position, which I have tried to show in my duty to your service every day since being awarded Commander of all the guards." Rhiannon gave a nod of recognition.

"I cannot deny, you have been outstanding in all of your duties bar one."

"One My Queen, pray tell me what I must do to correct my failure to you?" Rhiannon walked slowly down the three steps to her side, and turned her head to look at Luminaria who still faced forward.

"You know the one, the child tucked up safely with Bridget, why is she not here?" Luminaria felt the fear grow again inside her, and her heart rate quickened.

"I have tried My Queen, but Queen Bridget will not release her to our custody without more evidence." Rhiannon took several paces forward and turned to face Luminaria's back, she noted the slight tremble in her leg.

"I have told you that it was Ariel that brought down the Merle into this realm, this is my realm and I know everything that happens within it, this you know, why have you not expressed this directly to Queen Bridget."

"My Queen, I have to converse with Master Elgin, he is the only member of his people who has direct contact with Queen Bridget, and he has been quite clear that because of who the mother of Ariel was, Queen Bridget cannot and will not release her, they say it is impossible for a child of light as she is to do such a dark thing." Rhiannon gave a sigh.

"Even though your queen has told you otherwise, who do you believe their queen or your own?"

Luminaria knew she was in an impossible position, and she had no idea how she was going to answer to it. Rhiannon walked round in front of her and looked her right in the eyes. Luminaria felt the sweat building in her hair close to her scalp.

"Commander, you are either loyal to them, or loyal to me. I want Ariel here in our care, no, I demand she is brought before me, you say you are loyal, then prove it, get me Ariel." Luminaria bowed low.

"Yes, my Queen." Rhiannon smirked and flicked her wrist.

"Then go, and this time do not return alone."

Luminaria turned and walked down the hall staring at the door as beads of sweat ran down the sides of her face. She walked as quickly as was possible in the presence of the queen, her only goal was to get out as fast as she could. She approached the door, grabbed the handle, opened it, and slid through. Pulling it closed behind her, as she heard the lock meet with the frame, she gave an exhausted gasp, lent back on the door and closed her eyes with relief, and breathed in yet more air as her legs trembled more violently.

For a few long moments she remained where she was with her eyes closed, and regulated her breathing, for several long minutes she had held her breath before the queen, and her lungs had felt like they would explode. Once her breathing became more even, she opened her eyes to see the guard by the other door watching her, his face looked white.

"How bad was it Commander?" She regained her composure a little, and walked towards him.

"Whatever you thought it was, times it by one hundred, and then add more." He looked scared.

"Shit!" Luminaria walked past him.

"Language Corporal." He snapped to attention.

"Yes! Sorry Commander!" She smiled as she walked down the long tunnel back to her quarters to pack for yet another long trip to Florae.

Alone on the smooth flat surface of rock above the waterfall, Branna used her black book to recreate the ritual she had done on that stormy night in Avalon, when she had drawn down Roack from the Merle. Having the large black bird assist made it so much easier as she no longer required the use of a ten foot copper rod.

Her skill at creating a larger and more powerful veil to hide her and the surrounding area had grown tenfold, and as she chanted, she expanded the veil to cover the whole area, including the caravan in which Berengar was now sleeping. The black clouds swirled into the sky as the last of the sunset on a clear sky was blotted out, and the thunder began again.

High above the shape of a large black bird was silhouetted against the lightning, and with each bright strike, a puff of a smoke like mist fell from below Roack into the open jar. Branna chanted as the large smoky objects swirled within the container, and then opening her eyes that blazed red, she spoke out loud in a tongue not heard in the realm of men before. As the smoke flowed round the inside of the jar, Branna chanted out her command, and suddenly like the snapping of a twig, the puffs of mist separated into hundreds of tiny parts of the Merle.

Branna gave a gasp of air and sat back as the mists swirled round and round, she lifted the wooden bung off the floor and placed it into the top of the large jar, with a tap to ensure it stayed snug. She smiled knowing the jar was just for show, Roack flew down and landed at her side and inspected the jar.

"We all shall stay where you have placed us, none will leave until we hear you command it."

Branna gave a satisfied nod at the bird.

"Thank you, behold my friend, these will create all of your companions, now do me a favour, stop using your mind and use your beak, for believe it or not, you now have the power of speech." Roack looked at her for a second and her beak clicked, Branna gave a giggle.

"It will not come easily, you will have to practice, find the place that squawks inside you, and use the words you think to make them work."

The bird bobbed up and down.

"How?" Branna gave a huge smile as she heard the rough croaked voice of Roack for the first time.

"Just like that." She was not sure if it was possible, but she was sure that the bird actually looked shocked.

"We…Likes…This." She giggled.

"No, you like it, you are free of the rest of the Merle, you can connect to it whenever you want to, but you are now Roack the Raven, the individual, you are now what all life in this realm and the other realms have, you are a single entity under your own control of your own thoughts. You should say I can, I will, I think, because anything that crosses your mind now is exactly that, it's your own private thought." The bird bobbed around on the floor rapidly, it was clear Roack was happy, and yet she still spoke into Branna's mind.

"We will practice, we need time… No, I will practice, and need time to master this gift, I am grateful to the Raven Branna." She smiled.

"I am happy to hear it, now come on it is getting dark, and carrying your friends back safely is important, so you will have to guide me so I do not drop them."

Back in Florae Bridget Violet clung to her husband Malcolm and shook with fear, as another night terror had invaded her mind and pulled at her insides. She had awoken in a sweat feeling sick and violently retching, before he had been awoken at her side and grabbed her into his embrace.

"Why will you not tell me what is causing this Bridge my love, please again I beg of you, let me help you defeat these nights of terror, we cannot go on like this, why hide the truth from me?" She relaxed in his arms as the feeling subsided and he gave a sigh of relief, she turned and looked into his worried eyes.

"This was my task; it was my burden. I know you do not understand it, but this is my part to play in all things. Enaria saw this and she has guided me, there is no other in this time that can save our people. Please my love I beg of you, trust me this was written on the red stone to be my task, just hold me and believe in me and protect our children and grandchildren, especially Gwen, she above all must be kept safe." He gave a long frustrated sigh and pulled her tighter.

"Never has there been a time when I did not trust your wisdom above all others, but I fear deeply for you, you are my queen, but you are also that slip of a girl I fell in love with, and I vowed I would always be there for you, and be your strength in times of weakness. At the moment I have never felt so weak as I do, holding you in this moment." She smiled and raised her hand to the side of his face and stroked it.

"Oh, my love, you are so wrong, you have no idea of the strength you have given me to withstand all of this, without you at my side I would have fallen long ago, you are the reason I still live."

Chapter Twenty Four.

Revelations And Truths.

Luminaria had worked hard to get the rank of commander to the Marshals of Fae, it had not been an easy task, as she met and married and then had two children. Life at first within the new realm of Avalon had been reasonably easy, as she lived in the town of Avalonia and the fortress where she was posted was at the base of the mount, and just a few minutes' walk from her home.

The investigation into Ariel had become her greatest nightmare as she worked longer and longer hours, and had travelled far more than she had ever done, and it had taken its toll. Feeling caught in a trap between two queens, she was being pulled in every direction, and so eventually she decided there was only one person that she could confide in, her brother Fagan, who was currently the Maker of Avalonia, and overseeing many of the building projects around the realm.

It had been hot that summer, and Fagan had taken to sitting out by the back door of his house connected to his makers shop, in the cooler evening air of Avalonia. He had never expected Luminaria to ride up; after all she had not visited him for several years due to her command and duties. He heard the clatter of hooves of her white horse, long before she came into view, he leaned back on his chair and looked at his companion.

"Well, that be a horse in a rush, sounds like the bindweed is on its tail it does, ye better stay scarce for a while, if that horse belongs to it's owner, ye will be interested in what is said this night."

His guest gave a nod and slipped out of their chair, and entered the workroom attached to the house.

She arrived at speed and her horse slipped on the smooth white stone road. She twisted, sliding off the saddle, jumping down to the floor. Her long mane of golden hair wafted up as she hit the floor, her sword glinting in the evening light. She was tall for a woman, and slender from her exercise of combat, her uniform was the deepest blue of a commander with golden bars on her shoulder. She looked worried.

"Greetings Brother." He gave a nod, understanding immediately his guess was right, and she looked deeply troubled, he smiled as she approached him.

"Tis been a while since ye sort out my home, ye look like the cat that returned to find no cream, what ails ye?" She walked briskly towards him.

"I need your advice on a matter of great importance." He gave a nod.

"Looking at ye face, maybe we should retire out of sight, come, the walls have many ears out here."

He got up and walked towards the door, but Luminaria beat him, and was inside before he had a chance to move. Fagan walked in, where she paced up and down the small kitchen. He stopped and took a look at her, she looked very tired and worn out, and could feel the conflict brewing inside her.

"Ye look like a willow with root rot; maybe ye should sit a while and let the calmness of the evening wash over ye." She shook her head and continued to pace.

"Brother I am in trouble, I have disagreed with the Queen of Fae and it has not gone well, and I am at a loss as to what to make of everything." Fagan walked over to her, and gripped her shoulders and held her still.

"Ye are more skittish than ants on a sugar pile, whatever has ye so riled up? Come sit and take the air and then tell me all about it." She gave a long sigh and her eyes filled with tears. Fagan pulled her close, he knew her well, and tears was not something seen often with her.

"I feel ye insides churning like butter, Lumi, come calm ye and we shall talk." She wiped her eyes, and Fagan walked her to the table and sat her down.

"I think ye needs something with a little more buzz of the bee than tea."

He bent down, and opened the bottom cupboard and took up an earth coloured bottle and lifted two glasses, he turned back to the table, and sat down and pulled on the cork.

"Tell me what has ye so spinning like the wind ribbons?" He poured the dark liquor into the glasses, and slid one across the table towards her; she lifted it and took a long swig.

"Whoa Lumi, this stuff will take rust off cart wheels, go lightly with it." She looked at him, her face pale and her eyes sparkling from her damp tears.

"I have made a grave mistake." He gave a nod.

"The Ambassador, I figured as much, ye understand why she is innocent; does ye now? See how fruitless your actions were?" She gave a soft nod.

"She is the daughter of mother's teacher Enaria, I honestly had no idea. The queen told me it was her who was guilty, and I simply believed her, so I went to see Queen Bridget, they told me she was sick and not to be disturbed, but I barged my way in and we had such a row." She shook her head. "How could I be so foolish, she was so angry, and when she told me who this Ariel is, I could not believe it, what am I to do?" Fagan took a swig of the drink.

"I warned ye did I not? Caught between two queens, ye always did have a way of doing things big." She looked at him.

"It's not funny, Bridget thinks I deliberately targeted Ariel, and Rhiannon wants me to arrest and imprison her here, whatever I do is going to cause another rift like last time. Oh brother help, I don't want to be the one who splits the two Fae apart again, those two have only just repaired their rift."

It was an awkward place to be, and Fagan could feel the fear inside of her. He sipped his drink and gave the moment some consideration, then scratched his head of fluffy white hair, and leaned forward to look her in the eyes.

"The way I see it is this, the only thing that matters is the facts and ye feelings bout them facts, so does ye truly believe this Ariel called the Merle down to Avalon?" She shook her head.

"No, it had to be the other one, Branna." Fagan understood.

"Ye wanted to lean on her, to get her to tell ye about the Branna girl?" Luminaria took another large swig of her drink.

"From what I have found out, Branna was unhappy with the queen, calling her the golden queen, you know the gripes of the workers? Apparently, she had put in many requests to see the queen to present her work on the darkness, and had been rejected every time. There are reports of her voicing her dissatisfaction, and she was known to complain about the queen, stating she favoured those of golden hair, it was clear to me she was not the type to admit anything. I knew that Ariel was a soft hearted and gentle person, foolishly I thought to get to the truth I had to crack her, so I tried, but overdid it." He gave a soft smile.

"Well, ye never did much by halves did ye?" He shifted in his chair, and leaned back onto the table. "Ye know what Mother would say don't ye?" Luminaria gave a nod.

"Speak up and speak honest, even if everyone disagrees with you." He gave a nod.

"So ye thinks this girl is innocent, and that the other one did it?" She gave a nod.

"I do yes."

"Then ye know what to do, tell the queen ye are going after the one called Branna." Luminaria gave a long sigh.

"That's the problem; I was instructed to prove its Ariel no matter what." She looked at Fagan and he could see her pain. "Brother she is innocent; I cannot do as my queen asks; it is wrong." He reached across the table, and took her hands in both of his.

"It is right to speak up and speak honest, no matter what the queen thinks, ye have to be true to ye, if not, how can ye live as ye? I says go after this Branna and bring her back to face her crime, tis the only way I see ye proving yeself." Her head softly nodded.

"Being me is not so easy at the moment, but you are right, we have scouts everywhere hunting her down, and yes as always you are right, I will go and see her and tell her what I know. I do have scouts reporting sightings back on anything remotely suspicious, and I have also been out looking for signs of this Branna." He patted her hand.

"Ye has always been stronger than most, and ye has always walked the line of truth, and no matter what, I loves ye." She smiled.

"I love you too; you are a good brother, thanks." He gave a nod and knew she understood and would be true to herself. She poured another drink and downed it in one, then stood up.

"You always did have a way of clearing my mind, I am glad you are here." She took a long deep breath to compose herself and tried to smile. Fagan stood up and walked round the table towards her, he pulled her close and kissed her forehead.

"You have Mother's light within ye, take that light and use it well, it has always guided ye on the right road." She pulled him tight and held him for a moment, and then kissed his cheek.

"You have always been there when I needed you, I should visit more, and maybe bring the children round more often."

*L*uminaria released him and walked out of the door, within a minute he heard the sound of her horse as it clattered over the white stone road, and he turned to see his guest stood in the doorway, and smiled at him.

"I see ye ears heard it without me, does that answer all ye questions, Ye know her as well as I do Rayne, ye almost married her, she is in a bind and needs help, will ye help her?" Rayne gave a nod and smiled.

"I am grateful to you Master Maker; I will go after her and I will do what I can." Fagan gave a happy nod.

"Ye light is bright too, go on go after her and talk, she needs a friend like ye on her side."

Prince Rayne of Moon turned in the doorway and was gone into the night, moments later the sound of hooves raced past the Makers shop for the second time that night.

*B*ranna came out of the trees to see Berengar sat by the fire, with two rabbits cleaned and prepared, on long sticks over the flame as they cooked. She walked towards the caravan carrying her large bottle, he noticed the movement and turned towards her.

"I woke in a storm and you were not here, so I prepared the meat for eating." She smiled as she reached the caravan a few feet away from him, she could feel his curiosity. "What have you there?"

Branna stopped and turned towards him holding the large bottle so he could see it in the fire light. The smoke inside swirled away from the light of the flames; he leaned forward and frowned as he saw the contents.

"Why do you need a bottle of smoke? If you wish to make smoke, throw leaves on the fire." She gave a chuckle as she turned back to the steps of the caravan; the glass jar was surprisingly heavy.

"Trust me my lover, this is no ordinary smoke, this is how we make your tribesmen pay for their crimes against you."

She heaved the bottle up to the floor of the caravan and then pushed it inside. Berengar simply frowned understanding nothing of what she was doing, and looked to the meat to check its progress. Branna climbed up inside the caravan, and dragged the bottle to the side of the door, where she wrapped it in several thick shawls to keep it free of any light.

Branna returned to the fire a few moments later with a pan of prepped vegetables and edible leaves. She hung the pot above the flame to cook, and then sat beside Berengar; she could see his confused expression as he turned to her.

"It is not smoke we need; it is weapons and fighters." She gave a chuckle.

"Only one sword shall swing in that moment, and that will be yours, believe me when I tell you, I fight with unseen weapons, blood will spill, but it will not be yours."

He really did not understand, but he had grown to trust her, her methods made little sense, and yet she had healed him from a wound he knew had killed many men, and he trusted her without really understanding why. Branna leaned forward to check the sizzling meat as it dripped fat into the flames, his voice was soft, yet had a power to it.

"Elric and my father are mine to take; my sword will only be sated with the taste of their blood. No hand will touch my mother, if I am to be dragged down to the underworld of devils and demons for my life, I will go there willingly knowing she lives at peace and protected, this you must promise me Branna of the Raven." She turned and saw the fire in his dark eyes, and could sense the taste for revenge in his words.

"Your mother will live and be held in great praise, for she will be highly praised for giving birth to the legend and ruler of your people Berengar, this I swear to you here and now." He gave a satisfied nod.

"Then use your smoke and let me cleave those in sight of my anger, and we shall take back what is rightfully ours." Branna looked to the bubbling pan and lifted the wooden spoon to stir the contents, she gave a soft smile.

"We will break camp here at dawn, it will be a long road, but we have time to gain more strength."

*I*t had been a strange night with strange dreams, and even stranger inner feelings. All day Ariel had sat in thought, isolated from everything, unable to keep her mind on her work, the visitation or vision or whatever it had been of Branna had given her hope that she had a chance to be with her, and it filled her mind completely, she simply could not think or focus on anything else.

The years had dragged past, and in many ways, she had been

given hope, because no news was allowed out of Avalon as to the whereabouts of her. Deep down inside she had begun to wonder if Branna had been killed in the wilds of the world of men, and now just when she thought she should give up, all the depth of her feelings came flooding back in wave after wave, crashing over her and occupying her every thought.

Sat on her chair by the open window, she stared out into nothing but the darkness of the night, as her mind slowly tried to process everything, especially the words of Bade. Did she really have her mother's gifts? She had never felt that she carried any form of mystic ability, was Bade right, was there something in her mother's work that may open up something hidden deep inside her? The frustrating thing was she just did not know, in her own mind, she needed something more substantial. Why had Bridget not been clearer in the Whispering Falls, why did she not just tell her what was happening, after all she is the queen, she must know something of her mother's final moments.

Nothing made sense and it was agonising and frustrating. For the first time in a long time the twists and knots in her stomach returned, as the loneliness seeped into her inner being. The truth was that even though Bade had proven to be a good friend, when it came to Bran, she felt so protective of her, mainly due to the way in which Rhiannon had treated them both that she felt she could not really talk openly to anyone. When it came to Branna, she felt millions of miles apart, and was completely alone.

*B*ranna was many miles away; she was also in a different realm. As Ariel sat alone, she had just risen and was dressing and preparing to leave the country of Bohemia, on the long trek back to the high plains of the place known as Sachsen, and she was feeling very confident as she stepped out of her caravan to light the fire to cook a meal, as she packed up and began what she felt was the real start of her quest towards bringing justice for her people.

In the mind of Branna she had what she needed, she had control of the flow of power through Roack. She had learned much from Ariel about charms, spells and herb lore, and now she had the final piece of her plan, a warrior to stand at her side and command her armies. Her plan was simple, head to the village in which Berengar was raised, and defeat the most powerful tribe in the region, and then corrupt them to her will. If she was successful, within a year she would sit in a seat of power, and then she could plot the downfall of the Queen of Fae Ofmoon. It felt almost perfect, the only problem was, somewhere deep down inside, she felt a tug, it was a familiar feeling and one she had not felt for a long time, it felt almost as if she could hear her name being called on the wind from across the ocean, and it pulled at her insides.

Branna blew on the embers, and they ignited the finely clumped moss, she sat up and placed the fine twigs onto the small flames, and then from the pile at her side, as the flame grew, she added slightly thicker sticks. As the sun came over the horizon and the flames stood up and danced as the twigs crackled and spat, Branna who was lost in thought suddenly felt the feelings within her flow upward to her lips, and she quietly looked to the horizon and whispered.

"Ariel."

Ariel's eyes closed, and her head tilted slightly, and then with a jolt she sat bolt upright in her chair and her eyes sprang open. Before she had understood, she had drifted into sleep sat in the chair, she spoke.

"Branna!"

Chapter Twenty Five.

The Hidden Truth.

It was still very early in the morning, when there was a knock on the door to Ariel's apartment. She had stayed up very late, and had only been asleep for a few hours, and was curled up under her blanket, snug and warm.

As she slept, her mind was alive as all sorts of images passed through it, so the sound of knocking appeared to be just another part of her strange dreaming. Somewhere in the background she heard a click and then a voice, and then felt the pressure on her shoulder that shook her.

"Ariel…Ariel you must wake up!"

Slowly the sound grew louder, and she came out of her hazy slumber and back into the real world. She opened her eyes to see Bade leaning over her.

"Ariel it's important, please you must get up." She gave a long groan.

"Leave me alone I am tired!" Her shoulder roughly shook, and she tried to roll over away from the hand that shook her. "Go away Bade, I have had an awfully long night, just go and let me sleep."

"If this was any other day I would, but it is not, Ariel you have to wake up, Master Elgin has summoned you to his chambers." She groaned again, she was warm and cosy and really did not want to move.

"Can he not wait till later?"

"Ariel, it's Master Elgin, so no, you have to get up and now, look I brought you hot tea." She reluctantly opened her eyes again, and tried to stir and wake up. She rolled back over and looked up at him, he looked concerned.

"What is all this about?" He lifted the cup of tea into view.

"Prince Rayne of Moon just arrived with Luminaria, Ariel this is important and you have been summoned. Just the sound of

Luminaria's name was enough to make her want to stay in bed longer, and she gave an exhausted sigh.

"That bloody woman just does not know when to quit, what in all the worlds does she want now? I have told her a thousand times, there is nothing in Avalon for me, I am staying here." She sat up, and Bade handed her the cup as she tried to blink the sleep from her eyes.

"Just hurry and get dressed, I will be in the next room waiting."

*I*t was a little over twenty minutes later, when Ariel, dressed but still very foggy and irritated, walked hurriedly along the wide deck in front of the House of Scribes, pushed on by Bade, who was looking very flustered, as Ariel commented on the whole situation.

"Why the lords did she send her son, does she really think that he can sway my decision?" Bade herded her forward.

"I honestly have no idea; all I know is they arrived unannounced and were taken straight away to the guest rooms to be attended to. Shortly after that, Master Elgin requested you be brought here. Please Ariel, behave yourself, he is the son of the queen and brother to the future heir of that realm, promise me you be polite with them?"

As they reached the doors of the house, she gave a frustrated sigh, she really was not at her best, as she was tired and wanted as little to do with any of this as was possible. Bade hurried her through the entrance, where there was a lot more than normal activity as scribes hurried back and forth. Ariel stopped as Bade gripped her shoulders, and gasped behind her, as he tried to recover his composure and regulate his breathing. Behind her, she could hear him as he tried to take long slow steady breaths, and refill his lungs and reduce his mild panic. After a few short moments of breathing, he appeared at her side.

"Are we ready? Right then, let's do this."

Bade walked down the centre of the house, towards the guest apartments, and Ariel followed. Outside the door was a junior scribe who stepped forward as Bade arrived, and leaned in to quietly whisper something in his ear. Bade nodded, and the Junior gave a bow to Ariel and walked off, she looked at Bade as he prepared to knock.

"Why all the whispering, do you know something I do not?" He turned and gave a weak smile.

"I have no idea what all this about, I was sent to get you as soon as they arrived, and I have been at your side since. I guess we will have to just wait and see, just please be good." He knocked on the door looking white in the face, he gave another smile.

"I promise nothing, I hate that woman." The deep voice of Master Elgin came from inside the room, and Bade opened the door holding his arm out to Ariel, and instructing her to wait, he stepped through the door and she heard him announce her.

"The Lady Ariel of Erin is here Master Elgin."

"Wonderful show her in." Bade reappeared and smiled, he mouthed the words.

"Please behave." She ignored him and walked in through the door.

*T*he parlour room of the guest apartments was large, Ariel knew it well, on occasion she had met with Gwendolyn here for private conversations. As with most of the house, it was panelled in dark wood, and had a highly polished cedar floor. The walls were adorned with elaborate tapestries, and round the edges of the room there were several seats, with equally elaborate and ornate cushions on them.

The far end of the room had large triangular windows, that looked out onto the gardens of the house and the rising slope of the base of Mount Kivi that was tree lined. Luminaria stood at the side of a long wooden table that ran down the centre of the room, wearing her best pressed uniform, with a her long golden hair falling off her shoulders and down her back. Her face was difficult to judge, as she wore an expression Ariel had not seen before, it mattered not as her gaze did not hold long on the Fae Commander, as her eyes moved to the leader of the House Master Elgin. He gave her a hearty smile.

"Ariel my dear, please do come in, I am sorry for calling you at such an early hour, but I feel you will be heartened by this meeting, please if you may, I would like to introduce you to Prince Rayne Ofmoon, who has unexpectedly graced our presence at this early hour."

Ariel looked to the large window, where a young man looked out into the gardens, and turned at the mention of his name. She was a little surprised at how young he was at first glance, and she felt he bore little resemblance to Rhiannon.

Like Luminaria, he wore a finely tailored deep blue jacket with golden cuffs, and tight pale blue pants that dropped to his highly polished boots. His hair was almost gold, and was wavy, as it too ran past his shoulders and bounced down his back. He looked to have a kind face, and had the deepest violet eyes she had ever seen, which sparkled with life. It felt surprising to see him, as compared to her, he did not look that much older than a junior scribe. He smiled revealing snow white teeth, and a few lines of humour across his face. He gave a short bow and walked across the room to greet her.

"Lady Ariel, it is sad we never met when you were in Avalon, sadly I have been elsewhere and not as available as I should have been during your time there, I hope you can accept my apology." Just for a second, she felt momentarily wrong footed, then remembering who he actually was, she gave a bow.

"My Lord Rayne, I am pleased to finally meet you, although I am no longer in service to your mother's realm. I have taken another position here at home, and therefore I hope you will excuse me if I am uncertain as to why I was summoned here to greet you, I believe there is a new Ambassador to Avalon representing Florae now?" He gave a slight nod of recognition.

"Indeed, there is, and I have met with him, although he informed me that there is no one more qualified in the history of the lines of Fae as you, and so as a bit of a history buff myself, I have taken the liberty of indulging myself by requesting to meet you, I do hope you excuse my whim?" He was skilled in flattery that was for sure, and she gave a smile.

"I feel honoured, and yet still unsure as to why you would visit without prior arrangement, which is the duty of the house to arrange on your behalf." He smiled again.

"I have requested a meeting with Queen Bridget, to which your good counsel leader has arranged on short notice for me, as I say, your ambassador's praise was such, I simply felt it would be a waste to visit and not meet with you."

The smile and the manner of him felt genuine, and yet Ariel had little trust of him, especially considering he had arrived with Luminaria, she forced yet another polite smile.

"As I have stated My Lord, I feel honoured that you would think of me." Elgin stepped up at his side.

"I believe the time has arrived My Lord, Our Queen will see you now." Across the room Bade gave a nod, grabbed the door handle, and stepped through opening it wide. Master Elgin offered a hand to show the way, but Rayne paused and looked at Ariel.

"It was very nice to meet you, I do hope at some point you would do me the curtesy of meeting and talking with me?"

"I am available at all times in the house My Lord Rayne, I will look forward to it." She gave another bow, and Elgin led the way taking Prince Rayne Ofmoon with him. To Ariel's surprise Luminaria remained standing by the table looking at her, Ariel considered the moment before speaking.

"Should you not be going with him?" Luminaria looked very uncomfortable.

"No…I am here for other reasons." Ariel gave a slight nod.

"I won't keep you from your business then." Ariel turned and walked towards the door; Luminaria spoke.

"Ariel, please don't leave… I came here today to see you." Ariel turned and her voice sharpened, her dislike was more than a little obvious.

"How many times will we do this? I have not seen her, I do not know where she is, I have not heard from her, but if I did, I still would not tell you. Will you ever just go home and stay there and leave me alone?" Luminaria put her head down and gave a long sigh.

"That is not why I wanted to see you, I will never ask you about Branna again, I promise you that." Ariel was confused and her anger bubbled inside her, it came out in her voice.

"THEN WHY ARE YOU HERE? JUST LEAVE ME ALONE, I HAVE HAD ENOUGH, AND I AM SICK OF ALL OF IT."

Luminaria gave a nod of understanding, and took a long pause. Her voice was soft and low, and it was clear she was seeking the words and choosing them carefully.

"Ariel, I came here today to offer you my humble apologies. I was wrong, and I made you suffer. I am aware this is nowhere near good enough, and it will not make up for the wrongs that have been done to you, but I feel honour bound to face you and apologise in person…I am so very sorry for all the pain I caused you, I ask not for your forgiveness, it was important to me that I do this."

Such was the surprise that Ariel was dumb struck. She stood and stared unable to think or talk, her insides suddenly went into free fall as she searched to find a response, any response, but she could not fully comprehend what had just happened. All the days of crying, the loss of Branna the love of her life, her inability to finish her life's ambition of building the house, the trial she endured, arriving home bound in a bracelet and escorted by guards, the humiliation she had felt before the counsel, there just was not enough words to describe it.

Tears welled into her eyes, and Luminaria watched equally as lost for words but looking riddled with guilt Ariel felt momentarily paralysed, she was not even aware of the few words that finally found their way into her restricted throat, before they spilled out and croaked onto her lips.

"Just tell me one thing…Is she alive?" Luminaria took a step forward and her expression changed, a tear welled in each of her eyes.

"As far as I know…Yes." Ariel nodded.

"Thank you."

Her emotions welled up inside her like an eruption as her heart wrenched in pain, without really understanding why, she turned as Luminaria took another small step towards her, and she ran. Tears streamed down her face, as she bolted through the door into the long corridor, and a gasp of pain came past her lips. Somewhere behind her Bade's voice shouted her name, but she was unable to stop, she just wanted to flee, and she ran, she ran as fast as she could with blurred eyes, and her heart filled with pain, or was it just sheer relief? She really could not tell which, she just felt the emotions surging inside her and had to get away as fast as she could.

The next few minutes passed in a blur, she was out of the house running for her life down the deck, tears streaming down her face, sobbing uncontrollably, and then suddenly her arm jerked, she twisted, and a body wrapped round her, and even though she heard his voice, she understood nothing of what he said and she crumpled into his warmth and wailed.

*L*uminaria stood just outside the doors of the House of Scribes and watched. Bade held Ariel tight in his arms as she cried outside her small house on the front of the deck, and she felt wretched inside, her eyes fixed on nothing but the distress of Ariel. She did not even notice when the wise old figure of Elgin walked up to her side and viewed Ariel wrapped tightly in Bade's arms as she sobbed. It was a sombre sight to see. He looked to Luminaria, her eyes fixed on Ariel with tears in her own eyes, and he gently took hold of her arm.

"You have done the right thing here this day, I appreciate how hard that must have been for you, but you can rest assured, what you did was the right thing." Luminaria gave a sniffle understanding whom was speaking to her, and lifted her hand to wipe away her tears.

"If that is true, why do I feel so wretched inside?" Elgin watched as Bade tried to guide Ariel who was still sobbing, into her apartment away from those who had stopped to watch.

"The hardest thing Luminaria that any of us will ever face is having the character to admit we wronged some people. It is never easy to look deep inside ourselves and admit the truth of some of our actions. To do so, and then make amends is the truth of what real bravery is, this may not feel very pleasant, but give it time." She turned to him and he gave a sad smile as he saw Bade finally get Ariel inside her home safe.

"Today feels bad, but in a day or a week or maybe longer, you will be able to face yourself and admit freely, I am glad that I tried to make up for my actions. You will never forget this day Luminaria, and you will learn much from it, Lord Rayne will be some time, so come, walk with me and we shall talk more."

*B*ridget Violet, Queen of the Fae of Earth, sat in her parlour, as her maid tended to her. Master Elgin entered the room and gave a regal bow.

"Lord Rayne Ofmoon, My Queen." Bridget looked up and she waved her hand, and her maid stepped back and turned, walked towards the side door and left. Bridget gave a nod to Elgin, who opened the door wider and Rayne entered. He smiled and gave a bow, she smiled.

"So formal Rayne, I do believe your studies on the Violet Isle with my brother has greatly improved you." He gave a cheeky smile as Elgin exited the room.

"It is lovely to see you again; it has been far too long Bridget, I have been made aware that you have been sick, so it is nice to see you looking exceptionally well." She gave a giggle and pointed to the chair at the side of her.

"You have the flattery of your father, come sit with me and tell me what is so important that you would come at such an early hour." He walked across the room and took his seat a few feet from her, where he could see her up close, and his voiced softened.

"I have a few reasons for my visit, one being to ensure you are happy with the workmanship of our Masons, and also I wished to check on how you are feeling." Bridget gave a knowing smile.

"You have learned much of your mother's skills in diplomacy I see, but really Rayne, I know you have personally read my letter of gratitude for such skilled work creating the falls, and as for my health, I am sure your mother has all the details well and truly noted down.

I have known you all your life, and I must admit to come here at such an early hour on such a pretence is a little disappointing, I expect better of you." He gave a chuckle.

"My apologies, I should have known that to try and disguise my visit would be a pointless exercise." Bridget smiled.

"When you arrived with Luminaria you gave yourself away. Lumi is a very athletic and beautiful woman, I believe she is married with two children now, if you want my opinion, you were a fool to let her go. I see clearly you still have great affection for her, after all she has ended up in a very difficult situation, I think it is very sweet that you still care enough to come to her aid." Rayne gave a nod of defeat, he knew Bridget was far too wise to have tried to fool her, his face took a more serious look, as did his tone.

"Lumi is a decent woman, she can be brisk in her manner at times, but she has been a loyal commander in the Marshals to my mother, I doubt there is another who could replace her in the ranks." His eyes met Bridget's as he looked up. "She is caught in a trap and I want to help her." Bridget understood completely, her voice was soft and yet very serious.

"Caught between two queens, one of which who has great political ambition, you are playing with fire Rayne, does she really still hold so much value to you, that you would risk everything for her? Rayne she is married to another, and yet here you are taking the biggest risk of your life for her, this is not a game Rayne, even you have no protection from the wrath of your mother. Please trust me when I say, her ambition is great, and if you step in her path, she will not think twice about stepping on even you, after all the future of that realm is destined for Eleanor." He understood.

"Why do you think I came to you first?" Bridget smiled a soft smile; she saw his struggle and understood his motives.

"I am unsure of what I can do, I have little power in her realm, so tell me what do you know of this whole affair?" He gave a long sigh.

"According to all the reports and what Lumi has told me, my mother suspects that the Merle was some how contacted, and drawn down into her realm. She believes it is the fault of Ariel your adopted daughter. Lumi believes it to be the woman named Branna who was assigned a role of studying the Merle. Lumi actually thinks this Branna tapped into something powerful by accident, and as a result pulled down a darkness with evil intent to use against my mother." He gave another long sigh. "You know the reason, you alone confronted her about it." Bridget gave a nod.

"And it divided the two lines of Fae and created distrust between the two races, some of which still linger Rayne. Oh yes there is a lot of smiling and pleasantries, but deep down behind the scenes, you know of the resentment that exists, especially with your mother." Rayne fully understood the position; he had witnessed it first hand from his mother.

"She has a fixed vision and will not alter her path no matter what, believe me, I have had many conversations with her that have ended up with her getting her own way."

"I am sure you are aware of everything, especially the work of this Branna and the things she discovered, but this Rayne is far greater a complication than even you realise. If the truth comes out the reverberations will echo through history for a very long time. If I could advise your mother, which I have attempted to do, it would be to leave this Branna and Ariel alone and look closer to home." He frowned.

"Closer to home, I am not sure I understand?"

"That is my point Rayne, no one completely understands apart from the two queens of Fae, and we understand this perfectly, and that is why you are risking everything. Rayne your mother is as aware of this as much as I am, I have acted, she has not, and that is why this is such a big problem." He shook his head.

"But if this Branna did bring down the Merle, which again is only a theory, then all we need to do is find her and remove her, will that not solve the problem?"

"No!" He blinked.

"What?" Bridget gave a long sigh and paused to gather her thoughts. She chose her words very carefully.

"What would you say if I told you I have read a great deal about the work that Branna did, and as brilliant as she was, trust me the girl is exceptional, she made a fatal flaw in her research that I spotted from the letters that Ariel sent me. Ariel is the daughter of our most powerful mystic, and she has skills few realise at this time, but the flaw even evaded her sharp mind. I believe that your mother was always aware of the consequences of it, and did nothing, which is why she has tried to blame Ariel and divert as much attention from Avalon as possible. I am sorry Rayne, but if you ask me, Luminaria has become the sacrificial lamb in all if this, and trust me, she will suffer as a result regardless of what you do." He shook his head and looked to the floor, as his thoughts tried to understand things.

"I honestly thought coming to you would help, but now I feel more confused and conflicted than ever. I know my mother is hiding something." He lifted his head and looked at her. "I feel that she fears what she hides, and yet sat here with you, I can see you do not fear this thing whatever it is, and yet I do feel you are not being as honest with me as you have been in the past."

Bridget gave a long sigh and sat back; she looked tired and weary, and to him her face had paled and the darkness below her eyes was more prominent. She sat quietly for several minutes as Rayne watched in hope, her eyes fixed on the wall across from her. After what felt like an eternity, her eyes moved back to him.

"The Fae have too many secrets. I have always tried to cast light into our world to illuminate everything, but as the queen of this realm even I have learned that there are some things that must be hidden for the better of every race, not just Fae. Tell me Rayne Ofmoon, how strong is your loyalty to your people?" It surprised him.

"No offence but that is a stupid question, you know how I feel." She nodded.

"I do indeed, I have always admired your efforts on behalf of both races, but this question goes much deeper Rayne."

"In what way?" Bridget paused for a second. She went to speak and then stopped, and then after a short pause to rephrase her words, she asked the one question Rayne never expected.

"If I was to ask you to swear loyalty to this one thing, even though it goes against your oath to serve your mother loyally, and remain silent before all, would you be prepared to do it?" Rayne sat back in his seat.

"What the hell is this about that would make you ask such a question?" Her voice stiffened.

"Would you?" He stared at her.

"You really are serious about this, aren't you?" She gave a nod.

"Never more so Rayne." For the first time since arriving he suddenly looked a lot less calm and a great deal panicked.

"Give me some idea of what you are asking of me, and let me decide." It felt like a fair request, and she considered it.

"What would you say if I told you, the Merle can only be brought down if the person doing it already has a connection to it, no matter how minor?" She looked so serious and his mind felt like it would explode. His fear was evident in his low quiet question.

"Is that even possible?" Bridget looked at him intently, there really was no need for her to respond, he knew her, and he knew that she was always completely frank and honest with everyone; he stumbled a little on his words.

"Do the Ruling Counsel… Know any of this?"

"Do you swear?" He felt his heart rate rise, and the beads of sweat forming on his brow. Bridget did not flinch, she sat there looking at him with determination, and he knew he would hear no more unless he did the unthinkable, and swore an oath with her.

"Do I have a choice, if I want to end this?" She shook her head.

"No…Only with a bond sworn between us will I reveal what was told to me by Enaria days before her death. She saw this, and she shared a fatal secret with me, and I have held that secret since. Only with a bond of blood will I reveal what I know to be the truth, even Malcolm is unaware of what I know, such is the gravity of this knowledge."

*R*ayne knew better than to try and out manoeuvre Bridget, he knew she was resolute and would not budge an inch until he gave in, he had seen that in the dispute between her and his mother.

"I see I really have no other choice. What do you wish of me?" Bridget stood up.

"Come with me."

*S*he walked across the room and through a side door into the chamber of her Table of Power. The huge table of violet coloured smooth stone gave a pulse as she entered. She clicked her fingers and all the doors to the room closed by themselves and locked, she turned to face him.

"Here we are safe from all eyes, nothing can pass the defences of my table of power, now place your hands on its surface and swear to me that you will not reveal what I tell you to anyone other than those who know, which is both Queens of Fae, for there is no other living soul that knows the truth, and there is good reason for it."

Rayne did not hesitate, he walked up to the table and placed both his palms down on its warm smooth surface and they instantly stuck.

"I Rayne Ofmoon, swear to you, Bridget Violet Queen of Fae of Earth that I will protect your secret from all except those that already know, namely my mother, Rhiannon Queen of Fae of Moon. And I will bear this secret which shall remain hidden until such time as I am instructed to reveal the truth." His hands came free of the table, and with a gasp of relief Bridget sat down in her chair.

"I cannot deny this burden has been a great weight to me, to know there is another I can include is of great relief to me." Suddenly she looked very frail and his concern rose sharply within him, he lowered to her side and took her hand in his.

"Tell me, share your burden and allow me to share your load." Bridget closed her eyes.

"Forgive me for this, I have asked something great of you, and it will weigh heavily upon you." He squeezed her hand and smiled.

"I may be young, but I have broad shoulders." She smiled with deep affection.

"Rayne… As Enaria approached her death, I know you are aware of her story, so I will not waste time, she told me that our Goddess of the Moon had been infected by the Merle. Her spirit was unharmed, but her garment bore fragments of the Merle." He instantly understood.

"That garment was the largest part of the creation of our lines, the Fae have been accidently infected, there are Dark Fae my mother was right." Bridget shook her head and smiled.

"No Rayne…Some of the Fae have a connection, but the power of light within us subdues it, most infected Fae do not even realise it, and it has no bearing on their life. When Enaria visited the Moon realm after Tideguyde left it, she cleaned it completely, sadly by that point her garment had already been collected and was being recrafted by Eve. She placed a powerful symbol of protection in the heart of the realm, and that has prevented the Merle from ever entering the realm again." He began to understand.

"This small part of the Merle within us, is only dangerous to those who try to reach out to it, I understand now, and you know for sure my mother knows this." Bridget nodded.

"She does, it is the reason we argued. The Fae are golden in her eyes, why do you think that is." He really did not need to answer.

"Somehow, they are free of it, but those she forces to toil in tunnels and work areas, they have it which is why she keeps them as far from her as possible?"

"Yes, but there is more." She took a deep breath. "A time will come when the one that bears the red stone will rid this world of it, until such time all we can do is cleanse those that are infected. It takes a lot of power to remove it Rayne, only a Queen can wield such power."

It hit him hard, and he fully understood everything, and a huge wave of sadness washed through him and he squeezed her hand tight.

"You are dying, you have taken all of it inside you." He felt a tear in the corner of his eyes as she nodded and softly smiled.

"I love my people Rayne." It felt like his heart would break, she was loved so deeply by her people, he admired her so much for her fair hand and fair rule, he did not know what he should say or what he should do.

"I admire your bravery, and have nothing but love for the way you have always been kind and fair to me and my people, my mother should hang her head in shame. Tell me what should I do?" Bridget released his hand and took a long intake of breath; she turned her head slightly to look at him.

"Both our people are infected; I have taken all of it from this line in Florae, and as far as I know none of my people are now at risk. I have found a way with Enaria's star to take it with me, but you must convince your mother that not everyone has this sickness. Rayne if she takes it from them all, she will not live, but all the Fae will be safe from it forever, you must be ready to take control until Eleanor takes the throne, or you have children of your own who will rule." He stood up and leaned on the table so he still faced her.

"You say the one with the red stone, that is Eve is it not?" Bridget smiled at how fast his mind worked.

"One will come in time, and Eve will pass her the stone, it will happen in your life time, so all I can say is when she comes to this realm or others, give her your loyalty and protection." He nodded his head in agreement. "Sadly, my dear boy, I am very tired and in need of rest."

"I shall leave you now, and return to Avalon to try and convince my mother. I will return again to talk with you."

"Then for now, I bid you safe journey and good luck, and thank you Rayne, you have proven yourself to be of great value to your people, go to them." Rayne gave a regal bow of the utmost respect.

"May your reign continue for as long as possible, for your people have been greatly blessed to have you. Farewell Bridget Violet Queen of all Fae." She smirked.

"Better not let your mother hear that." He smiled and then looked very serious.

"I do not lie, I meant it."

*H*e turned and walked towards the door, Bridget clicked her fingers and they opened up, he walked through and turned for a second and waved with a smile. His pace quickened as he headed down the long corridor towards the large doors leading out onto the deck. As he walked towards the top of the steps, he noticed Luminaria stood talking with Master Elgin, she turned and gave a smile as she saw him. Rayne walked at a good pace down the steps towards them, before he was even close enough, he spoke.

"Master Elgin I am deeply grateful to you for such splendid hospitality, you have done your line proud." He drew level with Luminaria and grabbed her hand as he looked at her, and his voice lowered. "We have to go." He turned back to Elgin. "As much as I would like to tarry, I am afraid my time has been shortened greatly, please give my regards to Lady Ariel, with her consent I would like to return and meet with her as promised."

Luminaria felt Rayne's hand squeeze tightly onto hers, there was a blinding flash of brilliant yellow and Elgin stood alone. With another Flash luminaria stood beside Rayne in front of her house, she frowned and looked to him.

"What's going on?" He took her hands in his and stood before her.

"How deeply do you love your husband?" Luminaria looked shocked and her cheeks turned pink.

"Rayne, we did this years ago, I told you then, I will never love another more." He smiled.

"Go to him, take the rest of this week off I am assuming command for one week." He squeezed her hands. "Lumi, there are more important things than a command. You need rest, so take this time that I am gifting to you, and use it to its fullest, get strong and refreshed, I will see you in your office in one week."

He let go of her hands and turned and walked off down the white stone street, she had no idea what had brought that on, but after all, she knew him better than any, and so she understood there was good reason. She smiled as she watched him.

"You are a good man Rayne, one day you will change the world for a woman you finally commit to."

Chapter Twenty Six.

Time Alone.

Branna and Berengar packed up within a few hours and were back on the road. They had a long journey ahead of them, but this gave them time to talk more as they idled along the dusty roads. Berengar had seen little of Roack at the camp, there had been fleeting moments where he had come out of the caravan, and seen the bird on a rock a few feet from Branna, and it had appeared like she was talking to it.

At first, he had brushed the idea off as stupid, but after several encounters, it was clear to him that there was some sort of connection between the two, and so whilst on the road, he decided he would ask. It was midday and it was warm at the front of the caravan sat up on the covered seat, Branna fanned herself as he held the reins of the horse's, he looked at her and she noticed.

"What?" He was unsure of how to say it, so he just asked.

"You call yourself Raven, is that because you can talk to them?"

It surprised her at first, she had not thought he had noticed, but in a way, she was glad he had mentioned it, for some time she had pondered whether or not he would understand, after all, few people in the world of men would.

"My people have the ability to bond with animals; we draw a sense of power from their world, so we connect with them. I can talk to Roack, and she too can respond back." He gave it some thought; it was not really that big a surprise after all he had noticed over many weeks.

"This makes sense to me Bran, on the night of the storm as we lay together, I saw this Roack in the sky…Although she had grown in size and was as big as a man. Does this Roack have powers from the underworld?" Branna gave a chuckle.

"Roack like myself is from another world, although it is a higher realm, not one from under. We share a force that aides us both, my people have many magical abilities, Roack helps me increase the power of them." He understood.

"The bottle of smoke, those things you got with the help of your bird." She nodded.

"Yes…That smoke, is many parts of Roack's power, and I will use it to help you win back your honour and create an unbeatable army." He stared at the road ahead and thought about it, and it was over ten minutes later when he spoke again.

"Roack gave you the power to bond with me and enhance my life, her power helped you heal me, to me then that means she is part of our family, she is one of us is she not?" Branna smiled.

"She is, we are a family of ravens, united with the same bond, two maidens bonded to one man, you could even say we are your ravens Beren." He gave a mighty laugh.

"My ravens, the Ravens of Berengar, I like that."

The caravan slowly moved along under the trees as the dappled light illuminated the road ahead with shafts of light, he looked to her again and smiled.

"Tell me more of these powers and where they come from."

Berengar was a warrior, his life had been the law of the sword and the mighty, his time with Branna had shown him there was far more to the world, and so he decided that he would question all he saw, for Branna had a talent for things that were very much out of the ordinary. Already he had seen how her life was very different from his, her views on sex and marriage for instance. It made sense to him that she would befriend a bird, for she like all birds was very much a free and wild spirit.

She had a quality to her he had never known of in any other woman, and in his early time as he recovered under her care, he found himself drawn to her in a very powerful way, and yet he knew little of her life before she had picked him off the river bank.

*T*hat day began a long series of questions and answers that would last for most of their journey; the conversations they had would reveal more of themselves to each other and deepen the bond. Berengar had only ever trusted his bow or his sword, and it was during this journey that he grew to trust Branna more than any other living soul. He had no idea of the span of time before them, but he was sure all of it would be lived side by side.

Branna talked openly about the Fae, Rhiannon, and her ambition to finally destroy her. She talked of life on the Moon Realm and in Avalon, she even talked at length about Ariel, and yet in all of her conversations she made no reference to love, sex or relationships with Ariel. Branna at first was not sure why she never mentioned her deep love for her, or the promise she had made to reunite with her.

On those days when Berengar would drift off to sleep and Roack was off hunting, she would ponder her reasons as to why she did not mention these things to Beren. In truth she did not really understand herself when it came to Ariel, she knew that she loved her, possibly more than anything else, there had been many times when she had made love to Beren and others, and her mind had drifted to Ariel over the years. She questioned as to why she was unable to talk about her that way, was it to protect herself. Was she ashamed of what she had done since leaving, after all some of the things she had done would horrify Ariel, she just was not sure?

Her relationship with Berengar was different, she was not with him because she had fallen in love with him, her reasons for the bond with him were very different. He was a warrior of great power, he had the same lust for revenge as her, he could unite the most powerful tribe in the region and create an army for her. In her mind the union of her with Berengar was more of an agreement of protection and power, it was more political than feelings and love.

Yes, the sex was incredible, and she found it to be the most satisfying since leaving Avalon, but the simple truth was, she had felt the darkness inside him as he fought to live, and as strange as it was, she recognised something in him she had always been aware was also inside her. Their union all came down to that simple point, he was probably the only person alive who could understand and accept her dark side, and that was a powerful thing for Branna.

Branna was split down the middle, half of her was light, and the other half darkness, but of late it felt like the light was fading. She had grown very powerful since that night when she took the caravan, her Fae powers had increased tenfold with the mixing and blending of the Merle. In her youth she had dreamed of being allowed to study the Merle, and in Avalon her wish had come true, but as exciting and fascinating as it was, it had always been the study of something outside of herself.

Her black book contained the notes of her years of study, but it was almost full and she felt it was time to write another. Almost like starting the second chapter of a story, Branna knew that now the Merle was within her, this was no longer the study of something far away, this was now the study of something that was living inside her, in many ways, she was now involved in the study of herself.

*T*wo days had passed since the visit of Luminaria, and Ariel had not left her rooms. It had been agreed with Bade that she needed a little time to recover from the experience, although in all truth she had not really explained to anyone what had happened during her conversation with Luminaria. Elgin was aware as he has spoken to Luminaria, but he had spoken nothing of the event, apart from his comments to Bade, where he had advised him to say little, but keep a watchful eye over her. So it came as a complete surprise when Princess Gwendolyn arrived back from Avalon, and instead of going to the royal house, she walked straight down the long front deck and knocked on Ariel's door.

Assuming it was Bade with more supplies; Ariel answered the door, and was very surprised to see the princess of the realm smiling at her. Gwendolyn stepped in and pulled her into a long hug.

"Get changed and pack a few things, I want to show you something, but it will take a few days."

When the princess of the realm appears and asks you to visit somewhere, it is hard to refuse, so for Ariel who had not slept for two days or sketched, it was an impossible situation, as one does not deny a princess.

She packed some things into a bag along with her sketch books, extra parchment and charcoals, and then Gwendolyn took her hand, and in a flash of blue they were gone. They arrived on the shore of a long white beach, where the waves came rolling up to the sand with a gentle lapping sound. Birds flew in the skies above, calling to each other as they bent and twisted in the air, and in the distance on the horizon Ariel could just make out two large islands. She turned to Gwendolyn who was smiling.

"Are we on Sora?"

She nodded and pointed behind her, where Ariel saw a large wooden house, but it was not like those on the main island of Florae, she had no idea, but it was similar to a house she would visit in many years in the world of men, close to a mere in the woodlands of Loxley. Gwendolyn took her hand.

"Come on, come and look at the house, Gwynfor built it, this is where he intends to live when his work building the realm ends. He has let me use it often, I come here with Merlin so we have some peace." Ariel stopped walking.

"I am not a child; I do not need everyone running around and acting different with me." Gwendolyn turned on the steps of the house and looked at her with bright blue sparkling eyes.

"You are right, you are not a child, and as for treating you different, I always have, you are not some stranger to me, you played a huge role in raising me, you are family to me." Gwendolyn gave a sigh and sat down; her voice was soft and thoughtful.

"Ariel, you have suffered a great deal because of Rhiannon, I did not bring you here to pry into your thoughts or tell you great pearls of wisdom. I have watched you handle this with determination, I have seen the pain in your eyes, and felt the loss in your heart, and I have watched how you have endured great wrongs without complaint. The truth is you should have been allowed back into the house to oversee everything, it was your design, your dream and she took that away from you, it was wrong Ariel, she was wrong. I just thought that back there in public it would be harder to sort things out, here you are completely alone and isolated, here you can talk if you wish or stay silent, you can walk, you can sketch and you can sleep, things we both know are healing. That is simply what this is, me reaching out to someone who I care deeply about, and giving you a place to work everything out. You no longer wear the bangle, if I am wrong then head straight back; you are not here as a captive." She stood up, turned on the steps and headed for the door.

Gwendolyn busied herself in the kitchen area lighting the fire and setting a pot to boil, it was several minutes later when Ariel walked in through the door.

"I am sorry." Gwendolyn looked up from the stove where the flames were starting to catch to heat the water.

"You have no need to apologise, take this time for you and work things out, it is what I do here. You have the room at the top of the stairs, it's the door to the left, put your things there and get comfy, and then we shall have some tea. The place is pretty basic, you know Gwynfor, he likes the simple and practical life, but I also like it, there is no one fussing about how to do this and how we have always done that, this place is here just as a space to think, use it well." Ariel smiled.

"You have changed in your time away; I think Merlin has done you good." She shrugged.

"Merlin is Merlin, he has his way and he allows everyone else to have theirs, it is a very freeing experience being around him." Ariel lifted her bag and walked towards the stairs; she stopped and glanced to Gwendolyn who was setting the pot on the flame to boil.

"I am not unhappy Gwen." Gwendolyn looked across the room towards her.

"I asked her if Bran was alive, and Luminaria told me that as far as she is aware, she is. I guess what I am trying to say is that by saying that, I understood that Bran got away, and she is not in a prison or been sentenced to death, she is free. I had no idea, and just knowing made such a difference, and it got the better of me as my feelings overwhelmed me." Gwendolyn smiled.

"You still have hope of seeing her again, that is a powerful feeling indeed, I am happy for you Ariel, you deserve a break from everything. For years I have watched you dedicate your life to the people, and you left nothing for yourself. You know when you came to see me at the cottage in Avalon, I think that is the most relaxed and happy I have ever seen you, I hope you find her again one day, because if you do get the chance, Ariel take it. Life here will always go on, the house will run and affairs of state will be handled, do not sacrifice another chance to be happy because of paperwork, take it and run with it, be happy."

*T*rue to her word Gwendolyn gave Ariel space. She sipped her tea alone at the top of the steps to the house, then went for a long walk along the beach. It was sometime before she returned to the house. As she walked slowly along the white sandy beach with the soft breeze blowing through her hair, she noticed Ariel sat on a rock with her bare feet in the sand, sketching in her large book of parchment.

Ariel looked relaxed and happy, her eyes fixed on the parchment, her hand twitching or gliding with each stroke of her charcoal. Gwendolyn smiled to herself, Ariel had no idea of how much she admired her, to Gwendolyn, Ariel had an inner peace that gave her immense resilience, she had often wondered if that had been what had got her through intact. Rhiannon had shown an element of her true character in the way she had treated Ariel, and it had been a good lesson for Gwendolyn who would one day wear the crown of her own people.

Ariel had no idea of what she had done, simply being the daughter of Enaria, had shown the Queen of the Moon the true power of an individual's ability to point out the hypocrisy of a queen, who was supposed to be the wisest of them all. Gwendolyn now saw things with fresh eyes, and it made a huge difference to how she would rule one day.

She walked to the side of Ariel and looked down on her sketch, and it caught her breath, she crouched down to look closer.

"Wow she is beautiful, you are an amazing artist." Ariel gave a smile.

"She is, she is wild and different, but at heart she is the most loving person I have ever known. Rhiannon is a fool, Bran is wiser and smarter than all of her golden haired wonders put together, she has learned so much and Rhiannon was a fool to not give her an audience, she will regret ignoring her one day, I think it is the biggest mistake Rhiannon has ever made, she is a complete fool."

Chapter Twenty Seven.

Deals And Demons.

Sending Luminaria off on leave, the first she had taken in several years, Rayne was free to look deeper into her investigations. It was clear there was nothing at all to implicate Ariel, which as he already knew, meant that his mother was indeed using it as a way to get even with Bridget after her accusations. Rayne took the only logical course of action, and closed the case on Ariel down, sending a dispatch to Master Elgin to request he inform Queen Bridget. He was aware that this would displease his mother, but after all he was the Commander in Chief of the Marshals, and so therefore was the only person who outranked Luminaria. This would to a degree remove Luminaria from all blame, which had to be directed at himself, it was the only way to save her.

Having dismissed any idea of Ariel's involvement, he turned his attention to Branna. Reading through all the reports he found there was no direct evidence, the truth was no one was actually sure just exactly where the point of contact with the Merle was. There was evidence to show something had passed from the upper realm downwards into Avalon, but when it came to the location of the contact things became very vague. The only real information showed that it had occurred somewhere behind the Mount of the Citadel, but investigations into the house and the work station of Branna, had revealed no traces of dark magic at all, if anything they reinforced the belief that the whole area had been covered by the protection of the plaque on which was Enaria's Star, and with that being the case, Rayne determined it was impossible for any darkness to exist there.

Rayne's only problem was Luminaria, he knew her well, some would say too well, and having listened to her conversation with her brother, Fagan, he understood that she was convinced it was Branna, and the simple fact was he trusted her instincts. Her reports tracking sightings and strange occurrences throughout the realm of men were far more detailed than he had expected.

It was clear that some of the things that had been noted very much matched the abilities of most Fae Ofmoon, the question was, which one? Branna was not the only one from Avalon that had secretly slipped out and decided to live in the world of men. What did catch his interest was Luminaria's very detailed reports of sudden weather changes, especially large thunder storms and driving rains that were very destructive. The Marshals attending the scene had recorded traces of an unknown, yet powerful form of magic in the air surrounding these regions.

Rayne intensified the search across the world of men in hope that something would show, and prove the theory of Luminaria. Rayne agreed with Fagan, Branna had to be found and brought back to prove either her guilt or her innocence. For five days he worked, reading reports and making changes that overruled Luminaria, and to a degree conflicted with his mother, he knew at some point one of her many spies would alert her, and at that point it would be him alone that faced her.

*T*he confrontation came on the sixth day. Rayne was sat at his desk in the large office with several other officers, when the door crashed opened and Rhiannon walked in. She wasted no time as everyone snapped to attention.

"GET OUT ALL OF YOU!" The offices scattered, vacating as quickly as possible as Rayne sat back and smiled.

"Mother how nice of you to visit." Her grey eyes smouldered with anger, and her face was flushed with rage, she held up a piece of parchment.

"Just what exactly do you think you are doing, and where in all the realms is Luminaria?" His face remained cheerful.

"I am doing as you and father always requested, I am commanding the army and taking the position seriously, as for Luminaria, I gave her some leave to spend time with her children, she has worked very long hours of late and she looked tired, so I allowed her some time for the children." Rhiannon's Eyes narrowed.

"I have no idea what you think you are up to, secret meetings with Bridget and now this. Your scheming will not fool me, you are sticking your nose in where it is not needed and where you have no right. How dare you send a full pardon to Florae; I will send them an article to rescind your decision." Rayne leaned back in his chair.

"As queen you have every right to do that, but tell me this, just what reason do you intend to use when there is absolutely no evidence whatsoever to prove Ariel had anything to do with the events that led up to the Merle being brought down by a member of this realm? Think about the political implications of that, do you really intend to anger the White Lord again by dividing the Fae for a second time?" Rhiannon walked up to his desk and placed her hands flat on the wooden surface; she leaned over it, and brought her face up close. The anger on her face was very evident.

"Are you threatening me?" He showed no fear.

"No mother I am trying to talk some sense into you, yes Bridget confronted you with an uncomfortable truth, and you did not like it, but don't you think it is time you acted more like your reputation implies, than this vengeful and petty persecution of an innocent girl for no other reason than she is close to Bridget? For the life of Eve, Mother look at you, ranting and raving for what?" She stood up straight, her eyes narrowed at him.

"You have no idea what you are messing with, you could risk far more than you realise, you are over your head and you need to stay out of my affairs." She turned and began to pace across the room. "You have no idea of the things in the heart of this realm that have an effect on all of us, you are meddling in things you have no understandings of."

"So, enlighten me." Her head snapped towards him.

"You need to know your place, I will tell you this just once, stay out of my affairs and keep well away from the investigation of those two, it is my business not yours." Rayne stood up behind his desk; he could see her anger, and knew how little more he could get away with.

"You are supposed to be the ruler of this realm, you are supposed to be the one who protects all of us, but we know that is not true is it Mother? Is it not time that your rule of protection applied to the likes of Branna and all the others who lack the gifts of fair hair? Just why is that exactly, is it because there is a connection between the two, and you are afraid others will find out your little secret problem?" Her eyes exploded with bright white light.

"GET OUT…GET OUT WHILST YOU STILL LIVE!" Rayne knew he had gone too far, and he was dangerously close to getting struck by her powers. He walked towards the door, choosing his words carefully.

"So much for family, you are a fool, you are too blinded by the power you wield, and one day everyone will see it, just as Bridget did."

"I SAID GET OUT!"

"I am going, goodbye Mother." Rayne walked out of the room, and in a flash of yellow he was walking on the white soft sand of the Isle of Iona lost in thought.

Ariel had spent five days alone on the island of Sora in Florae. Gwendolyn was right, just being away from the main island and relaxing, had actually given her the space to really sit and consider everything that happened. Most of the days she had wandered alone on the beach, or walked into the deep woodlands that surrounded the cabin. She carried her journal or large book of parchment on which she did many sketches, many of them of her life in Avalon with Branna. The seclusion and peace calmed her deep down inside, and in the evenings, she had helped Gwendolyn prepare a meal, and they had sat and talked until darkness on the steps of the cabin.

Gwendolyn spoke of her grandmother and her concerns; she expressed her nervousness at becoming queen long before she felt ready, and most of all she spoke of her life in Avalon with Merlin and how they had spoken of marriage. Ariel could see the love in Gwendolyn's eyes and hear it in her voice as she spoke about him, and it gave her great joy just to witness it. The final night together was approaching as Gwendolyn would be leaving at dawn to return to Avalon. As Ariel walked out of the clear blue warm water of the sea, she lifted her clothes off the old tree stump that stood on the edge of the beach, and headed naked for the house. The sun was still very hot, and the damp droplets of water on her wet skin helped to cool her.

Inside the cabin Gwendolyn was already busy chopping up the green leaves and other raw vegetables for their evening meal, she smiled as Ariel entered the house.

"I got a communication earlier whilst you were swimming; it appears Rayne Ofmoon has issued an order to drop all charges against you, so it looks like your name has been cleared of all wrong doings."

Ariel was lost for words, as she looked at the open document written in a skilful hand on the table, Gwendolyn gave a broad smile.

"I like Rayne; he is very much like Eleanor, nothing like his mother." She gave a giggle.

Ariel really did not know how to respond, she had spent the week coming to terms with everything, only to find none of it had not mattered, as she had now been pardoned. Gwendolyn noted her look of confusion.

"Ariel whatever you decided this week alone, stick to that regardless of what has been done. I know the depth of soul searching that you have gone through, but this changes nothing, whatever you have chosen to do, stick to that." She blinked out of her daze.

"I am, this week has been an important moment for me, for the first time since leaving Avalon I really do know what I am going to do, and to be honest even this will not change that, although to be honest, it helps a little." She smiled. "So what are we having for our last meal here?" Gwendolyn gave a soft smile at her.

"Good, I am glad you have found your direction again, I have no idea by the way what this is called, Merlin makes it a lot and I am rather fond of it, I think you are really going to enjoy it."

*I*n a different realm travelling under the veil in her small caravan, Branna sat and watched the road ahead. The meadows had gone and the road was uneven and stony as it climbed slowly upwards towards the highlands of Sachsen territory. Since leaving the lands of Bohemia, Berengar had become more and more impatient, to the point where he had taken to sleeping during the day and driving the caravan in the dark of night using the moon and stars to light his way and navigate.

Branna heard the door at the back of the caravan close, and a few moments later Berengar came up the side of the wheels and reached out to pull himself up into the seat. She smiled as she saw him, Roack had flown off to scout and it had been quiet, she was looking forward to the company. He lowered his large frame onto the seat and looked around at the scenery.

"We should stop soon and prepare, we are only a few days away from the territory, they will have watchers on the tracks so we are better resting and preparing whist we are still a little ways out."

Branna could feel his apprehension, she knew how much this meant to him, but as yet he had not really seen her abilities at work, he had no idea of the power she now controlled, and she could feel that in his mind he was heading towards what he saw as a warrior's death. Her voice was calm and quiet, as she relaxed and handed him the reins.

"You fear more than you need to, you have not seen the true

power of my people yet, but you will, and you will walk from this fight victorious. I will not let you perish, and they cannot beat us, no matter how feared the Varisci are, they are no match for the powers of a Raven. Be at peace my lover, rest your mind and do everything as I have instructed to you, and you will take the day and become more powerful than Grembald and Vulgan put together." He gave a sigh.

"My mother will be spared?"

Branna turned to him, and saw the look of concern on his face, he obviously had a deep connection with her, but that was her greatest concern, she stretched out her arm and touched his leg softly.

"Have no fear, she will come to no harm, but I will warn you, she may not like what she sees. The power of the raven does contain darkness as you saw during the ritual; it will not be a pleasant thing for anyone to watch. When your mother sees what I can do, and she realises that we are now one, it may be a shock, for she may think you are in league with demons when we are done."

He understood, and he was aware that the magic of Branna would be disturbing to a woman who was in his eyes kind and loving, but there was one aspect of it he knew that Branna would not really understand, he placed his left hand on hers.

"My mother has suffered a great deal from my father, there were times when he was cruel and shamed and humiliated her. I understand that she may not like what she sees, but to me it matters not if she thinks you are a demon from the underworld, and that I am your slave or puppet. The only thing that matters now is to free her from the grip of my father, and let her be free of him once and for all."

Branna nodded softly at him and smiled. "It will be so, trust me, I gave you my word, and it is my bond, your mother will be unharmed, and free of your father forever."

Chapter Twenty Eight.

The Rise Of Berengar.

After several weeks of long boring days and nights of travelling, Berengar had grown in strength and power. His body had been weak before the ritual, as he had not recovered fully from his wounds, but over the last week he felt more powerful and stronger than he had ever done before. With his rapidly gaining strength, and the knowledge that he was heading back towards his home, his mood over the last few days had changed from quiet and sultry, to one of optimism, and a rapidly growing thirst for revenge.

The previous night he had pulled over to rest, and had slept well after a night of intense passionate sex with Branna, both had drifted into a deep sleep as Roack sat on the roof above the door of the caravan and kept watch. Berengar had risen first and started a fire, and placed a pot of water to boil, and whilst he waited for Branna, he pulled out his large sword and practiced for the hundredth time that week, feeling the weight of the blade and the power in his arm. He felt stronger and faster than he had ever been, and as Branna emerged naked from the caravan to wash, he felt the confidence inside him rising, as he saw the glint of his blade, as it whipped through the air like lightning.

Berengar was impatient throughout the first meal of the day; he gobbled his meal down, and wiped his wooden plate and returned it to the rack on the caravan side. Branna took her time, she knew they were only half a day's travel from his village, but she was calm and in no particular hurry, no matter how much Berengar tried to hurry her along. She looked up at him as she chewed the last of her meal, Roack sat on the roof pecking at the large chunk of raw meat Branna had thrown up to her. Berengar stood before her losing his patience, Branna thought it was amusing, she could see an almost boy like side to him.

"Have you got the robe ready." He gave a grunt.

"It is on the seat up front." Branna chewed on, savouring the flavour of her food.

"Good put it on, and do not remove it until I say so." He looked confused.

"We are half a day's travel before we arrive, the thing smells, and is irritating to wear." Branna nodded.

"I am aware of that, and for every minute, and every scratch, and every foul smell you have, allow the hatred of it to add to what is already inside you, now go and get it and put it on. It will make you far more alert, and also remind you of what I have planned, we must do this exactly as I told you, there is no room for error, do you understand me Beren?" He scowled like a scalded child.

"I know what is to be done this day, I am not a child, I understand the importance of this." She gave a nod.

"Good, now go get it, and wear it."

*H*e turned and stomped off round the caravan and she smiled. Roack looked down at Branna sat by the fire, her voice was slow and croaky, Roack was starting to get used to having her voice, although it had taken some time for her to adjust.

"I feel the hate and anger within him, it might not be wise to anger him more, there is great power within him." Branna stood up and kicked dirt into the fire.

"Beren is a proud warrior, he understands the rules of combat, and he also understands how timing is essential in a surprise attack. Today is his day, he will rise up and take his seat as the leader of my army of ravens, he must be alert, swift and mighty, so that all who see him, will understand the true nature of his strength. No male warrior wants to be ordered around by a woman, so today he also must see my power, and understand we are one and the same, only then will he truly swear his full loyalty to me for eternity, and remain at my side." Roack bobbed up and down on the roof.

"You show great wisdom for one so young; I shall look forward to watching the start of your rising in power to match the woman of light you hate so deeply. My eyes shall be yours as we travel there; you will have no care of what they have to greet you." She gave a smile.

"They have nothing that will make me fearful, they are men who think women are weak, and today they will learn otherwise."

*T*he journey from the camp site to the village was slow much to the irritation of Berengar, who was wearing a long thick heavy black robe, which made his skin itch. The road was steep and the horses panted as they pulled them slowly up. The scenery began to change as more and more rocky outcrops appeared on either side, and the caravan swayed from side to side on the uneven floor, making Branna and Berengar lurch constantly in their seats. With each sudden lurch and change of seated position, Berengar scratched at his arms and grumbled, Branna smiled.

"Is your anger rising my lover?" His voice growled below the thick heavy woollen hood.

"Grrrr! Much more of this and there will be no need of your skills, if it is a demon driven by hate you want, then you shall have your desire this day. When I cast off this wretched garment, I will be driven by all the hate in the underworld, and none shall stand before me and live." Branna gave a little titter.

"We are close, I see the cliff drop and the narrow road on its edge, soon my lover you will have your heart's desire, be still now and hold in your anger for your blade, for the time to swing is almost here."

They passed through a small ravine where the sides rose up in pale grey stone, littered with old and weather ravaged trees, and then suddenly to their right the rocks fell away leaving an open trail with one side to their left that was flat and smooth, and the other side fell down a huge cliff to a river far below.

The road curved round the sheer wall and Branna saw a pass on the other side where the land expanded out lined with giant boulders and ancient trees of pine and spruce. The caravan slowly made its way along the high cliff track, and into the ravine, where the sun was blocked out and a cool breeze blew with the heavy scents of the trees that surrounded them. Branna pressed on the brake, and Roack flew down and landed on the roof of the caravan with a thud, she turned to Berengar.

"Is this the pass?"

He peered out from below the hood and gave a stern nod, and turned to look at the familiar sight of the track leading away from the high cliff towards his home settlement.

"It is, a little further on; the path will open wide and reveal the plains that my home is built within. We must be wary, for it will be well guarded, they will already be aware we are here, and sent runners to the village, they will be waiting to meet us." Branna spurred the horse on, and the caravan gave a slight jerk, and rolled on the dry stone road way.

"Remember do not move from this point onwards, and do not reveal yourself until I say so, as far as they are concerned, we are traders looking to trade goods for meat." He grunted.

"I trust you, but I am in need of losing this robe from hell, and the swing of a sword. The time for reckoning is upon them so do not fail me Branna, I have placed a belief in you, and if it is a bad judgement, we will die this day."

"As you will soon see, my magic will not fail you, and before the sun falls, you will have an army to stand beside you, and a loyalty you have never known from fighting men to support you. Swing at only those who betrayed you, and leave the rest to me, for today your kinsmen will feel the cold fingers of the Raven inside their souls, and you will finally rule as you should have done. This is the day when the name of Berengar will be on the lips of men who will quake with fear as they speak it."

In the settlement, the runners had arrived and informed Elric, the second in command, and the word had spread of a mysterious wagon on the trail. By the time Branna and her cloaked companion rolled into view, all around the large circular settlement, Varisci warriors had taken up their positions with longbows and swords.

In the centre of the circle was the large long house that was now the house of Vulgan, the leader of the tribe and Berengar's father. Vulgan stood leaning on his carved walking stick, and watched from the top of the five steps that led into the long house, as the cart slowly trundled towards the centre of the large settlement. Elric, the head warrior and defender of Vulgan walked out into the centre of the circle to meet them. Berengar could see little but the dusty floor, but Branna and Roack had a good view of everything, and noted the wide circle of Varisci tribesmen all armed and ready, she almost breathed her words to Berengar, who she could feel the tension within building.

"Hold your seat and focus, wait for my signal, not much longer now, and you can reap your vengeance."

Branna applied the wooden brake, and the caravan slowed to a halt. She lifted her eyes, and smiled at the scarred and shaggy haired fighter in front of her, who was stood staring at her with malice.

"Greetings friend." Elric looked back to Vulgan, who gave a nod; he turned with a stern face to Branna.

"Who are you, and what is your business here?"

Branna stayed sat in her seat, her dark eyes glinting, her long black shaggy hair blowing gently in the soft mountain breeze. She eyed the man before her, and then cast a glance at all the heavily armed men that surrounded the outer buildings of the village, in her estimation there were at least four hundred men, heavily armed and waiting for an order to kill, and deep inside she felt calm, as she sensed the silence around her. She smiled again.

"I am Raven." She poked a finger towards Berengar. "This is my demon, and that up there is Roack. We are traders looking to trade with the Varisci. We were told you are devils in men's skins, but wealthy, and I have a fondness for wealthy devils, they make me richer." She gave a laugh, and Roack above her gave a screech. Elric looked unsure and glanced back to Vulgan, who gave him another nod, he turned back to Branna.

"What is in the cart?" She rose slowly from her seat to show she was unarmed, and dropped down onto the dusty floor.

"I have goods to trade, herbal cures, and many items of fine things to attract the eyes of the ladies; I seek trade for food and supplies for my long journey back to the lands of Hispanica. Come I will show you."

Elric was nervous as he viewed the hooded and cloaked figure, she had called her demon. "Bring them and let me see." Branna shrugged as she dropped from the seat to the floor, and turned towards the back of the caravan.

"If you wish."

She calmly walked to the back of the caravan, and looked around at the warriors all brandishing their weapons and looking fierce. At the windows she could see women and children, all trying their best to view the scene. At the back of the caravan, she calmly folded down the steps, stepped up onto them, and undid the latch of the door. The door swung inward revealing the large glass jar with a wooden bung, and filled with hundreds of what looked like swirling shapes of black smoke.

She gave a heave, and pulled the large bottle towards her. It had a net bag of rope around its base, and slipping her fingers into it; she lifted the bottle and lifted it out of the caravan. With the bottle on full display in front of her, Branna gave a grunt and carried the large bottle round from the back of the caravan. She walked past the horses, and placed it gently on the floor in front of Elric, who looked at it with a very confused look, as she smiled, and looked over his shoulder to Vulgan.

Elric eyed the raven sat on the roof with suspicion; he could feel the hairs on his arms bristle as it stared into his eyes. All around, the warriors moved from side to side curious as to what was in the bottle. Elric could not understand what it was he was looking at, and he lifted his head to the smiling Branna with a stern stare.

"What is this trickery?" Vulgan who could not really see what was happening limped with his stick onto the steps, and bumped down them to the floor.

"What is it?" Elric turned to face him looking puzzled.

"She has a jar of smoke."

"Wisps!" Branna corrected him; she turned to look at Vulgan.

"They are Wisps." Vulgan limped a little closer.

"What do they do, we have never heard of these things before, and what use are they to us?" Branna shrugged as she watched Berengar's father for the first time and took the measure of him.

"I hear many rumours on the road, and if what I hear is true, that the devils in skins kill their own kin, then all of you need Wisps, for they purify the soul. It is the reason I made such a hazardous journey round the cliff tops, for the souls of the Varisci it seems need to be cleansed."

Elric scowled at the jar, the others in the settlement fidgeted as they watched, and Vulgan grew angry, and his stern face turned red.

"What is this madness? You have got a nerve girl, to walk into here with your half truths and lies about the honour of this tribe. I should kill you where you stand." Branna looked at Vulgan with a blank expression and shrugged, Elric was looking even more unsettled. Branna was calm, and simply spoke as if talking to a person on the road, there was no hint of fear in her at all, which puzzled the Varisci as they looked on. They had become accustomed to people quaking with fear in their presence.

"You cannot do that, my demon will not allow it, he rose from the depths of the dark places he was sent to, in order to protect me. It was he who suggested I bring the Wisps to you, for he alone knows of the treachery that rots all of your souls." Vulgan's temper rapidly rose as his face turned redder with his rapidly growing anger.

"TREACHERY!! WHAT IS THIS TREACHERY YOUR DEMON SPEAKS OF? SHOW ME THIS DEMON THAT CANNOT DIE, AND I WILL SHOW YOU A MAN IN A CLOAK THAT BLEEDS RED LIKE ALL MORTALS!"

Berengar stood up from his seat and cast off his cloak, and there were gasps all around the village. He jumped down from the wagon and in one swift sweep of his sword, he stepped towards Elric as the sudden silence was broken with gasps and looks of amazement, and brought his gleaming blade out of its sheath and high into the air.

He strode with great strides towards Elric, who was far too shocked to react quick enough, and with a thunderous sweep of his blade, and a roar like a demon returned from the dead, the head of Elric who had betrayed and stabbed him, flew into the air before the shocked tribe, and fell with a splat on the floor and rolled towards Vulgan.

Roack gave a mighty screech, and the wisps of dark smoke flowed out of the jar through the glass by the hundreds in the direction of every warrior accept Vulgan, who stood staring and lost for words at his son. Having never seen anything like this before, the warriors froze unable to understand the scene, as wisps of dark smoke flowed towards them and then expanded and stretched before each warrior, forming a perfect copy of each of them. The warriors stared with horror as the smoky forms floated towards them, and then stretched out their arms to embrace them. It felt like time had momentarily stopped as the hard brutal men of the Varisci, felt the cold and icy tingles of death float towards them.

As the smoky figures embraced the first of the men, and slipped within their skin, disappearing inside them, the men shuddered and began to scream with horror, and fell to the floor clasping at their heads and convulsing violently. Other men seeing what was happening, panicked and dropped their weapons, as they tried to get away from the icy cold wisps of smoke that had formed into the replicas of them, and floated towards them with their arms outstretched. It was utter chaos as Berengar walked slowly towards his father.

"YOU BETRAYED ME; I WAS LOYAL TO THIS TRIBE!"
Vulgan stood his ground, his wife ran out of the house at the sight

of her son, and watched with horror as the tribe were slowly being absorbed, and screaming on the floor for mercy by the Wisps that were devouring their souls. Vulgan did not blink.

"You were loyal to Grembald, you protected him as others suffered, I did what was right for our people." Berengar lifted his sword and pointed all around him.

"They are my people now, see what you brought on your own people because of your own greed, you never forgave me for being ambushed. You never forgave me because you got wounded saving me, when it was you who forced me to go out on that hunt for your meat. All this time you have punished me for your mistake, and it cost you the head place of the tribe. It was you who took the road of dishonour, and arranged an assassin to slay me when my guard was down. Well today father, you will pay for your crimes, and I will take this tribe back down into the under realms of darkness with me to suffer for eternity.

Berengar walked up to his father, and plunged his sword into his heart, and pushed it through to the other side, and it appeared out of Vulgan's back with a gush of blood. Berengar looked into the eyes of his father as he held his sword fast.

"I will meet you in hell when I am done."

With that he pulled back on the sword and it came slipping out, dragging with it bone and tissue. Vulgan collapsed with a horrified look set on his face, and hit the dusty floor dead.

*B*erengar's mother stood with tears in her eyes, as she looked at her son who she had believed to be dead. At his feet lay the slain body of his father, he gave a nod to her.

"You are free now and under my protection, never again will you suffer his cruel words or his beatings. Tell my brothers that I am back from the dead and home again, and they too shall be under my protection."

She cried stood frozen as she saw what was happening to those all around her, and her legs shook and her tears streamed down her face, and she sniffled as she spoke.

"They are imprisoned for they disobeyed your father and went looking for you." Berengar felt yet more rage build inside him.

"Go…Free them and bring them to me." She turned on the top step and ran across the back of the village to the cells to release them, and also to escape the fear of seeing a tribe devoured and jerk on the floor.

Berengar stood upright in the centre of the settlement and viewed the scene; he threw back his head and wailed out the Varisci war cry. Branna stood calmly and watched as the writhing men on the floor grew still, and then slowly rose back to their feet. She watched as Berengar turned to her.

"You are true to your word Branna the Raven, I am yours forever, and bound to you as your demon and protector." She smiled and walked slowly towards him.

"No, I am your queen and you are my king, for this is the centre of the empire we shall build together. Look around you Berengar, look at the men who rise as my raven did, they are your men, your army, yours to rule for eternity at my side. Look my lover, these are your ravens, all of them, for they are your Ravens of Berengar."

Chapter Twenty Nine.

The Rise Of The Raven's.

*T*hat night the village of the Varisci appeared as normal as ever, no one who entered would suspect anything, families continued as they always had, any difference in them were completely unnoticeable, but scratch beneath the surface, and there were some very different personality changes. One man who lived with his wife and her widowed sister, took both of them willingly to his bed, something that would never have been tolerated before.

Children who were obedient and quiet, became slightly colder and more brutal with each other, almost as if overnight they had become sadistic, and the most obvious change was everyone's extreme loyalty towards Branna and Berengar. They were treated like the king and queen they were going to become, and no one found it odd that the large black bird that sat above the doorway to the long house in the centre of the village, could talk to them. Children left offerings to the bird of scraps of raw meat, and a once suspicious tribe that feared the Raven as a bird of ill omen, had miraculously adopted it as a symbol of good fortune.

Berengar's brothers, Otto and Vladimir were brought home from the cells where they had been badly abused and left to rot. They were welcomed and praised as they walked through the streets, and Berengar's mother Filiberta, welcomed her family back with open arms, albeit with a slight fear of Branna, who appeared to have an unnatural loyalty from her son. Branna sensed it, and decided to help her cook a large meal from the family. She went to her caravan, and came back with herbs and sweet wines for all of them, and then joined Filiberta at the side of the central fire pit, to show her a few things that she had learned as a young Fae cook.

Berengar sat at the table and talked with his brothers and thanked them for their loyalty, and told them the tale of how Branna had saved his life. Filiberta listened carefully as she stirred the pot, and her son talked of the dark dreams and pain he endured during his time riddled with fever. As suspicious as she was about Branna, it was hard not to be grateful, for now she understood that her son had not died as she had been told, but when he was on the edge of dying, it had been Branna that had dragged him from the river and up the riverbank and saved his life.

Everything appeared normal as the candles were snuffed out in the village that night and darkness covered all. Alone in the darkness, Roack sat high up on the roof and considered the day's events, amazed that Branna had been able to successfully separate the Merle and blend them with humans to create a whole army of separate entities. It was a strange experience to realise each of these people had a part of themselves within them, it was even stranger that since the ritual where Branna had joined their lives together for eternity, Roack had felt individual, and had even started referring to what she always called "Us," as "Her."

As the sun rose, and the village slowly came to life Branna was already wide awake and back in her caravan, which had been placed at the side of the long house, and the horses had been stabled. She returned to the house and lit the fire, then wrapped in a shawl of black wool, she left the house following her senses as she wove through the trees towards a strong sense that drew her mind towards it. Roack flew down to her shoulder, as she walked through the trees to the edge of what was a high drop off, and she looked across the wide gap and saw that the canyon or valley was almost a perfect round circle, with a huge column in the centre, which was topped in a flat wide circular plateaux. She smiled as she looked on it.

"Roack, this is perfect, this is where we will build an empire."

The giant hole in the land was at least a thousand feet deep, with sheer dropping rugged walls of grey stone, she bent down and ran her finger along it, and the stone broke apart in a perfectly straight line, she smiled.

"This is perfect for my purpose, it yields to my powers, but is unbreakable by any of the means of men. Roack this stone will weather many ages before the spirit of the land can wear it away."

The Raven took to the sky, and crossed the wide gap and landed on the smooth flat surface of the central wide pillar, and Branna could see how smooth the stone was, it was perfect. She watched as Roack walked round pecking at snails, and quietly spoke out her thoughts.

"This will be our new home, this will be where we will grow and plan, and I will one day see my revenge for all of those of my line who have suffered. This is where the golden queen will fall, but first I will hide everything within a circle of darkness, and she will never know of the enemy growing right in front of her eyes and under her precious moon. From this day forth, I will work my thoughts into a reality so cold and brutal, that when I am finally revealed, it will be the day that foolish and ignorant white queen dies."

Roack lifted into the air and flew back to her shoulder. She landed softly and spoke in her new croaky voice, which she was still getting used to.

"This place has no name, and is unseen to most but this tribe." Branna smiled.

"I will name it and one day people will quake when they hear it, for here will be the Castle of Berengar, and from here I will create an army of little ravens, who will grow and spread, and undo all of the work the Fae has done. They dream of a world of peace, I will bring chaos, pain and destruction to everything they touch, and all of it from here unseen. Roack it is perfect, we will be happy here, Berengar has his army of slave soldiers, and I have the mind to create a world fit only for us, soon more of the Merle will flow to me, and from here out into the world."

Branna stood on the very edge of the high cliff, and looked across to the pillar in the centre and the pictures in her mind began to form.

"Roack, we span this gap of five hundred of men's yards with just one bridge, no one will enter without us seeing them, and across there on that smooth pillar, we will tunnel into its depts. We will create a labyrinth of passageways and tunnels to house an army ten times bigger than the Fae. We will learn more of the skills of others, and between us we will breed a whole new line of beasts of fear, and I will bring down more of your friends to fill my beasts with darkness, creating fears the world of men has yet to see. Here will be our home, our roots where the Fae of Ofmoon and the darkness join together in union against the corruption of their precious white queen." She turned and walked towards the trees.

"Come let us go and gather what we need, I have an empire to build for my future husband."

*T*rue to her word, Branna started that day as she organised the

village, and men were sent into the high forests to cut down the trees
for timber, and the blacksmiths were set to work smelting ore from
the valley basin. The Varisci whilst still a formidable fighting force
with a reputation for fierce combat would be set the task of building
the centre of her new realm, and once everything was sorted out and
organised, Branna left Berengar, Otto and Vlad to organise, and she
returned back to the site of the deep canyon and tall pillar of stone in
its centre with Roack.

Hidden from all eyes under the veil of darkness, Branna knelt
down as her eyes filled with a deep almost burgundy light, and as
she touched the floor it began to vibrate. Roack sat on her shoulder
connected to her mind whispering quiet words of power, and before
them the rocks rose up from each and began the start of a new bridge
of stone.

Deep below in the canyon, rocks cut themselves free of the walls
and glued themselves together, and created two vast angular pillars
that grew out of the walls of the cliff and the central pillar, and
rose upwards until they met in the centre of the wide gap level with
Branna.

She gave a gasp of relief as she rested her mind a while, and then
moved a little further away where she repeated the process. This time
one foot thick large slabs rose up from the floor of rock, and slid
slowly across the gap to meet where the two angular columns from
below met, and they shuddered to a halt creating a wide bridge of
smooth thick stone. Happy with her efforts she sat back and rested
and ate from the supplies she had carried in her bag, she felt tired but
knew this was a good first effort and made an excellent start, and was
satisfied it would serve her purpose.

The following day she returned, and continued her work, and as
each day past and she perfected her abilities, Branna grew stronger
and stronger, and slowly over the period of five months a crude and
rough looking castle grew out of the pillar cutting pathways and
stairwells below the surface creating a mass of inter connected rooms
inside the column. Once the stone was in place, the men of the village
laboured with wood and metal and moved into the castle to fit it
out and create a castle fit for their king and queen that would rival
anything built in Avalon by the white queen's slave workers.

All around the region, Branna sensed the stone and marked places
for men to toil and chisel, and soon veins of gold and silver were

discovered, and the power and wealth of the Varisci grew. It took over a year before the castle was completed using labour and magic.

When it was finally finished, all assembled in the great hall, where two seats of stone were set up high on a platform with four steps before it. Decked out in the deepest of red, with a tall golden perch set above in the centre, Branna and Berengar dressed in deep burgundy robes with long flowing cloaks of black raven feathers, walked into the great hall to tremendous cheers and applause, where they walked through their adoring masses and stood before the two seats.

Once seated as the room fell silent, Otto and Vladimir came up the steps, and placed a crown of gold feathers on each of their heads, and they were pronounced king and queen of all the ravens of the Varisci and the land of Sachsen. They sat smiling as the room filled with cheering people sat down at long tables, and feasted until they were sick. Wine flowed and the day began as they would forever, and as the feast began, it became the first of one loud riotous celebration, that progressed into a debauched night of sexual lust and desire. No man or woman cared as they fornicated openly on the tables and the floor taking whoever took their fancy and could sate their desires. And as things became more and more debauched, as they laughed with joy, Branna and Berengar joined by his brothers stripped off their clothes and joined the masses, and cavorted alongside their other ravens.

The ritual of the ravens became an annual event which would in time be known as "The Gathering," and it would be held in tribute to the raven sat high on its perch as it viewed the masses below, it became a ritual devoted to the praise of Roack, and the powers of the Merle.

True to her word, Branna had risen to power, and was building an army that would rival Rhiannon, the rise of the raven of darkness, could have been avoided if it had not been for the folly of a queen who wished to protect her own vanity and political ambitions. Branna had set off on a journey to flee the realm of Avalon with a raven containing a darkness that would corrupt her very soul.

She fought hard to control the darkness inside herself, and as a result the darkness did not notice that it had one single flaw, and it was the same flaw as her arch rival Rhiannon. With Rhiannon the wisest and most powerful member of the Fae was a tiny speck of darkness that fought against the light within her, and within Branna there was one tiny piece of light that fought her darkness. Rhiannon and Branna were equals, although neither would admit that, and that small flaw was indeed their greatest weakness.

*O*n the night of the third Gathering at the Castle of Berengar, Branna felt something she had not felt in a long time, and left the event to walk outside the castle. She walked for a long time through the ruins of the old village of the Varisci, which had been burned down on the completion of the castle and out into the ancient deep woodland. There in trees within her circle of darkness created by the veil, Branna dropped her defences and spoke in her mind for the first time in many years.

"Ariel hear me, I am ready."

Ariel shot up in bed with a huge jolt, and there at the end of her bed stood the figure of Branna dressed in a long feathered cloak. She rubbed her eyes hoping this was not a dream.

"Bran is that you?" The figure whilst almost transparent in the moonlight smiled at her.

"Ariel I am sorry it has taken so long, but I did not forget my promise." Tears filled Ariel's eyes.

"Nor I too, you have been in my thoughts and my heart since the day we parted." She sniffled into the sheets as she saw the wonderful smile of Branna. "I miss you so much Bran." The vision of Branna opened her arms and beckoned to her, with her voice that sounded distant, and unearthly.

"Then come to me again Ariel, come into my arms, and feel me once again embrace you."

Ariel did not hesitate, she slipped out of bed, and grabbed her already packed bag as her premonitions of late had shown her a meeting similar to this, many times in the past year. With a bright coloured flash, she left Florae, and appeared deep beneath the trees to see Branna standing with open arms. Ariel dared not to hope.

"Is that really you, is all of this real because if it not I am not sure I could take it?" Branna chuckled.

"You have not changed a bit? Yes, it is me; I told you I would let you know when I was safe."

Branna walked towards her and embraced her, and Ariel felt that familiar feeling as she was wrapped within her arms, and relaxed and breathed out a sigh of joy and contentment. Branna pulled her face round to her, and kissed her deeply, and Ariel responded as her body became alive. Within seconds they were peeling away each other's clothing, kissing and touching each other, as they slumped to the floor amongst the tall ferns and enjoyed the feeling of being together, as they once had in Avalon. For over an hour they made love, and as the sun rose over the trees, they lay together exhausted, happy, and curled around each other and slept.

*R*oack swooped in and landed on one of the tallest trees and looked down, she bobbed about on the branch feeling the disgust growing inside her and talking to herself.

"No good can come of light, she will destroy all of it. I hate the light and those who bring it, you are a fool Branna the Raven she will bring your end."

Roack's mind lit up with the voice of Branna.

"She is mine, touch her and I will destroy you and all your ravens. She stays and you tolerate her, otherwise I will send you back from where you came and you can go back to we again, do you understand?"

Roack lifted into the air and gave a loud squawk.

"You are a fool, nothing good can come of this, keep her away from me is all I say."

In another realm under the cover of night, and set within the abundant tree lined mountains, a terrified scream wailed into the realm of Florae, Queen Bridget was having night terrors once again.

*F*rom one small part of the Merle no bigger than your hand connected with a particle of the Merle, no bigger than a speck of dust deeply hidden within a disgruntled member of the Fae Ofmoon, hidden within a circle of darkness, and covered from sight by a veil created by Tidegyde for her future lines, was all it took, and it would lead to murder, deception, and complete chaos for over a thousand years.

It would eventually begin a conflict that would take one man and his wife on a journey to seek out all of the lost heirs from the past of the kingdom, before the full truth was finally revealed. Before that could happen, darker deeds had to be done, so that those who live in ignorance, would take heed, and finally look to the east and the mountains of an old world renamed Saxony.

Deep below the ground, within a fast flowing stream of water, that thundered down into an abyss, around a wide round plinth of smooth stone, a soft voice gently spoke.

"It is as seen… Be brave my child, for now my light will flow towards you, and you will be protected always by it. All is not lost, for within you is a truth none can stand against, and through you, as I predicted, a queen of light will fall. The truth of all is coming, look to the red stone and await her."

Ariel gave a happy moan in her sleep, and snuggled up closer to Branna.

Chapter Thirty.

Gone In The Night.

Ariel opened her eyes; and the sky was blue, through the gaps in the deep green leaves of the canopy far above her. Her body felt warm, and heart felt at peace for the first time in many years. She gave a long sigh of relief, and turned to see the mass of black tatty hair hanging across the tanned face of her naked companion Branna. She lay there in the grass and crushed fern, gazing at her with pure joy and love, so many years had passed by them both, and here she was once more at her side. There had been so many days of doubt and grief, and yet here again at her side, she no longer doubted anything, for this was the love of her life, sleeping peacefully after a night of love making.

Ariel sat up as Branna slept, and her mind began to swirl back to the night before. For months she had been having dreams and visions of Branna, and they had been so real that three times she had rushed into her arms, only to find herself stood alone in her room. Weeks ago, she had packed her bag with clothing, drawing parchments, and charcoals, which is how convinced she had been that Bran was calling to her, and now sat beside her under the trees, she could see how right her dreams had been. Her mind echoed the voice of Gwendolyn.

"I hope you find her again one day, because if you do get the chance, Ariel take it, life here will always go on, the house will run, and affairs of state will be handled. Do not sacrifice another chance to be happy because of paperwork, take it and run with it, be happy."

She thought about her words, as high above the birds chirped in the trees, and the gentle sound of Branna's breathing appeared to surround her and comfort her. Had Gwendolyn seen something in her own future that had not been in her own dreams? She was aware that Gwendolyn had become a powerful seer for the Fae, so had her words held a much deeper meaning than Ariel had at first realised?

She was not sure, all that could really guide her at the moment was the power that surged within her to reconnect with Branna. This was not at all like her, she had never been a reckless person, her life as the historian had always taught her to be cool and calm and think every last detail through, and yet look at her now. She smiled and gave a small chuckle as she shook her head slowly.

"Am I crazy?"

*I*t did appear insane compared to who she had been, but deep down inside she knew that she was never going to be that person again, after all, she had packed her bag ready, and when the time came, she had not for one second even given the moment a single thought. She had grabbed her bag and jumped to Bran, and after an age of not seeing her, her heart had raced and the heat inside her had boiled up from nowhere, and before she had realised, she had been in her arms, kissing her, biting her lip, caressing her tongue in a manner of which she had never thought she was capable.

Her heart began to beat faster as the memory of the previous night flooded into her, had it not been her that tore at Branna's dress, pulling it from her as she dragged her down onto the floor? She had no idea of what had possessed her, all she knew was the moment she saw her, she had wanted her more than she had ever thought possible, and she had dragged her down, pulling her clothes off as she kissed and sucked and bit the body of her lover, and it had been intoxicating and wonderful as her desires had taken her to a level of passion and lust that she honestly had never thought she was capable of.

Ariel gave another little chuckle, had it not been everything she had thought of alone in that house on Florae, had it not been glorious to throw back the formal Scribe and just devour the woman she loved? She turned to look at Branna lay on her back her eyes closed, and her thick mane of tatty black hair spread out across the flattened grass and fern.

Her face was paler than it had been in Avalon, and she looked more rested than she had been, working all hours on her research. She had lost a little weight, but it suited her, as her body looked more toned than it had before, her eyes ran down her torso from her soft medium sized breasts, down her flat stomach to that patch of closely cropped dark hair, to Ariel she was without doubt the most beautiful person she had ever met. She leaned down and softly kissed her on the lips.

Branna gave a groan followed by a slight sigh, and then her lips responded, her arm came up as she stirred, and her hand touched the back of Ariel's head and pushed it closer to enjoy the kiss. Ariel felt her heart race and the heat within her rose up again, and her kiss intensified, she knew that she had not done yet, and she slipped slowly down to the side of Branna as their lips separated to allow them to breathe.

"I have missed you so much Bran."

That familiar feeling ran across her and down between her legs, it appeared Branna also was not done, and they had all the time in the world to finish. Ariel felt the pulse run through her body and gave a breathless gasp.

"Oh Bran!"

Malcolm Lord of Fae stood at the top of the steps, in front of the House of Scribes, with Master Elgin of the counsel, as Bade came hurrying up towards them. Malcolm had a stern look as he noticed Bade give a shake of his head to Elgin. He gave a sigh.

"This is not good, the queen was adamant if Ariel left, she would be going into peril, she will not take this news well." Bade arrived gasping for air.

"There is no sign of her… I am not sure, but I think she took some of her belongings with her…I cannot sense her in the realm; she must have gone in the night." Elgin patted Bade on the shoulder.

"This is ill news, but if she chose to leave willingly, there really is little we can do, we all know how she feels about the girl from Avalon, if she has been in contact with her, then I fear Ariel has stepped onto the path of her own destiny." Malcolm gave a heavy sigh.

"I must find her and bring her and this girl back here, at least in this realm we can protect them, when the Queen of Moon hears of this, I am sure she will go looking for them, we must find Ariel first and protect her." Elgin agreed, as Bade regulated his breathing and nodded in agreement.

"She must be made to understand the danger she has put herself in, her only protection for now will be here, no matter what the Queen of Moon may say, she is not the type to give up. I fear when this news reaches Avalon, Rhiannon will release all her hounds in search of Ariel, this is not a simple matter for her, she sees this as personal."

Malcolm knew all too well the power of Rhiannon, he had heard far more on this matter than any, and he knew how important it was to Bridget to protect Ariel. There had been many long nights like last night, where the terrors of the night came to Bridget, and he had been her only companion in those dreadful moments.

The long conversations that followed those panic filled hours had revealed much to him of Bridget's thinking, and especially her disagreements with the moon queen, his mind raced as the group walked back towards the meeting room deep within the House of Scribes. He knew that something had to be done, the problem was without knowing where Ariel had run to, there really was little he could do. They entered the room where the servants hurried to set up a table of food and drinks, Bade who had recovered his breath, spoke quietly with Elgin, as both of them watched the servants. Elgin gave a nod and looked to Malcolm, it was clear he was holding his words back, and gestured for them to sit.

*T*he three of them were seated at the table, and then waited until the servants had attended to them, before Elgin dismissed them. He lifted a freshly baked cob and broke it apart, as the last of the staff cleared the room, then broke some cheese from the block and took a large bite. Malcolm was lost in thought, as his mind retraced everything that had happened over the previous years, his eye caught the gaze of Elgin, and he stirred from his thoughts.

"What?" Elgin swallowed.

"I was saying that I think we need to contain the news of Ariel's departure, I feel it would be more prudent to keep things quiet, after all, Ariel has been known to travel throughout the realm in the last few years, so it is not uncommon for her to be away for a few weeks at a time, it may give us time to decide what to do and act." Bade gave a long sigh.

"But we have no idea where she has gone, I cannot find a single trace of her, she must be using a veil to hide her location from everyone." Malcom gave an agreeable nod.

"Although if memory serves me well, didn't Luminaria make reports that we have stored, of her reports of this Branna's movements?" Bade understood.

"Well yes she did, she was convinced that the girl left the mainland and crossed across the continent to a place called Hispanic, via Gaul, I believe the last reports came from the southern Sachsen region heading into Bohemia." Malcom gave a nod as he thought.

"The way I see it, compared to our living standards the world of men is crude and unsophisticated, a member of any Fae race will stand out, I will start there." Elgin frowned.

"You will?" Malcom gave a nod.

"I promised the queen I would watch over her, and so I feel duty bound to go after her, get me those reports Bade, I wish to study them before I set off." He rose from his seat. "I will talk to Bridget, Ninian and Erin can care for the queen in my absence, I will head first to Avalon and consult Luminaria, before I head out across this world of men." Elgin was unsure.

"I am not sure you would be a very welcome guest of Avalon considering the circumstances."

"My granddaughter is in that realm with Merlin, I shall pass it off as a visit, I am sure Merlin would offer good counsel and some assistance. Have no fear, I will create no unrest or bad feelings and conduct myself as I always have, as the regent of my queen. Prepare the papers Bade, I wish to consult a few good friends to accompany me, it will have to be a small party so as not to arouse more suspicion, and remember no matter what, keep the news of her disappearance to a minimum, well at least for now, it will buy us time."

Malcom turned and strode from the room, Bade watched on unsure.

"Are you sure this is wise Master Elgin?" Elgin gave a soft smile.

"Our lord regent is a powerful man Bade; he understands the workings of the Fae better than most. I would also add he is a man of great honour, and he has sworn not just to our queen, but his wife that he would protect the child they raised together after the loss of Enaria. Do not underestimate the power of Malcolm, for it was under his guidance that Queen Bridget led us all from the Forest of Time, through the trials of the land of Erin and onto the Violet Isle. Malcom has singlehandedly supervised the building of this realm, and trained his son to continue his role here. I am sure that if anyone can find Ariel it will be Malcolm of Fae, and if he does not find her, I fear we may never see Ariel again.

*N*o one realised at that time, how the words of Master Elgin would ring to a certain degree with truth, and like many other stories of that time, the mystery of the disappearance of Ariel and Branna, would fade into history, and become a forgotten act, and nothing but a story, that at times the older ones would tell their children to pass the hours of winter's darkness. Malcolm would leave his wife and search all the realm of men, and return seven years later looking older and worn, to face his wife and ailing queen, to report of his failure to find the child they raised as parents, as a duty bound favour to their beloved friend Enaria.

Within the year, Malcolm died, leaving the weakened queen of the Fae, broken hearted and declining rapidly. Some say he died of a broken heart, destroyed by his inability to keep his sacred promise to Bridget, and Enaria, to protect the heritage of the Fae of Earth, by ensuring the line of the mystics. Others have told of how he returned a lesser man, broken by his heart breaking search, facing the wild tribes of the men of earth, which left him exhausted and depleted. The simple truth is no one knows, the older recorded facts were that he returned half the man he had been when he left. Whatever the cause, it had a huge impact on Bridget, for he was the love of her life, and her greatest support.

Bridget Violet, beloved queen to the fae of the Earth, fought on, but shortly after her granddaughter married the lord Merlin, she rose one night, and walked high into the mountain range of Florae, and entered the sacred cave of burial, at the peak of Mount Bridge, where she fell to her knees, before the ornate tomb of her husband Malcolm. To its side, was the long white empty tomb, carved from white marble, in ornate design, and lined with the white crystal of protection, which she had prepared long in advance. On her knees, fighting with all of her last energy, she summoned the White Lord to attend to her, and prepared her final moments.

*A*cross the realms in Avalon, Gwendolyn felt the chill run through her bones and sat up abruptly in bed. Merlin opened his eyes and looked up at her.

"Gwen, what is wrong?" She wiped her brow, and turned to him.

"Something is wrong, I cannot explain it, I have to return home, there is danger."

He sat up in bed and pulled back the covers, he did not question, he simply trusted her, and stood up and reached for his clothes.

"Hurry and dress, we should make all haste and get you there." Gwendolyn nodded, and slid out of bed and reached for her dress, Merlin slipped on his sandals, and hurried out of the room. He too sensed something, but he was aware of that feeling and knew who waited beyond his door. He walked briskly down the hallway, and pulled back the bolt, and as the door swung back, he saw his master dressed in a long tatty robe, and bowed.

"Master, what is it that I must do?"

The dark figure stood still the tip of his hood moving gently in the breeze, his voice was soft, but carried with it the urgency of the moment.

"Prepare her, for her destiny will begin this night. Go to Florae, and wait by the falls, for this night, her people will finally be free, and she will be needed to unite them, a time of great darkness approaches, and she must gather her strength and take the seat, for her lands will endure great pain, and she must be there to ease their sadness, the future of her line depends on her more than ever." Merlin gave a bow.

"I understand my Master, I will be by her side and aide her all I can."

A streak of white shot into the sky, and Merlin turned at his door, Gwendolyn came out of their room pulling her long blue cloak around her, she looked afraid.

"What did he say, I felt his presence?" Merlin walked slowly towards her and took her hand in his.

"It is time, we must go to the falls and await her time, Gwen her time is over and it is now the right moment for you to respond and comfort your people." She shook her head as her eyes filled with tears.

"I cannot… I am not ready, not yet, I have matters with her to arrange." Merlin gave a sigh.

"All has been done my dear, she is far too weary to remain, your people must look to you from this night. Gwen, we knew this time would come, it is time for you to stand in her place." He squeezed her hand softly, and pulled her into his embrace, and just for a moment he held her close, and could feel her trembling. Gwendolyn gave a soft sob into his shoulder.

"Help my love for I feel my strength is deserting me, I cannot bear the thought of her not being here, I am but a pale replacement for her." He gave a gentle smile, and tightened his embrace.

"Gwen, you must trust in this, in yourself, she has taught you all she knows. Time cannot be altered, now is your time, and whether you believe it or not, you are ready, it is why she feels secure, knowing she can leave in peace. Do you really think she would leave you unprepared?"

Gwendolyn swallowed hard, as her tears ran down her cheeks.

"I still have such doubts, how can I rule in her shadow, there will never be another like her? My love, I fear I cannot fill her shoes, I need Ariel, she is the only one who could advise me, and she is gone and hidden from all of us, she has the lines of wisdom I need. She alone understands the legacy of my grandmother, how can I rule without her?"

"Gwen, you have no other choice, the time is upon us. Wipe your doubts away with your tears, for your people need you, and trust in yourself and you will arise a queen of great standing in her likeness. Trust all she has taught you, now more than ever before, believe in her and trust her, she knows what will become of her realm."

It was several long minutes before Gwendolyn took a deep breath, fastened her cloak, and lifted her bag. Merlin smiled and holding her hand, the young frightened figure of Gwendolyn walked out of the door and into the cool night, and with a faint pop, they disappeared, and reappeared in Florae.

All over the realm bells rang out, and people wept openly as they gathered below the steps of the house of scribes, where Bade stood on the uppermost step, holding a royal proclamation delivered to Master Elgin. He stood before the gathered crowd and swallowed hard, and looked at the parchment written in the hand of Ninian, he took one last breath, and the bells stopped and silence descended, broken only by the murmurs of those who had realised what was about to befall the realm.

"People of Florae, and of the Earth, I stand here, as instructed by the line of my queen, with the sad tidings, that upon this night, our cherished and beloved Queen Bridget Violet has made her way to await the moment of her passing, beside her beloved husband Malcolm." He felt his voice tremble and tears formed in his eyes.

"The realm is closed, and her family have been summoned, bow your heads, and mourn, for the brightest light of our people, will soon diminish."

He fell to his knees and silently wept, as all over Florae, the Fae of Earth did likewise, as they looked to the floor, and openly wept in the streets and fields. It was a heart breaking display of open affection for a queen who had loved and nurtured her people, and saved them by gathering them together in a new realm, where they had flourished.

*H*igh up on the mount the tall black robed figure walked down the tunnel and into the vast cave, to see Bridget crouched on the floor before her husband's tomb, she looked up as he entered.

"My Lord, I fear I have not the strength to stand, now is the time to fulfil the oath you swore to me. Help me, for I can endure this no more."

The was an air of sadness to the lord of time, as he walked over towards her, and gently rested his translucent hand upon her shoulder.

"Here, let me give you the strength to fulfil your chosen task, arise from the floor, and be their queen one more time." Bridget smiled, as she felt the strength return to her legs, and she gave a nod as she finally lifted herself up, and once more stood proud as the Queen of Fae.

"Thank you, my dearest of friends, I have cherished our times together, since the passing of Enaria, you have been a great strength to me."

"I think she would have been very proud of you for the sacrifice you have made for your people, you can rest assured that I will watch over your line and guide them when I can."

Bridget took a deep laboured breath, and opened her hand, to reveal she was holding the black star of Enaria, she looked down on it.

"It looks so small, I hope Enaria was right, for I feel a great deal must go into it. Promise me you will keep this safe, and my people will never be threatened again." His hood twitched.

"I have given my word to you, even though you hide much from me, and I cannot deny, in somethings I am mystified as to why you feel you had to do this alone, but I have sworn my oath. I stand by my word, and will uphold it and stay true to my word, not because I have to, but because it was requested by someone whom I hold great respect for." She smiled; it was a mighty compliment indeed.

Bridget lifted the black star shaped stone and held it close to her heart. "When this is done, protect it and ensure no other ever finds it and uses it. Gwendolyn will take my place, and she will do great things, even though she fears the task, guide her for me and show her the depths of what I have taught her… I am ready My Lord… Now is the time."

Bridget Violet, First Queen of the Fae of the Earth, stood upright, and held the black star in her right hand against her chest, the White Lord opened up his arms, and stepped forward to embrace her. "Goodbye my sacred friend, rest well."

A flash of bright blue brought Merlin and Gwendolyn onto the road before the tall central buildings of Florae. Holding hands, they began to walk at speed towards the gathered crowds, who had filled all the open court before the House of Scribes, and surrounded the large central open space where the waters of the realm poured from the many streams down into the huge cave below, creating the Whispering Falls.

Gwendolyn's bright blue eyes looked to the House of Scribes, set to the back drop of the peak of Mount Bridge, she walked quickly her heart pounding towards the people she would soon rule over. No one really noticed her at first as everyone bowed and looked to the house, she hurried forward, and then above the peak above the city, a stream of bright white light exploded into the air, and cut through the sky and up into the darkness. Gwendolyn stopped and felt her heart break.

"No… No, I am too late."

She turned and she burst into tears, and Merlin gripped her hard, as she flung herself into him and wept bitterly. As she wept in his arms, Merlin watched as the thick column of white light gave a pulse, and radiated out, and as everyone looked to the sky, they saw a bright white dome form over the whole realm. Bridget became the protection of her people, Merlin smiled as he understood what she had done, and he marvelled at the skill that she had used. Although, at that moment, he had no idea that Bridget would never be seen in any other realm again, as she had chosen to become the barrier of white, that would hold out the darkness forever, the White Lord had kept his promise, and honoured his oath to her.

As Gwendolyn wept, Merlin watched as before him a single beam of light fell down from the sky, and before him the light expanded to create the form of Bridget, he patted Gwendolyn as she sobbed into his chest.

"Gwen, face your future." She swallowed hard and looked up at him, and saw his face shimmering in white, she turned and felt the shock run through her, as the shimmering form of Bridget stood before her. Bridget smiled.

"Hush child, you are to be queen, for you are the one I chose to follow me. Dry your eyes, and know, that your people will prosper under your rule." Gwendolyn wiped her eyes.

"I am not ready; I did not want you to leave." Bridget smiled a loving smile. Neither of them realised that the people of the realm had fallen silent and had turned, and were watching as the young slender figure of Gwendolyn shared her last moment with her grandmother.

"Gwendolyn my child, you are more than ready. Never forget, that you like all your subjects at heart, are just a simple member of the Fae, hold that dear to you, and your rule will be balanced and even. Who you are now, is who you should always be, even whilst wearing a crown, for then you will understand the life of your people and they will prosper. Gwendolyn my child you saw me as a queen, yet I always saw myself as a mother, and a simple grandmother, I never saw myself as a queen, and in that I lived amongst my people with true understanding of their life, and therefore could make the choices that was best for them. Never forget, it was I who named you, my heir."

As the people of Fae watched in awe, they saw Bridget lift her arm, and command Gwendolyn to kneel. Merlin stepped back as Bridget smiled, and as she twisted her wrist above Gwendolyn, a white circle appeared in the air above her. The people watched as Bridget turned, and face the gathered inhabitants of the realm, her voice was loud and clear.

"People of Florae, I give you a queen, take her to your hearts and embrace her as you did me, let it be known, that I chose her to follow me, and name her White Circle." Bridget turned as Gwendolyn looked up and she gave her a loving smile. "Arise Gwendolyn White Circle, new Queen of Fae of the Earth."

The hovering circle of white light dropped to the earth around Gwendolyn, and she was instantly engulfed in light, and the people fell to their knees, and covered their faces such was the purity of light that surround her. Master Elgin stood and watched as the light was slowly absorbed into Gwendolyn, and he smiled, and spoke quietly, so only Bade who knelt at his feet could hear him.

"Goodbye my precious queen, you chose with great wisdom, but there again you always did, I shall miss you, and was honoured to serve you, and now I will serve your chosen one with the equal honour."

The bright light around Gwendolyn gave a pulse and then slowly was drawn into her, and there was no sign of Bridget. Gwendolyn rose to her feet feeling nervous, before her people were standing and watching her. Behind them came three loud bangs as Bade thrust his staff into the floor of the top step. Elgin's voice echoed all around the valley floor.

"The queen has passed, long may our new queen reign. Arise and welcome Gwendolyn White Circle, your new Queen of Fae." Merlin appeared at her side, and lifted her arm into his.

"Your highness, your people await you." She swallowed hard.

"My Love, I am terrified." He smirked.

"Good, you should be." She glanced at him and he smiled. "All the great queens are you know." She smiled.

"I am so glad you are here."

Gwendolyn walked towards the House of Scribes and Royal Lodge along the road, and the people parted to create a wide open path, as she approached they bowed with great reverence, and she felt awkward and uncomfortable, even as a princess, she had never felt as on the spot as she did now, it felt strange and surreal. Merlin smiled as he walked at her side as she approached the steps up to the house where Elgin awaited her, she came slowly up then feeling apprehensive, and Elgin gave a regal bow.

"My Queen, as your servant and master of the house and council, I offer my life and my service. Your council awaits as we prepare for your coronation." Gwendolyn gave a nod, and took a deep breath.

"Thank you, Lord Elgin, would you kindly lead the way." He gave a nod, and Bade gave a bow and hurriedly walked towards the door, he banged hard on the brass plate with his staff.

"Open the house, your queen awaits entrance." The mighty doors swung open, and Gwendolyn new Queen of Fae followed Elgin, and holding the arm of Merlin, she entered the house, and the people roared with their cheers into the air, for a new era had begun.

Ariel sat on a rock at the edge of the bridge and looked out into the woodland. Branna came walking down the long bridge and stood beside her holding a goblet of silver with wine in it.

"You feel it too?" Ariel nodded.

"She has passed, I feel it, and I feel the sadness in my heart. I should be with Gwendolyn; she will need guidance." Branna understood.

"You can go to her, but if you do, you know what will happen."

Ariel gave a sigh.

"I know Bran, she has never given up and she never will, for as long as we live Rhiannon will search for us. My hope lies in the strength of Gwendolyn, and that as a second queen, the power that passes is stronger and gives her greater wisdom, for only then do I have hope Rhiannon will stop." Branna gripped her shoulder softly.

"Gwendolyn will not stop her, there is only one that can, and one day I will. I bide my time, but a day will come when we walk in Florae again, you will see, I promised you that I would find a way to return you home, and I will not fail you." Ariel stood up and turned to her.

"It matters not Bran, not today, Bridget was my Queen, and she was also a mother to me, I am Fae of Earth, and we differ from your line. I am not ungrateful Bran, I love being back with you, but this is not Florae, and today I need to be alone, there are things I wish to do to honour the person who saved me and raised me, and I would like to do that." Branna gave a smile, she did understand.

"You must honour her, I do understand you know, I walked away from the traditions of my race, but you are free to choose your own path. Ariel you are not a prisoner here, yes this land is veiled, but it is not a cage, it is the only way I can live free of her grip. Go and honour Bridget, she deserves it, she was good to her people."

Ariel moved close and kissed her softly on the lips. "I will be back soon." She turned and walked into the forest to gather herbs and prepare her private ritual. Branna watched as she disappeared feeling a sense of sadness inside her. Roack flew down and sat on the stone rail.

"The woman of white clouds your mind, ignore her." Branna's eyes moved to the bird.

"You have what you wanted, Beren has his army and his three children, and you have an army of dark souls to play with, Ariel is mine, she is all I have ever truly wanted. I have told you Roack, if she is harmed in anyway, I will send you and all of your legion of dark souls back, so leave her alone to follow her way of her people and do not interfere."

The bird gave a disgruntled squark, and lifted into the air, and Branna moved her eyes back to the trees and stared onto the path Ariel had taken.

Chapter Thirty One.

The Passing Of Bridget.

Albanlin loosened his arms and she slipped onto his arm. He lifted her up, and cradled her like a small child, as he looked down upon her. Her face was restful, and the dark lines below her eyes, had appeared to have faded away. "Such a loss, be at peace Queen Bridget, I shall miss you. You taught me much in your time, of the ways of your people, and I will be forever grateful to you."

He walked slowly around the tomb, and lowered her inside, onto the bed of silks, and rested her head on her pillow. Her arms were folded onto her heart, and as he gazed upon her one last time, from under his sleeve a translucent hand slipped out, and gently slipped the black star from her grip.

"You are free of it now, and cleansed for all time, how sad those who saw you as lesser, did not understand your wisdom. Your legacy will not die my good friend, I will ensure it."

He stepped back, and lifted his arm, and outside the cave tunnel, where a wall of pure light prevented entrance, Bridget's son Ninian, with his wife Erin of Kell, waited. As the light dropped, they walked inside, and down the long tunnel towards the tomb. Albanlin walked to the far side of the large cave, as he heard them approach, and his robes faded into the wall, and the cave was empty as Ninian limped inside.

Moments later Gwynfor arrived, and knelt on the floor at the side of his mother's tomb and wept bitterly. Outside the air flashed blue, and Gwendolyn appeared at the side of Merlin, and as she appeared, Eve stood in a long red robe, and pulled her into her embrace, and Gwendolyn burst into tears.

"My sweet child of the White Circle, I feel the pain that hides within you, let it free, her torment is over. Her loss is bitter, but her wisdom and love for her people ran deep, I feel it within you. I feel her presence around you, cast off your doubts and use all she taught you in her place."

Gwendolyn pulled her head back and wiped her tears. Eve smiled a warm and loving smile, as Gwendolyn looked her.

"I was not ready to say goodbye to her, she was the life of this realm, and of our people, she gave so much of herself to protect all of us, I fear I cannot match her, for her love was vast." Eve nodded.

"It was, and she gave so much of it to you. Dig deep and look within you, for I see all of her love as it flows through you. Trust me White Circle, you have so much to give to your people, carry it round and share it as she did and you will succeed." Eve took her hand, and gave her a smile.

"This will be hard for me for I loved her dearly as a sister, walk with me my child and let us stand together and say our goodbyes." Gwendolyn swallowed hard, and took a deep breath, and at the side of Eve, she walked into the cave, and down the tunnel, and entered the chamber of her grandfather and grandmother, to see Bridget one last time, and say her final words of heart broken departure.

*A*riel walked into the woodland, the feeling of loss within herself was strong, this was the first time since leaving Florae she had felt homesick, because she knew that in the House of Scribes preparations would be underway for the crowning of Gwendolyn, who to Ariel, was almost like a daughter.

Knowing Bridget had gone forever felt painful, she had lost her mother as a child, and now the woman who took her in and raised her beside her son Ninian, had also left her, and she felt very much alone in the world.

Returning to Branna had made her so happy, although she had not been happy when she first saw the crude castle that was being built, it gave her a strange sense within herself, and she felt fear when she entered it, so much so, she lived outside the castle near the old village in Branna's caravan. It actually suited her better, she had grown solitary in her isolation on Florae, and the castle was loud and noisy with the men, who she found crude and cruel.

Branna was a regular visitor, and she would stay with her many nights talking of her life of travels and her aims to protect her people. Ariel felt torn, part of her was still the Branna she knew, but she was different, especially around Berengar, who whilst always polite with her, gave her the impression he was not that keen on her being around Ariel.

Alone in the trees, she sat on an old fallen tree and wept her tears, and her thoughts focused on Bridget as she wandered through her thoughts, as she drifted through her memories of her final days on Florae, and her last meeting with Bridget. They had walked in the trees high up on the slopes above the House of Scribes.

"How are you doing with your mother's journals?" Bridget smiled and her violet eyes shone with life, although below her eyes were still black, and she had aged, with a thick white stripe now a feature of her long dark hair.

"I have learned a great deal about her life, and my father before I came along. It has been nice to understand their bond of deep love, and the skills of my father, I have noticed similar patterns of his within myself, and it has comforted me."

"I liked Bryant, he was a dedicated writer of runes, but he also had a very strong inner strength. I remember when your mother first met him, she was captivated from the moment she first laid eyes on him, as was he, they loved each other deeply from that moment on. I think for you it was similar with this Branna you lived with in Avalon." She stopped and took Ariel by the hand.

"Ariel, you are like a daughter to me, and I know you, and I can see how much you miss her, why stay when you are free to go as you please?" Ariel gave a smirk.

"Am I though? If I leave this realm, I will be in Rhiannon's grasp within the day. I am not unhappy here, but since returning, I do not feel like I fully belong anywhere. My life was planned to be at her side. I swore to her it would be, and because of Rhiannon she was forced to flee or suffer the return to her home realm, where she would be a prisoner. I really do understand that my fellow scribes have trouble understanding me, but they have never experienced the kind of life I had with Bran, and I want that again. It may make no sense, but one day when she is safe, I know she will send for me, and even if those here do not agree, I will go to her."

Bridget understood, her bright violet eyes watched her intently, she lifted her hand to her neck, and unfastened a chain. It slipped from her neck, and she pulled it free and held it up before Ariel. Ariel looked down at it, she recognised it straight away, for it was a silver star set in a circle of Amethyst, Bridget turned her hand and it slid from her palm into Ariel's.

"On that final day, when we left together, your mother gave me this. She told me there would be a shadow across your life at some stage, and it was important that at that time you had a connection to her. I sense your unease, and it is growing stronger, and I feel the shadow she saw is drawing near, take this and wear it always, and in a time of need, you will not be alone."

Ariel came out of her thoughts as she fingered her pendant, so much had happened since that day. It was not long after, she returned to Branna and spent that night in the woodlands with her. The following day, Branna had told her of her new life and the kingdom she would build, and introduced her to Berengar. She sat in her room in the crude castle, where work was still going on to build it, and explained the story of how she found Berengar and nursed him back to health, and then swore a pact, that she would help him, and in return he would help protect her from Rhiannon.

It made little sense until the day she met Roack, which for Ariel was shocking. Tying her life to a raven was considered a penalty punishable by death to the Fae Ofmoon, for only a queen was given that power. The memory slipped into her thoughts, as she turned and looked at Branna, sat on her large bed.

"How in all the realms could you be so stupid, have you any idea what will happen if Rhiannon finds out?" Branna shrugged.

"What can she do, it is too late, I have the same power she does, and now I have the strength and the means to protect us. Ariel, in Avalon I was at her mercy and look what happened, she tried to imprison you, and I had to flee, I was too weak to protect the only thing in my life I had left that I loved. Have you any idea how I felt?"

It caught Ariel's breath, for a moment she felt stunned, Branna had never really admitted deep feelings, she had always joked and fooled around, but stood there seeing the resolve in Branna's eyes and the passion that had flowed out with her words, she struggled with her thoughts and words. Ariel took a breath and tried to calm herself.

"Oh, for the lords of all the realms look at us, I love you as deeply Bran, my life without you has been a misery, you will never know of my nights of anguish missing you so deeply it tore at my being. Bran the bird has been tied to the Merle, you cannot ask me not to worry, it frightens me, I cannot lose you again, I will not survive it. What if it corrupts you? Bran if just the little I know from what you speculated back in Avalon is true, it could consume you to the point where even you see me as a threat. My mother was Enaria, she was a power of pure light, and whether I want it or not, the Merle will see me as its enemy." She shook her head.

"It cannot, Ariel I am Fae, we live on the Moon realm surrounded by the darkness, our abilities are such we can control it, there are rights and rituals we do not share with others that allow us to isolate other forms of power and control, so we remain intact. Don't you see, that is why I have full control, she knew all along that it infected her lines, it is why all children are taught the containment charm when they are young. Rhiannon knows some of those in her line have a Merle infection, and she has hidden the truth. Ariel, I can teach it you, and we can be joined properly."

Ariel walked over and sat with a thump on the bed, she took Branna's hand in hers, and softly squeezed it.

"No, of all the Fae of Earth you chose to fall in love with, I am the only one who cannot be joined to you. Bran my blood is from the line of pure light, my whole body is the weapon that could be used to destroy you, no darkness can enter me, actually I am the one person who can live here and not be affected by it. We can never join in that way, what we have is all we have."

"I do not care, Ariel, I just want you, I want you here with me I want the life we had in Avalon. Beren is my protector, and a means to children nothing more. I have no feelings for him in the way I do you, we are friends indebted to each other, who share the same feelings of vengeance for the evil done to us. What I have done I have done to be truly free of her and her Marshals, no one can hurt us here." Ariel gave a slight smile as she looked in the sincere dark eyes of Branna.

"I understand I really do, I just wished you had waited until I got here, there are other ways I could have helped you, that did not involve using the Merle."

Ariel left and went back to her caravan to consider what she had learned and spent the night alone. Branna gave her three days of space before she came to her, and that day and night sat in the caravan, Branna explained how it was the only way she could prevent Rhiannon from finding them, as it allowed her the power to create a veil across the whole region and hide her from the moon.

They ended up in bed and made love, and for a whole week Branna remained at her side and spent her time walking in the woodlands talking with her, as she spoke of her dream to build a tribe and live free protected by Berengar and his army. She talked of how she would raise a family using Berengar, as the seed for her new family line, and how Ariel would be able to help her raise them at her side. It was true the Varisci were fierce and ruthless as warriors, but at least both of them would always be safe.

*F*rom that day forth, time slipped by, and Branna gave birth to her first son, whom she named Amand. Her second child Dagaric soon followed and then three years ago she gave birth to Maud, her first female of her line. Maud was a strange child, she had none of the qualities of Branna, and she was dark and brooding as a baby, making little noise but always aware. Berengar showed little interest in her, she was small and stunted and shamed Branna, telling her the child was cursed.

Ariel was aware Berengar knew little of the lines of Fae, and he had no knowledge of the passage of power in the female line. Branna doted on the child for it was clear, like all fae the child had been bestowed with gifts, and yet Ariel sensed something more within her, something powerful, and yet sinister. She felt guilty because she was only a small child, and yet there was something about the child's eyes, a coldness, a darkness, and even though Ariel entered the castle each day to attend to her, she felt afraid of the power within Maud.

Ariel had heard a great deal about what Berengar referred to as the gathering, Branna talked little of it, except to say, it was a feast and a meeting of the tribe. Ariel was seen as an outsider, and during their first shortly after her arrival, Filiberta had taken her outside the castle, and told her never to attend it. She knew that Ariel was kind and filled with love, and warned her to stay in her caravan, and stay as far from the castle as possible. Ariel listened, she had always sensed the good in Filiberta, and so heeded her advice. On the night of the gathering after the meeting and the feast, Branna came to Ariel in her caravan, and stayed with her until the sun rose.

Ariel knew there was something happening Branna wanted to hide, but over the years she grew tired of asking what, as all Branna would ever say, was that the tribesmen acted like fornicating animals, and it was not something that should be witnessed by the pure of heart. Ariel was no fool, and had once entered the large round room by mistake, where a circle of seats with perches above them were arranged in a large circle, it had not taken long to realise, each member of the family had been tied to one of the many ravens that lived in the castle.

Branna spoke little about Berengar's brothers, and it had been Filiberta who had spoken of her son's, many were wary of Otto, he was rumoured to be cruel and sadistic. Yet when she met Vladimir, who travelled a great deal with his own group of warriors, she had found him to be polite and respectful, if not a little flirty at first. Otto spent a lot of his time leading raids outside the castle, so was away for long periods, and often returned in the night, only to leave the following day.

It felt very strange to Ariel, she was not unhappy, and yet there were stories from those who came from the villages scattered all around the valleys to trade, of the coldness and cruelty of Branna's army. Branna had appeared to be colder than Ariel had known her to be in Avalon, but over her time, Branna had warmed and become caring and loving towards her. After several years, she was not unsimilar to how she had been in the house in Avalon, and for Ariel that had become all that had mattered to her.

Branna was her centre of everything, and living in her caravan, with her writing and drawing, she had become used to the rough warriors around her. Most of the time they ignored her, and just went about their duties. Ariel helped with the children of the tribe and schooled them, in the ways of scribing, so all of them learned to read and write Runes. It was enough, it was a simple life, and Berengar provided plenty for her, and she had Branna to herself most evenings, Berengar was after all, just her lover and regent in the castle, Branna assured her, he was never short of women to warm his bed. Life went on and eight years passed by, and Ariel had found she had grown contented with her solitary life.

Today was hard, she had felt a sense deep within her, all day, and that afternoon, Branna had sought her out and told her of a rider who had arrived at the castle, with the news of the death of Bridget. For most of the day she had wandered alone through the woodland, remembering home and those who had loved her. In many ways it had felt like Avalon, she had arrived and met Branna, and suddenly her thoughts of Florae had diminished, until of course today. She gave a sigh and stood up still fingering her pendant as she remembered

Bridget, her queen.

*S*he found the path that led her back to the old village and her caravan, and was walking along lost in thought, when she remembered a moment from the day she left Florae to head to Avalon as an ambassador. She had met with Bridget to collect her papers and have one last meeting about her reports. They talked for an hour, and then as the time came close for her departure, Bridget had lifted a box and walked to the table with it.

"Ariel these were made by your father and charmed by your mother, there were five when she gifted them to me, Gwendolyn has one, and Gwynfor the other, and I have one as well as Malcolm." She opened the box, which was lined with red fabric, and there were four empty spaces, but in the fifth, was a small dagger of steel, engraved with intricate runes.

"When we moved to the land of Erin, I always carried one in the back of my belt. Your mother told me, if attacked, if would inflict a severe wound, especially from any who had a heart for bad deeds. As queen I have never felt threatened, and yet I took note of her words and have always carried one. My children have one each, and you are like a daughter to me heading into the unknown of a new realm, I feel in my gut this may one day play a part in your safety, so I want you to take this last one, and carry it always in Avalon." Bridget lifted out the small dagger in its sheath and handed it to her, Ariel took it, and admired the craftsmanship of it.

"I will be an ambassador; I am sure I will be safe and protected. I understand the rift between you and Rhiannon, but I am sure she will ensure my safety at all times."

"Nevertheless Ariel, I will feel more at ease if you take it, it will put my mind at rest."

Ariel took it and slipped it into the back of her belt, it was light and small, and under her cloak completely out of sight. She came out of her thought of remembrance, and slid her hand round the back of her waist and felt it, and knew it was secure if required. This place was filled with warriors and yet she felt safe, she knew Branna had ordered she must be protected, and kept unharmed at all times, but even so, she was taking no chances.

*I*n Florae as the evening approached Hearne and Eve, joined

Gwendolyn with Merlin and other officials as the family of Bridget, brought everyone together in their time of grief. In the large hall, the table was laid out ready, as everyone gathered in a large side room. Outside the people mourned their queen as tributes were placed along the road, in the form of flowers and lanterns, and people openly wept as they knelt or walked the long road to the Royal Lodge sharing tales and remembering their lost queen for whom they held great love.

As the light faded, a bright burst of light appeared at the bottom of the road, and riders in blue rode out carrying large silver horns and played a fanfare. The Fae of Earth were startled and scattered into the fields, as a long line of horses rode along the road carrying the Marshals of the Fae Ofmoon in the centre of which was Rhiannon on a pure white horse. Her husband accompanied her, and before her rode Rayne and her daughter Eleanor.

At the front rode Luminaria in her full ceremonial uniform, as she commanded the Marshals. They rode towards the Royal Lodge as Bade watched alerted by the fanfare, he turned to guard the on the doors.

"Send a runner and inform the Princess that Rhiannon has arrived, it's a little late, but none the less she is here." He turned and watched the long procession. "Eight years I have managed to hide the fact she left, and now she has arrived, I just know she will demand her presence."

Master Elgin walked out of the house and to the side of Bade and watched as Rhiannon approached. He shook his head and gave a sigh.

"Even in the death of our queen, she has to show her power, to ensure the new queen will know her place. Why am I not surprised, this should be a day of mourning for all of Fae, and yet she has to appear, and exert her dominance? I saw this coming and have advised our future queen to meet her in the day room, which is the normal protocol of all state visits, at least that way the Queen of the moon is deprived of her tactless glory." Bade understood, and gave a slight nod.

"I hate to bring it up, but how do we explain the absence of Ariel, she has been gone eight years, and we have managed to keep that quiet?" Elgin smiled.

"As far as Rhiannon and her entourage are concerned, Ariel is on private business ordered by the last queen in another part of the realm and is not to be disturbed until her task is complete, I have already alerted Princess Gwendolyn to that fact." Bade gave a sigh of relief, and was grateful to his master of the house.

"Thank you, I wish I knew where she is, but wherever that is, at this moment in time it is safer than here." Luminaria gave her command and dismounted from her horse, as her Marshal lined the sides of the square. The people of Florae who had gathered to watch, all moved back as the Marshals moved in, Elgin scowled as he watched, and whispered under his breath so just Bade heard him.

"She has got a nerve, our people have more right to be in that square than she does."

*R*hiannon's party arrived, and steps were provided for her to dismount. She came down off her horse assisted by Rayne, and turned towards the steps up to the house and royal apartments. Elgin swept into a regal bow, as Rhiannon with Phwyll walked up the steps, closely followed by Rayne, Eleanor, and Luminaria.

"Your Highness, we are honoured by your visit, and we wish it could be under better circumstances. Our Queen in waiting, the Princess Gwendolyn, will see you immediately in her private royal apartment. If you would care to follow me, I will show you the way."

Rhiannon smirked, as Elgin swept his hand towards the door and led the way. The large doors opened and he guided the royal party through the chamber of the council and queen, where flowers decorated the throne, and had black ribbons adorned to it, and a black flag was draped over the large emblem of Bridget. Rhiannon noted it, and looked round the large chamber, she had not seen it finished, and was very impressed.

*G*wendolyn waited with Merlin, as she stood at the far end of her chamber. The door opened and Bade stepped in, he gave a regal bow.

"Your Royal Highness, the Queen Ofmoon has arrived to pay her respects." He stepped back and pulled wide the doors, Elgin arrived, bowed and stepped to the other side, and Rhiannon appeared in the doorway, Gwendolyn gave a curtsy.

"Your Majesty, I am honoured by your visit." Rhiannon swept in and dragged her into a tight hug.

"Gwendolyn, you poor sweet girl, such a burden to be placed upon you at such a young age, this must be such a difficult time for you. Simply know, I am here, and will always offer you counsel in your times of need. Your Grandmother was such a great woman, it will be difficult filling her shoes." She released Gwendolyn, who gave a polite smile.

"You are very gracious, and I am deeply relieved to know that I will have your support and counsel." Rhiannon appeared happy as she gave a courteous nod to Merlin, who did not bow, but returned his nod of acknowledgement.

"It is good of you to offer such support Rhiannon, at such a difficult time for the line of the White Circle, it is greatly appreciated by all of us." She smiled.

"Queen Bridget was a sister to me, I am deeply wounded at her loss, and could think only of paying my respects to the new queen of this realm. Nothing is more important than this, for the union of the two houses of Fae is strong."

Bade stood outside with his ear to the door, Elgin smiled at his side, as Bade looked up.

"If this was all she could think about, then why did it take her all day to get here?" Elgin gave a chuckle.

"My dear Bade, she is a political animal, every line she will use this night, had to be rehearsed first, so it flowed naturally and appeared sincere, you should know that." Bade gave a nod.

"She is a hypocrite, whatever it was she argued with our lost queen about, she knows has been buried with her and she is off the hook." Elgin raised his eyebrows.

"I am pleased to see you understand the way these things work; it will stand you in good stead one day. Never underestimate the ambition of that woman, her tongue slides freer than a snake. Come, we will alert everyone there will be more guests for the ceremony, and the banquet, we have work to do and a reputation to maintain for our future queen, let us both ensure we do not let her down, tonight will set the scene for the rest of her reign."

Chapter Thirty Two.

Family Rule.

The passing of Bridget was marked with a huge banquet, where people talked of their encounters and celebrated her long life. Eve was tearful as she spoke with great love about her close friend, no one spoke of her dreams or night terrors, it was almost as if they were afraid to.

Rhiannon visited her tomb, and paid her last respects in private, and the night ended late with Rhiannon and her party leaving afterwards to return back to Avalon. Luminaria had enquired as to Ariel, and Elgin explained her absence and her deep sorrow, and informed her of how she had left to another part of the island to carry out her queens last wishes suffering from grief.

Gwendolyn was relatively quiet, and wept a great deal as others told their stories, and for the whole night she watched the Queen of the Moon, something Merlin noted. On her return to Avalon in private Rhiannon fumed, she was no fool, and had received word that Ariel had left the realm, she had her spies everywhere. In a fit of rage, she signed the papers and ordered the immediate return of Luminaria to a new post on the Moon Realm, and her older brother Stenlow, was brought down to Avalon as her replacement.

One moon cycle after the passing of Bridget, as was the custom of the Fae of Earth, Gwendolyn White Circle was crowned Queen of the Fae of Earth, with a huge celebration, as she sat above the steps of the Royal Lodge, and was crowned by Eve. Life for the Fae began to return to normal, as the new queen took up her seat, and under the guidance of Elgin, she began her rule.

The days slipped into years for Gwendolyn, as they did for Ariel, and became part of the history as recorded on the parchments of the Scribes of Florae, and talk of Dark Fae and Branna and Ariel faded out of the memory as other pressing business replaced the day's events. The world of men became restless and unruly, and tribes started wars, and for many long years, all the continents saw turmoil.

Even for Branna, times changed, as tribes grew together and unrest right across the lands of the Germanic became the focus of that time. Otto and Vladimir joined Berengar, as defence of their realm began, and with Branna on watch as her powers improved, the war for land became the focus of everything, and the line of Berengar became a name of fear, as the ruthless army stormed across the continent.

With Berengar away for long periods of time, Ariel and Branna spent more time together. Ariel started to stay over and sleep in Branna's chambers, and with the castle calmer and quieter, and under the influence of Ariel, Branna grew softer and more loving, and a lot of the woman she had been in Avalon came out of her.

Roack was very unhappy, and would talk to the other ravens and voice her hatred of the woman of light, and slowly the word got to Maud, who had grown into a small, squat, unattractive figure of darkness as she reached her eighteenth year. Maud grew bitter and twisted, and very vocal about Ariel and her dislike of her, and on several occasions Branna disciplined her, which incensed her as she screamed at the top of her voice that Ariel would be her downfall.

*A*s a result, the relationship between Branna and Maud became strained, and Maud would sneak off to the basements and study her dark lore, as she looked to find a way to remove Ariel from their lives forever. In her dark basement, she cursed and swore and talked with her raven Rajani, who in turn, talked to Roack.

*B*attles raged, and Berengar was victorious, and his returns home were loud and wild, as all the men celebrated, with food and wine, and endless sexually fuelled escapades. Each time they returned Ariel would slip out back to her caravan and enjoy the quiet isolation away from the men and their lustful stares.

With each return, there were more prisoners, and it confused Ariel, as over time they would swear their allegiance to Branna and Berengar, and became as loyal as any Fae. There were days Ariel would talk to some of the staff, who would quietly express their fear, and yet within the month, they ignored her, or avoided her, and only expressed their love towards Branna, who they started to call their queen. It did not add up, and soon Ariel started to ask questions.

The torches were blazing in the castle, and it was filled with the wild screams of drunken men, as Ariel sat up in bed sweating as Branna lay back smiling. She turned to look at her.

"Bran, I know you told me not to ask, but I am troubled, and have a strange sense within me." Branna sat up and flicked back her long black matted hair.

"Are you having the dreams again?" Ariel shook her head.

"No, it is not that sort of a feeling, I have had the dreams since I returned to Florae, and they still continue here, I think that is my mothers' line within me. Bran I am worried about the captives, they arrive filled with fear, and hatred of your men, and yet within the month they grow into loyal subjects with only praise for you. I know you hate me asking, but Bran that makes no sense to me, you were a slave of sorts in Avalon, and your hatred of Rhiannon still to this day drives you to build an army to defeat her. You could never be subdued by the Fae, how are these captives turned so quickly into loyal soldiers?" Branna watched her with dark eyes, she sat up at her side.

"Ariel, please do not pry, you are safe here under my protection. Look I understand your concern, it is in your whole line to care, we do not kill them, I work very hard to spare lives, but as I have said before, there are some things here you are better off not knowing. Ariel, I love you, I love my life with you, please just do not ask." Ariel gave a sigh.

"I am sorry, I love my life with you too, it makes no sense that someone who I love so dearly because her will is so free, appears to be allowing the taking of the will of others. I guess I never thought that would be you." Branna slipped off the bed, and reached for her goblet of wine.

"As I have said, in order to survive and avoid the golden queen, I have had to do things that were necessary, and some of those things I am not proud of, and do not want to share them for fear of losing you." She turned and looked at Ariel as she sat in the bed.

"I want my life with you, if I am honest, you are all that I want, I do not care about the castle and the gold and all those other trophies. When you left me in Avalon, it broke my heart, because in truth, I was so happy there, I wanted to spend our whole life sat under the apple trees, or growing food in the garden and swimming naked in the river. I was so content and she took you from me, and it twisted my insides and I hated her for it. My brother and my parents are still on the Moon Realm, and for all I know she has them locked away. Ariel, I want to be the person you see me as, but I am caught with a foot in both worlds, and in order to enjoy this simple life here alone in this caravan, I pay a mighty price." Ariel gave a nod, and smiled.

"I know, I have felt the conflict within you since the day I returned, you have a fight of light and dark within you. I understand that Bran, I see how you struggle with it, and I am not ungrateful. I know the price you paid to have me in your life, and I know how you face your family who would rather I was not here, and stand up for me. I am not blind Bran, I see it."

Branna took a swig of her wine and moved back to the bed, her long hair fell down her back as she flicked it back, her skin was as white as snow. She lifted Ariel's hand and took it in hers, and gave it a gentle squeeze.

"Ariel, I need you, you probably do not fully understand, but your return saved me. Long ago I made a grave error, and it almost cost me, as I lost sight of the love I held for you. I started to understand that my love for you was also my protection, it was your love that helped me control the darkness. Through you, I mastered complete control of it, so it responds to my command, it is why Roack avoids you, she wanted all the control. I cannot lose you, just know that this life we have, is my saviour, please I ask you with all my heart, do not question them, not openly. I rule it is true, but it is a very fine balance." Ariel leaned onto her shoulder.

"I wish we could leave; I wish we could go back to our little house and be free of all this." Branna lifted her arm and pulled her close.

"It is why I fight so hard, Ariel whilst she remains in her seat, we will never be free, not in Florae or Avalon. There is no other realm we can go to, this is all we have and it has to be enough for now, but one day I will defeat her, and we will leave here together." Ariel kissed her shoulder.

"Alright Bran, I will not interfere, but please heed my warning, the line of men is weak, and the darkness will eat away at them. There may come a day you may have to choose, them or me, and you may face a challenge from someone you never expected, just be aware always, the darkness has a way of plotting the downfall of others."

Branna put down her goblet, and smiled as she turned, her eyes gave off a twinkle in the candle light. She slid round and pushed Ariel back to the sheets.

"I am aware, it is not unseen. Roack is loyal as she is bound to me, I know what lurks in the deep of my castle and what she is playing at. Trust me, she has no idea of the power I harness, Beren may have his own bird now, but he is joined to me, and if needed, I will strike and he will protect me. I have always assured that only I can rule, without me they will fall into dust. Ariel you are the love of my life and I will protect you."

She leaned forward and kissed her, as her hand slid over Ariel's soft smooth skin, and Ariel responded with passion.

"Oh Bran… Oh yes."

*B*ranna was right, she was in control, and once again she had proved that she was acting with full awareness of everything, although she was responsible for the captives, who each in turn were introduced to the cold shadowy figures of smoke that consumed their souls, which was why they were such loyal warriors.

Below the castle, potions bubbled and experiments were tried, as Maud delved deeper into the magic, her only real annoyance was that Branna had written her black book in code, and she could not decipher it. Deep down below Maud planned her own future, something that was only halted to enjoy the sexual violence she inflicted on her captives. She was an unattractive woman, stunted in growth, who many were repulsed by, and so she took out her frustrations inflicting sadistic pain in sexual acts, as she forced the captive men to pleasure her.

*A*riel settled down, back into her normal life teaching the children and helping out Branna with ideas to improve the castle. Branna had never worked the stone on the Moon Realm, but as a child she had been taught by her father, so her crude attempts to work the stone with her mind, had created a rough hewn castle, which appeared crude and frightening to look at. To a degree it served its purpose, as many of the locals feared it, which enhanced the reputation of the Berengar family.

Vladimir and Otto, spent most of their time on the front lines, where reports came back of more ground gained. The region of Sachsen was growing by the day, as unhappy tribes were supressed and beaten into submission, and for Filiberta it appeared the influence of Grembauld on Berengar was starting to show, as he ruthlessly led raid after raid to expand their territory.

The years moved slowly on as Berengar returned home on occasion filled with stories of conquest, and his soldiers talked with pride of rape, torture, and the burning down of villages, all of which Ariel found disturbing, although she did notice that Branna took little joy in the tales of her partner, although she still entered his bed when he was back for his short visits.

Ariel often found their relationship curious, there did not appear to be the deep loving intimacy between them, and yet they were as close as best friends, and he did to a degree make her laugh and smile. It was almost as if there were two sides to Branna, the deeply passionate and loving side that Ariel saw, and the fun loving disconnected side that she showed around Berengar.

*M*aud grew into her thirtieth year, and it was decided she should look for a husband to have children, but such was her manner and stature, no one would take her. Branna often pondered the problem, she wanted the line of blood to thrive, and her family to grow. It was true that Amand and Dagaric had plenty of illegitimate children, but she started to talk family, and setting down roots in the territories they had conquered, and so began a grand plan, to move outwards from the castle and expand the family, but her biggest problem was Maud.

One night as Branna lay at the side of Ariel and talked in her chambers at the top of the northern tower of the castle, she shared her thoughts with Ariel.

"I am tired of all this war, I never wanted to fight the lines of men, Berengar is going too far. It is time to pull back and grow the family, Berengar wants more children, but what is the point if all they do is give their seed to others to raise? I told him he needs to find something else to occupy his time, and lay his sword to rest for a while, all he talks about is killing, and I am starting to get so bored of hearing his stories of war. Ariel there has to be more to life, something more than just bloodshed."

Ariel turned onto her side, and watched Branna, she could feel her frustration deep down inside her.

"Bran, he is a warrior, one I may add who is connected to darkness, death is all he knows. If I am honest, Rhiannon was not much different, but she turned her mind to power and wealth. If as you say, you want to rise to replace her, then now must be the time to look to other things like trade. There is joy to be gained from good trade, and it is certainly less blood thirsty, maybe he needs to build up an empire of wealth. I have no use of greed, I live a simple life, I always have, but at least it is a lot less bloodthirsty, even if at times it is cut throat." Branna turned and smiled at her, and her dark eyes sparkled.

"You know that is a brilliant idea, there are many in this world who trade up great riches, it might just appeal to Beren, I know it probably sounds strange, because he is stronger than ten men, but I do worry about all the battles he has gone into. It is not love, well not romantic love, but I do care about him, I do not want him harmed. He is a strange man, but he does have great humour, and he makes me laugh a great deal. I do not want him harmed Ariel, I just want him safe and happy, he clashed with Fae marshals not long back, and he found them difficult opponents, you know the skills they have? I fear they may kill him." Ariel understood, she knew well the powers of the Fae, especially Rhiannon's Marshals.

"Never forget, he is of the line of men. Bran his life is tied to a raven, but even with the darkness inside it, the bird still has weakness and will one day die, and when that happens, he will decay and be as vulnerable as all men." Branna gave a sigh, and lifted her goblet, and took another drink of her wine.

"That is why it is important they build a family, pulling back from the fighting, and using the blood of this line is the only way to survive as a whole. Ariel if one dies and there are others to follow, it will continue the legacy of what I have tried to do. I don't want the killing; I want them to live."

"Then it is up to you Bran, to paint a picture of a land united under the rule of the Berengar family, that prospers through trade and reaps great wealth, power and status through governance. If you ask me Otto is pointless, he is cruel, sadistic and vile, if you want to win over Berengar, convince Vladimir, he is clever, and has a taste for nice things, especially women. With two of them on side, Otto will fall into place. Your problem is, the only female of your line is Maud, and she is so horrible no one wants her for a bride, and unless she marries, the chances of children are slight."

Branna understood that, she stared at the floor and lowered her voice, Ariel watched her carefully, she could see that Bran had something on her mind. Branna spoke quietly.

"Beren has suggested Maud marries Otto, he caught them together, and as he told me, they are very similar in personality, they would be a perfect pair, although I cannot deny, it churns my stomach to think of it."

Ariel felt a jolt of shock run through her; it was a sickening thought.

"Bran he is her uncle, I am no fan of Maud, but would he seriously wed his own daughter to his brother? What did you say when he told you, what did you even think of when he mentioned it?" She put down her goblet and lay back on the bed, and closed her eyes.

"I told him the thought sickened me, but he sat and talked, and said that there is no other who would touch them. Roack told me their line will be strong because of the union, and as I have found out, Maud is not opposed to it. Otto has taken the Castle of Fey to the north of the Gaul lands, and he aims to rule the lands as regent, she will have everything from the wealth of the estate, and will live a life of great comfort, and she is eager to travel there. Ariel if I prevent her, she will do it anyhow, I feel my hands are tied. If I allow this, it may go some way to winning her allegiance back again, and as the most vocal opponent of you, that will go a long way to protecting the unity of the family." Ariel turned to her as she looked down.

"Bran I cannot advise you on this, the thought sickens me, you are the head of this family and you must be seen to be stern but fair, you must act as you see fit." Branna gave a sigh, and lifted her hand to her eyes, and covered them, she felt tired, and needed to focus.

*I*t was four months later when Berengar returned with Otto and Vladimir, and Branna summoned them to meet in the room of the gathering. For two days they sat and talked of the future, as Branna laid out her plans for the future of the family, there were disagreements, but Branna was resolute that the family needed to take a new direction, and use other means of control such as manipulation and exploitation of wealth. Vladimir was intelligent and saw the sense in it, and a great deal to show the riches that could be took from the land they owned. Otto was for crushing the opposition and taking what they wanted, but Berengar sat at the side of Branna, and listened very carefully to her words, he could see the skill and the sense, which Branna applied to expanding the family to ensure strength and survival.

Otto scowled at Branna, and sneered at her suggestions, the meeting came to a head when Otto stood up abruptly, his distaste written across his face, his voice was disrespectful and crude, as he stared into the dark eyes of Branna

"I have heard enough of this pandering to the likes of those broods down the valley that quake at the notion of our riders on their paths. It is clear that this nonsense is the scheming of your white whore, she has softened your mind. This world is ruled by men, hard men, warriors, and we do not sit and negotiate, we take what we want with the edge of a sword, I do not need the counsel of a woman." Branna stared at him.

"You will sit down; I am not done yet." He scoffed and turned.

"I have heard enough of hiding behind woman's skirts, I will tolerate this no longer, I have battles to win." The temperature in the whole room turned ice cold, Branna's voice was soft, yet had iron to the words.

"When I command you to sit, that is what you will do… NOW SIT DOWN!"

$\mathcal{H}$e turned and saw her stood before her seat, her face was as white as snow, and her eyes burned red, she glared at him, as the goosebumps ran up his arms. He had gone too far and he knew it, Branna took a long inward breath.

"When I came to this village with your lost brother, while you hung in irons at your father's request, I could have released the wisps into you and your brother, so you would do my bidding without hesitation, and yet I did not. I spared you the icy touch of the darkness those that opposed us fell to. Remember brother, it was I only that spared you, and you have lived here in my home, which I built, and had the spoils of everything lavished upon you. It would take but a snap of my fingers and my wisps would seek you out, and you would no longer be a problem. I rule this land, because I took it, and do not ever forget that, now sit down and listen, and when I am done, I will allow you to leave."

He shuddered and walked back to his seat and sat down, he looked nervous and afraid, the others said nothing, there was no doubt in the room who had all the powers. He gave a slight nod.

"I say what I think, it is no secret that there is talk about the danger of the woman of light, she will be a threat to us one day, and your cavorting with her concerns many. I only say what I hear, and there are those who feel you are softening because of her." Branna gave a nod.

"Ariel is mine and mine alone, you have your endless whores, and I hope you washed before violating my daughter… Yes Otto, I am aware of your night time activities in my home with Maud. I could take your life, and no one would blame me for the treachery you have bestowed upon me. One command to Roack, and she would tear your raven to shreds as I watch you beg for mercy on the floor. So, in future, when you sit in this chamber, you will honour the pact of this family, and keep your vile opinions inside your crude and defiled head, do you understand me?"

He looked down and gave a slight nod of his head, Vladimir smirked. Branna sat back in her seat and the icy atmosphere around the room lifted, she flicked her hair back over her shoulder, and lifted a goblet from the stand at the side of her seat.

"Right, now I have your undivided attention, this is what I wish for the future of this family, and whether you like it or not, this is what I aim to do."

*T*hree hours later they emerged from the gathering chamber and were all smiles, Branna had mapped out her plan for the future, of which Otto would marry Maud in four months time, which he was not opposed to, and actually happy about. Berengar appeared relaxed, and Vladimir wore a permanent smirk.

Branna walked to her chambers and laid back on the bed and closed her eyes. Beren entered and saw her, and gave a smile as he walked towards her, and pulled off his shirt.

"You showed me great wisdom this day, I too have a loyalty to family. There are many things that my father and I disagreed about, but one was never our faith in our family." Branna opened her eyes and sat up, she looked at his side and ran her finger along the thick white scar.

"Beren, there is a lesson to this scar on your side. Your father taught you the skills of a warrior, but Grembauld taught you the skills of a powerful warrior leader. Both had their merits, but both were flawed. Grembauld became too drunk on the glory and power and lusted for more, you father dwelt on the injustice of losing his place, and wallowed in his defeat to the point where his loyalties were blinded by those who whispered dissent. You must not repeat the mistakes of the past, or you will suffer the same fate. We are strong, and we rule, but we need more than just the sword to hold power. My way balances everything out and brings peace to the region as the people prosper. You are a warrior, I understand that, but there are other ways to hold honour, and family is one of them. Now is the time to regroup, we end the last battles in victory, and then we administer fair rule and bring back trade, people with full bellies do not whisper dissent." He gave a laugh as he leaned over her.

"I knew when I woke from my torment of demons you were a powerful woman, and I swore my loyalty and it will never wane, most days I marvel at my fortunes, that I was lay dying in the road, and in flew a raven of immense beauty and power. I have not forgotten my saviour the raven, and never will, even if I live a thousand lifetimes." She smiled, and looked up at him.

"We are all ravens my lover; we are all the ravens of Berengar." He leaned down and kissed her.

Chapter Thirty Three.

Light And Darkness.

Battles raged for another year, but Berengar chose men from his ranks, to put in place to rule, and oversee new trade within each region, as the Berengar family rose up victorious, and over time, slowly the family grew in stature. They were not as loved as Branna would have liked by those they defeated, and were seen mainly as an occupying force, but ultimately, they achieved their goal. The family grew wealthy, and trade expanded into other nations, but the name of Berengar was feared.

Maud and Otto married, and moved to Gaul and the Castle Fey, where Maud gave birth, to Ivor, and two years later Victor, and then after six years, Ulric. Her sons were strong and powerful men, who Otto trained in the art of combat, and it was clear they shared the same line as Berengar, Victor looked very like him.

Otto and Maud lived a life of luxury and excess, their sexual exploits were well known and they attracted many to them, who shared their same sick and perverse sexual tastes and appetites, and around them grew a group of vile and evil individuals. Even Vladimir would comment when he returned from a visit, at the life they lived in the remote castle, where villagers hid their daughters after dusk, for fear of losing them to the depraved antics that were rumoured from the castle.

Ivor and Victor were regular visitors, and Branna doted on them. Ariel taught them how to scribe and read runes, and also educated them with other skills such as herb lore and farming, both of which were essential to the territories in which they would one day rule as lords over their own destiny's. Ariel liked Victor, he was far more intelligent and less likely to pull out his sword, she found it strange considering who his parents were, that his disposition was so different, and he reminded her very much of Berengar himself. He had a good mind for business and understood the ways of people, especially the politics of privileged life.

*L*ife once again underwent a long period of settled life, and Branna had another two children, both boys, who she named Gundobauld, and Merwig, but during their long walks, she voiced her frustrations to Ariel.

"Maud has grown in power, but she has a nasty and vile streak to her, is it wrong to wish for another daughter? Oh Ariel, if only we could mate, nothing would make me happier than to grow a child of yours inside me. The structure of life is cruel, I would love a baby of yours to grow within me, I would love it so much." Ariel gave a chuckle.

"There is a reason a man mates with a woman, and we have enjoyed the pleasure of each other for a long time now. Bran you know how deeply I love you, but honestly, I would not wish for my child to be raised tied to a raven, and filled with darkness, it is better we cannot have a child between us." Branna stopped and looked at her.

"Am I so bad, am I seen as evil by you?" Ariel stopped and gave a sigh.

"No, you are not, if anything I know that within you there is great light, there always was Bran, even back in Avalon. I know you pulled down the darkness, but you are Fae, and so therefore you can resist most of it, but the lines of men are not as strong, and Berengar's lines are seduce far more than you ever will be. It is the thing that has surprised me most about Maud, I honestly thought that as your powers passed on through your blood into her, she would resist the darkness more, and yet she has not, and I find that puzzling." Branna shrugged.

"I have a powerful mind; I have trained it for a long time to resist the urges of the darkness so it is I who have control. Maud has not the power of thought to separate the two within her, it is why I crave another daughter, so that I can train her mind to be stronger. Ariel one day I will pass from this life, and I will need a strong woman to replace me, my hope now lies in another child, for I feel Maud is lost to the darkness, as is Otto."

She made sense to Ariel, but in the back of her mind, Ariel saw things differently, she pondered the thought for a moment, and then looked at Branna who was watching her, Ariel was uncertain as to voice her mind, Branna smiled, she already knew what Ariel was thinking.

"You may as well say it, I have thought it too, it is the most obvious aspect of all of this." Ariel felt bad, she did not want to hurt her.

"Bran, if you have another daughter, Maud will do everything to destroy her, she will never allow another female to rule. I am sorry, but I would imagine, she would be a threat to the life of any other female child you brought into this family. She aims to rule one day, and I feel she will destroy everything you have built." Branna gave a nod and smiled.

"You are so clever, and so wise at times, I do greatly heed your counsel. I know what I am doing Ariel, no one will hurt any child of mine, I would never allow it, not even my own daughter."

*I*n a way, hearing Branna say that, gave Ariel some relief. She had always felt unsafe around Maud, her senses around her worried her, for she sensed pure malice within her. Walking through the woodland with the sunlight beating down, felt so far away from anything sinister for Ariel, and yet she knew through the trees, less than an hours walk away, stood the large brooding castle, filled with the guards that all had darkness in their hearts. They walked along holding hands, and Branna was more relaxed than Ariel had seen her in some time, she noticed Branna watching her, and she smiled.

"What?" Branna chuckled.

"You notice too much, but I have been wondering about something, it probably sounds strange, but I suppose I need to know." Ariel stopped and faced her, Branna looked like she was struggling to ask.

"Bran just say it." She looked her deeply in the eyes, her tatty long hair wafting off her shoulders.

"Why me Ariel, why did you come back, and why have you stayed?" She looked uneasy. "You know, being here you are shut off from your own world, I have no home, my family are trapped in the Moon Realm, even when I was there, I was not allowed to see them. I was alone in Avalon, but you have a home, friends, a family of sorts, and yet you came here and left everything. Why… Why do all that for me, I am not worthy of it, I have done things I am ashamed of?"

Ariel took her hands in hers and held them tight, as she gazed into those dark bright eyes of Branna, her face was so pale, as were her lips, and yet in her eyes there shone such life.

"Bran leaving you as I did in Avalon was awful, it hurt so much.

Had I known I was going to go home to be imprisoned, and accused of letting the Merle into Avalon, I would never have left you, and I would probably have run with you, and escaped both realms forever. But the honest truth is two things, firstly I am the daughter of Enaria, and so I have always known that my blood carries huge protections, and so in a way, I have always known that no matter what I face, I will be safe." Branna blinked.

"But Ariel, your mother was infected on the Moon realm and as a result she died when she returned, even you cannot be safe from the Merle, you have no idea of its power."

"That is actually the other thing. My mother encountered something that killed her on the Moon Realm. Bran I sat alone for a very long time and thought, and then the dreams started to come, I kept quiet about my theories and never mentioned them to any in Florae, but when I read some of my mother's journals, I realised I was right." Branna shrugged.

"Right about what?"

"Rhiannon, and Bridget. The sickness that infected Florae whilst I was in Avalon, a sickness no healer could cure, and yet Bridget would visit them, and they would emerge cured within days, the melancholy, the fever, the way my people lost their will to live. There were only two people who lived, that saw my mother like that, one was Bridget, and the other was me, and then in Avalon, after the storm I saw it again in you. I knew then that the Merle had infected the garment of Tideguyde, and both of the lines of Fae were created from them, and the first two made were its queens. I realised if Bridget had worked it out, then Rhiannon must have also, and that explained her hatred of half her people." Branna shook her head.

"But there is no proof that Rhiannon knew, even I did not think so, until Roack let slip that the Merle had tried to communicate with others before." Ariel smiled.

"She is supposed to be the wisest of them all, and yet she was not in Avalon that night, and Gwendolyn told me, Luminaria had informed her that all of Avalon was cut off from the Moon Realm, and when it was restored, there was no evidence at all. So, I will ask you this, if Rhiannon had no contact and could not see inside her own realm, why did she act so fast, and accuse me of being a Dark Fae?" Branna shook her head.

"She must have felt something, after all she knew it was the house, which is why she came after you." Ariel smiled and shook her head.

"No, the house was protected, remember the symbol of light above the door, had she seen it she never would have made the accusation. Bran, Rhiannon never went anywhere near the house, and yet from a locked out realm with no evidence, she claimed the Merle had been brought into the realm of Avalon, and there were Dark Fae, it is impossible to form that opinion based on the visible facts. She made the accusation, because she was well aware the Fae were tainted, she has always known, which is also why she sent Luminaria, if she had visited Bridget, both of them as powerful queens would have sensed it in each other. Bridget's accusation about the treatment of her people was so much more than based on hair colour. Bridget knew she was infected by the Merle, and I think she worked out as I did, Rhiannon knew about it, but covered it up. That is the reason Rhiannon acted so outraged with Bridget, she thought the truth would come out." Branna gave a sigh.

"That still does not explain why me." Ariel gave a chuckle and leaned in and kissed her softly on the lips.

"Simply put, I fell deeply in love with you. That day after the storm, when I helped you home, you struggled at the door as if you did not want to enter, but you were weak and I pushed you through it. Once you were inside you could not remember, the light within you was still strong enough to resist the Merle. Alone in Florae, I knew if I left you alone then you would be consumed and I would lose you to the darkness. Bran I had to come back, I was the only thing that would save you. I have my mothers' gifts of light, as long as we are together, no darkness can harm you, and I love you and want to protect you, I had to come back in order to save you, and I really wanted to save you, so I am here." Branna smiled and then looked at her, and frowned.

"It makes sense to me, but I thought the light destroyed the darkness, how do you explain that?" Ariel simply stared at her, and then smiled.

"I met him."

"Huh… Who?" Ariel giggled.

"A man of extreme kindness, a man who was created by equal parts light and dark. As I sat in my room on Florae, I simply thought of Merlin, and when I did, I knew that your love would fade without me, and when it did you would be in danger. I waited for you to contact me, knowing that as soon as we made love, all those feelings would grow again, and you would be saved. Merlin's full name is Merleline, in the old language of runes, in the modern tongue it would be Darkline. If Merlin can live with both within, and be kind, so could you, because your Fae powers are strong, it made complete sense to me."

"You really do amaze me, you always have, your mind is so deep and filled with such ability. It has always drawn me to you, I love how you think and work things out, I saw it every day in Avalon. I always thought I was the only one to use my mind to work everything out, but then I met you and it left me speechless, so much so, I wanted to get as close to you as I could."

Ariel took her hand, and they started to walk again, she smiled as she looked up at the trees and took in their beauty, as the birds and bees flew all over the canopy of sweet nectar filled flowers.

"I am only a simple Scribe Bran, Florae is filled with many like me, we read the runes and write down their meanings, and we record everything we see and hear. If I ever return to Florae, I will spend my time there writing about us, just as you have written your life in your black book, I shall write in the runes of blood, so only my line will ever truly be able to understand their full meaning."

They walked along taking their time and talked quietly, as they made their way slowly back towards the path that led to the caravan. When they arrived in the ruins of the village, not far from Ariel's caravan, soldiers were gathering, Branna looked to the senior warrior.

"What is going on?" He gave a regal bow.

"My Lady Raven, your daughter and her husband have arrived with their sons, there has been an attack on the Castle Fey, and many are slain. Lord Otto is arranging a party to head back and take revenge on the villages that joined together in the uprising against him." She looked to the road towards the castle.

"Stand down your men until you hear word from me, I want the full story before I give the lives of my men to battle." He bowed but looked worried. Branna gripped Ariel's hand, and walked briskly towards the bridge, the last thing she needed was yet more senseless war for wars sake.

*I*nside the castle men were preparing for the long trip and another battle, as captains shouted out their orders, with Ariel at her side, she burst into the great hall, where Berengar, Otto and Vladimir stood at the long table looking at maps. Ivor and Victor stood watching. She walked up to the table and glanced down at the map rolled out across the table.

"What is the meaning of this?" Otto gave a scowl.

"This family was attacked, and now we shall seek revenge for their actions." Bran looked at Berengar and then the others, and back to Otto.

"How many men did you lose?" Otto looked displeased at having to answer, Branna looked to Vladimir.

"You were there Vlad; how many were slain?" He looked cool and calm.

"At least a thousand." Branna nodded and looked to Otto.

"That is almost all of your men, and now you ask to use all of mine, to do what, lose again?" He scowled at her and turned up his lip.

"That was my home, my land, and they rallied behind some priest, and he filled them with faith and destroyed it all." He looked at Berengar. "You are my brother and a warrior, and yet you allow this woman to question me, father would have laughed at you, why do you stand there and say nothing when she talks to me with that whore of light at her side? Tell her, this is not her place." Branna pushed Ariel behind her, and her eyes burned red with her temper.

"How dare you speak out such in front of me, THIS IS MY HOME, AND MY ARMY."

There was a sudden flash of red, and Otto was blasted off his feet and landed with a thud, and slid on the polished wood thirty feet up the room. Branna walked slowly towards him.

"Your crops failed, the lime and stone you sold gave no profit as you and your deviants drunk it away. Your warriors were drunks, incapable of fighting, and that lies on you. Do you think my eyes are not upon all of this families' lands? I know everything that happened as you and your friends fornicated with the villagers, raped the innocent and tortured the leaders for sport. You then had the nerve to crawl back here through your own incompetence, and you try to take my men to die for what, your vanity?" He lay on the floor staring at her with hate.

"All men of honour would defend their land; how dare you think you can overrule my brother." She leaned over him, her eyes blazing and he was clearly afraid, she laughed.

"Honour, what do you know of honour, a man who sneaks into

his nieces' bed to fornicate behind her parents back, because he had grown bored of his whores. A man who sits and drunkenly laughs as the crops to feed his people die leaving them with empty bellies, a rapist of virgins and killer of innocent men. You dare to lie there reeking of your lust and stale wine, and question me in my own home? I should kill you now just for your insolence." She lifted her hand and he shrank back on the floor, and she smirked.

"A warrior of honour, look at you now, you disgust me, if it was not for the fact that you married my daughter, I would have killed you the moment I walked in, for the shame you brought to this family. Get out of my sight, there will be no return to your castle, and none of my men will die for you." She stepped back and turned to Berengar.

"Call off your war, any who leave will die by my hand before they get a mile away. Roack, call in all the ravens." Roack gave a squark from her perch, and flew off and out of the window, Branna took a breath and calmed herself as she looked at Berengar.

"He is your brother, sober him up, and clean him up, and then show him and Maud back to their rooms, they reside here from now on." Berengar gave a nod and turned and walked from the room, Branna looked at Vladimir.

"Take his sons and teach them properly, show them what a real Varisci is." He nodded and stepped back, and turned, he gave a nod to the two men who stood watching, and they followed him out of the door. Branna took Ariel by the hand and led her quietly away, she took her up to her chambers, and held her close, and just breathed in.

"I am sorry, I meant to hold in my temper." Ariel squeezed her tight.

"Many men will live because of this day Bran, a little temper is a small price to pay, I felt your anger, and honestly, I did think you would kill him in front of me." She shook her head.

"I did not want that, as crazy as it sounds, I want to spare lives not take them." Ariel kissed her softly.

"You were right to act, and right to put him in his place, although having me there may not have helped." Branna scoffed.

"Having you there is the reason he lived."

*O*tto was very unhappy as he stormed round his room cursing, he reached for the bottle and stopped to pour a glass, he drank it down in one huge gulp. He slammed his glass down, and took a deep breath, and then walked out of his room, heading towards the main hall, and food.

As he walked along the corridor, still fuming, he noticed Ariel coming smiling out of Branna's chamber. She was relaxed and smiling, as she blew a kiss through the door and slid out backwards, and then turned to head for the stairs, lowering his hand to his belt, he hurried as quiet as a mouse behind her, slowly slipping his dagger out.

Ariel walked softly towards the stairs on route to her caravan outside the castle, she passed the room that had once been hers when she arrived at the castle, and gave a smile remembering those nights before the castle filled with returning warriors. Her senses suddenly alerted, but it was too late as an arm came round her and a knife slipped to her throat. Before she really understood what was happening, she felt a jerk, and the door crashed open as she was dragged through it backwards, and gave out a squeal that was muffled into the hand that covered her mouth.

"Just scream whore and I will slit your throat."

She felt the knife push into her skin, as her eyes widened in fear and she was forced face down on the bed. Otto sneered as he pushed her hard holding the knife hard against her throat. She was panicked, and her mind swirled, and was not able to think, her skirt came up as he leaned on her. Panicked flooded into her, as she tried to push back with her arms, but he was just too strong, and she was gasping trying to breathe, her mouth filled and stifled by the covers, she wailed out into the soft blanket that filled her mouth.

"NOOOO!"

Then she felt him as he thrust and she screamed in pain, her ears filled with his laughter as he pushed the knife harder into her neck, and he thrust again and again laughing and jeering.

"This is what a woman is for, not ordering or controlling the guards, this is what you get when you stick your nose in my affairs whore."

He pounded harder, more violently, and she screamed again it hurt so much, her mind was flustered she needed him to stop, she had to stop him, but she was not strong enough, her thoughts turned inward, he roared out into the air, and stiffened, and she felt him throb, and suddenly her eyes blazed with her fear, her panic, and her hatred of Otto.

The room flashed in brilliant white as he relaxed and his seeds stopped pumping into her, and he breathed out sated from his vile lust. As he closed his eyes with a scream blinded, Ariel pushed as hard as she could, as the bright light exploded out of her, twisted, pulled her knife from above her waistband, turned on Otto, and plunged the knife into him.

She missed his stomach, but it jammed at speed into his thigh, and went right down to the hilt. The scream of pain and agony was horrendous, as he hit the floor blood spraying everywhere. Ariel saw her chance and fled, she exploded out through the door, as guards came running from every direction, and Ariel ran blindly towards the stairs. Two guards appeared in front of her and yelled for her to halt, she lifted her hand and her palm flashed white, their hands snapped to their faces as they screamed in pain and they fell to their knees, Ariel swerved past them and ran for her life.

At the main gate four guards fell blinded, as Ariel filled with terror, raced across the bridge and headed into the trees. By the time she stopped, she was gasping for air and fell into the high fern sucking in air her arms outstretched and on her knees.

Branna lay in her bed drifting, unconcerned with the racket, she was happy and relaxed, when her door opened and Berengar stormed in.

"You need to get out there, your woman of light has almost killed Otto." She sat up rapidly.

"What?" Berengar pointed.

"He is in her old room with her knife in his leg, and he is bleeding to death as the knife will not come out, it is charmed and none of us can touch it." Branna slipped out of bed and reached for her robe, her voice was harsh and filled with her anger.

"What did he do to her?" Berengar frowned.

"Why does that matter, he is going to die?" She stormed past him, out of the door and walked down towards the room.

Inside Ariel's old room, there was blood everywhere, Otto writhed on the floor, his pants round his knees, the knife sticking out of his thigh, as his blood pumped out, screaming as Branna walked in, she stared at him with hate, as he looked up at her and screamed.

"SEE WHAT YOUR WHORE HAS DONE TO ME." Branna smouldered with anger and her eyes flickered with red light.

"What did you do to her, tell me or I will stand here and watch you die.”

The guards stepped back as small flashes of red emitted from her fingers, the temperature in the room dropped and turned icy. Roack flew in through the window and landed on her shoulder, she looked down at Otto and saw the red meat around the knife, that had gone clean through the bone, and bobbed its head.

“His bird says he did the flesh thing with her, he coupled against her will.” Branna fumed.

“Is that true, did you rape her?” Her eyes intensified, he swallowed hard, and said nothing. He looked at his thigh, and the huge pool of blood on the carpet.

“LOOK WHAT SHE DID?” Branna stepped forward and leaned over him.

“Answer me or I will kill you now, did you rape her.” He looked terrified, and looked toward Berengar.

“Are you going to allow this, I am bleeding to death, and I am struck with a pain like I have never known?” Berengar looked at him coldly.

“I told you to stay clear of her, I told you she was for Branna only, everyone here knows that. I warned you what would become if you messed with her, I told you Otto and you refused to listen, and now look at you, like father you have allowed your pride to take your leg. She is Branna’s, why do you never listen?”

Vladimir watched from just outside the door, and gave a nod of agreement. Otto looked at Branna as she stared at him, her eyes red with her rage, he felt angry and betrayed, as his face contorted and he spat out his words through gritted teeth.

“I am family, I am blood, and she is a whore from the light, so yes, I took her and showed her what a man is really for, and what she truly is, now kill me you bitch and have done with it. I will die laughing knowing I defiled your precious whore of the light.” Berengar shook his head.

“You fool, you have no idea of the damage you have done. Bran he will die if his leg is not fixed, the knife is cursed with the magic of light, it is beyond the ability of our healers.”

She looked down at Otto and lowered her hand, as she thought of Ariel, and clasped the hilt, he jerked as the pain burst into his leg, and he screamed. Branna smiled as she very slowly pulled free the knife, bit by bit making him feel every last inch. Otto screamed and wailed like a child, and thrashed his arms on the floor as Branna gave a chuckle.

"Feel it Otto, feel it grate on your bone, as it withdraws, and the next time you decide to take a woman against her will, remember this, for this is what you did to her, feel it Otto."

He screamed out in agony, his face red and contorted, Branna twisted the blade, and his screams intensified, Vladimir turned away in disgust and covered his ears, so did the guards. Berengar watched Branna, and understood the lesson she was teaching him. Branna slipped the knife free and Otto crashed back into the floor, soaked in his sweat, and trembled like a frightened child.

"Ariel is mine and mine alone, if you even look at her again, I will kill you on the spot, do you understand me?" She stood up holding the knife, with fragments of meat hanging from it. Otto lay panting as she pulled off a chunk, and fed it to Roack on her shoulder and smiled, as the bird swallowed it.

"This is my home, my region, and my family, and now you know your place, stay in it." She turned for the door, and Berengar reached out to her.

"Bran, he must be healed." She looked back at him with no pity whatsoever.

"He is so fond of proving the role of women, let his wife attend him, it will be good practice for her powers, but I will not lay a hand on him ever again. He is your brother, not mine." Branna walked out of the room and hurried towards the stairs, as Berengar sent a guard down to tell Maud what happened, and get her to rush and attend to Otto, Branna left the castle and walked towards the caravan.

Ariel faced the floor holding herself up with her arms and wept, her pendant swung in front of her, and it gave off a pulse of light. She slowed her breathing and sat up, and lifted her hand to it, her eyes flashed, and her mind filled with a calming soft voice.

"Veil yourself my child, hide, and get away." Pictures filled her mind as she remembered a moment many years ago, as she stood in a meadow filled with flowers, and her mother stood in front of her smiling with soft grey eyes, and her long golden hair flowing down her back.

"Ariel the veil was never ours, but it is important in the life of all Fae, I am sure the moon queen is not happy to know we learned of it, but like all knowledge, if it serves us, then we should not discount it. There will be times in your life that you will need to isolate and remove your presence from the world, and it is at those times you should use it. The charm I have been teaching you is modified, for it will eliminate all eyes from you, so do as I tell you, and follow me in the ritual, and walk under the veil."

Ariel relaxed and focused her mind as she listened to her mother, without realising she whispered the charm as she lived through the memory, the chain round her neck containing the pendant Bridget had given her, began to shimmer, as with her eyes closed, she recited the charm taught at the age of nine summers.

Branna turned outside the caravan. "Ariel I am coming." She made to move and then stopped, she sensed the air, and the feeling of Ariel had gone, she shook her head. "No please Ariel, do not leave me, please I beg you."

But it was too late, all sense and feeling of her had completely vanished, her eyes filled with tears, and she fell to her knees and wept.

Chapter Thirty Four.

The Depth Of Love.

Branna went into Ariel's caravan, and lay on the bed that was strong with her scent and wept, she could not understand why Ariel had gone, did she not know she was coming to her to help her? She had felt her, and was ready to run to her, but suddenly she had gone, and Branna knew what that meant. Ariel was kind and loving, and had been violated by that butcher, and Branna understood the pain and devastation that would course through Ariel, and she felt helpless and lost, unable to help her or hold her as she wept.

For several long hours she lay still and quiet, until her hurt had lessoned enough to move. She sat up on the bed, where for years she had laughed and loved and talked with her, and it now felt empty and cold, devoid of the life and love of her precious Ariel. Finally, she got up and took a deep breath, and left the caravan, closing the door and walked slowly back towards the castle her heart filled with grief.

She walked onto the bridge and looked at the castle, suddenly it felt alien and dark to her, she had always been so proud of her home, but within these four walls, an horrendous act had taken her joy from it, now it looked cold and dark and devoid of life. She walked slowly over the long wide bridge towards the gates.

Maud saw her and stormed out towards her, her face was bitter and twisted as she marched with a fix stare on her face, she pointed behind her a look of anger and hate on her face.

"How can you let that whore you bed do that to him, I need you to fix his leg, I have tried but as it stands, he will never walk again?" Branna stared at her coldly, feeling unconcerned.

"You wanted him, and you got him, he is now yours, you married him, so it is up to you to fix him, that is marriage, so if you do not know what to do, lift a book and learn." Her face looked black as thunder as she looked at Branna.

"Mother you are the only one who can do this, he will be a cripple for the rest of his life if you do nothing." Branna gave a smirk.

"Good, finally my maids will be unmolested. Maud, you wanted this, I chose Beren and I nursed him back to this world from his darkness, if as you say one day you will rule, then learn to do what I did and get him fixed, if not he can hobble forever, for I will never lift a finger again to help him."

"What because he hurt your whore?" Red flashed and Maud screamed as she slid across the floor, and Branna looked down at her with red angry eyes.

"Hold your tongue around me, I am tired of your flapping. Ariel was mine, I wanted her, I brought her here and this is my home, in it you will show me respect or you will leave or die. Do not think I cannot push out another to replace you, children come easy to me with Beren. Be glad he still lives, that was my gift to you, because when I found out what he did, I wanted him dead, I still do."

An hour later Branna stood high up on the top of the castle, on the balcony of her room, Roack flew down and sat on her shoulder.

"I feel the pain within you, I have no understanding of this, why is the woman of light so important?" Branna gave a sigh.

"I know you fear her, but she would never hurt you. Roack, I know this makes no sense to you, I chose the darkness within me, but in order to continue, I also need some light, and she was my light." Roack bobbed up and down on her shoulder.

"We knew she would not hurt us; I heard her words in your ear, I was not far away as I watched over you. Your man sent riders to look for her, but she hides in the light, it is a light I cannot look into. The men she used the light on, their birds died, and they are dying, there is bad feeling in your rock, none of them want her back." Branna stared out over the woodland, and felt the tears in her eyes.

"I know you do not understand feelings Roack, but I really do love her, and not seeing her or holding her, is painful. She is on foot, and within days she will pass under my veil, and I will never see her again, I am not sure how I will live after that." Roack bobbed up and down on her shoulder.

"These feelings, this love, the yearning you talk of, is this the same as when I first came to you, and I was one with all of them and wanted to be a oneness, and you called out and made me a one, you made me a Roack and I wanted that badly, is that the same as your need of the woman of light?" Branna wiped her eyes and smiled.

"Yes Roack, it is something like that." The bird bobbed on her shoulder.

"I understand that, I understand your feelings of love. Branna the Raven, you have a power, if this woman of light will leave soon, stop her." Branna sighed.

"How can I Roack? I do not know where she is, I cannot feel her, she is wearing her veil." Roack flew off her shoulder and pecked at a snail, she picked it up and swallowed it, Branna shuddered.

"You wear what you called a veil, your home has a veil, make it stronger, I can show you, and no one will come and no one will go, and the woman of light will not leave. You can hunt, so you can find her."

Branna realised what Roack was suggesting, why had she not thought of that? The veil kept her hidden, but it could do more, she just needed to make it stronger, she looked at Roack who sat watching her from the balcony rail.

"You are right, I need to make our protection stronger, will you help me?" Roack bobbed up and down on the rail.

"You gave us all a oneness, we will help you find this woman of light and give you back your need to continue, all of us need you Branna the Raven, the women of light will allow you to help us. If you want to do this, you must get higher, go high and look across all your kingdom."

Branna understood and headed into her room, she crossed it quickly, and headed out of the room for the stone steps up to the top of the tower, above the gathering room. The stone steps wound round the outside of the wall, and there was no rail to stop her if she fell, but regardless of the hight and the strong breeze, she ran as fast as she could, winding round the tower, until finally she reached the top, and the one foot wide ledge that encircle the large glass window.

Roack flew at her side, her mind connected and guiding her, the bird could see what Branna saw, and feel her footing. Branna looked out across the vast open land, filled with valleys and trees, her breathing was laboured, but she knew, everything for miles within her sight, was hers. This was her empire, this was hers to command, and out there alone, Ariel was lost and afraid, and she had to find her.

Ariel stood up, she had no idea where she was or which direction she had ran. In all her years here, she had not walked these paths. Looking up through the trees, she could see the sun, and thought it must be early evening, and if it was, she was heading west, which she knew led through the lands controlled by the Berengar family. She looked down at the floor and path she was stood on, and that is when she noticed the large red stain on her dress.

She was bleeding, he had been so aggressive, he had made her sex bleed, she gave a sob, and felt the tears in her eyes, she had no idea what to do or where to go. She felt dirty and unclean, and tried not to think of what he had done, but deep inside she could feel the pain eating at her, and building up inside. She had to move, she had to get away, as much as she loved Branna, she had to leave, Branna could no longer protect her.

Ariel started to walk following a path that she had no idea of where it led, she just knew if it went west, it was away from the castle, and every step she took, was yet another one away from Otto and his vile disgusting leer. The air around her felt electric, and the hairs on her arms started to raise, somewhere ahead she heard water, and yearned to clean herself, and then suddenly, the air above the tree exploded as lightning streaked and thunder roared across the realm shaking everything.

*B*ranna stood at the top of the tower as Roack instructed her, her eyes burned red and the wind picked up, as the large black raven sat on the wall and spoke into the mind of Branna.

"Focus, let the power build, think of your veil, picture it in your head, see the boundary, feel its edges, and everything hidden below it."

Branna closed her eyes as the air around her began to swirl, Roack's croaky voice spoke gently in her mind.

"Good… Now thicken it, push your power into it, see it darker, stronger and focus on it. Can you feel it as it flows from you, do you feel the power you hold?"

Branna focused her thoughts as she held the image of a veil so dark and so thick no one would pass. Roack bobbed up and down as she watched the air rippling and flowing as the deep dark red light flowed from Branna and swirled around her in a thick mass.

"This is good, you have grown stronger than I ever thought you could, now hold it, hold it firm in your head, and do not let go."

Roack watched feeling happy, the darkness swirling round was becoming so thick, it was getting hard to see Branna, but she could feel the power flowing from her, Roack spoke in her croaky harsh voice.

"Hold on to it my dark raven, and now feel the pain, feel the loss of the woman of light, let your pain and anger flow into the veil, and prepare for it to mix, for within you the powers that mix will be stronger than any who try to pass. Let your hate of the man who harmed her flow into you, and take that hate and the pain you feel and put them together, let them flow together around the veil."

The sky grew darker as the wind shifted and clouds rolled in, blotting out the sunlight, all round the castle others turned and looked to the sky. Berengar stood at the end of the long bridge and sensed her all around him, he turned and looked back, and up to the tower, and could see the thick black clouds swirling around, and he knew it was her. Roack watched feeling satisfied, and bobbed up and down, there was no light at all, and her only point of contact was the red light that flowed out of Branna like a fiery aura.

"Look to the west, and release it, let it flow from within you and out into the veil, scream your pain and unite the darkness with this land, and no one will enter or leave without your command."

Branna shook as her pain came bubbling up from deep inside her, and the agony of losing Ariel shot out of her mouth as she wailed into the air, and the sky exploded in its agony, and lightning shot from the skies and rocketed to the floor, in one almighty wail.

"ARIELLLLLLLLLLLLLLLLLL!" The darkness was instant, and the sky exploded with lightening. Ariel turned and looked back.

"Branna!"

Her heart beat faster as more tears rolled into her eyes, and she felt the tug of separation, and just for a second, she dropped the veil, Branna's head jerked.

"Ariel is that you?" Ariel turned back to the path, and ten yards in front the air rippled and Branna appeared, she stopped as her breath caught in her throat. Branna looked at her with tear filled eyes.

"Ariel, I found you, I thought I had lost you." Ariel sobbed, and shook her head.

"I cannot go back Bran." She looked down and sobbed even more, as Branna saw the blood on her skirt that had run from her legs. "Look what he did to me, I am stained forever by his filth, I am sorry Bran, I can be here no longer." Branna shook her head.

"Please Ariel, do not leave me, I love you, I need you, I will not survive here alone, we promised we would be together always." She took a step forward and lifted her arms.

"Ariel, I promise, I will leave all of it. We can go anywhere, come with me and we shall leave, all I want is you at my side." Ariel wept bitterly, and shook her head.

"Bran there is nowhere else we can go, we both know this was the only place we could be together, but it is no longer safe here for me. Bran they hate me, they fear me, I can feel it in everyone I am around, they do not say it, but they all want me dead and out of your life. Bran I love you, you are the love of my life, you are my life, but if I stay, they will kill me."

Branna gave a mighty sob and shook her head, tears streamed from her eyes. Her voice was soft and showed her heartbreak.

"Please Ariel, I am begging you, do not leave me, do not give up on me, you are the only part of me that is still living, and I want it to keep on living. I will protect you, Ariel please I need you." Ariel wept and the tears dripped from her face onto the dry hard soil.

"You cannot protect me, I know you want to, but you are fooling yourself, the darkness has taken them all and it will get worse. Bran please if you truly love me, let me go, and live for the memories we have made, it is the only way left now, please my love, let me go." Branna fell to her knees and cradled her face in her hands, as her tears dripped down through her fingers.

"Ariel I cannot endure my life alone without you, with all of the powers I have gained, I am not strong enough to let you go. Without you, there will be no life, and no light, and I will be lost to the darkness forever. Please Ariel, I beg you, do not leave me alone here to endure eternity without you."

Ariel could not take anymore, her heart was crushed and she felt her whole life was scattered and broken as she watched Branna, who she had always seen as being so strong break, she lifted her hand and wiped her eyes as she took a deep breath.

"I am sorry my love, I truly am, for it is now the destiny of both of us to walk this life broken and alone. You cannot leave here, because if you do Rhiannon will kill you, and I cannot stay, because if I do, then Otto or Maud or one of the others will kill me. Either way, we will end alone with only our love and memories for comfort, neither of us has a choice. Branna you are no fool, you know this, even Roack cannot help you protect me, the evil that grows in your line, has killed what little of the Fae they had, and now they are consumed as men to be dammed forever. Love me enough to let me go.”

Behind Branna the sound of many hooves pounded the soil, her army had zoned in on her and were heading towards her, Ariel looked up the path.

“See, it matters not where you go, they are joined to you and will always follow, I will never be safe at your side again.” Branna stood up and turned, and looked back down the track, and Ariel said the charm and the veil of the Fae and Enaria was cast back over her, Branna sneered as the riders approached.

“WHY ARE YOU HERE, LEAVE ME!”

She turned back and her breath caught in her throat, Ariel was gone, and any sense she had of her was gone with her. Branna knew she had put back her veil and she would never find her as long as she wore it, she did the same the moment she left Avalon, and it had kept her secret, and out of Rhiannon’s sight since.

The horses came to a halt and the warriors looked round, Branna scowled at them, red light flickering in her eyes.

“I SAID LEAVE!” There was an almighty flash and the horses reared up, and in a puff of black smoke, Branna was gone.

Ariel lay in the long grass and ferns as a large man held her softly down and held his finger to his lips.

“Shush… You are safe, you will not be harmed.”

She had no idea why, but she sensed he was good and nothing to do with the men of Branna, she lay still and did not move as he watched the riders regain the composure of their horses. The warriors settled down their mounts and then turned back on the path, their mistress was gone, and so they spurred their horses on, and galloped back up the path. The large man watched until they were far off in the distance, and then turned, looked down at her and smiled.

“You are well known of white lady, there are some who say you tamed the raven, you are safe now and free of her.” She took a deep breath and sat up as he released her, the woodland all around was empty.

“Who are you, and why are you here?” He smiled as he stood up and offered a hand.

“They call me Cezar, I am travelling through to a land that has been my home for many a year, I know of your kind, as I do the Raven’s, for

I too was once captive in the moon realm." Ariel gave a gasp.

"You are Fae." He winked.

"I was, but no longer, I left the life many long moons back, come you will be safe with us." Ariel looked round as she stood up.

"Us, I see no one." He chuckled and lifted his fingers to his mouth, and gave a short shrill whistle. Figures rose from the tall grass and ferns all around her, they all looked around, and they headed over to him.

*B*ranna sat on the upmost top of the tower and wept, as her heart break ripped through her, even Roack who did not fully understand, felt she was better left alone, and stretched out her wings.

"Let out the pain, your land is sealed, stay a while, none should see this, they will call it a weakness, but they have no idea of the power it holds. Let the woman of light flow up in you, for it can only enhance the power you hold." Roack lifted into the air and flew down to the balcony outside of Branna's room, where the bed still smelt of her love making to Ariel.

Branna curled up on the small ledge and wept until she was exhausted, and then made her way slowly down to her chamber, where she locked the door. She walked to the bed, lay down and hugged the sheets and the pillow, and wept more tears, letting her grief and anguish scream into her pillows. Worn out and exhausted, she cried herself into her sleep knowing she was now alone for eternity, with no light to save her, from now on, she too would be consumed by the darkness.

*A*riel was taken by Cezar and his men to their camp, which was deep in the valley, far below the range of the castle, where there were caves lined with crystal through which no eyes of power could pry. In the large caves, in which their wagons were circled, Cezar introduced Ariel to his wife, who was the leader of the tribe, Crina. She too was Fae of the Moon, but she had golden hair, which surprised Ariel.

They were on route towards Bohemia, where they had been settled for a few years, the group had travelled for trade, and were now heading back to sit through the winter. That night, Crina took Ariel to the river, and helped her bathe, and wash away the blood and filth of Otto, once again there were many tears, and Crina understood the pain she felt.

They returned with Ariel wrapped in a towel, and Crina took
her into her caravan, and gave her clean clothes, and tended to her
wounds, for Otto had been so brutal, he had torn some of her skin.
Ariel sat up and talked, and gave a brief version of how she had met
Branna, and their life in Avalon, and then the story of how she had
return to Florae and been imprisoned, and how when Branna had
reached out, she had come straight to her, and they had lived here, her
in the caravan, and Branna in the castle.

It was hard to talk of what Otto had done to her, and she broke
down, but Crina knew of what the men of the family could do, she
had met many who had been raped and used by the vile warriors.
Ariel then went quiet she had no need to talk of her final moment with
Branna, Cezar had seen and heard all of it, and had already spoken
with Crina. It felt strange to Ariel that Crina had not judged her, she
simply smiled and nodded her head.

"There is no stranger thing than love, to truly love is to see past
everything, all the faults and all those habits that others hate, and you
look deep into the heart of this person and see the real truth of who
they are, and you cannot help or stop yourself. I have been interested
in your story, for it sheds a light on many things. This Branna is known
to us as The Raven, the queen of the line of Berengar, the talk is that
she is evil and wicked and filled with only darkness, and yet what
you have told me paints a different tale. I believe you are right, this
Branna is clever, but I also think she has a naive aspect to her, for she
called something she had no real knowledge of, and I think it did take
advantage of her. The lines of Fae are strong, and if her love for you
is as strong as you say, then maybe there is a side to her that might
have played a role in the Berengar's stopping their wars. Ariel I am a
mother, and I care for my children, as all mothers do, and maybe any
other would have been killed for their stupidity, but as hateful as this
Maud may be, Branna would not kill her husband, no matter how vile
he was, if she had, you would still be there at her side."

Ariel sat on the bed listening as she thought of Branna, deep inside
her there was a painful ache that would not go away, and she already
knew what it was, she had felt it once before when she had been held
in her room in Florae, it was the pain of separation. Crina patted her
leg and smiled.

"Love is never easy, especially one as strong as the love I feel within
you. The way I see it, you have two choices, you can flee and return to

your people, or you can return to Branna, I will not stop you whatever you decide, and I will add, there is no rush, these decisions take time, with us you are safe, so use your time well. You are exhausted and you should not make a choice with a tired mind, rest in this bed, I sleep in my hammock in the cave on nights this warm. You need rest, so for now do that. Your injuries will heal, and there is no damage that rest, good food and herbs will not heal, sleep well Child of light, and I will see you on the morrow."

Crina left, and Ariel slipped into her bed, rested her head down, she turned to the wall, and thought of Branna in those last few moments, and she knew that Branna showed her the truth of who she really was and the depth of her love, and it felt bitter and heart breaking, and she pushed her face into the sheets and wept.

*T*he following day, Branna stayed in her room and sat on her balcony, and stared out over her realm. The sky was darker than it had been, as her veil filtered out the bright sunlight, and somehow it fitted her mood, as her sunlight Ariel was gone. Her only reassurance, was she knew that Ariel could not leave, and that out there, in the trees, she was still close by, and not in the realm of Florae. As long as Ariel remained close to her, she had hope that one day, they would meet again.

Berengar tried her door, but it was still locked, he knew better than to force her to open it, he understood the importance of Ariel to her, had he not felt the same on the cold nights in battle when Branna was not at his side to comfort him?

Maud struggled, she was not as good at her art as she first thought, and although she had managed to close the wound on Otto's leg, she knew the bone was badly damaged, and if it was not healed properly, he would never walk again. She stood outside the door of Branna and begged for her help, but the door remained locked, as Branna sat alone, lost to her grief, weeping and looking at the dagger Ariel had used, it was all she had left of her.

*A*riel rose inside the caravan, the day was busy, scouts were out, sent by Cezar to try and gain information, but Ariel did not feel the need for company, and so sat on the steps of the caravan out of the way, as Crina watched her from a distance.

Ariel's mind was filled with the pictures of the broken hearted

Branna as she begged her to stay, and in truth she wanted to, and she felt such a huge conflict inside her. Once before she had been parted from Branna, and she did not want the pain that came with that, but she also knew, that she could never look upon Otto again, because she knew to do so, she would kill him, and break her vow of never taking a life.

$\mathcal{S}$he slid her hand to her stomach, as Crina walked up with food and tea, Crina gave a sigh as she looked at her.

"The seed has taken; you know it and I know it. We are Fae, we feel these things, what will you do?" Ariel looked up at her unsure of what Crina wanted to know.

"I know… I cannot contemplate that right now; it is too awful to think about." Crina understood.

"Ariel, you know there are ways to be rid of it." Ariel shook her head, and felt sick.

"No, I cannot do that, as much as I hate him, and I do, the child will be half of my line, and that blood is sacred to my people, and in that there is goodness. I must hope the power of my mothers' line will be enough to cleanse it, but there is one thing I know, my child will never be tied to a raven." Crina gave a nod.

"I sense there is more to you, but it is hidden from me. If your blood is so sacred, then you must be of a high line, is it a secret that cannot be revealed?" Ariel smiled.

"I feel strange and yet relieved to be around the people of Fae, my mother was highly regarded, myself, not so much. In Florae, I was but a simple scribe to the house hold of my queen. My mother was Enaria." Crina gave a huge gasp.

"The mystic?" Ariel nodded, and gave a chuckle.

"So many hold her in such high regard, and yet to me, she was simply my mother, a mother who I lost when I was a young child." Crina nodded and smiled.

"Your story makes more sense to me now, I cannot say I was not puzzled last night, I was, but I see now, the daughter of Enaria would have a powerful force of light within, and in that she would be immune to the darkness. You know, you have probably saved her from far greater darkness up until now, but with you gone, she may slip deeper, and in that, you will lose her forever." Ariel felt a huge surge within her, and she lowered her head.

"I am aware that leaving her will condemn her to a life she has never wanted, all Branna ever yearned for was to live a free life, and in her naivety, she was taken by the darkness, and now it will consume her, and she will die alone surrounded by evil. If I go back, I will lose the child to the same darkness, and I must at all costs spare the child that. Crina this cannot be known, not to any, if one of your men is taken, they will find out, I must hide the child from them."

*M*en started to arrive back in the camp around mid afternoon, Ariel sat on her steps, and Crina and Cezar sat a few feet away, preparing the meat brought in earlier by a hunting party. Two men walked up and Cezar looked up as he filleted the meat with skill.

"What do we know?" The men gave a bow, the shortest one glanced at Ariel, and then looked down at Cezar.

"Our news is not good, the haze and dimness of the day, is something to do with the Raven, she has covered the skies and land. Out west on the trail through the valley, all looks clear and bright, but when you walk towards it, you hit a barrier no eye can see, and you cannot continue on. It alerts her guards, and they appear, we were lucky to get away. We think it surrounds all the land, we are trapped, none can enter, and none can leave." Ariel understood straight away.

"It is a veil, she is Fae Ofmoon, and she has corrupted it with her darkness, her land is sealed to protect her line. She fears attack from those who destroyed the castle of Otto, and she aims to keep me held prisoner here to force me to return to her." Cezar sat back and gave a sigh.

"Pass the order, we establish camp for definite here. The Lady Ariel is of high standing to her people, and as such, I have given her the protection of this camp and my word to aid her. If this Raven feels she can force her to ground, we will ensure no one ever finds her, she is one of us now, and we will sit this out and wait until we find a way through." Both men gave a serious nod and broke apart to spread the word, Cezar turned and smiled.

"My father once met your mother, and he held her in the highest regard, he talked often of her beauty and her kindness, here in this camp under my watch, you will have the same regard, regardless of the life you have lived. Our line will protect yours, until this is over." He gave a nod and returned to the meat, and Ariel sat back and spoke quietly to herself.

"As much as I yearn to hold you in my arms Bran, I cannot return now."

Chapter Thirty Five.

The Veil Of Enaria.

Branna spent three days in her room before she emerged. The first place she went to, was the room of Otto, where Maud was attending to his dressings, Otto had a fever and was in a great deal of pain. Branna stood at the end of the bed, and looked at his face, and then down at his leg as Maud removed the bandages.

"You did well to seal the wound, but you have a long way to go before your skills at healing rival mine, sadly the one person you need, is the woman he raped. Even Otto with his vile and sadistic manner towards her, would have had the best care from Ariel. All of you were blind to her powers, all of you moaned and complained, and yet look at you now, three days of hammering at my door begging for his leg, and Ariel was the only one who could have saved it." Maud looked at her.

"He will never walk again." Branna smirked.

"He is alive, that was my act of charity to you my daughter, the price of his leg, was the cost of disobeying me. If a day comes when you rule, you will understand that, this is my land and my home, I built it, and I rule it. Never ever allow him to challenge me again, for that will be the day his life ends." She turned and walked towards the door, and Maud felt her anger rise inside her.

"You are the coldest and darkest of us all." Branna turned and looked at her.

"Now I have lost Ariel, yes, I am, I have nothing left to be warm about, my whole existence is coldness and darkness. She was my light, and he took her from me, if it displeases you, get used to it."

Branna left the room and walked down to the main hall, where Berengar came to her. He held her by the shoulders and looked into her eyes.

"I will find her, your realm is sealed, and I have men searching for her." Branna gave a smile.

"She will hide and stay hidden, she is Fae of the Earth, and has skills my line never knew, you search in vain, she can never return whilst Otto lives, and I owe my daughter her husband, and their sons a father. I have lost her forever this time Beren, and I know it." He gave a nod.

"I will still look."

It was strange in a way, they were simply lovers, and Berengar could bed any between their moments alone. Branna placed no demands on him at all, he was her partner in all of it, and loyal to her in ways none would ever understand. There was a deep bond between them, but it was not Romantic love, it was respect, for he admired her above all others. Berengar had heard the stories of Ariel, Branna had often shared her life with Ariel, and spoken of the deep feelings between them, and he had never been jealous, if anything he had admired her honesty, and as a result respected her more.

The one thing he knew, was around Ariel she was happier, she was less brooding and irritable as she had been in their early days together. Branna smiled more around him when she had spent the day with Ariel, and she had always been more passionate when she had left Ariel's bed and come to his. With her gone, he saw the return of her more irritable side, and also sensed the pain she felt deep inside, and he also felt that deep down inside she was lonely without her, and there was nothing he could do to ease that. He looked her right in the eyes.

"You should have killed him, he deserved it, all of us knew she was yours, not one of us tried to seduce her, she was a fine woman Branna. I would have taken her to my bed, but she was yours and yours alone, he should have died for his violation of your trust, and her body." She smiled.

"I know, but Ariel hated me killing people, I was trying to honour her by letting him live. I will not fix his leg Beren. I know he is your brother, but he will crawl on his belly every day, and even may beg for death, but for every moment he lives, he will regret defying me, this is our home, and we rule, and that is the lesson he needs to learn, as do any others who feel their queen is not up to the job." He nodded.

"Your crown is safe; none will harm you whilst I live."

*T*hat day everyone was summoned by Branna, and gathered in the large hall where she sat in her seat and addressed all of them, and laid down her rules and her laws. Branna spoke of her plans for the expanding of their realm through trade, and how everyone gathered would one day rule a province and build up great riches. She exerted her dominance over all of them, and made it their law, in which in any who defied her, would suffer under penalty of death. She also made it very clear, that if Ariel was found, not one hair on her head was to be harmed, and any who disobeyed her would die that hour.

In her final show of strength, she ordered Roack to bring her a raven, any raven, and when the large black bird flew in, there was panic, as Branna held it up, and asked for its owner to step forward. The crowds parted and a captain of Vladimir came forward to claim it, and as she looked down at him, she spoke loudly.

"All of you have your ravens, if one dies, both die, that is the bargain you all made for a longer life, and any who disobey me, will suffer, as this man will. Let this be a warning to all of you, I am your queen, and I will be obeyed."

She held up the bird as it struggled and tried to squark, and with a flash of her eyes the bird screamed out loud, and the captain gripped his skull and screamed in pain, and fell to his knees. The assembled mass looked on with horror and stepped back as they saw the blood flow from the captains' eyes and foam flowed from his lips, and he screamed out in agony and thrashed around on the floor. Branna watched coldly, showing no care at all, and then with a flick of her hand, the bird turned to dust, and the captain fell still and quiet.

Branna looked down at his lifeless corpse, and shook the dust from her hand, as she looked up and back to the mass of her realm.

"That is the only warning you will ever have, there is no room in the realm for leniency, obey me or you will all suffer the same fate." She turned, looked down.

"Clean that mess up."

*S*he walked through the centre of their mass, and they divided and watched nervously as she passed them. She made her way onto the long bridge, and into the woodlands, where she walked under the trees lost in thought, her heart filled with sadness. She stopped in the dim gloomy woodland and stood staring at the trees, feeling lost and alone, and she looked to the darkened sky, where the sunlight no longer burned brightly down, her voice held her anger, as she forced her words through gritted teeth.

"I will never forgive you Golden Queen, I will never forget how you drove us apart, and one day I will return to your realm and will destroy your heart as you have mine. All I ever wanted was to walk free with her at my side, and because of you, I had to flee and leave her behind. Look at what you made me, it cost me her love, and you shall pay, oh Golden Queen, you shall pay with your heart, and then your life. Hear me, as I stand here on the spot where she returned to me, and I swear before the sky my oath of vengeance for the loss of Ariel." She fell to her knees and wept.

*F*orty feet away, sat in the tall grass, Ariel covered her mouth, and held in her pain, as her heart broke. She had hoped to sneak back to her caravan to recover some of her things, but had been waylaid when she understood where she was, for this had been a place they had visited many times, it had been here alone they made love on many occasions. She had not expected Bran to appear, and she had not expected to see her break as she did, just for a second, she had thought of standing up, but the throb in her stomach made her realise, and Ariel held back her sobs, as the tears fell from her eyes, as she watched the love of her life weep.

In her mind she spoke loving words to Branna, knowing that her veil would not let them pass to her.

"I love you my dark raven, I always will for I will love no other, and you will have a child by me, for your line and my line will be joined, and I will make sure she will be everything you wished for, but she will not be dark, she will be the brightest of the light. This I promise, goodbye my love."

As quiet as a mouse she slipped backwards, until she was out of sight, carefully moving through the trees, and made her way down towards the valley floor, leaving Branna to weep alone. Branna sat up and dried her eyes, just for a second, she had felt a strange feeling, she stood up and looked round, but the woodland was empty. She walked forward several long paces and looked round, and she spotted the flattened grass, and leaned down. There on the floor was a small piece of fabric, with a delicately woven lace edge, she recognised it instantly.

Branna reached out and lifted it up, it was damp with fresh tears, she lifted it to her nose and sniffed it, the smell was one she knew well, it was Ariel's scent. She looked into the woodland, but knew she was gone, her voice was soft, almost to herself.

"Goodbye my love, knowing you are near, but hidden from me is a comfort, I will cherish my time with you and never forget you." Holding Ariel's handkerchief, she turned, and walked back through the woodland towards the castle. Ariel was still in her realm, and just knowing for sure, made a difference.

*A*riel returned to the cave, knowing she was trapped here forever unless she could find some way of escaping. She was Fae of Earth, and had many skills unknown to Crina and Cezar, and with the realisation that for now they were stuck, Ariel began to share the knowledge of her people so that they could live unseen in the realm of Branna and her ravens.

The rocks and high places were searched, and many caves that ran deep below the surface were found, and Ariel showed them how to make smokeless fires and harvest certain plants and trees, for food and medicines. The men hunted, and food was dried and stored, and stronger weapons were made, and as the months passed with Ariel at Crina and Cezars side, the group began to flourish.

Others were caught on the land, and Berengar's men slowly rounded them up, and where possible, Cezar found them and took them to safety, and three large deep caves became camps, each watching a specific area of the land of the ravens, under the dim light of the ancient woodlands that surrounded Berengar's castle.

*A*s Ariel talked survival, Branna organised. A better road was constructed to the large wall of rock that led down the valley, and using the skills taught to her by her father, Branna started a tunnel that would lead through the rock face. Once she had a hole about five feet high through, men moved in with chisels, and began work cutting a new road, so that the thin path round the mountain top, which she had travelled in her caravan that first day with Berengar, could be blocked, to ensure there was only one way into their realm below the veil.

By the time it was complete, Ariel had given birth to a daughter, and she was four years old, whom she named Ena in tribute to her mother. She was dark haired and dark eyed, and even though she was the daughter of Otto, Ariel thought she had a look of a young Branna, which gave her comfort.

*T*he rumours spread that Branna was often seen alone walking in the woodlands, and how she would sit between two mighty trees and talk to herself, but Ariel knew different, and many times she too would sit hidden and listen, for she knew, this was Branna's own way of dealing with the loss of the love of her life, which was also why Ariel would secretly watch. It was midsummer and Ariel sat alone watching, and listening, Branna appeared and walked into the space, which now had short grass as it had been worn over time.

Branna sat down with her bag, and for a while she was silent, and then she looked at the bag.

"Some would call me foolish, but my dreams tell me my words reach you, I know you wear the veil of your mother, but I am stronger now. Ariel, I am darker than I wish to be, but my feelings of loss, and the way I miss you, has increased the process. I am sorry my love, but I am losing you slowly, I am fighting so hard against the darkness for you, I want to keep you inside, but I fear now the darkness will completely take me. I know I have lost you, I hate it so much, but I have accepted it, and soon I will come here no longer." She gave a sob, and tried to hold back, she looked up and her tears filled her eyes.

"You were right to leave, Otto and Maud have grown strong, they think I do not know, but I hear all the evil things they say about you, and one day I fear, they will hunt you down and kill you, for that is their wish. I do not blame you Ariel, you need to know I understand. I want only good for you, and you should walk in the light, but sadly for me that is no longer possible, so this is goodbye forever. I am leaving my bag, for I have brought your books, remember one day you said if you got back to Florae, you would write about me, and tell the truth of my story? Ariel, I have read what you wrote and you wrote the truth, so here they are, take them from this land, for if I fall the veil will lift, it will not be for long, so use it well, take your books and finish them." She stood up and looked down at the bag, and wiped her eyes.

"I wish I could have held you one more time, and looked into your grey eyes and felt that love, for I am afraid I am losing the pictures I have fought so hard to keep clear in my mind. When you leave here, because one day you will, remember me with love, and try to excuse my darkness. I am sorry I let you down, I was a fool and did not realise what I was studying, and by the time I came to my senses, it was too late. My only happiness and joy were the cherished moments with you, please never forget me."

Ariel had no idea why, but as Branna turned she stood up, and as

Branna started to walk, she felt a huge surge within her and cast off her veil.

"Bran wait."

Branna turned and her eyes filled with tears, she smiled.

"I knew you could hear me; I knew this was not in vain. I miss you so much, but I am dangerous now, you must get away from me my love, I do not have much time before I am consumed." Ariel nodded at her.

"Your dreams are right, I have sat here often and listened to you, I heard all your words and cherished your love also." It mattered to Branna, and she wiped her eyes.

"I never wanted this Ariel, I wanted to keep my promise, I wanted to be at your side, it was important to me you understood that." Ariel took a step forward.

"Bran I always knew that, it is why I waited so long in Florae for you, I wanted it too. It is not too late, open the realm and run with me, let me take you away from here. Bran leave all this, your family rule now, your legacy will live on." She shook her head.

"Ariel, I want to, but I cannot. Maud is powerful, if I leave, she plots behind my back, and will bring horrors untold to this and all the lands. I try to honour your words and I have stopped many from dying, but if I leave the whole world will suffer, and this was never about merciless killing, it was always about repayment for Rhiannon alone. I long to be with you, I do, but I have to stay, can you understand that? It is you who should leave, but without Roack I cannot lift the veil, and Roack fears what will happen to the Merle if I do. Ariel a new power is rising in the world of men, and the Ruling Council work to seat a man of power to rule all lands, Beren plans to stop him, and is busy planning as I speak. My ravens have flown far, and we have gathered many, it has gone too far for me to stop it, and the darkness within me fights to aid my consort and defeat this new power."

She understood, and as she looked at Branna she felt the tug at her heart, she had not changed much, her face was whiter, her hair much longer but still as unkempt, and her eyes still burned brightly, but she looked thinner and worn, and under her eyes was darker. Ariel walked into the gap between the trees, and stood a few feet apart from her, and Branna smiled.

"I am happy to have seen you one last time, you are as beautiful to me as always, and I will cherish this memory forever." Ariel smiled and took another step closer.

"Fight the darkness Bran, never surrender completely to it, you must fight always, it is my hearts desire that you never let it beat you. I fell in love with a fighter, so if I ever meant anything to you, fight it Bran, and to aide you, remember this."

She took another step forward and pulled her into a kiss, and Branna felt her breath trap in her throat, and slid her arms around her as she kissed her back. It was long, loving, and passionate, and she felt a warmth inside her grow, and closed her eyes taking note of every second of the moment. She could feel the power of the darkness as it struggled against the light, and she felt the warmth of her happiness as it filled her.

When Ariel pulled apart, Branna stood with her eyes closed, and swayed as her head felt disorientated and cloudy. She opened her eyes, and Ariel was stood back in the trees, and smiled at her.

"I gave you what light I could, make it last and fight with it. No matter where I am or where I go, know this Branna of Moon, my love will always be yours, for I will love no other. You are and you always will be the love of my life."

Branna breathed in and swallowed the air, she slipped her hand in her robe and lifted out Ariel's lace handkerchief, and wiped her eyes. Ariel smiled when she realised, she had dropped it that day, and Branna had known she had been there.

"I will walk your dreams always my love, never give up Bran, our love was worth more than you losing to the darkness. I will always be inside you holding your light, nourish it often and in remembrance of me, and keep the light bright as you did in Avalon. Goodbye my love."

Ariel turned, shouldered the bag, and walked into the trees, and Branna watched her as a single tear ran down her cheek. Ariel faded away, and replaced the veil that surrounded her, and then turned, and walked in the opposite direction, where she knew she would be safe.

Branna never returned to the site of Ariel's arrival again, and what was now the site of their final parting. She called no guards and let Ariel walk free, and Roack flew down from the tree and sat on her shoulder, as she turned back towards the castle.

"I have kept my part, and now you must keep yours. The family needs another female, go to your man, for if you mate this night, a female will come to your line."

Branna did not really hear her, she was too busy reliving the memory, that was a reminder of what she had lost because of Otto, and she was also cherishing it, and playing it back in her mind, Roack did not like how it felt, and lifted into the air.

"You must break the connection, the woman of light hurts me, think of her when I am not around, I do not want her inside me." Branna smirked as she walked at a good pace, and somehow the darkness below her eyes appeared to have lessened.

*A*riel returned to her caravan, and unpacked the bag. Inside she found her dagger, still stained with the blood of Otto, and her book of parchments, her silver quill tips, and a tiny bottle of fresh ink. She smiled as she looked at it, and opened up the book, and there inside on a piece of fresh parchment she saw Branna had written.

'You were always the light that guided me, and one day your light will lead me back into the light of all things, and I will atone for all I have done. It was your love that saved me, and it will lead your dark raven home again. My love was always, and will forever be yours. Bran.'

Ariel sat for a long time holding the parchment, and in her mind, she could see the memory left by her presence, of the moment Branna sat alone with the book of Ariel's detailed notes of the life of Branna. Branna smiled as she dipped the quill in the ink and wrote the note, she then lifted it to her lips and softly kissed it. She was not sure how, but somehow, Ariel knew this was not a thought, it was a vision of the past, and was something connected to her blood, that ran directly from her mother, did she have the same gift as her mother? She was not sure; she just knew that what she saw happened.

*T*hat night, Branna stood beside Berengar, and watched as the caravan of Ariel burned, she turned to Berengar, as the flames flickered on his face.

"See, every trace of her has gone, every paper, every line she wrote, is lost to the flames. Ariel will never return Beren, she cannot, she is the purest of light, just like her mother. For her to return would bring an end to your line, she has nothing to return for, the last traces of her lie smouldering in the fire, it is done." He gave a nod and looked at her.

"I know of the love between you both, but you chose this life, not a life with her. This will bring calm, to see the last of her gone forever will calm the fears that she stalks them in the night. We live in the darkness now, remember we are all your ravens, this family is all we have left now. This empire we build it is strong, and one day we will rise at your side and defeat the Goddess of the Moon, and then we shall rest. This was the vow we swore to each other, and I will honour it all."

Branna took his hand in hers, and turned from the fire, she knew at last Maud and Otto would calm down, but she also knew, that out there in the trees, Ariel lived and had her words, and also a shawl that she had made Branna in Avalon. She would wear it forever, she would always be wrapped in black, as a symbol of her raven, and the love of her life. Branna smiled as she walked away, the truth of Rhiannon would be known, she knew Ariel would ensure it.

*T*hat night Branna lay with Berengar for the first time in many years, and in the darkness a child was conceived. Berengar was planning with Vladimir to start a large campaign, word had come to them that a man of political interest was rising in the tales of a distant land, which Branna had once spoken of. The Isle of the Anglo was filled with riches, and where Branna had run from to evade capture, and Berengar aimed to attack and defeat it, and increase his wealth.

His army had grown large and powerful, and through trade he had made many friends, so as his army assembled, he briefed Vladimir and Otto's son Ivor, of his plans to conquer the small isle. Branna was uninterested in it, and focused on building up a large library of parchments, and she spent many days alone reading of lost lands and the lore of others. Victor the second son of Otto was a frequent visitor, and Branna had grown very fond of him.

Victor was intelligent and well read, and Branna would sit and talk of many things with him, and late one night after a long discussion on the tales of the land of the Gaul's, she turned to him and smiled.

"Tell me, you know of the plans of your uncles to take the land of my home, what are your thoughts on this tribe they call Celt?" Victor sat back, as he held his wine.

"I know little of these people, apart from the few tales you have told me in my youth. I have heard that they organise well and are mighty fighters. Some say that they were trained by your Fae lines, I fear if there is a war, many will fall." Branna smiled, he was good with words, but it was clear, he was no fool and was not convinced battle would serve their purpose. Branna leaned forward in her seat.

"What would you say, if I told you there was another way, a way where less men will die, and more power can be gained?" He smiled.

"I am listening."

So began Branna's story of a small village on the coast, of a place named Tintagel, and her story of how she saved the life of a small child by teaching them of the dangers of infection from fleas. She talked late into the night, and into the early hours of a new day, of how a man of intelligence could take a whole area, simply by arriving, and instead of invading, helping the local people improve their lives. She talked of how such a man would find a place, where a fort could be built from local stone, and how few would be able to take it, such was the nature of the land and the formation of the rocks. Branna gave Victor the means in which he could be a saviour to the people, a local hero, and as such he would be loved, and the people would defend him, rather than attack him, and one day he would govern over all, and his subjects would be loyal, and all the lords would come to him for aid and security.

When they were done, Victor smiled, for Branna made more sense than Berengar, and understood, that if he used his sword to defend the people, not conquer them, they would see him as a lord and protector. From that would be gained greater power and greater wealth, and the region would be taken with little blood spilled. What Branna did not know, was that soon she would have a female child who lacked power, but through Victor, finally another raven would rise to power, and she would become the woman Branna had always dreamed of as a daughter.

In a strange twist of fate, Branna would unknowingly, bring forth a new raven of power, but Ariel had already given birth to the means to stop her. Sat there as the candles burned, and without understanding the series of events that would unfold, Branna was planning her own demise.

Across the realm as the sun rose and the camp in the cave stirred, Ariel walked with her daughter Ena towards the river. Ena was tanned and slender, yet because of her games with the boys she was strong. Ariel smiled as she sat down on the grass at the river's edge, and patted the floor for her daughter to join her.

"Come Ena, for today I want to tell you the story of a great mystic of the peoples of Fae, you will be five summers old soon, and when I was that age, I sat with my father, and he told me of the line of Tideguyde, and the creating of two races, one for the moon, and one for the Earth. They were made to fill the world with beauty and love, as they carried the gifts of fellowship and earth." Ena sat down at her side.

"I am Fae, I know that, like you are Fae, who is this great mystic?" Ariel smiled.

"Her name was Enaria, and she was your grandmother, it is why I gave you the name of the first three runes of her name, because one day, some of her gifts will be passed on to you, and when that happens, you will need to know how to recognise and control them. It will start with dreams that come true, and then when you master them, other gifts will come to you." Ena gave a nod, she understood, Ariel smiled, she could see the intelligence in her daughters' eyes.

"Enaria grew to be a great Mystic, and she fell in love with a man called Bryant, which in the old tongue of our line, means strong, and he was. Not strong as in he could lift heavy things, although in that aspect he was very strong, but strong as in his mind. He had a very strong will, and he knew a great many things, and through that he gained great wisdom at an early age. Your grandfather Bryant, used his hands to craft many things, this ring hung round my neck was made by him, and my mother placed many charms into it. One day you will own it, as it is a cherished artifact of our line, for it was made by two Fae who had the greatest love of each other, and all the realms." Ena smiled.

"You loved him, didn't you?" Ariel gave a large smile.

"I love him deeply, I was a bit of a daddy's girl, oh Ena he was such a wonderful man, I followed him everywhere, and I learned many things from him, which as you grow, I will teach you. Today, I want to tell you of Enaria, your grandmother, for she took a charm from the Fae of the moon, and she increased the power of that charm, and now they are gone as I talked to you about a few days ago, when I told you my parents died, the only person who can use this special charm is me, and today I am going to teach it to you, for it will be the most important thing you learn from me, and it is Enaria's charm of the Unseeing Veil."

"Unseen, will it make me invisible?" Ariel gave a happy nod.

"If someone is beside you, then they will see you, but if someone is looking for you, they will not find you. Ena, members of the Fae can feel the presence of others around them, but under this veil, no one will sense you or your presence. To them it will be as if you were never there, and there will be times when you will need to use it. Ena this is serious, it is blood magic and I will need you to learn it quickly, do you understand, because a time will come when you will need to run and hide, and it will be at that time you will use it. I will teach it you, and one day you will teach your children, for only the line of Enaria can use it." Ena nodded, she understood.

"The boys talk, I know we live in a land of darkness and that the raven is looking for us, I promise I will learn fast, and use it to protect us." Ariel smiled and reached her hand to Ena's.

"You are a bright girl, and you must always remember, you come from the line of one of the most powerful mystics of the Fae. Ena, I have the dreams, I see things, so when I tell you something important, learn from it. I may not always be at your side, so you must learn quickly, and always use it to stay safe until I can come to you. Never forget how deeply I love you, Ena you are the most important thing in my life, you are my light."

Chapter Thirty Six.

Avoiding Detection.

As the years ticked by, Branna became more and more isolated, and was either in the library, or down in the lower cellars of the castle below the gathering chamber, where she studied her herb lore, and experimented with her powers. Her black book grew thicker as she documented her progress and began to look back and study all of her research, of which she noted she had made some serious errors in her judgement.

The most obvious aspect of Branna, as Ariel had always pointed out, was that she was a highly intelligent academic, but at times, she had allowed her emotions and especially her hatred of Rhiannon to cloud her judgement. The Merle was far more intelligent, and powerful than she realised, and in her rush for revenge on Rhiannon, she had got carried away, and lost focus. That had been the opportunity it needed, and when the Merle through Roack, had seized its moment, to infect her more.

Ariel's comment about Merlin, and how he balanced the two forces of light and dark equally, had played on her thoughts for years. Having met Ariel one last time, and felt the huge surge of power flow into her from the kiss, she started to seriously study the balance of the two powers, and look for an answer, that may allow her to regain control once more over the growing powers of darkness within her. It was to be a long battle, for the answers were not easily found, especially as at times, to hide what she was doing, she had to disconnect from Roack, to prevent her from understanding her aim.

The large black raven would sit on the walls outside the crude window, and eat snails as Branna worked. All through her pregnancy she studied the effects on the light and the darkness, and when her time came to give birth to her daughter, she realised the power that Ariel had given her in that final kiss, had not only saved her, but it had also affected the growth of her child's powers, and her daughter

Rosamund, was born with little ability to use the magical force within her.

It did not take long after the birth, to understand, that in many ways, Ariel had saved her daughter. Had Rosamund been gifted, it was clear Maud would have killed her to prevent her from taking over, and replacing her. On the night Rosamund was born, Maud visited to meet her new sister, and when she held her and felt she was lacking in magical gifts, she smiled and was satisfied she would never be challenged if anything should happen to Branna.

Branna grew stronger after the birth of Rosamund, and returned to her rooms of study, and worked more and more on controlling the power of the Merle, as her force within her increased. She noticed the lines on her face and the heavy dark rings faded, and her skin became smoother. For all the time that she worked, she remembered the last meeting, as Ariel appeared before her, and she held the picture and her feelings of that day, which had surged up within her as Ariel pulled her close. Another new aspect of Branna alone since that day, was she cried a lot more in secret, as she held onto the feelings she had from Ariel, and over time, she felt parts of her memories return, and her moments with Ariel in Avalon, or in her caravan near the castle grew clearer and less hazy.

Berengar appeared less interested in Rosamund, it appeared he was more interested in the males of his line, yet his mother Filiberta, revelled in the small baby girl, and lavished her praise and love on the child, much to the joy of Branna. Filiberta had been a solitary figure around the castle, her sons were respectful, but did not really pay her much heed, and Branna in her loneliness began to spend more time with her and her infant. Branna had always felt Filiberta saw her as a demon, and avoided her, and yet one day as they walked outside in the woodland close to the castle, Filiberta stopped and turned to her.

"You have never married my son, and yet you have his children, but I know he has other women, does he treat you right, are you not scorned by his behaviour." Branna smiled.

"No, not at all. I saved him from the river and we swore an oath to each other, but it was understood, we would both live as free people. Filiberta, I do not want to own anyone, I am not the devil I have been painted, but I cannot feel the deep feelings of love for him, that maybe some of his other women feel. We lead a tribe, a family as the leaders, nothing more. He is a good man and good father, and so I am happy to have his children and raise them alongside him, but what we have is merely an arrangement, a pact to rule and build something no one can take." She watched Branna carefully.

"You do not love my son, but you can love deeply, I have seen this. The woman who left, the kind one, she was the one you loved, and she loved you deeply, that I saw, it was clear to my eyes. Now she is gone, you are lonely, I have heard you weep, I am glad my son did not hurt you to cause that, I wept much because of his father."

Branna smiled, she honestly thought no one cared, in a strange way, it felt nice to know that someone else appeared to understand her. Her children didn't, and she had for a long time thought Ariel was the only one that ever truly had.

"I knew Ariel long before I met Beren, she was the love of my life, but we had to be apart for a while. When she came back, I was very happy, Ariel understood me in ways no other ever will, but her powers are a threat to this family, and after she injured Otto, it became impossible for her to stay. I do care for Beren, never think I do not, he means a great deal to me, and I will always be by his side to protect him, as I was when he confronted his father. You know Filiberta, that was painful for him, to know his father betrayed him, was the greatest pain he had ever felt, I know they argued, but he cared deeply for his family, and he did respect his father."

"Vulgan was blind to his son, he was blind to all of us. He only ever thought of himself, and never his sons. Beren was right to do what he did, and as for your friend, this Ariel, she should not have stabbed Otto in the leg, the dagger should have gone through his heart. I am ashamed my son would treat such a kind woman in such a way, and I have told him, not that he cares, he is like his father. I am sorry my son has caused you such pain, you should not have let her leave, you should have kept her closer to you." Branna gave a soft smile, and swallowed the emotion that had built up inside her.

"I wanted her to stay, I begged her to, but I also understood why she felt she could not. Maud will never forgive her for what she did, and Ariel knew eventually Maud would try to kill her, Ariel did not want me to suffer that. Knowing she is alive is a comfort to me, I could not have watched her die."

Branna and Filiberta walked for most of the day, as they talked of the plans for the future. Branna explained Berengar's plan to storm the isle of Anglo, with Armand and Vladimir, but reassured her, he would be staying at the castle in Gaul. The castle had been left standing, and men had been despatched to rebuild it and establish order and trade again. Berengar would oversee the final stages and liaise with the armies that invaded the Anglo Isles. As they walked across the bridge, and back into the castle, Branna took hold of Filiberta by the arm.

"Thank you for today, I was feeling lonely, and your company brought me relief." Filiberta smiled at her.

"We live in a world ruled by men, and yet here they take the rule of a powerful woman. If talking to me keeps you strong, I am pleased. My family has flourished under your guidance, and I owe you deep gratitude for that. I too enjoyed today, I felt like I had a daughter, and it was nice to feel that."

Across the lands and sea, on the small Island of Iona, Gwendolyn walked along the beach with Merlin, she was relaxed and calm, as she linked the arm of Merlin, the sound of the water lapping onto the shore. High in the air the gulls screamed out, lifting and falling in the wind, she wiped back her long golden hair, glanced at him and gave a chuckle.

"You have not heard a word I have said, are you unhappy at our news?" He blinked, and came back to the present.

"I am sorry, my mind is preoccupied, I am delighted with our news, no one is happier than I am, it is time for your line to produce an heir." She smiled at him; she knew him so well.

"Yet, even my news is dwarfed by the concerns of your thoughts, can I help?" He gave a sigh.

"I am sorry, the world of men is becoming unstable, the clans and tribes are increasing and joining together. I cannot explain it, call it a feeling, but the men of the Norse are growing in number and looking to other shores. I have heard talk of the tribes in the Germanics growing in number and great power, and with the Roman forces on the shores of this isle, and swarming the lands, I fear that Avalon's welcoming attitude is drawing attention, and too many see this isle as rich pickings." Gwendolyn understood.

"Rhiannon has grown far more powerful than any expected, she trades with all who come to her door, I hear the outer reaches of the realm are now filled, and a hive of industry. Her prices are high, and yet there is no shortage for those who seek skills and trade with their trinkets. My grandmother always said that handing her Avalon was a mistake, she said it would be the downfall of the realm of men." Merlin agreed.

"Bridget had great wisdom, and far sight, I spoke often with her on such matters. It concerns me the natural tribes of this Isle will be wiped out, the Romans have brought culture, but the price in lost souls is great."

"My brother has talked often of this, he misses Cille, he always admired him for uniting the lines of the tribes. During his time there was peace, alas, his death and force for stability has fallen by the wayside, and there is no single man with the power to unite everyone again to one banner."

Merlin gave the matter some thought as they walked further along the golden sands. He stopped after some time and looked at Gwendolyn.

"Maybe that is what we need, one man to rise and take the role of leader, all of the tribes and the clans of this land are divided, which is how they have fallen, the Romans especially have used divide and conquer to great effect." Gwendolyn smirked.

"He would have to be a mighty man, and he would need to be marked so, in order to unite the tribes of these lands. Galliant tried diplomacy and gained no footing, all he did was attract attention and get all eyes looking this way. Sadly, the lines of men speak only with a sword these days, to unite these lands, he would have to be a mighty warrior indeed. I am not sure one so mighty exists, and he would have to carry great honour, I have seen most of the tribes in action, honour is not a quality I would attribute to any of them." Merlin stopped and gazed into her bright blue eyes, and his green eyes twinkled.

"There is one clan of the dragon lands, who believe in great honour, and they raise mighty warriors. They have united all the tribes of their lands and they do conduct themselves with great skill." Gwendolyn frowned.

"There is, who, I have not heard of any, although my time out in the other realms is lesser these days, the affairs of my own realm take much time?" Merlin was thinking and got that thick stare in his eyes again, she knew his ideas were forming in some form of action plan.

"The line of Pendragon is a line of high honour. They have the backing of many on both sides of the border, and they have held back the Romans with great skill. I am sure, there is one in their line that could prove to be a man of great leadership, and to be honest, hand him a sword of fable, and all would follow him." Gwendolyn looked at him in astonishment.

"A sword of fable? Oh, you can be so sly, I know what you have in mind, have you any idea of how difficult that is to make, it is why it is Fae legend?" He gave a smirk.

"But you know how to make it." She shook her head.

"Oh, my love, you have no idea what you ask, I would need a circle of makers to create it, and a lot of magic." He pulled her close and smiled.

"You have the time, your duties will be lighter than normal whilst you are with child, and the Norse sword maker is well known of, and the son of Sequana, has excelled in his ability for the Marshals of Avalon." Gwendolyn looked at him and felt doubt.

"My love, this would be a powerful weapon, to hand it to a line of men could be dangerous. If it fell into the wrong hands, it could be fatal, even the Marshals of Avalon would not stand against it." He gave a nod, and winked.

"Then we would set them a test, and if they failed, they would not receive it. A test so powerful, only a one true king could take it. If I am right, there could be such a man in the house of Pendragon."

Gwendolyn gave a smirk, she knew him so well, she walked along at his side and once again she could see he was lost in thought, and enjoyed walking in the soft white sand, listening to the sound of the waves rolling across the bright blue water.

*M*uch had changed for Gwendolyn, in her years ruling she had matured, and even though she had struggled at first with the heavy burden of care of all the Fae of Earth, she had with the support of Elgin and Bade found her feet. As the time approached, she parted with Merlin, who wanted to talk with each of the council, and was heading to talk with Rhiannon in Avalon, and Gwendolyn made it back to Florae. It was evening and everyone was settled for their meal time.

Gwendolyn walked up the steps to the house and in through the large doors, and thought of Ariel, it had been such a long time since she had thought of her, but as she walked into the hall of the archive, she smiled to herself.

"You had such vision, I hope you found your lost love, and are happy, you deserve to be, but I do miss you, this place feels strangely empty without you Ariel." She turned as she looked round, and smiled, Bade was sat in his seat at his desk, and was wavering half way between being awake and asleep. She walked towards him, and he jumped in his seat, she noticed the picture on his desk, and she lifted it up before he realised who she was.

"She was such a talented artist; this is an excellent self portrait of herself." She handed it to him.

"Bade, do not dwell on the past, I have always felt the love you hold for her, but after all this time, I do not think she will return." He looked up at her with sad eyes.

"Do you know something, is she still alive?" Gwendolyn sighed, and shook her head.

"Bade, I have told you before, I have no sense of her anywhere, she is the daughter of Enaria, we all know from her notes that her mother perfected a veil more powerful than any the Fae of Moon created. If she was dead, I would know." He shook his head.

"Not if she died wearing the veil, it has to be lifted by whomever placed it." Gwendolyn patted his shoulder.

"Love is an admirable quality Bade, but life is about living, one day you will have to accept, that she was in love with the woman from Avalon, and when she got her chance, she ran to her. I hope she found the happiness she so desperately sought, after everything that happened, she deserved it." He gave a nod and looked down.

"Bade, go and get some sleep, you are tired, I am heading to my quarters to write, I will need nothing more tonight, the Lord Merlin has travelled on to Avalon on other matters. Get some sleep, you look like you need it."

She made her way down the long hall to the rear of the building, and entered her royal apartments. Gwendolyn closed the door and walked to her private desk and sat down, in front of her was the heavily bound book of correspondence between Ariel and Queen Bridget Violet, these were the real letters, the ones her grandmother hid, and they were very illuminating indeed. She opened the book on the page she had left off on, and slid out the long white feather she used as a book mark, and started to read. This was the truth of her life with Branna, and what she saw, and it was clear to Gwendolyn, Bridget was right, and Rhiannon could not be trusted.

*I*n the castle of Berengar, Branna turned in her room, her face looked stern, as she stared at Berengar, stood by the door.

"Two years, why will it take that long to launch an attack? What if the Anglo tribes find out, have you any idea how hard it will be to hide a campaign as big as what you are planning?" He stood resolute.

"It is my plan, my army, and I want to be close when the attack comes, I have worked long and hard on this, I want to be there when they set sail." She sat back on the bed, and gave a sigh.

"Beren you do not know what lies ahead, this will not be like the valleys and villages here. Many realms connect to the Anglo's, and do trade with them, a full on attack will see them come to their aide, and you are no match for the Marshals of Avalon, Rhiannon has weapons and armours that will dull your blades and arrows."

He walked across the room and took her hand in his, he gave it a squeeze. He looked stern, and yet she could sense his concern for her in his tone of voice.

"I need to do this; I need to show them I am their leader and still a warrior. Can you understand that? Branna, I have asked little of you, and have served you with honour and loyalty, if this goes to plan, we shall have riches that will ensure our future in a changing world. There are romans of great culture to learn from, and the man of cross is rising in power, and acts against the likes of us. This will give our family line greater power than ever before, as gold and gems, hold great sway in the world that is growing."

She turned slowly and looked at him, he had aged, and she could see the maturity on his face, and the most annoying thing was, most of what he was telling her, he had learned from her. She took a deep breath, and gave a soft smile.

"I do not want to lose you, Asim stays here, as long as your raven is safe in my keep, no one can truly harm you. I want to travel with you and place a veil on your army, if I can keep you hidden, I will have peace of mind. Once I have done these things, I will return and wait for you here. Otto will not be a part of this, and so I will return quickly, I do not trust him Beren, and you should not either even though he is your brother. Otto will seat Maud if he can, and they will take everything we have built here." He gave a nod and squeezed her hand.

"If these are your terms, I will accept them, and I shall return victorious in praise of your land, and in praise of you my dark raven."

It was decided that night, and three months later, sat on a horse of black, and wearing a long black hooded cloak made of raven feathers, Branna rode out at the side of Berengar. With a veil cast over the whole army, they road east to the edge of their lands and the Castle Fey, just inside the boarder of Gaul, on a journey that would last a month.

Within the castle, the great hall was filled as guests arrived, and Otto and Maud made the most of their influence. Food was served, wine flowed, and there was a great deal of debauchery, as Maud frolicked with Otto and many consorts. Losing the use of one leg did not stop Otto, as he let lose his sick and depraved fantasies, and as the wine flowed, and the smell of money was in the noses of all, and trinkets fell from their lips from their devious hosts, there was no shortage of takers.

Filiberta took Rosamund, and locked herself in her room with her maids and stayed out of the way. Merwig was uninterested and avoided the festivities, although Gunderbauld did take a young girl to his room, and stayed there for two days with her. The few remaining soldiers were happy to join in, yet the guards of the castle, Branna's loyal protectors, watched on with emotionless faces and did nothing.

Branna was aware, Maud was cruel to Rajani her raven, and Roack ensured she was in touch at all times, and was guarding Asim. As Branna arrived at Castle Fey, Roack sat on her shoulder, and spoke with her mind, informing Branna of everything that was happening back at the castle.

The castle had been badly damaged when the villagers led by a priest, had risen up and attacked with no warning, taking Otto and Maud by surprise. Most of the guards had been drunk and easily slaughtered. Berengar's advanced team, had started to rebuild the castle, and added many more defences, although there was still a lot to be done. Branna looked out of her window onto the large courtyard that faced the entrance and the newly built draw bridge, it was clear, there would be no uprising again. Berengar had his elite force, which comprised of many of his original tribe of large fierce Varisci warriors.

She ran her hand down the smooth clear pane of the window, and turned to look at Berengar, as he unpacked his weapons on the table.

"This glass is of high quality, where did you get it?" He turned and looked.

"It is made in the village, there is a man here who comes from the Anglo Isles, it is knowledge he brought with him, he made all of them for the castle.

"It is Fae, this man is of my people, he must have fled like I did, and settled here. You should talk with this man and befriend him, he will be of good use to you, I think you will find you learn much off him. What was his name?"

Berengar polished his weapons, not really interested in the topic, he shrugged.

"I think he was called Ham." Branna nodded, and gave a slight smirk.

"He must not enter whilst I am here, do you understand? I know of this man, he worked this glass in Avalon, and he will know me, no one from Avalon must know I still live. Beren, it cannot be known I have been here, for if they find out, then they will learn I was with you, and they will come looking in the mountains for me, I was a fool to come here, I shall leave in the night and travel back." He gave a nod of understanding.

"I will make sure none know of your identity, there is a coach here, use that to return and none will see you. I will have ten guards accompany you, no one will stop you with them at your side." Branna smirked.

"I have Roack, no one will come near to me."

As the moon rose high, Branna cast the veil above the castle, and over the men, and then stepped into her carriage with her maids, and left with her escort, it was to be a long journey back, but she would stop as little as possible, she felt a strong sense of urgency within her, and she wanted to return to the safety of the castle as quickly as possible.

*I*n the vast valleys and forest, that surrounded Berengar Castle, the word was out around all the groups that were living in hiding, the Raven and her consort were away, and had left with the lion's share of their army. Guards still patrolled a large area of the forests, but Cezar had logged their routes, and spread the word around all the groups. Small hunting parties headed into the trees to grab whatever they could to dry and store. Five of the villages under the huge veil, traded goods and supplies with them for fresh meat, and so in Branna's absence, Cezar took his chance to load up all their winter stores.

Maud was far too busy with her cavorting to pay any attention, as she worked her way through many bottles of wine, and a lot of men. For a month there had been an endless stream of guests and frolicking, and such had been the intensity, three men and one woman had died from overtly aggressive sexual practices. Their bodies were dumped unceremoniously off the bridge, and dropped into the deep chasm below.

As the days grew warm, and with less guards out in the woodlands, Ariel was out with Ena, who was now in her tenth summer and had learned much from her mother, as they walked through the long grass and ferns back towards the valley that led to their camp. They were four miles away from the castle and according to Cezar's observations safe, and as they walked, they talked and laughed, enjoying the relaxed state that had existed for the last three weeks. Even though the sky was filtered through the veil, and it was gloomy below the trees, the sun was visible above, and it was clearly a day of pure blue skies.

Ariel talked of Florae and walking in the trees there, and the view from the top of the mountain, as Ena asked question after question, Ariel smiled.

"One day we will walk there together, you will see. If there is one thing my mother taught me, it is if you look hard enough, magic cast in haste has its flaws. This veil is not infallible, there is a way out other than the tunnel through the rock, we just have to look hard enough to find it, and I will not stop looking."

Ena understood, and she smiled as she looked up and the dim view of the sun above her, Ariel pattered her shoulder.

"You will love it when you escape, it is so blue on days like this, it will amaze you, and you will never tire of looking at it." She stopped, and listened, and looked round, Ena felt her mother tense up.

"What is it?"

"Shush… It is faint, but riders are coming. Hurry we must get off the trails and into cover, take my hand."

Ariel grabbed Ena by the hand, and both of them turned and ran away from the path into the deep ferns and tall grasses to get out of sight, and out of range of the guards' senses. The guards of Branna were not like normal men, they had abilities, unknown to mankind. Ariel ran, knowing the way to safe cover, holding Ena by the hand, it was hot and sticky, and she felt the sweat on her brow. Behind her the riders approached the place they had been, but they were still too far off to sense her, her footing was steady and sure, although Ena was panting, she slowed down a little, they were a good distance away. Ariel came to a slow pace as Ena panted, she smiled at her.

"It is alright, just get your breath back, if they pick up the scent, we head to the river, they will not be able to follow us there, and then we will swing back to the camp. Do not be afraid, if we get separated, do the charm I taught you and use the veil of my mother, nothing can find you if it is activated around you, for now you are safe under mine."

Ariel watched the path back towards the road, they had done well and made it a good distance away, she regulated her breathing and wiped her brow, and then turned, and walked on, and SNAP!

*S*he fell to the ground and twisted her leg, as the pain coursed through her, Ena gave a squeal and crouched down to her mother's leg, where the teeth of a mighty trap were closed tight on her leg, and there was blood all over her boot. Ariel winced as she looked at it, Ena leaned in and tried to pull the trap apart, she looked back terrified, as she pulled with all her strength.

Ariel breathed in and gritted her teeth, the pain was overwhelming, she tried to lean forward and help, but it was a big trap designed to hold boars and wolves, and filled with pain, she could not focus her mind, Ena heaved to no avail and started to cry.

"I am not strong enough Mother; it will not come apart." Ariel grabbed Ena by the wrist.

"It is too late, they have heard us and are coming, Ena you have to go, you cannot stay here they will get you. Hurry, wear the veil and go to Crina, and try and get help." Ena shook her head.

"I won't leave you; they will take you." Ariel breathed in and tried to focus her thoughts.

"Ena it is better they only get me, I am protected they cannot harm me, you are still young and have much to learn." Ena shook her head.

Ariel breathed in, the pain was intense, she grabbed Ena roughly by the shoulders and began to utter the charm of the veil, Ena understood what she was doing but did not want to leave, her tears ran down her cheeks, Ariel finished the charm and looked her right in the eyes.

"I need you Ena, I need you to be strong, and remember everything

I taught you. In my bag, is a brown book, it is small, but I have written all my charms my mother taught me in it for you, just in case something like this happened." Ena continued to cry as Ariel breathed in to try and overcome the pain.

"Ena you are of the line of Enaria, you must learn those charms and bring me aid, you are the only one who can, I will be safe and protected, Bran will not see me harmed. Ena, you have to go before they capture you, the man who raped me is in that castle, and if you end up there, you will become one of them, you must get away, I can fight them." Ena trembled, and looked very pale as she wiped her eyes.

"I am afraid to leave you." Ariel smiled at her.

"Ena you are my daughter, and I love you more than you will ever know, but you must leave me here, and return with Cezar when the time is right. Ena escape, work out how to get away, and go to Florae and talk to Gwendolyn, tell her who you are, and what has happened, and she will bring aid to me. Ena you can do this, think deep and think hard, I am inside you, and so are my powers, now go."

Ariel pulled out her silver dagger in its pouch, and thrust it into her hand. She pressed her fingers into Ena's temple, and for a moment there was a faint glow of white light.

"You have what you need, and you can do this, for ultimately, you will be the one to save me, now hurry and run as fast as you can, they will not come after you, I will not allow it." Ariel pulled her close and kissed her softly on her cheek. "I love you my daughter of light, go with great haste."

Ariel pushed her hard, Ena looked back behind her, where the sounds of approaching soldiers could be heard, she looked back at her mother.

"I love you, and I will come back for you." Ariel smiled.

*E*na stayed low and shot off as Ariel felt her fears rise within her, the noise of the guards was louder, they were alerted to the movement of Ena, and moved in closer to Ariel. She bit down on her lip to swallow the pain, and then sat up and raised her palms, she felt panicked and weak, but she needed to focus, and as the head of the first guard appeared, and she focused her mind a blinding flash of white erupted from her hand.

It hit him full on in the face and he screamed out in pain and was thrown back several feet, where he lay on the floor thrashing around screaming in agony. Ariel focused as the pain coursed through her, she was losing blood and felt faint, and needed to keep her thoughts clear. Sat in the grass with her blood covered leg, her hand up ready, she waited, to her left another guard appeared and she focused her thoughts and unleashed her light, as he fell to his knees and screamed out in agony, from her right side, a leather covered fist came crashing into her face, and everything went black, as Ariel hit the floor out cold.

*I*n the distance far away and undetected, Ena ran for her life towards the river, and a plan that had been rehearsed for all of her life. She knew there was little she could do, but as she ran, she swore revenge, and cursed the line of the Ravens forever.

Chapter Thirty Seven.

Alone In The Darkness.

*T*wo days after the departure of Branna from Castle Fey, Victor the second son of Otto, set sail to the western side of the Isle of the Anglo's. With two ships, and four hundred men, all hand picked by himself for the mission, his destination was Tintagel. He had convinced Berengar, that he could provide a decoy, to lure all eyes from the east, when Vladimir and Ivor, planned to land, to start their conquest.

Victor had the task of sending back information to aid Berengar, so he could update the real conquest to the east, but his real plan, was to execute the advice of Branna. At dawn two days later, Victor landed three miles below Tintagel, and unloaded tools and supplies, his men were armed, but had been instructed only to defend themselves if attacked, apart from that, they were to try and befriend all those they encountered. Victor had taught them as much of the language as possible, which had been taught him by Branna, so as they landed and talked of coming in peace to the fishermen, who were on the beaches, they were welcomed with open arms.

*A*riel's head was cloudy and fuzzy when she woke up, she opened her eyes feeling weak and in pain. The side of her face stung, and her leg throbbed. Her eyes flickered in the dim light, where a single torch burned on the wall in the distance. It took a few moments to realise she was hanging by her arms on chains, and she felt the pain where the shackles bit into her wrists. As her mind cleared, she noticed the dark figure silhouetted in front of her by the torch. Her head spun and she felt sick as her eyes cleared enough, to realise she was looking at Filiberta. She lifted her head from her chest, and looked round.

"Your leg was badly hurt; I have done the best I can with the little I have. I am sorry but I asked them to leave you on the ground, but Maud refused. Lady of white, your mistress is not here and you are in danger, my granddaughter has you in her dungeon, I will help where I can until Lady Raven returns, but know, that Maud aims to make you suffer."

Ariel looked round as her eyes focused properly, she was in a cell, with a metal mesh door, and hanging from a large bolt drilled into the roof. She licked her lips, her mouth was so dry she could hardly move them, and her voice was a hoarse whisper.

"Thank you, I am in your debt." Filiberta gave a nod.

"I have to go, if they find me here you will suffer more."

Ariel understood, she had taken a great risk to help her, and gave her a nod of appreciation. Filiberta slid back out of view and left Ariel hanging, she breathed in and tried to move her leg, the pain coursed up her, and she winced with the intense pain, and passed out. Round her neck, below her blood soaked dress, the pendant given her by Bridget gave off a faint glow, the protections of Enaria, were waking up.

In the darkness of Ariel's mind, there was a faint spot of light, and a soft voice whispered to her through her jumbled mind.

"Focus my child, I am here, I have always been here, focus on me and build your power, for within you is the key to all things. Focus Ariel, focus on me, I am here waiting for you." Ariel's mind struggled, as she tried within herself to understand, she hung in the cell with the flickering flame, and whispered more to herself, as there was no one there to hear her.

"Mother… Mother is that you?"

Somewhere in the back of her mind, she stood in a garden of bright flowers, next to a small building of stone, and in front of her stood her mother, with her long flowing golden hair, those grey sparkling eyes, and her smile of pure love and kindness.

"Ariel again, say the charm of protection, but this time, say it with complete belief."

"I am trying mother; I really am but it is hard." Enaria crouched down and smiled a beautiful smile.

"I know my darling, but we have to keep doing this until you can do it with your mind closed. Ariel one day this charm will save your life, now try again, and believe it with all of your heart."

"I am mother, and I do believe it, I really do."

"Good girl… Now come on, try again and let's see how you do."

In the darkness Ariel whispered quietly to herself, and the pendant around her neck gave a pulse and grew brighter. In her mind the happy voice whispered.

"Keep going… Oh my darling you are so clever, think harder, it is working." Ariel muttered to herself over and over, and slowly the light grew brighter out of the pendant, and the light surrounded her. "Oh, you clever girl, I am so proud of you."

The light gave off a huge pulse, and the whole of the cell filled with light, and surrounded her as she hung from the roof. Without realising, and in her state of unconsciousness, the light of Enaria grew out of her, and created a space no darkness could thrive in, Ariel for now was safe, but she was very weak and it would not last forever.

*R*oack flew down to the window, as the carriage swung from side to side. The bird dropped onto the seat, as Branna wavered between wakefulness and sleep. She gave a loud croak, and Branna's eyes instantly opened, and she jerked in her seat.

"What is it?" Roack bobbed up and down on the seat at her side.

"The woman of light has been captured, she is at the mercy of your daughter and her husband." The moment and urgency ripped through Branna, as she realised what could happen.

"They will kill her, and we are still too far away. Roack you must fly to the castle and tell Rajani, to talk to Maud and tell her if Ariel dies, both her and Otto will too, I will not have her harmed." Roack bobbed up and down on the seat.

"Two guards died when they tried to capture her, she fought well and used the white light, they died in great pain. Everyone at the castle wants her dead, be careful you may lose a great deal if you go against their wishes." Branna understood.

"She will live until I arrive, if not, many will die. Go to Rajani and let them know I am coming and she has to live." Roack jumped onto the window of the carriage.

"As you wish."

She spread her wings and took off into the air. Branna sat back, her heart was beating faster in her chest. She had to get back and soon, if only these horses could go faster, she cursed herself, she had known all along not to leave the castle, and yet she had gone against her better instincts, which she now regretted.

*E*na wept in Crina's arms as she looked at Cezar, he had that look, and she softly shook her head, all around she could see the others watching her, she gazed round in a wide circle, she knew what they had in mind.

"Give me some time with this poor girl, and then we shall form a circle, eat, and look at what can be done."

The circle was their way of sorting things out, all who wanted to be heard, could sit round the fire, share a meal, and speak their part, and after a debate, and an agreement by all parties, a course of action would be taken.

One hour later, after Ena had cried herself into a sleep, Crina and four of the women prepared the food, and set it to boil over the fire. Cezar had stumps and seats for all to be seated and measured out a huge circle in the centre of the cave. Wine bottles were placed, and as the food simmered, all of them took their seats, and prepared to debate how to rescue Ariel.

*C*ezar sat with his son of eighteen summers Dorin, behind them sat close and listening was his youngest son, Maxwell. Crina sat by the pot and ladled food into the bowls and passed them around, until everyone was sat with a bowl, and hunk of bread. Wine was poured and shared, and as they began to eat, Crina watched them all, as she dipped her bread in the bowl.

"There is only one way in, and you all know that bridge is guarded by her elite guard, none of you will make it into the castle. We do not even know if she lives, the two dead we found, had the scorch marks of a powerful Fae, if she is in there, she will be fighting and protecting herself." Many of them understood and gave agreeable nods. Dorin looked round.

"That is meaningless, it is just hope, we have to find a way in." Cezar smiled as he scooped up stew on his chunk of bread.

"Show me a way in where we will not all die, and I will take it at your side." A tall thin elder man gave a smirk.

"I admire your courage Dorin, but your father is right, we have spent several years watching and learning all of their routines, but the thing is, the Raven, is no fool and runs everything with precision. I know, I did most of the watching."

Dorin looked downhearted, he looked round the circle, and his eyes fell on a large rough looking man, with short scruffy dark hair, and a thick beard.

"There must be something we can do, Falk, you are no slouch in a fight, I bet you could take a good few down?" He raised his eyebrows and smirked, and rubbed the thick thatch of his beard.

"Dorin, we all love her, she is one of us, and if there was a way in, I would be there now with a trail of bodies behind me, but Crina and Sven are right, the bridge is impassable. I know we have tried; we even went under it using ropes at night, but even under there she has eyes. We have all learned much from her, and I for one want her back, that little one over there needs her, but how Dorin?"

Cezar swallowed his food and lifted his cup to drink, he patted his son on the shoulder, and gave a smile.

"I admire your spirit lad, but the truth is, we do not know if she is alive or dead. What I do know is we have been hiding too long, and so firstly, we need to get into the villages and ask some questions. We have people in the village that aid us, and some of their people work in the castle, so we find out if Ariel is alive first. Secondly, they have taken one of ours, so I say we come out of hiding and take a few of theirs back. We strike and we strike hard, and we make their lives harder than they have to be, they have had everything their own way up until now, so the way I see it, if we are stuck in here, we make a stand and fight for our space."

Many in the group gave a nod, Crina watched counting them, she looked back at Ena asleep on the blanket on the floor, and then turned to the group.

"It is decided, we ask for eyes in the castle, and we hit them on their patrols, and we make a stand as I may add Ariel often advised. When we find out the truth, we will meet here and look at what can be done. Pass the word round the other camps, that we will coordinate with all of them."

They lifted their drinks and emptied their cups, then stood up and made their way across the cave to their bunks, tomorrow would be a busy day as they organised, and hoped that Ariel was still alive, just in case they found a way in. Cezar took Dorin to one side, and spoke quietly.

"You know the rock all around the castle, map out the caves for more storage, we will collect their weapons and armour then store it, and if you do find a way in, come straight to me and we will talk."

Dorin felt more relieved, he still believed that they should try to save Ariel, but he also understood the impossible odds they faced. He grabbed two of the other boys, and they headed out into the night, it was better to move under the cover of darkness, especially whilst the guards had been scarce, as they had these last two weeks.

From what little they had seen and heard, they knew that many visitors had been arriving on a daily basis, and some of the villages had reported that large quantities of wine had been brought in on carts with large barrels. Dorin knew, whilst the parties continued, all of them had a window to really investigate the area, and he intended to do it as thoroughly as possible.

*I*t was quiet in the caves below, the torch had burned out, and the only light was through a barred window just outside the cell. The moon cast a pale blue line across the floor, as Ariel stirred, and lifted her head wearily off her chest. Her leg throbbed, and her shoulders and arms ached, as she slowly came round, and understood what she had thought to be nightmares, were true.

Her mouth was dry, and she tried to lick her cracked lips, but it was impossible. The wall in front of her was large iron squares, with a door, the spaces were not wide enough to climb through, even though she was thin. Beyond the door, was a table and a large water vat, it had a leak, and dripped onto the floor creating a puddle, and she tried to swallow. It felt like torture, her mouth was so hot, those drips would quench her throat, and having to watch such precious liquid seep into the floor, drove her insane.

The floor was dark, but there was movement, somewhere below her, small feet padded on the stone, and scurried around, she was not sure if it was mice, or rats, just the sound of their feet was enough to add to her misery. A she hung watching, she felt her eyes adjust to the dim light, and made out straw on the floor, and the lines of the edges of the large stone slabs. The cell was not large, about the size of her room at Florae, her neck hurt, and she leaned it back as far as she could and looked up at the ceiling.

It felt almost like a relief just to hold her head up, and she turned it from side to side to try and get some sort of movement into it. She could just make out the chains and shackles round her wrists, and tried to wiggle her fingers which felt numb. She winced as she moved them and felt the pain of stiffness in every joint, it really hurt and she wanted to cry out, but her voice was hidden in the dryness that ran down her throat. She closed her eyes, and felt utterly exhausted, and in her mind, she spoke the words her mouth could not muster.

"Oh Bran, why did you leave me to them, where are you?"

There was a fluttering noise, and then silence, she looked to the door of the cell, but all was still and quiet, was she starting to imagine noises? A small dark shape moved on the floor at the side of the cell entrance, she stared through the darkness, as a bird like form appeared and looked through the opening in the bars towards her. Its eyes glistened even though there was little light, and she heard a rough croaky voice.

"Your lady is coming, she told me to tell you not to die." Ariel breathed in with relief, as she watched the bird, she tried to speak, but her words were faint, and lower than a whisper.

"I need water, without it I will die."

"You must not die."

It felt helpless, why was she talking to a bird? She tried to swallow and again lick her lips; her mouth was so dry it felt difficult to form her words. Her words were a little louder, but not much.

"Roack, I am dying, I cannot survive without water."

The bird turned and walked across the room, it hopped up onto the top of the table. Ariel watched feeling hopeful, but she also did not understand completely.

"Why are you helping her, would it not be better for you if I was dead?" The bird turned.

"I do not like the white light; it hurts my kind. I know what your blood did up on the rock in the sky, I saw her there. The Raven wants you to live, it makes her strong, I need her strong, so I help her, not you."

Ariel understood, as she hung from the ceiling watching the black bird on the table. The power of the Fae was enhanced with love, and her love for Ariel had given Branna the strength to wield the darkness, and in doing so, she had given Roack what she needed, which was more of herself. It felt strange to understand that in some strange way, the three of them were bound together, and each was dependant on each others survival. If Branna died, so would Roack, and she would be devastated, like she had been in Florae, not knowing where she was or how she was. It was true, she had ceased to live and feel without Branna, and had only felt her life return when she came here to her that first night.

Roack flapped and lifted off the table, she gripped a small wooden beaker in her left claw, and then flew above the water vat. Ariel felt hope as the bird lowered to submerge the beaker. Roack was a large bird compared to others, and as was evident, was far stronger than any ordinary raven. Roack flew to the cell bars, and the beaker bumped on them, as she landed on her right foot and folded her wings, Ariel felt her breath hold for a second, the thought of water was driving her insane.

Once through the bars, the bird flew up in front of her, Ariel leaned back her head, as Roack hovered above her, the beaker touched her chin, and she felt it drag on it, as the beaker tipped.

The water was cold as it filled her mouth, and she swallowed the first mouthful, and felt more pour in as she breathed in rapidly through her nose trying not to choke. The beaker emptied, and she tried to hold the water in her mouth long enough to revive her tongue, the bird fluttered off, and headed back to the table where it dropped the beaker.

It was nowhere near enough to quench all her thirst, but she held what she could in her mouth and swirled it round, and felt the relief flow into her as she moved her tongue and felt some relief. She swallowed the last drop and gasped out, as she moved her mouth to bring it back to life.

"Thank you Roack."

The raven sat on the table and watched her, its bright shiny eyes studying her, Roack bobbed up and down on the table watching.

"I did not do it for you, I did it for her, you must live. I have orders to give, so you will continue to live, and then I will return to my raven." Ariel understood, the bird was loyal only to Branna, and as much as she hated Ariel, Branna had requested she do it.

"I understand your hatred of my line Roack, nonetheless, I am grateful for the little you have done for me." Roack flapped her wings.

"I must leave now."

With a flutter she was gone, and Ariel hung in the dim light and watched Roack's shadow on the floor, as the bird landed on the window and then flew outside. Ariel watched as the square of blueish light appeared on the floor, with the shadowed outlines of the bars on the window, and as odd as it felt, she could feel a little hope grow within her.

Outside, Roack circled the castle, spotted the room at the top of the long east wall, which had a light in it, and swooped down to the open window. Inside the room, Merwig sat at a desk and wrote, behind in the bed, a naked woman slept peacefully, he noticed the movement and turned as Roack hopped off the ledge and landed on the floor, he gave a sigh.

"Oh dear, what the hell does she want now?" Roack bobbed on the floor.

"The woman of light is dying, your raven demands she be saved, I was told to seek you out, and tell you to go to her and help her." Merwig put down his quill.

"Why me, I would have thought Lothar was more the hero type. She is aware her insane daughter is in charge at the moment, and has a murderous intent towards her, once she has slept with most of the castle?" Roack stared at him from the floor, her voice was harsh and croaky.

"She told me you. Go get Filiberta, and take aid to the woman of light, those are your orders."

He slid back his chair and gave a deep sigh, Merwig hated living in the castle, he never had the time to study enough. He lifted his papers and slipped them into the drawer, and then looked at the bird.

"You tell her, I do this under protest, go to Filiberta and tell her what she must do, I will meet her outside her room shortly." The raven bobbed on the floor, turned, and flew to the window.

*A*riel heard footsteps, and felt her heart start to beat, was this going to be her final moment? They grew louder, her judgement told her that there was at least four, and she felt very weak. Somewhere in the large room outside her cell, large bolts were dragged from their brackets, and there was a soft squeak as a door swung open. The light flooded into the room, and Ariel blinked as it drew closer and brighter, her eyes had become accustomed to the dark, and she closed her eyes to save them from such brightness. A voice spoke that she did not recognise.

"What a shit hole. Open it up and take her down, put her on the bed. You attend her and care for her wounds." Large shapes appeared in the doorway, as two guards unlocked the door, and came in.

Ariel heard a box scrape on the floor, and then in front of her a dark shape loomed up that smelt of an unwashed body and alcohol. A pair of hands gripped her waist tightly, and lifted her up, and for a second the strain lifted from her arms, and she gave a slight moan of relief. Around her wrists there was a click, and her right arm fell to her side feeling numb. She wanted to move it, but it was stiff and difficult. Her left arm fell, and her weight was taken in the strong arms that held her waist, and then she felt herself lower, and before she realised, the guard swung her up into his arms, and carried her to the back of the cell.

Ariel hung limp as she was lowered onto a soft bed of straw, and saw a female figure hurry in with a bag, as the guard stepped back. It was still a little too bright as a torch had been placed in a bracket just outside the cell, but she could sense the woman and it felt familiar, she understood it was Filiberta.

Ariel lay back feeling a sense of relief, as Filiberta tended to her leg, and a guard came in with yet another beaker of water. He held her up slightly in a sitting position, and beckoned her to sip. It was hard not to gulp it, but she listened to his words and did as he instructed, just enjoying the simple pleasure of cool liquid in her throat.

Three beakers later, she was feeling more awake, and sat up slightly as Filiberta worked on bandaging her leg. She had smeared a thick pungent smelling paste onto her wound, and it felt surprisingly good, as the burning within the wound cooled. Ariel watched as the older woman she knew to be the mother of Berengar tended to her.

"Maud will be very unhappy when she finds out you did this, be careful, she is not a woman to trifle with." Filiberta nodded as she tied off the bandage.

"My instruction was straight from the Lady Raven, if Maud is unhappy, she can argue with her mother. You have a fever, and need food, even Maud did not want you to die here in the dark, she wants to kill you herself." Ariel gave a smirk.

"Maud is not strong enough to kill me, well not alone she isn't." Filiberta shrugged as she dug in her bag.

"She will try, and if she fails, she will just hate you more." Ariel nodded, she understood that.

"Branna will protect me." Filiberta lifted out some bread and cheese, and placed it on the bed, she looked at Ariel in the dim light.

"Branna is seen as the one to rule, and at the moment, most of the people here want you dead. They fear the power of your light, do not put all your faith in Branna, I know she loves you, but she must be seen to act in the defence of this family. There may come a time where what she wants, and what she has to do to keep unity, will be two different things. If you love her, tell her to help you escape and never come back, for that will be the kindest thing for her. I have done what I can, you have food and a skin of water, I must go now." Ariel understood, she knew Bran was now in a difficult place, she looked up at the sad eyes of Filiberta.

"Thank you, I am grateful for your help, and your advice, you are a good person." Filiberta shrugged and walked towards the cell door.

"I no longer know the difference, all I know is death will come for me some day, and I will go willingly."

The guards closed the doors and locked them, and Ariel watched as they all left the room, she lifted the skin and drank some more, and then felt the pang in her stomach. Sat in the dim light, she lifted the bread and tore off a chunk, then noticed an apple, and her mouth began to water, as even the dry bread felt like the best food she had eaten in a long time.

High above her in the castle there were wild screams and the laughter of the drunk, as the wild behaviour raged on, for now she was safe, as long as there were festivities, she knew she had time to recover her strength. At some point, Maud would hear about it, and come down in her rage to take out her revenge. Ariel knew she had to be prepared, Branna was not safe yet, and she had trials to face before she did, for Ariel this would be the real start of her fight for survival.

*R*oack landed with a soft thump on the roof of the carriage as it hurtled along through the night. Branna had ordered them not to stop, and to keep going. Two of the guards rode at the side of the lead horses keeping them on the track in the moonlit sky, Roack spoke with her mind to Branna.

"They heard your words and have acted. She will be cared for and tended, and will live this night through." Branna gave a nod as in her head she spoke back.

"How do you mean, this night?" Roack sat still watching the road ahead.

"You are still many days away, when your daughter hears of this night, she will strike to try and kill her before you return."

"Then she will die too."

"If she does, you will lose everything."

"How so?"

"She is a woman of light, she can kill all of them, I know you know of the power inside her. Branna the Raven, if you want to rule your people, you must act for them, they do not want her to live, and you have to decide what you will do when you return. I know you know of the spell; your line has used it before. Sleep is better than death, and it takes away fear."

Branna sat back in her seat and thought about it, Roack knew far more of the Fae of the Moon than she had realised. Branna's eyes moved up to the roof of the carriage where she knew the bird sat watching.

"I do not wish to do that to her." The bird bobbed up and down.

"Then you must kill her, for you no longer have a choice. If you wish to rule, you must sacrifice her for their sake. I know you know this to be true." Branna closed her eyes, and felt the turmoil inside her.

"I have time, and I will find a way through this, watch the road and keep us safe Roack, I need to sleep, and we must get back as soon as possible."

Branna felt caught in the trap of her own making, as she sat back and looked at her life. She had been in such a rush to get her research completed before the queen arrived that she had made some fatal flaws. Those flaws threatened to rob her of the only thing that had ever really brought her true happiness. She had to sit as the hours passed, and every yard took her closer to her return to the castle to seriously decide what she was going to do. Maud and Otto were her problem, she was responsible for the darkness inside them, and ultimately, she had to deal with them. She closed her eyes and gave a sigh.

"Why Ariel, why do I have to eliminate her, when it would be so much easier to just rid my line of Maud and Otto?" The croak from above made her realise she was not alone; she was never alone these days.

"Your daughter is the future, if you want to protect your line, you need to protect her, Rosamund has not the gifts you needed. There is power in both lines, you have to unite this family, and wait for the one who will rule one day."

She understood that, but she could not kill Ariel, she would kill herself before doing that. Roack croaked again.

"You know the spell, use it, and for now, the family will unite."

Chapter Thirty Eight.

The Trial Of Ariel.

As the night wore on, exhausted and in pain, Ariel slipped into her fevered state. Alone in the darkness, lay on a bed of straw, her skin burned as if it was on fire, as above her Otto and Maud finally passed out and fell into a deep slumber.

The carriage with Roack sat on top, sped along through the darkness, where within Branna wrestled with sleep, her mind filled with the fear of what would become of her only love, left to the mercy of her ruthless and corrupted daughter.

As dawn approached Filiberta returned to the cell, and sat with Ariel, she had a pail of water brought into the room, wiped her face, and tried all she could in vain to cool her burning flesh down. She used the few herbs she knew of, and had hot water brought to her, and made a tea, and alone with Ariel in her cell, she did her best to get her to drink it, and as the hours slowly crawled by, she felt she was losing Ariel.

By mid morning, Branna was awake and slowly filling with panic. She arrived at an inn, her horses steaming and lathered, as her guards hurried to help the driver change the team, whilst Branna paced up and down the track, unable to rest or relax. Roack swooped down to her shoulder, and spoke in her croaky voice quietly.

"You must calm down; it is not good to let the guards see you in this manner. You hold the power of this family; you can never show weakness. The Raven that leads, must always appear strong. The Lady of White is cared for, Merwig knows to keep your daughter away from her, your wishes are known, and will not be disobeyed."

Branna gave a sigh as she turned her back to the carriage and looked into the trees. "I cannot lose her Roack, you know of the power that grows within me around her. It is her love that sustains me, and through that I find the strength to rule and control everything. If

Maud does anything to harm her, I am not sure what I will do.”

“You need to stay calm, but you know how they fear her. I feel your anger rising within you, and you must not let it out, this is a time to be in control, for the future of our family is at stake. Listen to me Branna the Raven, you cannot lose all you have built in a moment of anger, use your wisdom, think this through carefully.”

Branna stared at the trees as tears filled her eyes. “I know you do not understand Roack, I know she is from the light, but don’t you see, I need the light within me too, and she is my light, without Ariel, all will fall.” She swallowed hard and took a long breath. Roack bobbed on her shoulder.

“I will go to her and watch over her, not for her sake, but yours, we have too much to lose. I will tell her you are closer, and to live for you. We have made much ground, and you will be there soon.” Branna gave a nod and wiped her eyes.

“Thank you Roack, I know this is hard for you, you are a good friend and companion.” The Bird bobbed its head, and spread out her wings and lifted into the air above Branna.

“We are one, we are the Ravens, and we rise with each other. Make haste, and use your mind, this family must thrive not fall, you know the spell.”

*F*or several minutes after Roack flew off, Branna took deep breaths to calm her churning insides. She knew that Roack was right, Mauds hatred of Ariel had caused her a great deal of problems. She had to focus her mind and think things through, but of one thing she was very clear, Maud had done much in secret to undermine her, and that had to be stopped once and for all.

She turned to the carriage, as new horses were finally harnessed, and walked slowly over towards it, her mind filled with her moments of life with Ariel. She still had time before she arrived back at the castle, and she knew Roack was right, this was one time she had to be very careful in how she approached things, but she also knew, no matter what, Ariel would not die, that was not an option, no matter what anyone thought.

*W*ithin minutes, Branna was back on the move at speed, and she sat back feeling the frustration, as the day crept onward at a pace not fast enough for her. In the castle the day slipped past, and Merwig arrived and stood at the door, as Filiberta attended to Ariel and tried to reduce her fever. Ariel moaned on the bed, muttering in her delirium, as she spoke to Branna and Bridget, and also talked with her mother. Filiberta looked at Merwig.

"She is not improving; I fear for her life. She should not be here, she should be in better surroundings, this is no place for a sick woman." He sighed.

"This is Maud's wish, she sees this woman of light as a threat to all of us, and everyone else within the castle agrees with her. It is the wish of everyone that she is killed for her crimes of killing with the light, she has a power that could kill all of us, you know of the fear she instils. To be frank, I feel this is the only place she is safe for now, I would take the keys, and if they come for her, lock yourself in to protect her until our Lady Raven arrives back. I aim to lock my door with a young woman inside and get drunk, this has been a distraction I did not wish for."

Filiberta sat back, and gave a sigh. "I care not for what the others think, the Lady Ariel has a heart of goodness, she only tried to defend herself, those guards should have been more careful. Tell me this, if you are attacked on the road, would you not defend yourself as she did?" He shook his head.

"That does not alter the fact that she has only to lift her hand, and she could kill all of us, no matter what you may think, we are all at risk whilst she lives, she is a danger to this family." Filiberta stared at him in the doorway.

"And yet she has lived in this castle for years, and never harmed any of you. Do you not think that if she had come here to destroy you, then by now she would have done? You should listen to Branna, not Maud, Otto was told to leave her alone, he should have listened, Ariel could have killed him with a flick of her wrist, and yet, even as he raped her, she did not."

Merwig shook his head. "This is why I stay out of it all, I have no wish for this woman to be harmed, I feel no love for my older sister and her vile husband, but things have changed, even you have to agree, that now she has killed, the threat will always be there hanging over all of us." Filiberta shook her head.

"You are wrong, Ariel has no stomach for the taking of life, she is from the light, to protect those who live, is the path of her life, she is no threat to anyone as long as they obey their mistress and leave her alone. You may not understand, but this woman is the strength of your Lady Raven, and if you kill her, you will destroy everything."

Merwig watched the eyes of Filiberta, she was his grandmother and he respected her, but if he was honest, he really wanted no part in any of this.

"I was told by Roack to protect her, as that is the wish of my mother, and I am here, but if I am honest, I want nothing to do with any of this. When it is all done and over, I feel I will leave this castle, for life here has made me weary of the endless politics of this family, I wish no part in any of this."

Behind him guards walked down the steps, Merwig turned as they entered into the chamber. The lead guard walked up to the cell door, which was currently blocked by Merwig.

"My Lord, I have been instructed to take the prisoner up to the main hall, there is to be a gathering and the prisoner will be put on trial." Merwig stood fast.

"The Lady Ariel has a fever and is in no condition to be moved, she is sick from her wounds, by whose authority is she to be placed on trial?" The Guard looked uncomfortable.

"My Lord, it is the express command of the Lady Maud, we must obey her, in the absence of the Lady Raven, it is her right to rule." Merwig turned back to look at Ariel lost in her fever and covered in sweat as she burned.

"I have been sent word that the Lady Raven is on route back, and the Lady Ariel is not to be touched, go back and inform my sister she is acting against the wishes of the head of this family." The Guard shook his head.

"The Lady Raven is not here, and my orders were very specific from the Lord Berengar, that I was to follow her instruction in the absence of the Lady Raven. I am sorry My Lord, but I have to take her to stand before the hall to be tried, if you wish to speak out in her defence, then you have that right."

He pushed past Merwig and entered the cell, Filiberta looked afraid, as she was roughly pushed aside, the other guards entered the room and helped lift the limp figure of Ariel off the bed. She was unable to stand, and one of the guards lifted her up, and she hung limp in his arms. Filiberta looked at the lead guard.

"What is your name?" He looked at her.

"Why does it matter?" She stared at him.

"I want to know the name of the man that is taking Lady Ariel to her death." He frowned at her.

"It matters not, I am following the orders given me by my mistress, but if you must know, I am Wernerbrand." She gave a smile.

"I shall ensure the Lady Raven is aware of it on her return, I am sure she will wish to have words with you." He stepped back from her, and looked unhappy.

"I am a loyal servant of this family, and I am following the commands given by this family, I have nothing to fear." He turned and left the cell to catch up with the other guards as they took Ariel up to the large hall. Merwig turned to Filiberta in the empty cell.

"I am going to my room and locking the door, I have done all I can, I would advise you do the same, I fear an ill wind approaches."

*I*t did, Branna was moving at high speed towards the castle, as Ariel was taken up into the hall, where the crowds had gathered, as Maud paced up and down on the high platform of the thrones. Otto sat scowling on Berengar's seat, as the crowd parted and the guards walked through, with the limp body of Ariel hanging from the arms of the one who carried her.

Otto smirked as he saw her, finally his moment of revenge was upon him, and with Branna gone, he could finally seek justice for his damaged leg. Maud walked with an air of superiority, and a smug expression, as Ariel was lay on a prepared table and strapped down in full view of everyone before the thrones of Branna and Berengar.

The murmur around the large hall was loud, as cursed words were spoken at the sight of Ariel, many looked up to the platform and the smirking face of Maud, and expressed their approval to each other. Maud walked round the table looking down at Ariel who lay there her face burning red dripping with sweat, she smiled a grisly smile, and her eyes moved to Otto who gave her a smug nod.

Maud was loving the attention and support, to her it was clear, all she had to do was speak, and the whole castle would follow her. In her mind, she could see how one day she would be the ruler of this land, and she could not help but think, that it could be sooner than she imagined. All she had to do was take it from the lap of Branna, and it would be her domain for eternity, she looked at the gathered crowd and lifted her hand, and the loud mutterings began to die down to silence.

Maud stood before them all, stunted at only Four feet and eight inches high, her rounded plump figure with her sleek hair tied back into a tight bun, her dark eyes scowling malicious intent, and yet they held a sparkle gleamed from the power she felt. Her face was a fixed frown, that was made less attractive by her sinister smile, she faced them all, feeling the power she held and spoke.

"Here lies the whore of light, brought before you as I promised, to be judged for her crimes."

*I*nside the carriage as it sped through the start of the valley on the borders of the lands of Sachsen, Branna felt a strange feeling build within her and became alarmed. She had no idea how, she just knew, Ariel was in great peril, and her heart started to thump in her chest. She moved quickly from her seat and leaned out of the window and screamed.

"STOP… STOP THE CARRIAGE!"

The driver pulled hard on the reins, and applied the break, and the carriage shuddered and rocked, as it came to a juddering halt. Branna jumped out, the feelings of panic growing strong within her, she just knew time was running out for Ariel and she had no choice but to lift the veil and jump to the castle. She walked briskly round the carriage and looked up at the driver.

"Make haste to the castle, I will use other means." She had no idea how right her feelings were, as ten miles ahead, three trees had been felled under the instructions of Maud to prevent the carriage reaching the pass to the tunnel that led to the Castle of Berengar. The driver whipped the horses and the carriage moved off as Branna stood, and closed her eyes.

"Ariel, please live, I am coming." The veil came down and thick black smoke swirled around her and she was gone.

*I*n Avalon, Rhiannon sat bolt upright in her seat and stared towards the east. "There you are, you foul dark little witch!"

*M*aud gave a smirk, as the crowds roared with their approval, and as the noise died down, she walked round the table, her voice was loud.

"This whore of light, has taken the use of my husband's leg, and has used her power to kill good men of our line, and yet our supreme ruler says she should live and not be harmed by any here. I say that is wrong, a life for a life, a limb for a limb."

The crowd roared their approval even louder and raised their arms in salute of her. Maud gave a cruel and twisted smile, she was enjoying her moment and feeling the true power of a queen as she walked casually round the strapped down burning body of Ariel, she whispered as she leaned over the face of Ariel.

"Not so powerful now are you whore, no one assaults my husband and lives, your death will bring me great pleasure." Ariel face burned hotter as she mumbled her eyes flickering as she was lost in her dreams. Maud looked up at the happy jeering crowd and raised her voice.

"I SAY A LEG SHOULD BE TAKEN FOR A LEG, WHAT SAY YOU?"

Maud gave a nod, and Wernerbrand walked up onto the platform carrying his axe, Maud looked to the crowd, as they screamed out their delight.

"She took the leg of Lord Otto, I say we take one back, so she can see the pain she has inflicted on this family. Is there any here who would want to bed a one legged whore?"

Wernerbrand lifted his axe, and looked down on the heavily bandaged leg of Ariel, Maud's eyes danced with delight, as she watched filled with exuberance, revelling in every second of her glory and power, as the crowd screamed with delight and lifted out their weapons and waved them in the air, all joining in with the mass hysteria, that was sweeping the room. From the back a loud voice boomed out.

"I WILL!"

*E*veryone turned to look behind them, not understanding who would possibly say that, and silence fell, as the black smoke cleared and Branna walked forward with Roack on her shoulder, holding another raven in her hand. Maud scowled with hate and turned to Wernerbrand quickly.

"DO IT!" Branna squeezed and Wernerbrand exploded into dust, and the axe fell to the floor with a loud clang, and clattered down the stone steps to the front of the parting crowd. Maud turned back and stared at Branna with hate, her temper flared.

"She has no right to live, she took the life of good men of this tribe, you know the laws of the Varisci, a life shall be paid for with a life. She has maimed Otto for life, her leg should be his, it is the rules of the life we follow."

Branna stared at her as she walked slowly down the long hall as the parted crowds stepped back further from her. Branna looked from side to side, her eyes flickering red with her anger, she moved them back to Maud who stared at her with hate from the platform of the thrones.

"I made it abundantly clear to all of you, she is mine, no one shall harm her and live. Tell me daughter, seeing as you are suddenly so very indulgent of the rules of this tribe, what is the penalty for disobeying the queen of this land?"

Branna walked closer to the platform, as the silent crowd swallowed hard, as her long black feathered cloak, swished on the floor behind her. Roack watched from her shoulder, her dark eyes watching carefully. Maud looked red in the face, as Otto behind her scowled with hate, Branna stared at both of them, as she reached the base of the steps.

"Well, my daughter, will you not answer, as you can see, your followers await a response?" Maud fumed inside, as Brann slowly walked up the steps towards her, with eyes flickering red with her anger, Maud knew better than to take her on, and stepped back in fear.

"Would you kill your own daughter, is that whore more important to you than I am?"

Branna reached the top step, and leaned down close, and lowered her voice to Maud.

"At this moment in time. Yes! I warned you what would happen, I told you to stay away from her, but you refused to listen, tell me, why should you live now?"

Her eyes flashed with deep red, and Maud stepped back away from her, and shook with fear, Branna stood upright and turned to the crowd.

"To disobey a direct command of your queen, is punishable by death, one has already paid for their part today, what say you, who are so keen to see someone die, should my daughter pay for her betrayal with her life?"

The room was silent, as everyone looked down and at the floor, Branna smirked.

"Look at you, so happy to see a defenceless woman strapped to a table die, in your so called trial for justice. You made enough noise as

I arrived, in support of a semi powerful leader, and yet look at you all now, faced with the power of a real queen of the realm. Look how you lower your heads in fear. Tell me, how is any of this justice?"

*B*ranna stood tall, as slowly they raised their heads to look at her. Branna shook her head. "You call yourselves loyal, and yet the moment my back is turned you flock below the skirts of my daughter, and whimper like dogs when I return to show the true power of the Raven. I thought Varisci were unshakable in their devotion to their leaders, how sad it is to see I was wrong. Berengar would be disgusted to see how quickly you turned from us, he would slaughter all of you for such disrespect."

Branna stared at them all as her hand raised behind her. "His seat is not even cold, and yet you fill it with that poor imitation of a man." Her palm flashed red, and Otto screamed as he was lifted into the air, and blasted off the platform. He landed hard and screamed out in yet more pain, and slid up the centre of the room, as Branna stared down at him with disgust.

"You demand justice for what Otto, because one of the many women you raped fought back? You sicken and disgust me, you have no idea of justice, your only law is take what you can get and be damned to all others. I cannot believe this tribe for one moment would think that you could lead them. You would take what you could get and desert them, leaving them to die as you did at Castle Fey, when you ran whimpering back to the protection, under my skirt."

Branna lifted her head. "Otto raped Ariel, and she fought back and stuck him with a knife in his leg, that is the reason he hobbles and limps round the castle, he got justice, he was told to leave her by his queen, and he disobeyed me. I should have taken his life, but as a kindness to my daughter, I allowed him to live. Where was the justice for Ariel, as he tore off her clothes and brutalised her?" She gave a laugh.

"How many here have done the same, and carry a scar from the girl that tried to fight back, should I round them all up and have all of them put to death? You call for justice but none of you have any idea of its meaning." She pointed to Maud.

"Ariel took the lives of four men using her power of light, all of them Varisci, and all of them whilst they attacked her, and you call for her death, and yet there stands my daughter, how many men of the

Varisci have died during her antics of sexual perversions, only to be tossed from the bridge at dawn. More men of this tribe have died in her bed than were ever taken in defence by Ariel, and yet you pander to the wishes of this pretend queen for a day."

Branna turned to Maud, her eyes blazed with red as her anger rose.

"THERE IS ONLY ONE QUEEN OF THIS TRIBE, AND IT IS ME, AND I WILL BE OBEYED."

The blast that came from Branna was huge, and Maud was lifted off her feet, tossed across the room, and slammed into the far wall of the hall where she slithered to the ground unconscious. Branna stared at everyone who looked up at her with fear.

"I am your queen, and for any now that want to disobey me or dethrone me, now is your chance, face me and die like a Varisci warrior should. Ariel is mine, and never ever forget that again." She pointed at a soldier who looked up at her with terror in his eyes.

"Unstrap her, and take her to my quarters, and stand outside by the door and allow no one to enter. If anything should happen to her, I will eat your raven with my evening meal… Now go." Branna looked up as he ran up the steps and started to unbuckle the restraints on Ariel.

"Everyone else… GET OUT!"

*B*ranna stood and watched as the room cleared, Maud was lifted up and carried to her room, and two men assisted Otto. Roack leaned into her ear.

"You have stamped your authority back on this land well, but I fear in their hearts they still fear the woman of light and wish for her death. You have to act to show you have their best interests for this family in mind at all times, you will always have turmoil whilst the woman of light resides here. She has to go, I know that you know this, it is the only way to bring back full unity." Branna gave a sigh.

"For now, Ariel is ill and she needs me, I will go to her and heal her, only then will I decide what the future will hold.

*D*eep in the halls of Avalon, a commander of the guard walked briskly towards the steps as the room cleared of all the servants and advisors of state. He stopped before his queen, and dropped to his knee. "My Queen."

Rhiannon watched as the last doors closed, and the hall was empty apart from the both of them, she looked down at the officer on his knee.

"Give me your report Commander."

"My Queen. We found a carriage, and four escort tribesmen, and a few ladies of service, nothing more. No one there matched the description of this woman Branna, all of them were of lighter hues of hair. The carriage belonged to a warlord of a tribe known as Varisci, named Berengar." Rhiannon looked displeased.

"Were they Fae?" He shook his head as he stared at the floor.

"No, My Queen. All of them were of the line of man." She gave a nod.

"Where are they now?"

"All were slain as was your orders, the carriage was burnt, and the horses set free, nothing remains to prove this was a deed of Fae."

Rhiannon walked up and down at the top of the steps as she thought, she gave a sigh and flicked her wrist.

"Thank you, Commander, you have done well, your men will be rewarded, you can go."

Rhiannon returned to her seat and sat down and watched as the Commander walked through the door, closing it behind him. She gave a sigh and spoke quietly to herself.

"I know it was you, I am not sure how you evaded my elite guards, but I am closer and I will find you and remove you, your days are numbered Branna of the Moon, I am watching, you will not slip so easily away next time."

Chapter Thirty Nine.

The Rise Of The Raven Queen.

The fever upon Ariel was fierce, lost to her dreams, she burned up, as Branna sat with her and wept as she attended to her. Knowing in the castle there would always be a threat to her, Branna moved Ariel down to her private workrooms deep below the tall tower of the Gathering Hall.

Below the floor of the hall, with her work room doors open, Branna had a bed placed in the large empty space, which was in view at all times as she worked. Outside behind her bolted doors, four of her most loyal guards, took it in turns to ensure no other entered the room of the sleeping Ariel.

As Ariel burned with her fever, Branna worked at her long table, her black book opened to the pages she wrote in Avalon, as she had documented the cures Ariel had used to help her fight her own fever. When she felt tired, she would curl on the bed around Ariel and hold her in her arms, and talk quietly to her in between her bouts of weeping.

For five days she exhausted herself working to cure Ariel. The spells she had used had cured her leg, and the bruises on Ariel's face had almost gone, where there was just a soft yellow colouring to her skin. Her temperature had come down very slowly, and as the day came to an end, and Roack sat on the high tower above the castle, Branna curled into her, and snuggled up, feeling exhausted.

"Please come back to me my love, I am so lonely without you." Her eyelids flickered, and she drifted off into an exhausted sleep.

Above her head in the room of the gathering, Maud quietly slipped in followed by Otto.

Maud helped Otto to his seat, and shortly after the other members of the family still resident in the castle arrived. Merwig looked uninterested, and Dagaric sat smiling as he leaned over his seat to the very young looking Rosamund. Maud sat back and lifted her wine.

"So, we are here, have we decided what we should do." Merwig gave a sigh.

"Why can you not let this go, you are both lucky to be alive. Look, as I have said before, I do not care what happens to the bloody woman, but in all honesty, we have all been around her for years, and apart from her rape and being taken prisoner, Ariel has shown no threat to any of us. If Branna wants her for her bed, why are we all so alarmed, it is obvious they just enjoy sleeping together." Dagaric agreed.

"Berengar is fine with her being around her, he told me she is good for mother, really Maud do we have to keep doing this?"

Ariel opened her eyes, and saw Branna sleeping at her side, she smiled, and then heard the voice in the room above her.

"I have letters from Amand, and Gundobarld, and have had word from Ivor and Ulric, they too feel her power is too dangerous to just be allowed to be free in this castle. She is a woman of light, her mother was Enaria, and I am sure all of your ravens have told you what she did to their race before they came down to us. She has to go, she has to die, she cannot be allowed to walk free of this realm, if she does, she will go straight to the Queen of the Moon. It was her guards that burned the carriage and killed our men, she is out there hunting us and drawing closer, and with Ariel here, we are all at risk." Otto agreed.

"The whore has to go, there are other whores to warm Branna's bed, while that whore of light remains here, we are all at risk, she cannot be allowed to get free." Ariel closed her eyes and lay on the bed feeling Branna snuggled up close to her.

Sensing Ariel awake, Roack flew down from the tall tower, and landed on the open window, her dark eyes watched Branna, Ariel sensed the raven and opened her eyes, and looked at Roack.

Roack noted it and flew to the bed, she landed softly and looked Ariel in the eye, as above her the family discussed their problem. Roack bobbed on the bed, her voice was low, so as not to awaken Branna.

"She kept her word, she came back, and you lived." Ariel could understand the bird, she felt the concern deep within it.

"I owe you my life Roack, I am grateful, but I hear what they say above us, there will not be peace with me here, it is why I left." Roack bobbed up and down.

"Branna the Raven needs you close, she draws strength from you, the realm is sealed but the queen of light walks its boundary with her men of blue. She is close and knows something here hides Branna the Raven from her, I cannot let her open the protections. The queen of the light will kill everyone in here, and I want Branna the Raven to live." Ariel felt the panic flood through her.

"The marshals are here, does Rhiannon know where we are, or is it just her combing all the lands?" Roack's eyes shone dark.

"Branna the raven threw off her veil to get to you, if she had not done so, you would have died, the queen of light felt her and came looking. She will not find us as long as the protections stay closed."

Ariel felt the fear course through her, even now after all of this time, Rhiannon had not given up, she never would until she found and killed Branna. Ariel understood the situation.

"Roack, you must tell Bran to kill me, I have a daughter, my light will pass to her. Roack promise me you will keep her safe, you must protect her, she has to live." Roack bobbed on the bed.

"You would die to save her, this is strange to me, why would a woman of light throw away her life to save one who contains darkness?" Ariel gave a soft smile.

"Roack, what does Branna mean to you?"

"I do not understand, we are joined and a part of each other." Ariel gave a slight nod.

"Would you die and leave her body to save her?" The bird stood still and watched Ariel.

"To leave her I would go back to the dark sky, I would live and she would eventually die." Ariel nodded softly.

"But would you do it knowing she would have a life for a while longer and not die?"

Roack stood still and thought about it, Ariel watched her carefully, her dark eyes blinked at Ariel.

"If the Raven Branna was dying and that would save her, I would do it for her." Ariel smiled.

"Roack, whether you like it or not, that is love. I love her Roack, she means everything to me, so if my death will save her, I will give my life willingly to ensure she has life." Roack's head tilted from side to side, her croaky voice held an element of wonder to it.

"That is love, I did not know that I could love, this is a new thing for me, I understand you woman of light, I know now what this feeling I feel when she is with you is. You do not need to die, if you wish to save her, there is another way, a way known only to her line, it is a way to live and die at the same time." Ariel frowned.

"Tell me of this spell I know nothing of."

As Branna slept, and above them, Maud hatched yet another plan to unseat Branna and remove Ariel, Roack whispered quietly about a way known only to the Fae of Moon, where a person could be held in a trance like state of sleep and sealed with a crystal tube. Roack told of how a person in that state would not age, or die, and how they could later be revived and continue to live a normal life.

Ariel listened carefully and took in everything the bird told her, and for the first time in a long time, she began to understand that not only would this way save Branna, it could help her find a way to remain intact until someone could come to her aid. Ariel knew that at some point Ena would find a way to escape, and when she did, her first job would be to find a way to get her mother free.

When Roack left, Ariel lay back and watched Branna sleep with a smile on her face, it was the only way to save them both, and she knew somehow, she had to convince Branna this was the only way out of the bind they were in. She drifted into sleep lost in thought, curled in the arms of Branna, it felt nice, and in her dreams, she walked hand in hand with her under the trees next to the river in Avalon and felt happy.

When Ariel woke the following day, Branna was overjoyed and held her in her arms for a long time, and wept. It was hard for Ariel to see her so emotional, as Branna talked of the pain she had felt being parted. For Ariel it felt ten times worse, as she knew at some point she would have to talk to Branna. She was still very weak, but her body was healing, and being close to Branna helped to speed up her recovery.

It was several weeks before she felt back at full strength, as she stood and looked out of the window at the walls of stone that led into the deep valley below them, and breathed in the fresh air. Branna had tried several times, but Ariel refused to leave the room and go back up to the castle. She had said nothing, but she remembered the plans being hatched above them whilst Branna had slept that night, and she knew that she would never be safe again in the realms.

Branna said little of her times above as she administered to the family and the forces that were garrisoned in the grounds, around and within the large intimidating castle. It was clear, Branna was under great pressure, as those who advised her, spoke of how the family and those living within the realm were concerned that the woman of light still lived, and as long as she did, there would never be unity, as they all feared that one day, she would wipe them out. Maud was skilled in her ability to spread dissent, and even though Branna had faced her out in front of everyone, her malice was such, she would not rest until Ariel was eliminated, and so behind closed doors, she whispered and planned, and unrest began to grow again.

*O*ne afternoon whilst Ariel sat on her bed writing, the door quietly opened and Filiberta looked in. She smiled as she saw Ariel, and then slipped in, the guard who was on duty had been the guard that had arrived with her that night in the cell, and held Ariel by the waist, as she was released from the chains.

Filiberta came over and sat at her side and took her hand in hers. "I wanted to see you, when I heard you had recovered fully, I was relieved, but I still fear for your life, which is why I am here." Ariel understood.

"I know of some of the things that have been spoken of, I fear for Branna, they will never accept me here, they will not be happy until I am dead, and Branna will be undermined for as long as I live. Filiberta she will not listen, if you have influence you must tell her, that as long as I live, they will continue to undermine her."

Filiberta shook her head. "I have tried, Ariel, she loves you deeply, and when you were gone, she became withdrawn and lonely, the truth is, she would leave here if she could and take you with her, but she will not leave Berengar my son alone. She is in a trap of her own making, and I fear there is no way out for her that does not lead to her downfall. The family has grown and spread wide within the world, and they all wield immense power, but it is Branna who holds everything together as their queen. I fear soon everything will collapse into ruin and this family will be wiped out." Ariel understood.

"Then it must be down to me to convince her, I am the only one she will listen to. I cannot leave this room, if I could, I would run and hide again, but I fear like last time they would just hunt me down again. Rhiannon will never stop looking for Branna until she has found her and killed her, and Maud will not rest until I am dead, no matter what, both of us are trapped." Filiberta gave a nod.

"My grandson is to be married, and I will leave here soon to visit him, Maud will be accompanying me to his wedding, it is but a brief moment, but you must convince Branna to make the changes necessary to undo the evil she has done whilst she is gone. Ariel, it is not a long span of time, but you must help solve all the problems before Maud's return." Filiberta smiled.

"I must go, I may never get another chance to see you again, protect yourself, you are a good woman Ariel of the Fae, your heart is pure, and it has been nice to know you, if only for a short time, stay safe."

Filiberta slipped out of the room and Ariel gave a sigh, whatever she did, it would cause great hurt and pain, she lifted her hand to her pendant. "I wish you were around to advise me Bridget, you had the same wisdom as my mother, I miss both of you."

A week later Maud departed for the wedding of her son Victor, she would be gone for two long months and Ariel knew the time had finally come to face up to the reality of her situation, there was nothing else that she could do, she had to confront Branna.

That night they ate a meal together, and then hand in hand they walked into Branna's sleeping quarters and closed the door, and slipped into bed together and made love. It was soft and gentle and filled with love, and yet there were also some moments of deep passion, as Ariel knew this would probably be her last time alone with Branna.

Once they had finished, and lay back happy and relaxed, Ariel gave a contented sigh.

"I feel so happy, and so loved at this time, I have sat alone in Florae and dreamed of days like this beside you, my love." Branna breathed out.

"If only everyday could be like this. All I have ever wanted is simply this, I was so stupid, and I have made such mistakes. This was all I ever wanted, to be with you, and be happy."

Ariel turned and stroked Branna' soft shoulder, as she stared into her bright dark happy eyes. Branna felt she wanted to say something and smiled.

"What." Ariel gave a slight laugh.

"Bran my love you are fooling no one you know. Do you really think that I, a daughter of Enaria cannot see the pressure you face because I still live?"

Branna rolled over and faced the wall. "Please Ariel, I am tired of talking about it, I have no intention of giving you up, I love you. The last time I lost you, I also lost me, and the darkness almost took me. If you had not returned, I would be darker than Maud now, and I do not want to be like that, I want to keep this family together, but not through darkness." Ariel gave a sigh and slid up closer to her, she lowered her voice to a soft tone.

"Bran, you have always said how important family is to you, but you are losing this family, it is fragmenting because of me. The last time we were parted, I was close, but not at your side, I know you know of a way to keep me beside you and safe, in a way that will stop all of them from dividing. Bran this is your family, I know it means something to you, it is all you could talk about in Avalon, why are you allowing so much division? Bran I love you; you are my world, I am asking you to save me from them, and save yourself at the same time." Branna turned over and her eyes were filled with tears.

"Ariel, you have no idea what you are asking. Yes, you will be here at my side, but I will not be able to hold you, or talk to you. Ariel, I have not the strength to do that to you, please, you cannot ask this of me, it is the curse of years of sleep. Ariel, I do not want to do this to you, I would rather you did it to me."

Ariel took Branna's hand and gave it a squeeze. "Bran you know that eventually, they will kill me, I am trapped, I cannot leave the realm Bran, and if I could where would I go? If I go to Florae, I will sit in my room missing you until Rhiannon finds out, and comes for me. Bran here I may be alone in a box, but I will be there at your side. Bran my heart is so filled with my love for you, I will lie back and dream of everything we have done and said together, knowing that your life will be at peace and your family will be united behind you. Bran, Maud is gone for a short time, you have to seize your chance, you know I am right." She smiled and stroked the hair from Branna's damp eyes.

"Do this, save me, and your family, and arise the Raven you need to be to kill Rhiannon, and when she is gone, honour your promise, wake me up and stay at my side forever, I love you, my wild and crazy lover, do you know that?"

Branna pulled her into her arms, buried her face into Ariel's shoulder and wept deep bitter sobs of pain.

"I do not want to live without you Ariel, I do not want to do this, please I beg you, do not ask this of me." Ariel stroked her long tatty wild hair.

"I know my love, but it is our only way out of this that gives us a chance of a life together one day."

riel held Branna in her arms and talked softly of her love for her, and once she had settled, she took her by the hand, and walked her into the bath pool, where they bathed together, and Ariel smiled as she washed Branna with love and affection. Once they were clean, Ariel walked her out of the pool, and into the large work room, where a bed of soft silk was ready and waiting.

Ariel sat as Branna took the brush and brushed slowly through her hair, and Ariel closed her eyes, taking every second into her memory, she gave a sigh of contentment.

CRASH!

Her eyes snapped open, and she turned round to see a row of smashed bottles on the work table, with the brush in its centre, she looked up at Branna who was in tears again, Branna shook her head.

"This is not right, it is not fair Ariel, what is the point of being a queen of these people if I cannot be happy? I do not want to do this, you are the love of my life, I do not want to seal you up in a glass box. I want to walk in the woodland with you, curl around you at night and laugh at your side, as we always have. I want what we had in Avalon; it is the reason I have done all this. Ariel I just want to be free and share every moment with you. If you are here sealed in a box, there is no point to anything I have done."

The tears streamed down her face, as she stepped back, and fell to her knees and wept deep painful sorrowful sobs. "I will have no life without you, I already know what that is like Ariel, I got swallowed up by the darkness. I was not living, I may as well jus have been dead." Ariel felt her own tears, watching Branna break like this was painful, she dropped to her knees and lifted Branna's face to hers.

"Bran, listen to me, this is not as before." She held her face in her hands, and softly kissed her. "Last time I was hidden from you, I was not around to remind you, but here I will always be on view, and at your side. Bran you are so clever, I know you can find a way, I have seen your notes and diagrams, I mean, they are coded but I can see how you are working to find a balance like Merlin's. Don't you see, with me here at your side as you work, you will see your reason to fight every day, and you will find a way through to a balance. When the time is right, I will be waiting for you to awaken me." Branna took a deep breath and swallowed back her tears, as she looked into her soft loving grey eyes.

"Ariel it is not the same, I was so alone without you, I just want us to be together always as we promised each other in Avalon." Ariel leaned forward and kissed her again.

"But we will be Bran, I will always be there in your heart and in your thoughts, can you not see, we can never really be parted, our love is too strong. Bran we have eaten a wonderful meal together, we made love, and then bathed together, it was a perfect day together for us. Remember today, hold it in your heart for me, for it was perfect and filled with love, but now I am tired, hold me until I fall asleep to dream of you. Let me fall asleep in your arms, and then do the spell, and let me rest a while. When it is done, then control the darkness, find the balance, and rule this family as an equal to Rhiannon."

Ariel released her and stood up, she dressed in her white robe, and sat on the bed, she lay back and Branna got in at her side and held her tight, and they talked quietly until Ariel's eyes fluttered, and she slipped into a happy sleep, with the scent of Branna in her nose.

$\mathcal{B}$ranna lay there for a while quietly weeping, and then with a heavy sigh, she sat up, and Roack flew down to the window. With tears in her eyes and sobbing, Roack joined with her. Together they did the spell, and as Branna spoke through bleary eyes, the crystal formed around Ariel's bed, as it rose up, Branna shook with her pain.

Once the Crystal box surrounded it and before the top came over her, Branna stopped and leaned over, she straightened Ariel's hair, straightened her robe, and made sure that her pendant was over her heart. Once everything was neat, Branna then leaned over the sleeping peaceful face of Ariel, and softly kissed her.

"Sleep well my love, and when the skies are bright and the time is right, I will bring you back, and I will never leave your side forever. I love you Ariel, my beautiful companion and the love of my life, rest well."

$\mathcal{R}$oack felt the pain rip through Branna as she stood back, and she flew to her shoulder. Together they finished the spell, and the lid of the box slid over Ariel, and sealed itself tight. Branna fell to the floor and wept, and Roack flew back to the window.

"Listen to me Branna the Raven, your woman of light was right. I feel the pain inside you, but think of what you have built and why, one day you will face the queen of light and defeat her, and then you can return to your Ariel, and you will have the life you desire. This is good, she has done this to save you, it was right for you."

Roack turned, and flew out of the window, and left Branna knelt on the floor, beside the crystal box within which Ariel was sealed for eternity. She flew up to the top of the tower and landed on the edge and looked out across the realm encased under Branna's veil. She gave a loud squark, and out of the trees came all of the ravens, they lifted into the air and flew around the tower top, Roack sat still and watched, all of them were small parts of the merle, and Roack knew, true to her word, Branna had created a land for her ravens, and now it was her task to help her protect it.

*T*hat night Branna lay alone across the crystal box, and looked through the glass haze of the lid, and talked to Ariel, who had been frozen in her final moment, as she slipped into a happy and contented sleep. Ariel had yet again made a sacrifice to save Branna, just like she had sacrificed her early life to aid the future of her people.

It was a bittersweet moment, because without knowing she had started a sequence of events that would allow Branna to rise to become a Raven of power. Sadly, in doing so, it would also lead Ena, her daughter, to vow to find her way out of the realm, and return with help to avenge her mother. It was a series of events that would lead to the fall of the Berengar family, before Ariel ultimately would be released and returned to her home.

*T*wo nights after Branna sealed Ariel within the crystal, still in pain at the loss of her love, and already feeling isolated and lonely, she climbed the steps to the top of the tower, and looked out to the west, as Roack settled on her shoulder. Her dark eyes watched the horizon through the haze of the veil, as her long shaggy hair blew around her shoulders.

"Roack you are all I have now my Ariel is gone, and I miss her already. It is just us once again, just like the days of leaving Avalon, and we need to organise. Rhiannon has taken my family, and my home, and now because of her, I have lost Ariel, all I have is you in my loneliness."

Her dark eyes stared at the west, as her pain turned to anger. "I hate her Roack, and one day I will face her, and I will kill her. She has lied to her people, and Ariel was my only hope of getting the truth out there, it is up to us now, we have to find a way to defeat her. When Berengar returns, I will send out all our ravens to build an army so large, no matter how many marshals she sends to sniff at our borders, we will overwhelm her." Roack bobbed up and down on her shoulder.

"I like this Branna the Raven, I will help, and you will rise above all of them, and be the queen of all the ravens for eternity." Branna gave a smile, her first in two days.

"Rhiannon has taken away the love of my life, it is time I repaid her, and I will, I will take everything she loves from her, she has stripped my people of all they love, and I will not rest until she is gone. If she wants to create a dark Fae, I will give her one, and I will be the darkest Raven she will ever meet. I am Fae, and I am darkness, and soon her world will reel from the length of my reach."

When Maud returned, Branna walked up the hall, dressed in her cloak of black feathers, and up to her seat. She sat looking dark and brooding as the family and tribe gathered, and then she rose and addressed the assembled gathering. Her face was stern, cold and white, and her eyes darker than they had ever been, as she looked Maud right in the eyes. Her voice was loud and harsh, and filled with power.

"Ariel is no longer a problem; you can rest knowing the problem has been dealt with. She lies below this castle sealed forever in crystal; you are all safe. Too many of you whisper in the dark corners of this castle against your queen, about what you think this family should do, so listen to me now. We have a gathering for that, and in between there is only room for one to rule, and that is me. I am the queen of all you raven's, you live because I allow it, never forget that."

She moved slightly on the spot, and her eyes moved to Otto.

"My word is law, disobey me, and I will not care if you are family, tribe or outsider, your raven will die, and you with it. I am the Lady Raven, I created all of you, defy me, and I will destroy you."

Roack flew down and sat on her shoulder, and Branna walked down from the steps and the crowd parted, as she walked slowly through them. Two of her guards went down on one knee, and slowly everyone followed and lowered to their knees. Maud watched with shock in her eyes, and swallowed hard, and she realised, somehow, her own rise to power was a long time away.

*B*ranna was the head of the family, and it showed, she was the Lady Raven and the true force of power at Castle Berengar. All of their lives were held in her hand, and once and for all, Maud realised that it would take but one squeeze of Branna's thumb, and all of them would die. As much as Maud yearned for that kind of power, she knew, that without Branna's black book, she was nothing more than one of many of the ravens owned and controlled by Branna.

*F*rom Branna, a force of power would flow out across the world, as the family of Berengar, would head to all lands to claim power and control. Dark deeds would be done, and deep down inside, as she fought to control the darkness, she knew, that no matter what, she would be the one that carried the blame, for at the end of the day, whether she wished it or not, she finally understood, it was her error, her miscalculation, that had allowed Roack to control her in her early days, and in doing so, it had corrupted her deeper without her understanding.

*I*t was too late to stop it, things had gone too far, and the price she had paid was mighty, but she was the one responsible, it was her task alone, and alone she was, she had no other choice now. Darker deeds would happen done by those of her line, and all eyes would look to her.

*B*ranna was their queen, and seen as the Darkest Raven of Berengar, and whether she wanted it or not, that was how history would see her.

More Author's
From
Violet Circle Publishing

Mike Beale. (Children's Book)

Crumble's Adventures.
ISBN: 978-1-910299-06-7
Digital ISBN: 978-1-910299-08-1

Colin Smith (Play)

Heaven knows I'm Miserable Now
ISBN: 978-1-910299-16-6
Digital ISBN: 978-1-910299-23-4

Ted Morgan. (Poetry and verse)

Wordsmith's Wanderings.
ISBN: 978-1-910299-04-3
Digital ISBN: 978-1-910299-09-8
Peregrinations of the Wordsmith
ISBN: 978-1-910299-18-0
Digital ISBN: 978-1-910299-21-0
Silhouette Soldiers
ISBN: 978-1-910299-19-7
Digital ISBN: 978-1-910299-22-7
A Menu of Memories
Digital ISBN: 978-1-910299-32-6
Digital ISBN: 978-1-910299-33-3

Robin John Morgan. (Fiction/Fantasy/Slice of Life)

Heirs to the Kingdom.

Book One, The Bowman of Loxley.
ISBN: 978-1-910299-00-5
Digital ISBN: 978-1-910299-10-4
Book Two, The Lost Sword of Carnac.
ISBN: 978-1-910299-01-2
Digital ISBN: 978-1-910299-11-1
Book Three, The Darkness of Dunnottar.
ISBN: 978-1-910299-02-9
Digital ISBN: 978-1-910299-12-8
Book Four, Queen of the Violet Isle.
ISBN: 978-1-910299-03-6
Digital ISBN: 978-1-910299-13-5
Book Five, Crystals of the Mirrored Waters.
ISBN: 978-1-910299-05-0
Digital ISBN: 978-1-910299-14-2
Book Six, Last Arrow of the Woodland Realm.
ISBN: 978-1-910299-07-4
Digital ISBN: 978-1-910299-15-9
Book Seven, Bridge Of Sequana.
ISBN: 978-1-910299-17-3
Digital ISBN: 978-1-910299-20-3
Book Eight, The Circle of Darkness.
ISBN: 978-1-910299-26-5
Digital ISBN: 978-1-910299-29-6

The Curio Chronicles.

Part One, Abigail's Summer.
ISBN: 978-1-910299-27-2

Find out more about our authors and their books at
www.violetcirclepublishing.co.uk